DEMON·QUEEN wants to *Paint*

AMBER ATLAS

DEMON QUEEN WANTS TO PAINT
BOOK 2

ISBN (print): 979-8-88993-095-2
ISBN (e-book): 979-8-88993-096-9

Edited by Taylor Kilgour
Cover Illustration and Design by FuyuDust
Interior Design by Tancgu LLC

Published 2025 by MoonQuill®
Arlington, VA
www.moonquill.com

Table of Contents

CHAPTER 1

PRETTY, PRETTY AZRAEL

Wet and shaking, Morrigan, Alphegor, and Azrael stumbled into her small studio apartment, dripping water onto the parquet floor. Small puddles formed underneath them, making the floor slippery.

"I am not a fan of this Overworld weather." Azrael took off his jacket and squeezed the water out of it right onto the puddles, connecting them.

"Hey! Go do that in the sink," Morrigan grumbled as she hurried to the bathroom to find some towels and a rag. There were some neatly stacked on the washing machine—she must have forgotten to put them in place after washing. She grabbed them and hurried out to the hallway.

Much to her surprise, Alphegor stood completely dry, despite being soaked just a few moments before.

"I assume you don't need this." She chuckled awkwardly and handed the towel to Azrael, who began wiping off the excess water. Morrigan threw the rag onto the puddle, allowing it to soak up the moisture.

"Let me help you." The king smiled and knelt down beside Morrigan, hovering his hand above the wet rag. It dried within a few moments, along with the floor around it. Then Alphegor put his hand on her head. A pleasant warmth spread from it down her body, and she felt the cold and wetness dry out and disappear. Half a minute later, she was completely dry.

"Thank you, Father," Morrigan chimed in, and Alphegor scooped her up in his arms, carrying her into the apartment.

"Hey! What about me?" Azrael called out from behind.

"If I recall, Eirwen offered to teach you how to properly apply fire spells to smaller outputs for drying and similar tasks. But you just wanted more power," the king retorted.

"Fine, but I am not staying in these wet clothes." The demon began taking off his clothes. As he removed his shirt, Morrigan saw the round mark on his chest—the oath he had sworn to her. However, when he began to take off his pants, she quickly hid her face in Alphegor's chest.

"Do you have no manners, Azrael? You are in the presence of a princess!" Alphegor growled, putting his hand over Morrigan's eyes.

Thank you! I have no desire to see Azrael naked.

"Where am I supposed to go? This place is so small!" Azrael complained, and the king glared at him. The white-haired demon shrank back a little and went to the bathroom, where he proceeded to undress.

"Princess, do you have any clothes I could wear?"

"Oh, for the love of all that is dark," the king said with a groan. He sat on one of the chairs, carefully placing Morrigan in his lap.

"No. I don't wear men's clothes," Morrigan called back, but an idea popped into her mind. She slid out of her father's lap, who observed her curiously. She winked at him and began rummaging through the closet. "Wait! Actually, I might have something suitable for you."

"Really? Bring it over," Azrael yelled from the bathroom, and Morrigan snickered as she pulled out one of her long summer dresses. The fabric was stretchy and light, so it would fit even somebody with a larger build than hers. Seeing what the girl had in mind, the king smiled and put one of his legs over the other, watching the scene with amusement.

She went to the bathroom entrance and stuck her hand with the dress draped on it inside while making sure not to look. Azrael took it, no doubt not understanding the foreign fabric at first, but after a moment Morrigan heard him gasp.

"This is a dress!" he spat in outrage.

Morrigan and Alphegor laughed. "Well, you asked for clothes," Morrigan said. "This is the only thing I can offer."

"Nuh-uh! I am not putting this on. I'll just walk around naked."

The bathroom door opened, and Morrigan hurried to cover her eyes. But before Azrael could properly exit, Alphegor lunged forward, pushing the young demon back into the bathroom.

"You will wear this, or you will sit out on the street naked," the king snarled.

"Yes, Your Majesty," Azrael squeaked, and Alphegor retreated from the bathroom. Morrigan almost felt bad for Azrael as she heard him whimpering—almost.

After a few minutes, the bathroom door opened again, and Azrael came out wearing a flowery white dress that seemed stretched to its absolute limits. Morrigan stifled a laugh, while Alphegor didn't bother to hide his sneer. For the first time, she saw something akin to a blush spread on the mage's face.

"It suits you," the king teased, and Morrigan lost her composure, letting out a hearty laugh. Azrael glared at her at first, but as she continued laughing, his expression softened and he chuckled.

"What doesn't suit me?" Azrael moved his hips like Morrigan had seen concubines do so many times when trying to catch Alphegor's attention, and she laughed even harder, to the point her stomach and cheeks began hurting.

"Enough, enough." Morrigan held her stomach in laughter, trying to regain her composure.

"Your Majesty, look at my giant breasts!" Azrael's voice turned eerily feminine, no doubt a work of some magic, and Morrigan snorted, completely unable to control herself. Seeing her laugh, Alphegor and Azrael laughed too. They enjoyed the light atmosphere for a moment, then Morrigan began to think.

"Once we go back to Doppelta, I'll have to properly learn to become a worthy Crown Princess," she said, thinking about all of her sisters who would no doubt give anything to take her place, and their mothers, who did everything in their power to catch Alphegor's attention.

"Yes, that is inevitable," Alphegor said solemnly.

"What if..." She looked at her father nervously, then continued with her gaze glued to the floor. "What if I don't want to be the Crown Princess?"

Azrael roared with laughter, the fabric of the white dress barely holding together under the strain. After a moment, he calmed down and said, "Why would you not want to be a queen? You get to rule over everybody and do whatever you want!"

"No, you have a responsibility over people, to take care of them and solve issues that could threaten their lives," Morrigan objected, but Azrael waved his hand dismissively.

"That's why you have the ministers do all that stuff for you. You just tell them what you want to do and voila! It gets done." Azrael sat on the bed and crossed one leg over the other, revealing more skin than Morrigan wanted to see. She and Alphegor sighed in unison and shook their heads.

"Father, are you sure he is over two hundred years old?" she asked. "Many humans my age understand that things are not so simple."

"I'm afraid Azrael stopped aging at twenty," Alphegor replied, then turned his attention to Morrigan. "I understand your concerns, Morrigan. It is no simple matter I am asking of you. However, with magic as strong as yours, there is nobody better suited to rule."

"But I—" she began, ready to reject the idea, but Alphegor raised his hand to silence her.

"Before you deny this role completely, give it some time. It is not something you have to learn today or tomorrow. You'll have hundreds of years to understand it," he explained.

Morrigan nodded.

If there is no rush, then I suppose it won't hurt for me to at least try. Perhaps in time I'll come to like ruling. Although currently it doesn't seem very likely...

"I'll give it a try, Father," she said.

"Good girl." Alphegor smiled, ruffling her hair gently.

"Hey, if she doesn't want to rule, could I maybe get a shot?" Azrael perked up, looking hopefully at Alphegor.

"I'd sooner let the Underworld freeze over!"

* * *

Morrigan stared at her bed, looking at it from one side to the next, assessing it from every possible angle. It was just a regular single bed. A bed meant for one person. A sleeping place that was made to accommodate the body of a single individual.

Then Morrigan looked at Alphegor and Azrael, who were sitting at the table, one flipping through her childhood photo album while the other messed around with her laptop, going from one program to the next and amusing himself with their features. Azrael had changed back into his clothes, which Morrigan had put in the dryer. Meanwhile, Alphegor had been learning everything about Morrigan's life as a human.

However, the issue was not with the activities they were doing, even if Morrigan wanted to pull her laptop away from Azrael and hide childhood pictures from her doting father. The problem was their size. They were two large demons. Fully grown male adults. Morrigan looked back at the bed again and groaned.

Where are we all supposed to sleep tonight? I don't think Father can even fit on my bed.

"Is there a problem, Morrigan?" Alphegor asked as he continued sifting through the photos with a smile on his face.

"Uh... I'm just trying to figure out where we are going to sleep tonight," she explained, and he tore his eyes away from the photos—although he didn't seem to want to—and looked at her.

"Surely there must be a space to sleep in this large mansion. I saw so many rooms on the way up here," Alphegor said, clearly unaware of the issue.

"Haha... Actually, only these few rooms over here belong to me. Well, not really. I am paying rent to live here, but it still belongs to somebody else. All those rooms that you saw in the hallway belong to other people," she said. Alphegor blinked in disbelief, and even Azrael paused his tinkering with the laptop to look at her.

"Wait... this tiny space is your whole living space? Just these three rooms?" Azrael asked, motioning with his hand to emphasize the smallness of the apartment.

"Yes. I'm not really rich or anything. I can't afford a bigger place," Morrigan huffed, sitting on her bed.

"No, Morrigan. You can afford to buy anything your heart desires. In fact, let's purchase this whole building right now." Alphegor stood up and walked towards the exit, no doubt to make said purchase. She quickly jumped up to her feet and ran after him, grabbing his hand.

"No, Father! It's not that simple. Each apartment belongs to a different person. You can't just go and buy the whole building all at once. And even if you could, the current tenants would have thirty days to move their belongings to a new home," she explained, and the king scowled.

"How convoluted. The human ruler is most inefficient."

"Humans don't really have a single ruler for a country anymore. Well, not in most countries, at least. The country is usually led by a group of people who change at least once every eight years."

"Every eight years? What can one even do in eight years?" Azrael barked out a laugh, then returned his attention to the laptop, losing his interest in the topic.

"Wouldn't that just create problems every time the ruling group changes? Normally, each ruler brings a set of big changes with their reign," Alphegor said, rubbing his chin in contemplation.

"Oh, it certainly does create problems. But enough about politics, we need to figure out where we can sleep tonight," Morrigan said, pointing towards the small bed to accentuate the issue.

Alphegor nodded in agreement. "Are you sure there isn't a place we could buy?" the king asked.

She was about to say no, but then she realized that there was a place they could buy.

"Oh, we could stay in a hotel!" She said the word "hotel" in English, as she didn't know the demon word for it.

Do they even have hotels in the Underworld? Probably not.

"A hotel?"

"Yes, it's like an inn. People can stay there overnight if they pay money."

"Are we going to see more of the human world? That's fun! Can I take this along?" Azrael beamed and lifted the laptop up, the opened internet browser window playing a video of cats. "It has moving pictures!"

Morrigan sighed. Taking two demons to the hotel would surely result in trouble, but she didn't have much of a choice.

I'll just deal with the problems once they arise.

CHAPTER 2

HOTEL TROUBLE

I knew there would be trouble, but I didn't expect it to happen before we even reached the hotel.

Having shifted into her human form, Morrigan walked through the streets, Alphegor and Azrael next to her. Of course, that didn't sound like it would be an issue. However, it was Saturday evening, which meant that the city streets were filled with people looking to relax and unwind after a hard week at work.

And all of their eyes were glued to the two charismatic men next to her—one cold and unapproachable, almost like a god walking on Earth, while the other was warm and inviting, his grin promising trouble.

"Seems like humans can recognize a good-looking demon when they see one," Azrael said, winking at a pair of girls passing by. They giggled and stopped dead in their tracks, watching Azrael and muttering among themselves as if wondering whether they had the courage to approach him. But one look at Alphegor made them take a step back.

"They don't know that you're a demon! And stop winking at every girl you see. You're drawing too much attention," Morrigan grumbled.

"You heard her," Alphegor growled, and Azrael clicked his tongue in displeasure.

"Can't even have a little bit of fun."

"I thought you hated humans," Morrigan muttered, remembering her conversation with Azrael before he had opened the portal to Earth.

"It's actually my first time seeing humans besides you, Princess. I can't help but be curious." Azrael shrugged as he looked from one shop window to the next, eagerly taking in the new environment. "Not to mention that they look nothing like humans in Doppelta."

"You're two hundred years old and you haven't seen humans before? How do you know that they look different, then?" Morrigan exclaimed, shocked by the fact.

"From books, of course," Azrael explained. "While the overall look is similar, the clothes humans wear in this world are really weird."

"Humans are prohibited from entering the Underworld, and usually demons do not wish to go to the surface," Alphegor added.

"Really? But... Why don't demons take humans as slaves if they take elves and dwarves who live on the Overworld?" Morrigan asked, though the topic of slaves always made her feel uncomfortable. If she had any say, she'd probably release all of them, but Morrigan also understood that the matter was probably more complex than that.

"It's a dark topic best left for another time. Is that large building over there not the hotel you were talking about?" Alphegor pointed towards the beautiful four-story building with large windows and many balconies that had lush greenery growing on them. This was one of the best hotels in the city and would cost Morrigan a lot of money just for a single night.

But I'll be going back to Doppelta soon, so it doesn't matter. Human money wouldn't do me any good anyway. It's just pieces of paper, after all.

"That looks much nicer than the house you live in," Azrael pointed out, and Morrigan shot him an annoyed look.

"Because this is supposed to be a luxurious place," she objected, grabbing Alphegor's hand and pulling him ahead. "Let's go inside, Father."

The foyer was neat and tidy, with an elaborate rug at the entrance and small palm trees growing in giant pots. There was a TV, which was playing a music channel, and even a coffee machine labeled as free to use.

"How may I help you?" said a friendly looking woman, approaching the group with keen interest.

"We'd like to rent three—" Morrigan lifted her hand up, showing three fingers, but Alphegor raised his hand and interrupted her.

"Two."

"We'd like to rent two rooms for a night or two," she corrected. The attendant looked at Morrigan, looking like her young, human self, and then at Alphegor, and a small smirk appeared on her face. It was there for just a few moments before she regained her polite, professional expression.

She just thought of something indecent, didn't she? Gross! He is my father. I know we don't look like parent and daughter with our current appearances, but still. Get your mind out of the gutter, lady!

"Of course. What sorts of rooms would you like? We have regular rooms without a balcony, premium rooms with a balcony, and VIP rooms that have a sauna in them," the woman said.

"What did she say?" Azrael asked as he sipped on a cup of coffee with a large dollop of cream on top. "This stuff is good, by the way."

"How did you...? Never mind. She asked what kinds of rooms we'd like—regular, premium with a balcony, or VIP with a sauna?" she translated into the demon language.

"What's a sownah? I want to try that!" Azrael exclaimed, his eyes shining with an excitement that only a young child could have.

"How much is the room with a sauna?" Morrigan asked the attendant sheepishly.

"It's five hundred euros per night," she replied with a smile, and Morrigan barely managed to contain her shock.

Five hundred a night? That's more than I pay for my apartment for a month!

"We'll take two premium rooms," she said, and the attendant nodded, retreating behind the counter.

"Did you get the room with the sownah thing, or whatever you call it?" Azrael pestered.

"No! That is too expensive. I got us premium rooms. Those should be comfortable enough."

"But I wanted the sownah!" he whined, tugging on Morrigan's sleeve.

Alphegor glared at him, and the demon quickly retreated. "Be grateful that Morrigan is paying for your room. She could have just as easily left you behind," the king growled.

That's a great idea! Shame I didn't think of that earlier.

"Tch... Fine." Azrael returned to sipping his coffee, delighted by the drink.

"Here's the keys to your room. I'll just need your name," the attendant said with a pen in hand.

"It's..." She paused for a moment, wondering which name to give, then smiled. "It's Morrigan."

"Unusual name. Are you a foreigner? I heard you speaking a different language," the woman added conversationally.

"Yes. We're foreigners," Morrigan confirmed, and it felt good for her to admit that. It solidified that she belonged in Doppelta, not here.

* * *

After teaching Azrael how to unlock and relock the door to his hotel room, Morrigan and Alphegor retreated to their own room. It was large, with two queen-sized beds, a giant TV mounted on the wall, and many potted plants placed strategically around the room.

"What a long day!" Morrigan groaned and jumped straight onto the large bed. It was soft and comfortable, and she could smell a faint hint of detergent coming from it. Her eyelids felt heavy and her body seemed to sink into the soft blanket. A few moments later, she reverted back to her demon form.

"You must be tired, little one," Alphegor mused, gently caressing her head. The proximity of his presence only made her relax more, forcing her eyes closed.

"Mhm," she mumbled, barely awake. Alphegor said something else, but she couldn't hear it. Instead, she vaguely remembered him tucking her into the bed and wishing her good night.

Morrigan woke up to loud music blasting from somewhere outside. She opened her eyes groggily and saw that it was definitely still nighttime.

"What is with that loud music so late into the night?" she grumbled, feeling Alphegor move next to her. She was a bit surprised to see him sleeping in the same bed, but didn't really mind. In fact, it was comforting to remain close to him.

"That infernal noise! Whoever dares to wake my daughter when she needs to rest will pay dearly." Alphegor's eyes grew as cold as ice, and he swiftly rose out of bed.

"Father, wait. I'll come too. You don't know human languages," she said, then quickly shifted into her human form.

"Very well. We shall punish the miscreant who dared to create such a racket." The king hid his demonic features and put on clothes in two blinks of an eye. He strode purposefully towards the exit, and Morrigan followed.

I just hope he doesn't try to murder whatever sorry fool decided to blast music so late. I'm surprised the hotel staff haven't intervened.

They followed the source of the music outside and saw a group of people dancing by the outdoor pool, splashing water, hollering, and being all sorts of annoying. Morrigan wasn't sure how to even approach the group.

I doubt anybody here would listen to what I say.

"Silence!" Alphegor commanded in the demon tongue, and the whole group of people stopped. All of them looked at him wide-eyed, each freezing on the spot and blinking like a deer caught in headlights.

Or almost all.

"Oh, Your Majesty, Princess! You have come to enjoy human fun, too? These drinks are great. And the music! I've never heard such great music before." Azrael cackled and giggled, clearly drunk beyond any reason.

"Azrael! Is this your doing?" Alphegor asked, and Morrigan felt the air grow chillier. The gathered crowd began to slowly disperse, no doubt people's survival instincts kicking in and urging them to move to safety.

"Yeah! Listen to this." Azrael went over to a nearby table that had a phone set on it and a giant pair of loudspeakers set next to it. He quickly tapped something on the phone and turned on club music so loud and with bass so low that it reverberated throughout the whole area, making Morrigan's knees buckle and shake.

"This little device is amazing! Not only does it have this magical internet thing, you can also connect it to this weird box using wires, and it produces this amazing sound!"

"Turn. It. Off!" she yelled, pressing her ears shut before the dreadful noise could damage her hearing.

"What?! I can't hear you, Princess! It's too loud," Azrael yelled back, moving his hands up in the air with the rhythm of the music.

Alphegor went up to the table, grabbed the phone, and smashed it against the ground, turning it into a pile of scrap.

"My phone!" one of the partygoers whined, but seeing Alphegor's cold glare, he just slumped and retreated back into the hotel.

"Aww, why did you have to go and do that?" Azrael whined.

Morrigan could see that her father was about to unleash some horrifying magic onto the drunken fool, so she went up to Azrael and grabbed his hand. "Enough for one night. It's time to sleep," she commanded, then began dragging him along.

"But I..." he whined, but she shook her head.

"If you want to live, then do as I say," Morrigan snarled, pulling him faster. Azrael didn't seem to get her hint, but was too drunk to object.

I swear, there are only so many times I can save you from Father's rage. I'm afraid we're about to reach the limit soon.

Chapter 3

Shopping

"I'm bored!" Azrael whined for the hundredth time, lying on Morrigan's hotel bed and switching channels on the TV in an attempt to find something interesting to watch. Initially, he was ecstatic about it, watching it for hours on end. But as he quickly discovered, television was filled with nothing more than ads with occasional snippets of movies and shows in between.

"Maybe there would be no need for you to be bored if you just opened the portal back to Doppelta," Morrigan complained, snatching the remote from his hands to turn off the TV.

"It's too early. I haven't recovered enough magic energy yet." He buried his face in the soft bed covers.

"You seem energetic enough to me," Morrigan grumbled, then poked his shoulder.

"You clearly have not trained your magical abilities enough if one spell can leave you completely useless for almost a week," Alphegor said as he took a sip of the wine that was inside the fridge.

"Hey, opening dimensional portals requires a lot of magic, and the magic on this planet is nearly nonexistent. Princess, don't you find it stifling?" Azrael objected, sitting up in the bed and shooing her hand away.

"Not really? I've spent more than twenty years here, after all."

"There is less magic here, but the little bit that I feel is very pure and strong. It should have rejuvenated you a few days ago," Alphegor reprimanded, but Azrael turned his gaze away.

"Not everyone has had thousands of years to perfect their magic," he grumbled, and Morrigan chuckled.

"How about we go for a walk around the city?" she suggested. In reality, the confines of the small hotel room were bothering her, but she had hoped that Azrael would have recovered his energy by now. However, if it would take a few more days until they could get home, she'd rather do something other than just stare at the TV.

"Yes! Let's go!" Azrael jumped up instantly, running for the door like a dog that was about to go for a walk.

"Calm down, Azrael. Morrigan said we'll go for a walk, not a sprint." The king drank the last bits of his wine, then got up. "If you do the same thing you did with humans the first night we got to this hotel, then I shall tie you to a lamppost until you have recovered."

"I'll be good, I promise!" Azrael snapped his fingers, and his demonic features disappeared. Morrigan also took on her human form while Alphegor's horns and tail seamlessly disappeared into thin air, as if they were never there to begin with.

"Why don't we first go to a shop? I feel like having a treat," Morrigan suggested, then skipped out of the hotel room, Alphegor and Azrael following close behind.

* * *

This was a huge mistake!

Morrigan watched in horror as Azrael pushed the cart filled to the brim with snacks, fruits, and whatever else the cheeky demon had managed to get his hands on. Even Alphegor's threats had done nothing to dissuade him from acting like a madman, so they had largely given up and instead took a shopping basket for their own use.

"I am not paying for all that," Morrigan muttered as Azrael added ten cans of corn and eight cans of beans to his cart.

"Obviously not. He'll be putting everything he took back in its place once we are done," Alphegor scoffed.

"What would you like to try?" Morrigan asked with a smile, trying to distract herself from the lunatic in front of her.

"I am not sure. All these things are completely unfamiliar to me. What do you recommend?" Alphegor smiled at her. She stopped and pondered what one thing would be that a demon wouldn't have tried.

While things in the Underworld are quite different, when it comes to food, there has always been something that was rather close. There's savory pies, salads, meats, fruits, and even desserts, so I can't say that I ever missed something.

Morrigan looked over the shelves of the stores, inspecting their contents and wondering what something truly interesting would be. Finally, her eyes landed upon the freezers on the far side of the store.

"I know! Follow me," she exclaimed, then headed straight to the freezers.

Unsurprisingly, Azrael was already rummaging through them and piling tubs of ice cream into his cart. "What is this cold stuff? Is it edible?" He skeptically poked one of the tubs.

"Yes, it is. I think we better take some smaller ones so we can try various flavors," Morrigan said, then put a few ice cream cones, popsicles, and ice cream sandwiches into the shopping basket that Alphegor was holding.

"Are these desserts of some sort?" the king asked, taking a chocolate ice cream cone to inspect it closer.

"Yes! I am sure you will like it, Father," Morrigan said, remembering how the king enjoyed his desserts during mealtimes.

"If you say so, then I am sure it is true," Alphegor said resolutely. He placed the treat back into the basket.

"Really? This cold thing? I bet it tastes no different than ice," Azrael scoffed, but he did nothing to remove the tubs from his cart.

"We'll see about that!"

Morrigan and Alphegor went to the cash register to pay for the ice cream, while Azrael was ordered to go back into the store and stack everything he took back onto the shelves. She didn't trust him to do the task properly, but hoped that he would at least put frozen stuff back into the freezer and the other things in the general vicinity of where they were before. Store staff would surely handle the rest.

"These human inventions are most unusual. They don't use any magic and yet they do things that defy all logic," Alphegor said as he intently watched the cashier scan each product. The young woman— a student, by the looks of it—was blushing under his intense gaze, not knowing where to look.

"Human devices run on electricity," Morrigan explained, then paid for the treats before the poor cashier could melt into a puddle like one of Alphegor's concubines.

"Electricity, you say? Most fascinating. So humans in this world are able to use electric magic," the king pondered.

"No, not at all. We harvest electric energy in various ways and store it in special facilities, power lines, and batteries," she explained, rather proud of human ingenuity.

"Harvest electricity? Can you do that too, Morrigan?" The king looked rather excited at the prospect.

"Me? Not really. It's something done by large groups of people, rather than just one person."

"I wonder if I could do that in the Underworld, too." The king scratched his chin. Morrigan chuckled nervously, wondering how to explain that it would require either a large body of flowing water or large plains with strong winds or sunlight. All things that the Underworld did not have.

"Hey, don't leave me behind!" Azrael ran towards them while a disgruntled-looking shopworker chased after him.

"What did you do?" Morrigan asked as she sped up her pace.

"I just dumped everything inside one of the icy boxes. I'm not sure what the guy is saying, but he doesn't sound very happy about it." Azrael chuckled, then began running at full speed, as if it were a game.

I'm sorry, mister shopworker! I promise not to bring this lunatic here again.

* * *

With the store far behind them and with their ice cream in tow, Morrigan, Alphegor, and Azrael strolled through a local park. Since it was the middle of a workday, it was fairly empty, with the exception of a few elderly people and mothers with strollers. Morrigan looked up at the deep blue sky, admiring how vibrant it was—almost blinding.

"I never thought the sky could be so... vast. It feels like it is never-ending," Azrael said, also admiring it.

"It *is* never-ending. There are millions upon billions of stars and galaxies out there, and we can see them as nothing more than dots," Morrigan said, wishing that it were nighttime so she could see the infinite galaxy.

"I've heard about stars, but I have never actually seen them. How come I can't see them now?" Azrael asked. He squinted, trying to discern something in the vast blue.

"Because it's daytime. The sun is so bright and so close that all the faraway stars just disappear," she explained.

Azrael turned towards the sun, about to stare straight at it, but Morrigan managed to grab his hand and pull him away.

"Hey, why are you pulling me?" he grumbled, freeing himself from her grasp.

"Morrigan is kind enough to prevent you from going blind. Never stare directly at the sun," the king scoffed, then eyed the treats he was holding in a bag. "Where could we enjoy these?"

"Why don't we just sit at the table over there?" Morrigan pointed at one of the many picnic tables littered throughout the park, and he nodded.

"I want the yellow one." Azrael pointed towards the lemon ice cream cone, his eyes sparkling with excitement.

He truly is just a kid. It's almost cute.

Morrigan chuckled and nodded, fishing the lemon ice cream out of the bag and handing it to the demon. Then she took the chocolate ice cream cone and gave it to Alphegor.

"I think you'll enjoy this one, Father. It's chocolate flavored," she explained.

"Humans in this world have chocolate too? That is reassuring," the king said, taking the cone. Morrigan grabbed a strawberry-flavored ice cream sandwich and quickly tore off the wrapping. Azrael and Alphegor stared at the plastic packaging, unsure of what to do.

"This isn't edible, is it?" Azrael asked as he pulled at the wrapping.

"No, it's just a package," she replied, then quickly tore open Alphegor's and Azrael's ice cream. They took out their treats and looked them over.

"It is as cold as ice," Alphegor noted, then took a small bite out of the treat. Azrael didn't hold back and instead took a solid chunk out of the ice cream.

"Ahh! Too cold!" he whined, swallowing the giant chunk. Morrigan watched in horror as the demon grabbed his head and began howling from pain. "Wh-What? Is this poison? My head!"

"No! You swallowed it before it had a chance to melt. It gave you a brain freeze."

"Brain freeze?" Alphegor asked as he continued to eat his ice cream slowly, savoring every bite.

"Yes. I don't really understand the science behind it, but if you eat too much ice cream—or anything cold, really—too fast, then it'll make your head hurt."

"Oh, it stopped," Azrael cheered. He continued scarfing down the rest of his ice cream, occasionally whining and grunting from the pain.

He must be a masochist. Nobody would intentionally hurt themselves like this.

As they continued eating the treats, the sun began to set, and dusk settled over the park. Keen to see the stars again, Morrigan suggested that they stay outside until nighttime, and both demons agreed. Azrael ran around like a little kid while Morrigan told her father about various things in the human world that Doppelta did not have.

"I have to admit that the human world has its charms. Especially during the night," Alphegor said, looking up at the vast night sky. Millions of tiny stars shone there, signifying the vastness of the cosmos around them.

"Father, is there a night sky like this in Doppelta, too?" she asked as she stared at the full moon.

"No," the king said, and Morrigan dropped her gaze. "It is far more magnificent than this."

"Really?" she asked, then looked at him. Alphegor nodded and smiled at her.

"Really. I'll show it to you one day."

"Speaking of Doppelta"—Azrael suddenly appeared before them, hair filled with stray leaves and tiny twigs—"I am ready to create a portal back."

Chapter 4

Return to Doppelta

Morrigan stood in front of the large Demon Castle, its magnificent walls stretching high up into the darkness of the Underworld, while the light from its windows brought life to an otherwise desolate-looking place. Alphegor held her tiny hand and carefully assessed the structure from its foundation all the way up to its peaks. Seeing that everything was just as it should be, he gave a curt nod.

Behind them sat a tired and dejected Azrael, his eyes downcast and sunken. His magic reserves were completely exhausted after creating the portal back to Doppelta. While he had already complained that the portal required a lot of energy, Morrigan had not expected that her usually energetic magic teacher would be so drained.

"Finally! We're back," Alphegor announced in his loud, booming voice, sending the message to all castle inhabitants. In a few moments, the whole castle seemed to rouse, excited chattering coming from the windows as the demons came to look at their King.

"We're back," Morrigan confirmed with a smile, admiring the castle. It was dark and gloomy, but it still felt like the building was welcoming her back as more and more castle lights sprang to life.

"I'm going to rest in my room," Azrael announced. He was about to turn into a shadow when Alphegor turned towards him and glared, stopping him dead in his tracks.

"I don't think so," the king said. With a wave of his hand, dark tendrils grabbed Azrael and tightened around him, making him unable to move a muscle. "You tried to get rid of Morrigan and your oath to her."

Azrael chuckled awkwardly as a bead of sweat rolled down his face. "She looked a bit miserable here in the Underworld, so I figured it might be better if she lived with her own kind."

"She *is* with her own kind!" Alphegor snarled, and the dark tendrils began to sink into the ground, dragging Azrael along with them.

"I'm sorry, I'm sorry! I was wrong!" Azrael squirmed and wriggled, trying to break free from his bonds. He looked so miserable that Morrigan started feeling bad for him and tugged on Alphegor's sleeve.

"Please don't be too harsh on him, Father. I know he wanted to get rid of me, but he didn't cause me any harm in the end," she said, and the tendrils slowed down a little. "He has also helped me many times in the past."

"Your Majesty, you have finally returned." Lucius materialized from a shadow right next to them and greeted Alphegor with a deep bow.

"Nice to see you, Lucius." The king gave him a curt nod. The Prime Minister straightened, and Morrigan saw how his eyes darted from Alphegor to her and finally to Azrael.

"Your Majesty, I am glad to see you return, but may I inquire about the current situation and the reason you were gone for so long?" Lucius asked, his head slightly inclined to show reverence.

"So long? I was merely gone for a week, Lucius." The king laughed, but Morrigan understood what the old demon was talking about.

"No, Father." She shook her head and pulled on his sleeve for him to bend down. He obliged, and she whispered in his ear. "Only two weeks passed on Earth during the whole time I spent in Doppelta. That means that while we were on Earth, approximately two years passed here."

The king appeared startled at first, but then he nodded solemnly and straightened.

"Your Majesty?" Lucius inquired nervously.

"I apologize for the wait, Lucius. Give a short report on the most important events."

"At once, Your Majesty." Lucius opened his mouth, but a loud cry resounded from the Demon Castle's entrance. Morrigan looked towards it and saw Deziara running towards them at full speed. She had grown taller, beginning to resemble a teenager.

"Father, Morri!" she called out from across the yard as tears fell down her face in a steady stream.

"Deziara!" Morrigan shouted, running towards her sister. The two girls collided into a bear hug, at which point Deziara began crying even louder.

"Where did you disappear to for so long? I thought I would never see you again," she said through tears, then looked down at Morrigan. "But... you haven't grown at all. What happened?"

"I shall explain everything later." Alphegor went up to both girls and placed a hand on Deziara's head.

"Father..." A new set of tears erupted as Deziara launched herself at Alphegor, who hugged her while gently rubbing her back.

"I told you I'd bring Morrigan back," he said, and Deziara nodded as she hiccuped and sobbed into his chest.

It's nice to see him care for Deziara, at least. Perhaps he'll be nicer towards our other sisters too.

"Yes! I am so happy you have returned." Deziara hiccuped while Alphegor pulled a napkin from within his coat pocket and wiped away her tears.

"I'm sorry, sister," Morrigan muttered, taking hold of Deziara's hand. But the girl shook her head and pulled her into another hug.

"As long as you are back, it is alright," she said.

More and more demons came running out of the castle, and Morrigan recognized her other sisters and concubines among them. The younger girls were bolder and came up to Morrigan and Alphegor, greeting them excitedly. Meanwhile, the older girls and concubines looked more reserved. They were staring at Alphegor, trying to catch his attention by waving their hands or smiling at him. But the king greeted the younger girls who came up to Morrigan first.

"It's nice to see you back, younger sister!"

"We missed you and Father both."

"Let's celebrate your return."

Morrigan was pleasantly surprised that other half-sisters besides Deziara had missed her. Their mothers might have put them up to this, but their reactions seemed genuine.

For now, I shall accept their greetings. No need to be suspicious of everyone the moment I get back.

"Lady Morrigan!" came a voice from behind the gathered crowd of demons. Morrigan tried to peer over it to find the source, but everyone was so much taller than her.

"Gunna?" she called out, and the demons slowly parted, allowing Morrigan through. Sure enough, there stood her loyal nanny, her eyes red and tired, her stocky hands trembling, while her beard and hair looked somewhat disheveled.

"Lady Morrigan!" the dwarf woman exclaimed, opening her arms wide for a hug. Without hesitation, Morrigan ran up to her nanny and threw her arms around her. She felt thinner than she remembered.

"Gunna, have you lost some weight?"

"Dear child, I was so worried about you that I could barely sleep. I feared I might never see you again," Gunna said, tears flowing into her beard.

"I'm sorry, Gunna. I didn't think it would make you so worried..."

"It's not your fault, Lady Morrigan. As long as you are back safe and sound, that is all that matters," the dwarf woman said, running her large, gentle hand through Morrigan's hair. The girl nodded, barely able to hold back her own tears.

I never should have run away. To think that Gunna would be so worried about me as to lose weight.

"I'm still sorry, Gunna," Morrigan said before noticing a distinct murmur coming from a nearby demoness. Peeking over her shoulder, she saw concubines and some of her older sisters sneering, or even laughing quietly.

Are they making fun of me because I am so attached to Gunna? Fine, let them. We'll see what Father will say about that.

"Aren't you all forgetting somebody?" Azrael whined, still snugly contained within Alphegor's dark tendrils.

"I think I heard a doggy bark," Lady Lily said as she approached the group, smiling at Morrigan. Unlike the other concubines, who just gave her the obligatory polite smile, she appeared genuinely happy to see Morrigan.

"It's nice to see you again, Lady Lily," Morrigan said with a small curtsy, and the demoness curtsied in return.

"Indeed it is, child. Deziara missed you dearly. Talked about you every day, hoping that you and His Majesty would return," Lady Lily said, affectionately patting Deziara, who had joined to stand next to her mother.

"Mom! You're not supposed to tell her that." The demon girl blushed and pulled on her mother's hand in mock anger.

"Sorry, sorry. I am not so young anymore. Must have slipped my memory." Lady Lily chuckled, and both girls laughed alongside her.

"Princess Morrigan! You have returned," a voice called out from behind the crowd. A cold shiver ran through Morrigan's spine, and she took a step back.

Asdeus... Will she try to act as if she has missed me greatly to get on Alphegor's good side? There's no way I am letting her get away with that.

The demons parted to let the demoness through, her signature heels clattering against the stone walkway as she hurried towards Morrigan. Fake tears were streaming down her face, and her face almost convinced Morrigan that she had missed her. Almost.

Morrigan deliberately took a few steps back, glaring at Asdeus. The demoness's gaze remained a perfect mask of worry, but Alphegor had already picked up on Morrigan's distress and in a few swift strides closed the distance between them.

"What's wrong, Morrigan?" he asked, his eyes darting from Morrigan to Asdeus, analyzing and trying to understand what was happening. Asdeus, however, had no intention of letting her speak. She rushed forward, making her act even more dramatic.

"I am so relieved to see you both return safely! I was so worried when I heard that Princess Morrigan had disappeared that I could barely sleep," she cried, reaching one of her hands towards Morrigan. But Morrigan quickly ducked behind her father's leg, safely out of reach.

Haven't slept? Yeah, right. Gunna is the one who couldn't sleep. You look like you had the best sleep in the world—your skin is almost glowing.

"Lies!" Morrigan muttered, and she saw Asdeus's mask slip for just a split second, glaring at the girl.

"What do you mean, Morrigan?" Alphegor asked as he put his hand around her shoulders, protecting her from the demoness.

"Your Majesty—"

"Silence!" Alphegor commanded, and Asdeus took several steps back, her previous facade completely broken.

Time for retribution!

"Father, Asdeus tortured me!" Morrigan announced loud enough for the whole Underworld to hear. The gathered crowd of demons gasped as one and began muttering among themselves. The demoness looked around helplessly, her mouth opening and closing like a fish out of water.

"I... I would never!" she tried to defend herself, waving her hands in the air. "I... Princess Morrigan is... She's not..."

"Silence!" Alphegor ordered, and the whole gathering of demons instantly quieted, looking at their King. His eyes had turned red in anger—there was a storm brewing within him.

It doesn't matter what Asdeus says now. Even if she were to scream that I am a human, nobody would believe it. It would seem like nothing more than a desperate attempt to save herself.

"How did she torture you, Morrigan?" Alphegor asked, his eyes never moving away from Asdeus. The demoness stepped back, looking like she was about to cry for real this time.

"Your Majesty... I..."

"If you do not let Morrigan speak, then I shall pull out your tongue where you stand." Alphegor's eyes were filled with rage, and Asdeus froze on the spot, her mouth half open.

"Father, she would inflict pain on my hand each time I wrote a letter wrong. She'd force me to write a single character multiple times, and for each wrong one, she would use some magic to make me feel pain," Morrigan said, and the surrounding demons gasped again.

"She tortured the Princess?"

"What are those barbaric teaching methods?"

"Has she been doing that to my child as well?"

The glares intensified, and Asdeus's hand began to shake.

"No, it's not true... I would never do that to a demon child. She is..." Asdeus tried to salvage the situation, but there was nobody in the crowd who would believe her. Even the concubines, who had always treated Morrigan with animosity, looked shocked.

"What else did she do, Morrigan?" Alphegor's voice sounded like a low rumble, and Morrigan felt the ground shake. The other demons noticed it too, looking around in confusion for the source.

What is going on? Who... Wait... Is Father doing that?

Morrigan looked at Alphegor's face, then jumped back. The anger that contorted his expression could not be described in words. It was like he was the god of rage, his fists clenched so hard that blood began dripping from his hands, while his gaze was solely focused on Asdeus.

Alphegor took a step closer to her, and Asdeus shook her head, tears streaming down her face. She fell as she stumbled back, but the woman did not hit the ground. Instead, a portal opened behind her, and she fell straight into it.

"You'll pay for this, cockroach!" Asdeus yelled at Morrigan as the portal closed behind her.

"Find her at once!" Alphegor ordered, and a dozen demon guards rushed out of the castle's yard to search for Asdeus.

Chapter 5

Princess Affairs

When Morrigan awoke and found herself back in her bed—her actual bed, in the Underworld—she nearly cried in joy. She hadn't been gone for longer than a week, but it felt like much more than that. Alphegor was sleeping soundly next to her, his usually tense face relaxed. As Morrigan got up to sit, he began to rouse from his slumber.

"Good morning, Morrigan." He smiled as he ruffled her hair.

"Good morning, Father," she said, allowing her hair to be messed up.

"It'll be a long day today. Are you ready?" The king sat up, brushing rogue strands of hair away from his face. Morrigan admired the sight of the disheveled Alphegor, not the perfect kingly persona he used in public. This part of him was something only she got to see.

"As ready as I'll ever be," Morrigan said as she jumped out of bed, ready to face the challenges ahead. Alphegor nodded at her and got up as well.

"Good. There will be quite a mess to clean up after two years of absence."

"What about Azrael? Hasn't he learned his lesson by now?" Morrigan asked, pointing towards the window. They both walked up to it and stared down at the castle yard where Azrael slept, still cocooned in the dark tendrils.

"He doesn't seem particularly bothered." Alphegor said, and one of the tendrils moved, slapping the sleeping demon awake. Azrael yelped, then looked around himself and began struggling against his bonds.

"Let me go already!" he yelled, looking up at Alphegor and Morrigan.

"I'll release him in a few hours." The king chuckled as he walked away from the window. Morrigan glanced down one more time and then turned to leave.

I suppose a few hours won't hurt him.

* * *

Alphegor strode into his office, carrying Morrigan in his arms. Lucius was already in the office, sifting through piles of documents and rearranging them in a particular order. Next to him stood Viana, carefully observing his work, as well as three of Morrigan's sisters. Viana was Alphegor's first-born daughter and was already forty-three years old. It sounded like a lot but in reality, demons were officially recognized as adults only once they turned forty.

Viana took many of her traits from her mother, Lady Viviana. Her wavy purple hair, red eyes, and impressive curves all came from her. Their personalities were also similar, both being incredibly charming and slick with their words. There was a good reason Lady Viviana was the first consort.

The other three girls were the daughters of other concubines. They were Rosalie, the third-eldest daughter; Miriam, the fourth-eldest; and finally Celiana, fifth-eldest. All of them turned to look at Morrigan and Alphegor as soon as they entered.

What Morrigan couldn't understand was why they were inside Alphegor's office. Nobody was allowed inside without the king's permission, except for Lucius. Morrigan looked towards her father for an answer, but his furrowed eyebrows indicated that he was just as confused about this as she was.

"Good morning, Your Majesty, Princess Morrigan!" Lucius greeted with a short bow.

"Good morning, Father!" Viana curtsied with a brilliant smile, and her sisters followed. But it was not lost on Morrigan that they had not acknowledged her presence.

"Why are they in my office?" Alphegor growled, and the girls bowed their heads.

"Your Majesty, allow me to explain," Lucius interjected, but the atmosphere in the room had grown so tense that Morrigan could almost feel it restraining her breath.

"Everyone leave!" Alphegor commanded.

Viana tried to pacify the king, but he was having none of it. "Father, I'd like to—"

"Do not make me repeat myself!" Alphegor glared at her, and Viana, along with the others, escaped from the room. But as they passed by Morrigan, they glared at her, malice oozing from their gazes.

This can't be good…

As soon as the door was closed, Alphegor turned towards it and drew a circle in the air. It shimmered for a moment and then hit the door, burning a circular symbol into the wood. A few seconds later it began to fade, until the door returned to its previously untouched state.

"Speak, Lucius! I know you wouldn't let anyone into my office unless there was a good reason for it," Alphegor said, setting Morrigan on the floor. She decided that it would be better to sit down and went to the small sofa, getting up onto its soft cushions.

"It's a long and complicated story, Your Majesty. I think it's best if we all sit down." Lucius sighed, then motioned towards the sofa where Morrigan was sitting. Alphegor gave him an appraising look and then sat next to her. Lucius nodded, taking a seat across from them.

"I'll start from the moment you chased Princess Morrigan," the old demon began, giving the girl an appraising look. Morrigan sank deeper into the cushion, feeling the quiet accusation in his voice.

"Do not blame Morrigan for what happened. It was my negligence as a parent that led to her running away." Alphegor wrapped his hand around Morrigan as if to shield her from Lucius. The old demon looked surprised at first, but then smiled and nodded.

"To think that you would actually grow into an admirable father figure. Love does work in mysterious ways." Lucius chuckled, to which Alphegor mumbled something incomprehensible under his breath.

"Get back to the matter at hand."

"Of course." Lucius's expression returned to his stern mask, and he cleared his throat. "After you and the Princess disappeared, people within the castle grew more and more anxious by the day. Initially, I was able to reassure them by saying that you'd soon return together with the Princess, but then the fact that you had gone missing spread outside the castle."

"So people began to panic." Alphegor rubbed his chin, and a deep crease formed on his forehead.

"Yes. Rumors went completely out of control—I suspect a party who opposes your rule aggravated the situation. Within a few weeks, demons were rioting outside of the Demon Castle, demanding your return," Lucius said, then his gaze dropped.

"Let me guess—nobles intervened," Alphegor growled.

"Yes, Your Majesty. They began suggesting that the Demon Kingdom required a new ruler. I did my best to object to their advances, assuring them that I could manage state affairs in your absence."

"But then they claimed that you were trying to claim power for yourself," Alphegor stated, then slumped back against the sofa. "I see what happened now."

Morrigan blinked, trying to understand the implication they

were talking about. She had no knowledge about politics, so whatever conclusion Alphegor had come to, she couldn't deduce.

"I don't understand. What does that have to do with Viana and my other sisters being here?" she asked, looking from Lucius to her father.

The old demon sighed. "It means that your elder sisters are now trying to acquire the position of Crown Princess," he said, rubbing the bridge of his nose. Looking at his face carefully, Morrigan noted that some additional wrinkles had appeared during their absence.

"How? Isn't Father the only one who can name the next heir?" she asked, looking up at Alphegor.

"Normally, yes. But due to our prolonged absence, your sisters could gather support from the nobles, who can push towards the selection of a new Crown Princess," the king explained.

"Yes. They were moving things along at lightning speed. Normally such matters would take years, but a few dukes were pushing towards the election of a new Crown Princess," Lucius added.

"Who? I should free their heads from their shoulders for treason," Alphegor growled, and Morrigan saw her father's eyes had gained that horrifying red color.

"Your Majesty, please be lenient. Finding a replacement for them now would be quite difficult. Especially with the festival approaching within the next decade."

"The festival?" Morrigan asked as she tried to rack her memory for an answer. She knew of many festivals on Earth, but hadn't heard about any taking place in the Underworld.

"Yes. It is a grand celebration that happens once every twenty years. I completely forgot that it is approaching. Is that the reason why the girls were here?" Alphegor addressed Lucius, who nodded.

"That, and they were also helping me with managing state affairs in your absence. Of course, I've kept their sphere of influence to a complete minimum."

"Good. That means it's not too late for Morrigan to make up for lost ground. I could completely shut down the matter entirely, but that might not sit well with the nobles, and I'd rather not have a civil war on my hands," Alphegor said nonchalantly, as if he were talking about an annoying chore.

Morrigan paled at the mention of war. As a human, she had lived in a completely peaceful country that hadn't been in a war since long before her birth. But she had seen enough news reports to know how devastating it was, especially on civilians, who arguably had nothing to do with it in the first place.

"Father, we can't have a civil war," she pleaded, grabbing his sleeve.

Alphegor smiled and gently patted her head. "Don't worry, little one. I believe we have returned just in time to resolve the situation peacefully."

"What should we do with the princesses? Allow them to continue their work?" Lucius asked.

"I have returned, so there is absolutely no reason for them to be doing that anymore. However, they may continue with their preparations for the festival," Alphegor announced.

"But the nobles? Won't they object if the princesses are suddenly cut off from state affairs?"

"I'm not so old that I need other people managing state matters for me. I'll put the nobles in their place at the earliest opportunity. Now, Lucius, give me a report of all events that require my immediate attention." Alphegor strode towards his work desk, leaving Morrigan alone on the sofa.

"What about Princess Morrigan?" Lucius asked, throwing her a look filled with pity.

"Not today, Lucius. She's been through a lot and needs to rest," Alphegor said, then snapped his fingers. "Azrael!"

The circle on the door lit up again and then disintegrated into shimmering dust. A few moments later, a disheveled and very annoyed Azrael arose from a shadow in the ground.

"I've barely managed to go to the bathroom and you've already summoned me. I already learned from my mistake, alright? No need for more punishment," the white-haired demon grumbled, but he kept his head lowered before Alphegor.

"We're going to intensify Morrigan's magic lessons," the king said sternly, and Morrigan shivered. While Alphegor was very demanding of others, he was always lenient towards her and never pushed her to do anything. If he was asking Azrael to intensify the lessons, then it was probably because there was no better choice.

There is no reason to appear incompetent anymore. In fact, this is a perfect opportunity for me to learn some actually cool magic.

"I'm ready, Father," she said resolutely, balling her little hands into fists. Alphegor nodded approvingly, looking pleased with her answer.

"Alright, now *that* is something I can understand. I'm on it, Your Majesty," Azrael said, his previously demure attitude gone. "Within a few months' time, this little girl will know more magic than all of your other daughters combined."

"Do not overdo it, Azrael. Teach her what she needs to know instead of just stuffing her full of magic that you deem to be *cool*," Lucius grumbled, crossing his arms over his chest in a disapproving sort of manner.

"Don't worry about it, old Lucius! When have I not been a good magic teacher?"

Morrigan could think of a few instances, but she decided to remain quiet for Azrael's sake.

He has suffered enough punishment for one day. Not to mention that

Father needs to cool down a little. I get a feeling that one more thing could send him into a rage.

"Focus on strengthening her independence. Her ability to protect herself should be your top priority," Alphegor noted, then walked up to Morrigan, kneeling beside her. "Do not hold back anymore. Give your lessons everything you got and trust me to take care of any problems that arise afterward."

He said the last sentence in a barely audible voice, and Morrigan nodded. "I won't let you down, Father!"

"You wouldn't be able to do that, even if you tried." He chuckled, then pulled her into a hug.

CHAPTER 6

BURNING WITH FIRE

Morrigan stared at the long row of magical gems in front of her, rubbing her chin as her eyes darted from one to the next. They were of every shape and color, a collection Alphegor had ordered to be brought out from the Royal Treasury. A troublesome task that was once again hoisted onto Azrael in addition to his previous punishment.

"How am I to choose just one?" She looked at Azrael, who was leaning against the nearby wall, his eyes closed and his body lax.

"It doesn't matter. You'll be able to learn them all in time. Just pick the one you want to learn today," the demon replied, not bothering to open his eyes.

"It does matter. It might take a while for me to properly master this magic, so it needs to be something useful. Something more important than other magics." Morrigan lifted the blue gem closest to her. "I don't even know what most of these do. Like what is this one?"

Azrael opened one eye briefly, then closed it again. "That one is a sapphire. It contains water magic."

"Water manipulation or water creation?"

"It's sapphire, a level nine gem. Of course it contains both," he grumbled.

No, definitely not water. Bathtime alone is a challenge. Dealing with water magic would force me to constantly relive the day I died.

Morrigan put down the gem and walked over to Azrael. "Will you stop sulking already and help me pick a gem, like a magic teacher should?"

"Nah," he replied curtly.

Morrigan jabbed a finger into his side. Unfortunately, the demon didn't even flinch, completely ignoring her attempts to rouse him. "You know that if I hadn't asked Father, your punishment would have been much worse."

"I know..."

"So help me out already! I don't know much about magic." She tugged on his sleeve, and Azrael finally opened his eyes and looked at her. His gaze was somber and tired, and she wondered what could have made this usually cheerful demon so downcast. "Did something happen?"

He looked at her for a long while, then ruffled her hair, his signature grin returning to his face. "Alright, let's get down to business!"

Odd. I wonder what put him in such a mood. I doubt it was related to the punishment. He got off rather lightly—as always.

"There was no need to mess up my hair," Morrigan grumbled, watching as Azrael strode to the long line of gems that were laid out on the training ground. He picked up three and then returned to her side. She wanted to ask what exactly had put him in such a bad mood in the first place, but decided against it.

It'll make him sulk again. I'll ask him some other time.

"I believe the best choice now would be to learn some offensive magic."

"Offensive magic? I don't want to fight anybody," Morrigan objected, shaking her head and taking a step away from the gems. "Why can't I have some paint magic or color magic, or something like that?"

"Because paint magic isn't going to save you when an assassin attacks. Many demons will surely want to remove you from the picture. Previously, you were the only candidate, and a young child at that, so the amount of attempts on your life was rather tame."

So there is some sort of paint magic? I'm going to have to look more into that when I have the opportunity.

"No, whatever you are plotting in that little brain of yours—stop. Things are going to get serious now. If you want to survive, then you need to learn how to defend yourself," Azrael said, then presented the gems to Morrigan.

Giving other princesses the chance to become the heir must have really riled up some nobles. No doubt they will do everything in their power to remove me as soon as possible.

Morrigan took a deep breath and steeled herself.

Azrael is right. I need to be able to protect myself, instead of just rely-ing on my father and him. They cannot be by my side all the time.

"What are these gems?" Morrigan asked, and Azrael's expression softened.

"The red one here is fire opal. Can you guess what magic it con-tains?" He snickered, and Morrigan laughed in response.

"Oh, I don't know. Perhaps rock?" she joked.

"That's right. How'd you know?" Azrael played along, then pointed to the blue gem that had golden streaks running through it.

"This one is a lapis lazuli—it contains electric magic. The clear one is an antarcticite, which contains ice magic, of course."

Morrigan carefully looked over the gems, trying to imagine how it would feel to use each type of magic and assessing which could be best used offensively.

Ice magic seems rather useful. I could easily stop any attackers in their tracks, create icy walls to block attacks, and... pierce them with ice. Not sure if I want to put people on an ice skewer. Also, how would I even remove all that ice afterward? Does it come with a convenient unthaw switch? Probably not.

The gruesome scene made Morrigan shiver, so she shifted her focus to the lapis lazuli.

With electricity, I could just electrocute enemies and leave them paralyzed. But how would I control it? Isn't it really difficult to predict where electricity will go? What if I accidentally electrocute a friend? I'd rather not.

Finally, she looked at the smooth fire opal.

Fire magic seems destructive, though it would certainly be very effective offensively. But it has the same problem as electricity—how to properly control it? It's probably easier to handle than electricity, but I'm not sure.

"Oh, and before you choose, remember that whichever magic you choose, you will also gain a certain amount of resistance to the corresponding element. So if you were to choose antarcticite, you'd be more resistant to cold weather, and ice attacks in general."

"Resistance, you say?" Morrigan pondered, remembering the unbearable heat she had felt near the lava river. Those were hardly a rarity in the Underworld, and she had never been particularly fond of hot weather, even as a human.

Having made her decision, she reached for the fire opal and engulfed it in her palms. She imagined its power seeping into her body, the gem slowly being absorbed. A few moments later, she felt the stone disappear, and a warm tingle passed through her.

"Good choice. Can never go wrong with fire," Azrael noted, putting down the other two gems. Morrigan nodded and took a deep breath.

"Alright, so how do I do this? Do I just imagine launching a fireball or something?" she asked.

"Pretty much." Azrael shrugged and leaned against the wall, watching over Morrigan. She took a deep breath, outstretched her hand, and imagined a fireball flying at the dummies on the other side of the training ground. But instead of a small fireball like she'd hoped, a giant sphere of fire grew in front of her.

She panicked and tried to stop the magic, but the ball just kept growing and growing. "Wha—"

"Princess, stop!" Azrael yelled.

"I can't!" she screamed back. The fireball was growing so big that it was threatening to swallow her and Azrael, so she tried to mentally shove it away from herself. The flaming monstrosity moved towards the poor training dummy and then exploded. Azrael lunged towards Morrigan and wrapped his body around her.

A moment later a wall of fire erupted around them. She feared that Azrael would take the brunt of the hit, but noticed a shimmering force field around them that protected them from the raging flames. They remained in that position for about half a minute until the fire began to disperse.

Azrael stood up, uncovering Morrigan and allowing her to take a proper look around the training ground. Everything in the room that was made out of wood—dummies, shields, training swords, and benches—was burned to a pile of ash. The floor and walls were covered in black soot, and even the door was singed. Only the magical gems lay on the floor unscathed. Even Morrigan's guards lay limp on the ground.

"Oh no! Did I kill them?" Morrigan ran up to the guards, searching for any vital signs.

"No. They're fine. But it seems like they exhausted their magic reserves in order to guard against your fireball," Azrael said, carefully stepping over ash. "This will be hard to explain."

Morrigan heard shouts coming from the hallway beyond the training ground, and less than a minute later a bunch of demons, mostly maids and servants, ran inside.

"Nothing to see here, folks! Return to your duties." Azrael waved his hands, trying to get the demons to move, but they stood stubbornly in their place, muttering among themselves and looking at Morrigan with shocked eyes.

"Morri! Morri! Are you alright?" Deziara came tearing through the hallway, unceremoniously pushing the servants aside and running up to Morrigan. "I heard a loud noise. What happened?"

"It's alright, Deziara. Nothing happened, really," she replied, forcing herself to smile in front of the gathered crowd. In reality, her heart was beating like crazy as she tried to comprehend the destructive power she'd just acquired.

What would have happened if I wasn't within the confines of the training ground? What if somebody who couldn't defend themselves had been hit by that?

"What happened to the guards? Did somebody attack you?" Deziara looked over the training ground, searching for any assailants.

"Nobody attacked us. There is nothing to see. Everything is under control," Azrael shouted as he began to physically push the crowd away. But people were resisting, not willing to move, and more demons ran through the halls, joining the already gathered mass. Among them were some of Morrigan's sisters, as well as curious concubines.

"What happened to the guards?"

"It must have been an attack. The whole training ground has been destroyed."

"Is the castle not safe anymore?"

"Isn't it clear what happened?" a feminine voice said, and everyone turned to look at Viana, who was walking towards the scene with her head held high and a faint smile on her lips. "My little sister lost control of her power."

The crowd gasped and turned to Morrigan. Their gazes were piercing and judgmental, and she felt the urge to turn and run.

No, if I run, then it's all over. I have to stand tall and show them that it was intentional.

"I'm afraid my eldest sister has jumped to conclusions. I did not lose control; I was merely testing the limits of my power," Morrigan replied, crossing her hands over her chest in a challenge. Viana was about to open her mouth again when all of the gathered demons bowed their heads. Alphegor was approaching, his eyebrows furrowed in a deep scowl.

"What's with the racket? What happened?" the king asked, glancing over the whole scene. When his eyes met with Morrigan's, she grinned sheepishly at him.

"Father, it appears Morrigan had a training accident," Viana said with her head bowed. The king just roared with laughter and let out a loud whistle, earning a scowl from Viana.

"Look at that power! At age four, when most demon children haven't even manifested their abilities yet!" Alphegor went up to Morrigan and picked her up in his arms. "You'll be a demon to fear one day!"

Morrigan noticed Viana bite her lower lip while the gathered demons relaxed.

"But what if Morrigan doesn't learn to control it? It could be really dangerous," Viana said, but Alphegor just waved his hand dismissively.

"Nonsense, she'll have it mastered in no time at all. Won't you, Morrigan?" he announced, and Morrigan could feel cold sweat form on her palms.

"Of course," she replied with as much vigor as she could, although Morrigan had no idea how she could ever control that fire. It felt like it had a mind of its own.

"Wonderful! Now, clean this up. Azrael, gather the gems and come to my office afterward," Alphegor ordered, then strode away, still holding Morrigan in his arms. As they retreated, Viana glared at her with such intensity that Morrigan felt like she might drop dead. Servants also didn't appear too pleased, seeing a large cleanup ahead of them.

After they reached Alphegor's office, the king put her down on the sofa, drew the same spell to block overhearing from outside, and waited. Unlike in front of the crowd, he appeared far more serious and thoughtful.

"Did I... mess up?" Morrigan asked, peering at him. Alphegor seemed to snap out of his thoughts and turned to her.

"No, this is not your fault. It's just not quite what I expected. I need to hear Azrael's thoughts on this."

A few long minutes later, there was a knock on the door. "It's Azrael."

"Come in," Alphegor ordered. The white-haired demon entered, his expression just as serious as Alphegor's.

"So—what happened?"

"It seems like the Princess has a natural affinity for fire magic. That, and her huge magical potential created a rather explosive effect." Azrael sighed, ruffling his hair.

"Do you think she could learn to control it?" Alphegor asked.

"Yeah, but how long it'll take and how easy it'll be depends purely on her," he said, looking at Morrigan.

"I'll... do my best?" Morrigan gave them a crooked smile and a thumbs-up.

"Change the training place to the dungeons. We can't have another incident like this happen where everybody can see it," the king said, and Azrael nodded.

"Wait, the dungeons? Is that really necessary?" she asked, remembering the dark, trap-riddled place.

"It's only a temporary measure. I promise to find you a better training spot soon," Alphegor said, then knelt by her side and looked her straight in the eyes. "I know this is much for me to ask, but you must gain control of this power as soon as possible. Your life may depend on it."

Morrigan nodded, and Alphegor gave her a quick hug before standing up.

"Now get to it. There's no time to lose."

Chapter 7

Lavabee Honey Cake

A giant explosion rumbled through the dark dungeon room, leaving yet another crater in the middle of the already massacred space.

"Why? I was imagining a tiny flicker of candlelight." Morrigan threw her arms up in frustration, her face covered in sweat and soot. No matter how hard she tried to control her flames and make them small, her mind always wandered back to the fainted guards and the judgmental stares of the Demon Castle's inhabitants.

"That sure didn't look like candlelight," Azrael said, sitting behind a tall stone wall that separated him from the carnage. He had a drink in one hand and a book in another, looking quite relaxed.

"You could try and teach me something for a change." She glared at him, considering whether he should become her next target.

"I can't teach you anything until you learn some basic control," he replied nonchalantly, then took another sip of his drink.

"But how can I learn any control if you won't even give me any tips?" she retorted, feeling the strongest sense of déjà vu. It was the same when she'd had to absorb a magical gem for the first time. Azrael had refused to explain anything, and she was left to boil in her own incompetence.

Why does he expect me to understand everything right away? Do all demons just do this instinctually?

"How did my mom teach you to control fire?" she prodded.

"She didn't have to. I was a natural." The demon grinned victoriously, and now she really wanted to burn him to cinders.

"Then how come you couldn't dry yourself off before?" Morrigan snickered.

"I have no use for servant magic. It's their job to dry stuff, not mine," Azrael retorted, completely unfazed by her attempted jab.

"Such a helpful teacher you are. I should get you replaced."

"Hey, now. No need to get hasty." Azrael closed his book and got up from his chair. "I can tell you what your problem is, but knowing that will hardly solve it."

"Knowing the problem makes it half a problem," Morrigan retorted, confident that even the smallest bit of information could help tip the scales in her favor.

"You are too emotional," Azrael said. He poked her forehead.

"Huh?" She stared up at him, dumbfounded.

"As I said—you are too emotional. You get riled up really easily, which messes with your mind and your ability to control magic."

"But I've never had any trouble with shadow walking or shape-shifting," she objected.

"That's because those don't have any levels of power that require control. You either can shift or you can't. But with fire, the results will vary greatly, depending on your mental state," Azrael said, then outstretched his hand towards her. "Enough for today. You need to cool down."

"I can do it!" Morrigan protested.

"No. I can see that you're still riled up. Let's try again tomorrow." He pushed his hand closer to her, and begrudgingly Morrigan took it. The demon teleported them in front of Alphegor and Morrigan's chambers, surprising Gunna, who was polishing one of the vases by the door.

"Lady Morrigan, you're back already." The dwarf nanny bowed to Azrael, who gave her a curt wave and then disappeared into darkness.

"Yeah. Practice was cut short today..." Morrigan said, her eyes downcast. Gunna instantly picked up on her sour mood and walked up to her.

"Why don't we have some nice tea and cake? I hear they baked some fresh lavabee honey cake."

"Lavabee honey cake?" Morrigan tilted her head quizzically. She had heard of lavabees before. Apparently, those rather large insects lived close to lava lakes and rivers and somehow managed to turn the hot goop into actual edible honey. But it was a rare delicacy, and Morrigan hadn't yet had a chance to taste it.

"Yes. Would you like to try it? It was supposed to be served to His Majesty after dinner, but I'm sure he wouldn't mind if you took a slice for yourself early."

"I would!" Morrigan nodded, and she felt herself getting giddy at the prospect of a nice dessert. Gunna hurried away to the kitchens while Morrigan retreated into her living room and waited.

After a while, the nanny returned, pushing a little cart that had the slice of the aforementioned cake. It had many thin layers of biscuits, and in between each sat a nice helping of orangish cream. Over the top, there was a drizzle of what Morrigan assumed to be the lavabee honey. It was slightly translucent, just like normal honey, but its color was rich and resembled hot magma.

"Here you go, Lady Morrigan. Enjoy!" Gunna said, putting the cake and a cup of tea on the coffee table. Morrigan grabbed the little dessert spoon, eager to dig in, but then realized that there was only one slice.

"What about you, Gunna?"

"I appreciate your concern, but I could not partake in a dessert that is meant for the king," the nanny refused with a smile, and instead motioned for her to eat.

"But..."

"No buts. You need this dessert more than I do," the nanny said, sitting on the sofa next to Morrigan. "Tell me: What weighs on your heart so heavily, child? You've only just returned home a few days ago and yet your mood is already so sullen."

Morrigan sighed, staring at the teacup in front of her. She took a moment to gather her thoughts and then spoke.

"It's just that when my father found me, he reassured me that I'd have all the time in the world to learn how to be a proper princess and heir. And yet the moment I came back, there was this political strife in front of me. I don't blame Father. I understand that even if he is a king, he cannot just do whatever he wishes. He cannot just force people to accept me and disregard other princesses."

Morrigan sighed, thinking of all the rumors that were circulating through the Demon Castle, and by extension, the whole Underworld. How maids and servants muttered among themselves that the eldest daughter should be the next queen instead of the youngest. How Morrigan's power was too unstable and dangerous. How it would destroy the Demon Kingdom.

I never wanted any part of this, and yet once again I am the center of attention.

Gunna's warm hand touched Morrigan's shoulder, bringing her out of her thoughts. "I understand that the burden you bear is great—but do not forget that you are who you are, and nobody can change that."

"But I can always improve. I can learn things, I can gain control over my weaknesses," she said resolutely.

"Or you could show to others that your weaknesses are actually your strengths." The nanny smiled, then pushed the cake towards Morrigan. "Eat it, child. You'll feel better."

Morrigan stared at Gunna for a moment, then turned her gaze towards the cake.

Turn my weakness into strength. How would I even do that? I didn't know that Gunna liked to talk in riddles.

The sweet smell of the dessert made her stomach grumble, so took a bite of cake. Once its flavor reached her tongue, her taste buds exploded with a mixture of sweetness from what tasted like condensed milk cream, the cake layers, which were less sweet and more neutral in flavor, and the explosiveness of the lavabee honey.

The honey was like a bit of magic on her tongue—just like those sweets she'd once tasted in Linberor Market. It was hot and spicy, but at the same time mild and not all harsh like a pepper would be. As she swallowed the first bite, the warmth of it spread down her throat and throughout her whole body.

"Gunna! This is amazing!" Morrigan said cheerfully, then took a sip of her favorite peppermint tea, which helped to soften the spiciness and cleanse her palate.

"I knew you'd like it, Lady Morrigan. Lavabee honey is said to taste like warmth, and is often given to people who are having a hard time," the nanny explained, then urged her to have some more.

Morrigan took the spare spoon that lay on the cart and scooped up a piece of cake. "You taste it!"

"Lady Morrigan, I already said that I—"

"Princess's orders. Eat it, or suffer punishment. Silent treatment for ten minutes." Morrigan puffed out her cheeks and held the spoon towards the nanny. Gunna sighed, then took the offered bite of cake. Her eyes lit up as she ate it, regaining the vigor that the nanny seemed to have lost over the years Morrigan had been missing.

"It is indeed delicious. Thank you. What a kind child you are!"

"Food always tastes better when shared with others." Morrigan smiled, then took another bite of the cake. "I just wish my troubles with fire magic would dissolve as easily as this cake in my mouth."

"If you're having trouble with fire magic, why not request an expert? Surely Master Alphegor would spare no resource for your sake," the nanny said.

He probably would find me a teacher if I just asked, but that could bring a different set of problems. The teacher would have to be trustworthy, and the training would still have to be done in some hidden place to avoid rumors. Also, Azrael will sulk if I get another magic teacher. Even if their specialty is just fire magic.

"An expert in fire magic, you say..." Morrigan drawled as she munched on the cake. "Wait... I know an expert! I have to go now. Thank you, Gunna!"

She turned into a shadow and, without hesitation, sped down the castle wall to the yard.

"Lady Morrigan, wait! What about your cake?" the nanny called after her, but Morrigan was too excited to turn back.

* * *

Morrigan rushed into the dragon stable, which were a good chunk bigger than before, and saw Haku curled up in a corner, chewing on a piece of wood somewhat apathetically.

The dragon had grown considerably since the last time she'd seen him—he was a good deal bigger than a horse. For her, it felt like no more than a few weeks, but she realized that the dragon had not seen her for two whole years.

How will he react? Will he be angry that I left him alone for so long? Will he hate me?

"Hey, Haku." She spoke softly to avoid startling the not-so-little dragon. He didn't react, instead continuing to chew on the wood.

Has he perhaps... forgotten me?

"It's been a while, Haku. It's me, Morrigan," she said, slowly approaching him. But the dragon didn't acknowledge her presence, acting as if there were nobody else there. Morrigan inched closer and closer to him while talking soothingly.

"How have you been? Has everyone been treating you well?"

When she was a few meters away from him, the dragon suddenly moved his tail in a sweeping motion, and she heard chains clatter. She paused and examined Haku's limbs—they were bound by chains.

"Haku, what have they done to you?" she exclaimed, then rushed to his side, throwing caution out of the window. The stable opened then, and one of the patrol guards came in. When he saw Morrigan crouched down near Haku, pulling at the chains, the guard rushed forward.

"Your Highness, get away from there! That dragon is incredibly dangerous!"

At his voice, Haku jumped to his feet and snarled viciously, his mouth filling with hot flames. The guard stopped, his eyes darting from the dragon to Morrigan, who was still tugging at the chains.

"How dare you chain up Haku? Where are the keys?" Morrigan demanded.

"Your Highness, get away from there!" The guard stepped closer, reaching his hand out. Haku roared, preparing to spew fire at the demon. She jumped out in front of him defensively.

"No, Haku! I know what they did to you is horrible, but if you hurt somebody, it'll only make things worse."

Haku blinked as if he had finally noticed her. The flames in his mouth died down, but his gaze remained sharp.

"That's right, Haku. Good dragon," she purred. Then she looked back at the guard. "Bring me the key to his shackles at once, or you'll become his dinner!"

The guard paled, then pulled the key out of his pocket. Morrigan went up to him and took it.

"Princess, please understand. This dragon went completely berserk after you disappeared."

"Well, clearly you don't know how to treat a dragon properly," she huffed, then went up to Haku. He watched her suspiciously but didn't object to her closeness. After a few minutes, she had removed his chains. Haku tentatively lifted his limbs, then looked at Morrigan.

"Isn't that better?" she said with a smile. But Haku roared in response, and his mouth filled with hot flames again.

Oh no... Is he mad after all?

"Run, Princess!"

CHAPTER 8

THE UNDERWORLD FIREWORKS

Haku's mouth opened wider, and fire streamed out of it in a steady current... above his head. Morrigan watched as the fire turned into little motes of flame that gently flowed down and then dissipated in the air. Before she could realize what was going on, Haku leapt up to her and licked her face enthusiastically. His tongue was a bit rough, but not as rough as a cat's. It forked a little at the tip.

"Yes, I missed you too, Haku." She giggled, then gave him a hearty scratch under the chin. Haku purred with delight, leaning into her touch. His tail wagged from side to side, sending the chewed-up pieces of wood flying all over the stable.

"Why don't we go out for a flight? I bet it's been a while since you've done that."

The dragon jumped up and down, then grabbed Morrigan by her scruff. She was a bit surprised by the sudden maneuver but relaxed as Haku gingerly set her down on his back. Sitting on top of him, she realized just how much larger he was than before. Her little body didn't cover his whole back anymore, leaving a large-enough space for another fully grown demon to fit.

"You've really grown, Haku. It's a shame I've remained the same," Morrigan said, regretting her escape from home even more.

I was so paranoid and foolish. I should have just believed in my father. He has never given me any reason not to trust him.

As Haku leapt forward, rushing out of the stable, Morrigan's breath hitched, and she began sliding backward. She frantically tried to hold on to him, but his scales were too smooth to grab. Thankfully, she reached the part where his wings grew out of his back, which stopped her from sliding farther.

"I think we're going to have to build you a saddle. Let's take it slow this time." She gently patted Haku's neck, and the dragon nodded in response, one of his green eyes looking at her. Morrigan had always been amazed by how intelligent the dragon seemed, but he appeared to have matured even more while she was away.

Haku slowed his pace to a trot, and Morrigan found a nook under his wings on which to support her legs. Then she wrapped her hands around him as best as she could and nodded. "Ready when you are!"

The dragon got a running start and began flapping his wings, slowly gaining altitude. Morrigan glanced down and saw how the ground grew farther and farther away. But she wasn't scared. The steady beating of Haku's wings and the warmth that radiated through his scales calmed her.

"I truly missed you, Haku. I promise that no matter where I go, you'll come with me," she said quietly. Morrigan had been sure that her scaled friend wouldn't be able to hear her, but a low hum escaped from him. She smiled as they rose higher and higher, going over the peaks of the Demon Castle.

Darkness engulfed them from all sides, and Morrigan felt saddened that Haku wasn't able to fly in the sky like a dragon really should.

"You know, while I was gone, I went to a place where you could fly endlessly up and not worry about hitting anything. A place where there are no limits."

Haku didn't make any noise, but she could feel that he was wholly focused on her. Taking it as a good sign, she continued. "I'm really sorry that I left you alone here for so long. I'm sure it was horrible for you, as even Azrael, who was supposed to care for you, was away looking for me."

The dragon let out a small puff of smoke that mercilessly hit Morrigan's nostrils.

"I deserved that. I know this will sound like nothing more than an excuse, but I was really scared at the time. I thought my father wouldn't acknowledge me and would abandon me, just like I was once abandoned before. But it wasn't true, and now I just feel foolish about it."

Haku huffed as his mouth lit up with flames. They traveled slowly out of his mouth like little flower petals and swirled around them as they flew.

"That is amazing, Haku! How did you do that?" She watched in awe as the fire danced around them. "If I could control fire as well as you, then all those nasty rumors about me being dangerous and unfit to be the Crown Princess would stop. Or least calm down a little."

The dragon cried out cheerfully before looking at her intently. She looked into his eyes, trying to understand what he wanted to convey. There was a nagging sensation in her mind—like a gentle tingle.

"You'll teach me?"

What surprised her wasn't his willingness to do so—she had expected as much. No, it was the fact that she understood him in a weird, almost telepathic sort of way.

Is this a draconic ability or mine?

* * *

"Princess Morrigan has gone insane."

"What do you mean, insane? She's merely four years old. Children her age do a lot of strange things."

"You haven't heard?"

"Heard what?"

"She is studying fire magic from that dragon of hers."

"What? Surely you jest. The dragon is her pet—she's probably just playing with it."

"No, I've seen it with my own eyes. She goes to the castle backyard every day and talks with the dragon."

"That is a bit odd, but she's still just a child..."

Morrigan couldn't listen to the maids yapping anymore and decided to emerge from behind the bookshelves, where she had been reading a book about fire magic. Once the maids saw her, their faces went as pale as sheets.

"What a nice day it is," Morrigan said, looking them directly in the eyes. Both of them trembled and bowed their heads low. "It'd be a perfect day to have a nice, long chat with Father. I wonder what topics he would be interested in. Perhaps the code of conduct that servants of the castle need to adhere to. I am not very familiar with it."

"My apologies, Your Highness! It will not happen again."

"Please, be merciful."

Morrigan snickered. It felt nice to put the rumor-weaving maids in their place.

"Get back to work," Morrigan commanded coldly, and the maids scurried away.

I have no time to deal with them anyway. Haku is waiting for me.

She turned into her shadow form and hurried to the dragon stable. Haku was already pacing near the entrance, expecting her arrival. They'd been training together for about two weeks, and Morrigan had managed to learn so much from him. It turned out that despite their inability to speak, dragons were quite capable teachers.

As Morrigan had realized during her time together with Haku, fire magic required emotional control over everything else. She needed to feel how strong the flame needed to be, so if her emotions were going berserk due to stress, it was impossible to control. However, time with Haku was very therapeutic and helped her to better understand herself, as well as him. It also helped that Haku could easily take control of any rogue flames.

"Hey, Haku," she said, wrapping her hands around him in a hug. His tail swished around, hitting against the wall with such ferocity that it felt like the stable would collapse. But since the structure was made out of solid stone, it held firm.

"Ready for some fire practice?" she called out, and the dragon leapt in joy. She chuckled, motioning for him to bend down. Haku lay on the ground and put his front paw out in a manner that would make it easy for Morrigan to use as a ladder to climb onto his back. She nodded at him in thanks before getting into the small saddle that she'd requested Azrael to get for her.

The saddle was specifically made to account for her size, as well as to make flight as secure for her as possible. It included a safety harness around her waist so that in case she lost her grip, she wouldn't be falling to her death. Morrigan checked that the harness was secure, then gently tapped on Haku's neck, signaling for him to move.

The dragon obliged, and they strode out of the stable, ready to fly once again. Much to Morrigan's surprise, she saw Deziara walking through the backyard, waving at them.

"Let's go and see what she has to say," Morrigan said, but Haku was already eagerly running towards the girl. Apparently, the only reason he had survived at all was because Deziara had taken it upon herself to care for him. She couldn't convince Lucius and Viana to remove Haku's chains, but at least she had kept him fed and entertained as best as she could.

And it showed—Haku always greeted her with great enthusiasm.

"Hello, sister!" Morrigan waved at her cheerfully, but her hands slumped as she noticed a rather serious expression on Deziara's face. "Is something the matter?"

"Morri, I think it's best if you skip your practice for today," she said, affectionately scratching under Haku's chin.

"Why?"

"Apparently Viana caught wind of your practice with Haku and decided to make a spectacle out of you. She organized a tea party and invited all the most prominent noble demonesses. I heard she even invited Father, although I doubt he'll show up," Deziara explained.

"What do I care for their tea parties?"

"She's organizing it in the castle yard. See the tables over there?" Deziara pointed to the far side of the backyard. While it was a good way away from the stable, her practicing fire magic with Haku would certainly be visible to everybody.

That little... She's trying to make a fool of me in front of all these prominent people. No doubt she intends to remove me from the Crown Princess's position. But I won't back off. In fact, I'll use this to my advantage.

"Let her have her fancy party. I'll give them a show they'll never forget," Morrigan announced, patting Haku affectionately. He responded with an approving roar, sensing her intentions.

"Are you sure about this, Morri?" Deziara looked at them with concern.

"I am! Be sure to watch," Morrigan exclaimed.

"If you're so confident about it, then I'll trust you. You've become far bolder since you've returned. I like it." Deziara chuckled, and Morrigan nodded in return. She urged Haku on and took off, flying above the castle.

They began the same way as always: Haku shot fire out of his mouth at various intensities, and Morrigan tried to mimic the size of his fireballs. Hers were almost always larger than his, but the fact that she could now control their size was already a testament to her improvement.

Once the basic fireball exercise was done, Haku began to fly more frantically, increasing and decreasing his speed randomly, gaining and lowering altitude, and overall making it more difficult for Morrigan. While he did that, she did her best to keep a steady stream of fire coming. Occasionally she would lose her focus and the fire would either disappear or become too strong, but it didn't take long for her to regain control.

Just as they finished this exercise to Morrigan's satisfaction, she saw a group of demonesses coming out of the castle, Viana leading them.

"No fire now, Haku. Let's observe for a while," she said, pushing on his right shoulder to indicate to him which direction she wanted to go. Haku obeyed, gently swerving to the right, away from the Demon Castle's lights. This way it would be harder for anybody to spot them from the ground. Not impossible, but they'd have to look really hard to notice.

Morrigan and Haku kept gliding in circles around the castle, observing the situation below each time they flew over the tea party. Then Morrigan noticed how Viana was looking up at them and pointing, drawing the demonesses' attention.

"How kind of my eldest sister to set up the stage for us! Haku, let's give them a show they'll never forget," Morrigan said, and Haku rumbled in reply. He began spewing fire from his mouth and made circles around the guests, making them visible to everybody. She could hear the gasps of the noble demonesses, even from high above.

Alphegor then exited from the castle, heading towards the tea party. As he noticed them flying above, the king stopped and smiled. Seeing this gave Morrigan the courage to continue, so she took a deep breath and then lifted her hands up. She thought of how she'd felt when she first saw fireworks on Earth. How they filled her with wonder and joy. She'd never had a chance to show her father any fireworks—their time on Earth was rather short. But she could try to create something similar.

Morrigan channeled the happy thoughts into her fire magic, and two wisps of fire shot from her arms. At the same time, Haku made the fire circling around them disappear, turning everyone's focus on the wisps. It climbed higher and then exploded in every direction, blooming in the eternal dark like a giant fire flower.

Morrigan shot two more wisps before following with more. One fire flower appeared after the next, then disappeared into the darkness. Morrigan saw that each time a flower bloomed, the demonesses gasped in awe. After she felt like her control of the fire was waning, she signaled Haku to descend, and the dragon landed right in front of the king.

"Father, I didn't think you'd come to watch my magic practice," she said, speaking loudly enough for the demonesses to hear.

"I wouldn't dream of missing it," he said, taking her in his arms. "Well done, Morrigan!"

"To think that a child so young could control fire with such precision."

"And while riding on a dragon's back, no less."

"Imagine what she'll be able to do once she's older."

Morrigan was thoroughly enjoying the praise of the noble demonesses, all of whom smiled at her. All except one.

CHAPTER 9

ART VS DUTY

Is the shadow under the bowl a bit too light? I think I need to make it a bit darker for contrast. And what about the light reflecting from the table's surface? I think I need to make it more prominent on the bottom of the vase.

Morrigan stared intently at the still life composition in front of her, doing her best to re-create it as faithfully as possible. She took dark blue paint and dabbed a little bit of white and then yellow in it, creating a lighter and slightly warmer tone. Then she took a brush with wide bristles and ever so slightly dabbed onto the painting, trying to create a bounce light on the vase.

She then looked at the dark blue vase in front of her, trying to understand whether the color she picked was the correct one. After comparing multiple times, she nodded in satisfaction, having ascertained the tone to be right.

"Let's move on to the flowers next," Morrigan said resolutely to herself, turning to the red and orange paints. A bright orange lava flower sat in the vase—one of the most beautiful flowers in the Underworld, in her opinion. In shape it resembled a lily; however, the petals' colors went from bright red in the center to yellow at the edges. It would be a challenge to properly re-create the color transition.

Morrigan hummed as she dabbed a round, soft brush into red paint and painted the basis of the flower onto the canvas. It was nothing more than a shape, merely a guide for her to continue applying colors onto. She took a smaller brush and then began to slowly transition from red to orange, making it as smooth as possible to mimic the real flower.

"Here you are, Princess!" Azrael stormed into Morrigan's little art studio, which was a repurposed storage room, appearing annoyed. "Aren't you forgetting something?"

"Nope," she called back. She cleaned her brush in the water jar and moved on to the yellow.

"Why, you little!" Azrael growled and stomped up to her. She had grown considerably over the past six years, now being ten years old, but Azrael still towered over her whenever he got close. Her red hair had grown longer, as had her horns, and she was also beginning to lose her childish features, slowly starting to resemble a teenager. "Because of you, I received an earful from Weisedun. Do you know how annoying that guy is?"

"I am well aware," she replied, taking the smallest brush and dipping it into white paint to create reflections of light on the flower.

"Then why do you do this to me? Why do you avoid his lessons? The old man won't ever give me room to breathe at this rate," Azrael continued.

Morrigan's brush stopped moving, a heavy sigh escaping from her lips. Never would she have thought that studying would become the bane of her existence in the Underworld. While she hadn't exactly been an honor student with perfect grades back on Earth, she never had trouble with her studies.

Here in the Demon Kingdom, it was completely different. As the next heir, she had to know far more than others, so her teachers were especially strict towards her. Things like history, math and languages weren't bad. The history of Doppelta was actually interesting, and

Morrigan wouldn't have minded learning it earnestly if the teacher actually bothered to change her tone at least once during the lesson.

Math, while not the most interesting subject, wasn't very difficult. In fact, it was much simpler than the difficult mathematical formulas she had to learn during high school. Languages was by far the most interesting subject, as it not only helped her strengthen her knowledge of the demon language but also gave her insight into other languages, like Elvish and Dwarfish.

But the lesson that she absolutely dreaded was politics. It was the first lesson that she'd had to learn as the Crown Princess. The first time, she approached it with an open, if a bit worried mindset. She thought she was ready to tackle the task of becoming the next heir. However, once the teacher began recounting one noble demon house after the next, she lost it.

There were so many names to remember and so many things to know about them. It all quickly turned into a jumbled mess in her head. Weisedun warned that it was only the first step and they would not be able to move on with their lessons until she memorized them all.

"Morrigan." Azrael poked her cheek gently, a slight smile finally creeping onto his lips. "You know you can't just skip it."

"But I just can't remember all those names! Duke of this, Count of that, Viscount of over there. Shouldn't I be studying geography first instead so I could at least know which places those nobles are ruling over?" she grumbled, swishing her brush in the water to get it clean. As it was done, she took the red paint and mixed it with black to create shadows in her flower.

"Well, children normally start with geography, but you're the Crown Princess, so you have to be better than others." Azrael shrugged.

"Do you remember all those names and places, then?" Morrigan asked, her voice filled with annoyance. But it wasn't Azrael she was annoyed at; rather, it was her inability to remember what was expected of her. It was her first true task as the Crown Princess and yet she was failing miserably.

"Of course I do. I am the head of House Ultimagi and the court mage, after all. If I didn't know that much, I would have never risen to this high a station." Azrael straightened, and his chest visibly rose up from all the ego that was inflating it. "But I guess it is too much for a little girl like you."

Her eyebrow twitched and her eyes narrowed at the white-haired demon, who grinned with satisfaction.

So you want to challenge me? So be it.

"Fine, I'll get to that lesson and learn all those names. How long did it take you to remember them all?" she asked, then carefully applied the dark paint, creating a popping contrast between each flower petal.

"Well, I could name all the duchies within a week, and within a month I could name every house down to the last baron." Azrael's purple eyes seemed to glow as his smile clearly issued a challenge towards her.

"Then I shall learn them faster," Morrigan retorted, pointing the dirty brush at his face. The demon appeared unbothered, radiating confidence.

"Oh, really? Well, you've already lost three days due to your little painting escapades. Can you really do it?" he teased, looking down at her from above.

"Just you watch me," she spat, then drew the last dark line on the bottom of the flower. The piece was complete—a perfect re-creation of the vase and flower in front of her.

"Is this done?" Azrael asked, leaning in to inspect the painting.

"Yes. What do you think?"

Azrael looked at the painting, then at the vase, and nodded. "Yeah, I can't see a difference. You've really improved over the years. I reckon with your artistic sense, you'll soon become the best shape-shifter this world will never notice."

* * *

I said I could do it, but this is impossible!

Morrigan scribbled down all the names of the nobles that Lord Weisedun was calling, but she was barely able to keep up with the demon. Even if he showed the location of the house on the three-dimensional map of the Underworld and explained what exactly the region specialized in and the general type of populace in it, Morrigan quickly got lost in the sea of information.

"This is the territory of Countess Shallren, whose house has been ruling over it for more than fifteen thousand years. As it is part of the Demon Kingdom, the main populace there is also demons, mostly succubi and incubi or those with the inborn ability to charm others." Lord Weisedun, a tall and thin demon with dark gray skin and red horns, illuminated the specific area on the map with a red light.

Morrigan looked at the spot on the map, but she had no idea where that actually was. The three-dimensional maps that demons used to chart the Underworld were something that completely blew Morrigan's mind the first time she saw them. Every cavern and turn in the giant underground tunnel was neatly documented and repro-duced into something that resembled a hologram of an anthill, only much larger and more complex.

There was only one thing that she understood in this map—the location of the Demon Castle. Sitting in the very heart of the Under-world, Linberor was located in the largest cavern that existed under-ground, so it was much easier to discern from other places. The lava river that flowed near the capital was also a good indicator of its placement.

But aside from this iconic place, every underground labyrinth looked just like the other. The only conclusion she could draw from the place Lord Weisedun was pointing to was that it was comparatively close to the capital.

"Alright, moving on to the next house." The demon lit up a completely different area way across the map, and Morrigan groaned inwardly as she tried to quickly finish writing about the previously mentioned Countess Shallren. But Lord Weisedun moved on so quickly that she barely managed to scribble down the name and location.

"Could you please slow down?" Morrigan asked, trying to keep her frustration concealed.

"Princess, I am afraid that this is of utmost importance. If you do not learn the noble houses as soon as possible, then we won't be able to learn about more serious topics." The demon appeared insulted by her interruption, pointedly glaring down at her.

"But what is the point of just listing all of the houses if I can't remember even one of them? You should go slower so I could at least write them down." Morrigan glared back at the man, and he took a step back in shock, covering his mouth with his hand like an insulted lady.

"Princess Morrigan! Are you doubting my teaching methods?"

Yes! They suck!

But of course she couldn't say that. Even though she was the Crown Princess, she couldn't just waltz around insulting everybody she didn't like, though a little voice in her mind suggested complaining to her father.

No, Morrigan. You are better than that. You can't run to Father because of every little thing that you don't like.

"No, I would never." Morrigan plastered on a polite smile, something that she was getting better at, and held the ink pen in her hand, showing her willingness to learn.

Lord Weisedun nodded in approval and turned back to his map.

"Then let us continue. I will not repeat myself, so be sure to listen carefully, Princess Morrigan."

"Of course," she confirmed, but groaned inwardly.

This isn't going to work. He could list all those names a hundred times and I still wouldn't be able to remember even one-third of them. I need to find a way to learn about these effectively.

As Lord Weisedun continued pointing out various places on the map and listing one noble house after another, Morrigan kept pondering on what she could do to solve her problem, hurriedly scribbling down the names.

Perhaps the reason why I am having trouble remembering all these names is because they are of demon origin. Even if I've learned the demon language for ten years now, their names still sound very foreign. What can I do to remember something foreign?

Morrigan began to doodle on the side of her notebook as her focus moved away from the lanky demon, who continued his lecture without any care. One line joined with the next, forming an oval shape, then some hair appeared on top before Morrigan scribbled in some vague facial features.

I got it! What if I were to request portraits, or at least drawings, of the nobles I am supposed to remember? Surely it would be easier if I could put faces to their names. Not to mention that then I would be able to study the art that they have in the Demon Kingdom. It's a win-win!

"Princess Morrigan, are you listening?" Lord Weisedun tapped on Morrigan's desk, his face filled with annoyance.

"Would it be possible for me to see the portraits of the heads of the houses?" she asked, excited by her own idea.

"Portraits? Whatever for?" the demon asked, his features softening.

"So I would be able to recognize them when I meet them. It would be embarrassing if I messed up their names upon meeting them, wouldn't it?" Morrigan said with a smile. She really didn't care how the most likely pompous demon nobles looked. But the art—now *that* was an exciting prospect.

"Oh! I commend your intentions, Princess Morrigan, but I'm afraid it would be quite troublesome to look through all the portraits one by one. It would take a long time to gather them and even longer to properly look through them."

"But..."

"Do not worry. You shall meet the nobles and receive proper introductions when the time is due," Lord Weisedun said, then returned to his speedrun of listing all the noble houses.

Fine, if you won't cooperate, I know somebody who will.

CHAPTER 10

SEA OF PORTRAITS

"Princess, I think this might be too much," Azrael grumbled as he heaved another five portraits into the ballroom. It was one of the smaller rooms, meant for minor occasions and parties hosted by the concubines, but was still large enough to fit about fifty people inside. Currently, the room was lined with portraits that were stacked on top of each other like construction materials.

"I never expected that there would be so many." Morrigan paled as she looked over them, wondering where she would even begin. While she had known that there were many nobles, which meant many portraits, she'd never expected such a ridiculous amount.

"What are they all even ruling over? A single lava droplet within some tiny lava river?" Morrigan complained, although she knew full well that the Demon Kingdom was larger than even the largest country on Earth in terms of size.

"No, there is a hierarchy. Dukes rule over marquises, marquises rule over counts, counts rule over viscounts, and so on, until we get to the tiniest baron ruling some far-off village at the edge of the Demon Kingdom," Azrael explained as he put down the last stack of portraits on a spare spot on the floor.

"Yes, yes, I get it. But is it really necessary for me to remember all of this?" Morrigan grumbled, pointing at the never-ending pile of portraits.

"No, you only need to remember the names. Not sure why you decided to make your task more difficult by remembering their faces," Azrael said, wiping the dust off his hand. Some of the portraits hadn't been touched in decades, making the ballroom smell of dust and old wood.

"There's no way I can just mechanically recite that giant list of names. It'll be much easier if I can remember their faces," she retorted, and Azrael sneered.

"Well, good luck. You have two days to go through all of these if you want to beat me." The white-haired demon smirked, then promptly left Morrigan alone with the portraits. She looked over them all again and sighed.

This will be a long day.

* * *

Three hours later a tentative knock sounded on the ballroom door, bringing Morrigan out of her contemplation.

"Come in," she called out, rubbing her tired eyes.

"How are you doing, Lady Morrigan?" Gunna came into the room, carrying a tray with what appeared to be sandwiches and tea. The nanny was smiling as she approached Morrigan, being careful to sidestep any portraits that had managed to slide out of place. At this point, Morrigan was almost as tall as the dwarf woman, albeit much more petite.

"This is wonderful, Gunna!" Morrigan replied excitedly as she took a sandwich from the tray, biting into it with much gusto. "Although these are all supposed to be accurate representations of each demon noble, the variation in art style and techniques used is astounding!"

"Art style?" Gunna asked, setting the tray on the floor and picking up the teacup to offer it to Morrigan. The girl scarfed down the sandwich, surprised by how hungry she actually felt, then drank the warm tea with it.

"Yes, Gunna! Look at this portrait, for example." Morrigan pulled forward the one behind her, which portrayed a blonde demoness with nearly black skin. "It clearly portrays all the important features of this person, showing her characteristics and enhancing her most attractive features. But when you look closely you can see that it was done with simple colors and using a minimal amount of shadows."

Morrigan carefully put the portrait aside and pulled another one forward, this time with a bulky demon man who had pale blue skin and horns that curved like those of a ram. "This portrait, however, focuses on every little detail. Every pore, every crevice, every single hair on his head is drawn in perfect detail."

She pulled the portraits such that they stood next to each other, holding each one upright with her hands. "Gunna, which one do you think is better?"

The nanny looked from one portrait to the next, stroking her beard in contemplation. She squinted, trying to discern something in one portrait, then the next. In the end, she shrugged. "I don't know, Lady Morrigan. They both look nice."

"Exactly, Gunna! Despite these two artists using such different techniques and styles, both pieces came out looking stunning, capturing the person in question perfectly. In fact, I'd say that these two went above and beyond. I can already imagine how these two people would act if I were to meet them."

Morrigan's felt herself get giddy with excitement. Gunna smiled at the girl, offering her another sandwich. She put the portraits down and took it, eating it just as hastily as the first one.

"So, I see your idea of learning the nobles' names by looking at their portraits is going well," the nanny noted, and Morrigan's expression fell.

"Actually, the name-learning thing isn't going as well as I had hoped," she admitted as she took the third sandwich from Gunna, biting into it and chewing it with deliberate slowness.

"Why not?" the nanny asked, offering tea for Morrigan to drink again. She took the tea and sipped it.

"Well, it started well enough. I looked at the portrait, looked at the name, and thought I had it memorized. So I moved on to the next one. The art style was different, so I compared the two. And then I looked at another one, and another one. And completely forgot about the names." Morrigan sighed, looking down into the teacup.

"Hmm... Perhaps we can find a different approach for you to learn," Gunna said, gently stroking Morrigan's shoulder. Her warm hand calmed Morrigan a little bit, but the problem still remained.

"Morri! Morri! Are you in there?" Deziara's voice came from the entrance, the girl obstructed by a mountain of paintings.

"Yes, I'm here!" she called back, and Deziara's cheery expression appeared from behind the pile. The girl was now seventeen and looked more like an adult than a child. Her black hair cascaded over her shoulders while her black eyes observed everything with the same sharpness as her father's. Morrigan thought that her sister had grown into quite the beauty.

"What's with all these portraits, Morri?" Deziara asked as she looked from one picture to the next. "Who are all these demons?"

"Leaders of every noble house in the Demon Kingdom. I am supposed to learn their names as soon as possible." Morrigan had changed her voice to match the strict tone of Lord Weisedun, and Deziara chuckled.

"Ah, yes. I had to do that a few years ago. I don't know how he expects anybody to just remember a giant list of names right off the bat. It's ridiculous." Deziara sighed, and her eyes landed on the sandwich tray Gunna was holding. "Do you mind if I take one?"

"Of course not. Enjoy, Lady Deziara." Gunna offered the tray to the girl, and she gratefully took a sandwich. Over the years, Deziara had grown to like Morrigan's nanny despite her being a slave, something Morrigan was really grateful for. She probably wouldn't be able to remain on good terms with her sister if she kept belittling the dwarf woman each time they met, like unfortunately most of the Demon Castle's inhabitants did.

"I know, right? How did you learn?" Morrigan asked, hoping to find inspiration from her sister.

"My mom helped me. She's a very good teacher!" Deziara announced proudly, then poked the nearest pile of portraits with her free hand. "Are these helping?"

"No. I keep getting distracted by the artwork and completely forget I need to learn their names," Morrigan admitted, and Deziara chuckled.

"Figures. Each time you see a painting you basically become glued to it for hours."

Morrigan pouted, although she knew her sister was correct. "I just hoped that tying an annoying task with something I enjoyed would help."

"How about I help you? I've learned all their names," Deziara offered. She took a large bite of the sandwich, munching on it with contentment. "This is really good, Gunna!"

"Thank you, Lady Deziara." The nanny bowed her head. "Would you like me to bring you some tea?"

"Yes, that would be fantastic. Something light, please."

"As you wish." Gunna smiled before hurrying out of the room, leaving the tray of sandwiches on the floor. Deziara immediately took another one.

"You'd really help me?" Morrigan stared at her sister with hopeful eyes. "It will probably take some time for me to memorize them."

"What are sisters for if not to help one another?" Deziara nodded, and Morrigan gave her a quick side hug, being careful to not knock the food out of her hands.

"Why don't I help you out as well?" a feminine voice said. Shortly after, Viana emerged from behind a portrait stack near the entrance.

"Did your mother never teach you that eavesdropping is rude?" Deziara grumbled, taking a deliberate bite out of her sandwich.

"Did your mother never teach you that yelling out your conversation for the whole castle to hear is rude?" Viana retorted, a pleasant smile on her lips. Her red eyes, however, were cold as they scanned the room, quickly assessing the situation. "Little Morrigan making trouble again?"

"I am not! I'm learning," Morrigan objected, crossing her hands over her chest. Viana always seemed to know how to get under her skin.

Viana arched her eyebrow and looked at the portraits as if they were piles of dragon dung, waving her hand in front of her nose to clear away the dust that was floating around the room. "Since when is dragging old, dusty pictures through the castle considered learning?"

"That's none of your business, Viana! Go annoy somebody else." Deziara snarled, making a shooing motion with her hand.

"How cold. I just came to check on what could have made my sweet little sisters so distraught, and yet they are trying to shoo me away as if I were some dog." Viana waved her hand in the air dramatically, then walked up to the closest pile of portraits and assessed it. "My, isn't this Baron Merkov?"

"You just came here to poke fun," Deziara grumbled. Morrigan nodded along with her, both younger sisters glaring at the eldest.

"Me? I would never. That is such a crude thing to do." A smile appeared on Viana's lips as she strode closer towards them, looking from one portrait to the next. "It seems like you have collected the portraits of all the leaders of the noble houses."

"So what if I have?"

Just go away already. You're beginning to remind me of Asdeus.

Although the horrid demoness had disappeared without a trace and hadn't been seen since the day Morrigan returned to Doppelta, she often worried that Asdeus might just reappear one day. It wasn't logical—she knew that. The Demon Castle had increased its security twice over and the screening of any new employees was so meticulous that even the most talented shape-shifter couldn't hope to get in. But the fact that Asdeus was still out there somewhere, no doubt plotting her next move, scared Morrigan. She was sure that the demoness would not remain hidden in the shadows forever.

"My, my, my, the prodigal Crown Princess is having trouble remembering a few names. How shocking!" Viana laughed gleefully, then walked up to Morrigan, standing just a few centimeters away, looking down with her penetrating red gaze. "I wonder what Father is going to say?"

"Father doesn't care about such petty things!" Deziara protested.

"Oh, no, of course not. But what is he supposed to say to his people when his heir can't even do such a basic thing as remember a few names?" Viana sneered, then turned on her heel. "I do hope you manage to sort this out, my dearest youngest sister."

"She will! Just watch!" Deziara yelled after her, but Morrigan began to ponder.

What can Father do if I actually fail my tasks as the Crown Princess? He cannot have an incompetent heir, no matter how much he loves me.

CHAPTER 11

FATHER-DAUGHTER TIME

With heavy steps, Morrigan trudged towards her room, each step on the staircase seeming more difficult than the last. After the whole fiasco with Viana, Deziara was doubly eager to teach Morrigan all the names of the nobles. She even tried using portraits, going from one image to the next, calling out each of them and describing their houses a bit.

Deziara's efforts certainly had helped Morrigan memorize many of the names, but she was still far from remembering the whole list. By the end of the day, she could recall around half of the larger houses and three-tenths of the smaller ones, and even that took great effort.

I never thought I would be so bad at remembering names. I didn't have this issue on Earth. But then again, I never had to remember such an extensive list of names. The sheer quantity of it is smothering.

Morrigan slowly pulled the door of her and Alphegor's shared room open, then slumped inside, sighing loudly.

"What's wrong, Morrigan?" Alphegor turned from his study desk, carefully looking her over. As the years went by, their living arrangements had also changed. The single bedroom was remade into a living room, where one side looked like a study, with all of the documents and books Alphegor needed, and the other side looked like an art studio, with shelves filled with art supplies and unfinished paintings.

On each side of this living area there was a door that led to Alphegor's bedroom and Morrigan's bedroom respectively, as well as their private bathrooms farther in. All of these could only be entered through the main living room, making it almost into an apartment of sorts. An idea the king had no doubt adapted from the human world.

"Father! You're already back? You usually come back later." Morrigan chuckled nervously and straightened, trying to hide her sour mood.

"I came back sooner to spend some time with you. I've been so busy lately that I feel like I've neglected you," the king said, then got up. Morrigan hurried towards him to give him a hug, which he returned without hesitation. Over the years, she had grown incredibly attached to Alphegor, and thanked Eirwen, her demon mother, for pulling her from Earth to Doppelta. It had truly been a blessing.

"It's alright. I know you have many things to take care of," she replied, enjoying the safety of his presence. Ever since their return from Earth—no, it was better to say that ever since Alphegor had returned from the battlefield—he'd been busy dealing with the Fallen Kingdom. From what Morrigan understood, they remained just as pushy, despite having their forces promptly beaten by Alphegor.

In fact, they used their defeat to plead with the neighboring Duergar Country for help, and the two had formed a sort of tentative partnership. Morrigan didn't fully understand the ramifications of that—after all, her politics teacher insisted that noble names were far more important than understanding the current state of things. But one thing she did understand was that it created a lot of work for Alphegor.

"Yes. The accursed Fallen Kingdom keeps stirring up trouble. Perhaps I should just wipe them out and be done with it. Then I wouldn't have to deal with all this paperwork and could spend more time with my daughters," Alphegor growled, glaring at the stack of documents on his desk. Morrigan feared they might just burst into flames from the intensity alone.

"I'm sure it'll all settle down soon, Father. Why don't we just rest for the evening?" she suggested, pulling him towards the sofa. He didn't resist, and just sank into the soft cushions, resting his head against the headrest. Morrigan sat down next to him, resting her head on his arm.

"I see you had a hard day as well. What troubles your mind, little one?" Alphegor said, gently caressing her hair. She leaned into his touch, letting the warmth of his hand wash away her worries.

"I just can't remember the names of all the nobles. Azrael said that he had all the big noble houses memorized in a week. I can't recall even half of them," she said. "Not to mention that Lord Weisedun keeps calling them so fast that I barely have time to register them, much less remember where they are and what their main strength is."

"Ah, yes, Weisedun has always been rather stubborn in his ways. Shall I find you a different teacher?" Alphegor asked, a hint of a smile playing on his lips.

"No. Then it'll feel like I've lost. If Azrael could do it, then so can I." Morrigan sat up straight, determined to follow through on her words. Even if she had no idea how to do it.

Perhaps it is time to pull out some old cramming techniques I used in school. It'll only work in the short term, but then I'll at least get Weisedun off my back and be able to move on to actually important things.

"The only reason why he learned the names so quickly was because your mother taught him. She was a phenomenal teacher," Alphegor said with a bittersweet smile.

That's unfair. Azrael got to spend so much time with Mom, but I didn't even get a chance to meet her. How I wish I could have spent even a little bit of time with her.

"Mom taught a lot of things to Azrael. They seem to have been really close," she noted somewhat bitterly. "Why is that?"

"Azrael lost his mother early to humans, and your mother felt really sorry for the boy. He had great potential but nobody to teach him. So she took pity on him and decided to accept him as her pupil."

"She sounds very kind," Morrigan said, feeling a bit of pride for her demon mother. And also a bit sorry that she had to put up with Azrael. He was a pain in the butt, even as an adult demon. Imagining him as a child made Morrigan shiver.

"Oh, yes. Eirwen was very kind. In fact, many demons called her weak due to this kindness, claiming that it was unbecoming for a demon," Alphegor explained, and Morrigan huddled closer to him, looking up into his eyes.

"Is it a weakness to be kind?" she asked. There were still many things she didn't understand about demons. While Morrigan was certain they were not the kind of villains fantasy stories made them out to be, they did have some cultural oddities she was still getting used to.

For example, the horns of a demon were their most precious thing. They were almost sacred, and unless they were a lover or a close family member, touching another demon's horns was forbidden, and could even be punished. Morrigan had once touched Deziara's horns while combing her hair, intrigued by their unusual texture. Her sister was startled by it, but since they were family, the incident was quickly forgiven.

"It can be your weakness and it can be your strength. Be kind when it is necessary, but do not be a fool by giving kindness to those who would spit on it," the king instructed, and she nodded dutifully. "Now then, enough of this heavy talk. I have some exciting news for you."

"Exciting news?"

"Remember the Nachtstern Festival?" the king said, and Morrigan noticed a glint of mischief in his eyes.

"Nachtstern? I do recall a lot of talk about a festival, but I didn't know you created a whole festival for our family." Morrigan chuckled, imagining Alphegor going around and ordering servants to make the grandest feast and attractions the Demon Kingdom had ever seen.

"No, not me. It was one of our first ancestors—Morax Nachtstern, the founder of the Demon Kingdom and the very first Demon King. He created the festival to celebrate the Underworld's triumph over the Overworld," the king explained, and Morrigan could see that he felt proud.

"The Underworld's triumph over the Overworld? But aren't they almost completely separate from one another?" she asked. "How and why would they even go to war?"

"They are separate now, but it wasn't always that way. Once, hundreds of thousands of years ago, the inhabitants of the Overworld ruled over all of Doppelta. They looted the Underworld for its treasures, enslaved the demons and other underground races to their will, and wreaked havoc on the underground ecosystem."

Morrigan felt taken aback by the sentence. Not the bit about humans wreaking havoc—that she was certain they were quite capable of in any world they lived in. No, what shocked her was the fact that Alphegor said that the Underworld had an ecosystem.

But there is literally nothing here? It's just darkness and lava and monsters.

"I see doubt in your eyes. What is it, Morrigan?" Alphegor looked at her, somewhat bemused.

"No, about the ecosystem bit. When I... When I ran away, I didn't see much of an ecosystem," she mumbled, still ashamed to remember the fact that she had run back to Earth like a fool, despite Alphegor showing nothing but affection towards her.

"Well, if you're going to zoom past it in your shadow form without looking, of course you wouldn't see much," he noted, and Morrigan blushed. But the king didn't appear mad and gently patted her head.

"There is more in the darkness than you might think. But that is a topic for another time. I'd like to explain more about the Nachtstern Festival."

"Yes, please do." She nodded, smiling.

The festival sounds like fun. When was the last time I even went to one? Sometime when I was just a small human child. I wonder what demon festivals are like?

"As I was saying, during the Nachtstern Festival we celebrate the Underworld's victory over the Overworld. Initially, it was more like an honorary day meant to celebrate the Royal Family, but over time it evolved into something that celebrated the Underworld as a whole. The length of the celebration has also increased from one day to five."

"Wow, that sounds interesting. How come I haven't seen it yet?" she pondered aloud.

"Oh, it happens only once every twenty years. Having such a grand festival more often than that would be excessive," the king explained, and Morrigan began imagining all the possibilities of demonic grandeur. Her mind went back to those delicious magic sweets she had tasted in Linberor Market all those years ago.

I wonder if there will be more things like that at the festival. I would love to eat those sweets again. Never had a chance to eat anything like it since.

Morrigan had once tried bringing up the matter to Alphegor, but once he learned that Azrael had taken her out of the castle, the king looked like he was ready to murder him. Again. She'd already lost count of how many times she had to ask Alphegor to spare him.

"I'd love to attend it, but doesn't it take place outside of the castle?" she asked.

"It does. And we'll be going together. It is customary for the king and queen to announce the beginning of the Nachtstern Festival." He ruffled her hair, and Morrigan's eyes lit up.

A chance to go outside the castle, and together with Father, no less. I won't have to fear any kidnappers or monsters or anything.

"I can't wait! Can you tell me what sort of things you can see there?" Morrigan's voice was filled with excitement, but Alphegor's mood seemed to drop.

"I can, but there is one issue." His expression became stern, as if he loathed voicing the words aloud.

"What issue?"

"The festival will have attendees not just from the Demon Kingdom but from other Underworld countries as well."

"But that's great, isn't it? That's how we establish friendly relationships."

"Yes, but this means the Fallen Kingdom will be attending as well. And you, as the Crown Princess, will have to meet them directly," Alphegor growled, the thought seemingly repulsive to him.

"Wait? As the Crown Princess?" Morrigan felt as if she had been struck by lightning.

CHAPTER 12

PREPARATIONS

Morrigan held her back straight and her head high, taking careful, measured steps across the ballroom. There was a heavy stack of books on her head, threatening to topple over from the smallest mistake. Her teeth were clenched and every muscle felt like a tight wire, stiff and unwilling to move the way she wanted.

"Princess Morrigan, please relax. You look like you are made out of stone," Lady Lily said, carefully observing her every step from the side.

"I feel that if I relax, all the books on my head will fall," Morrigan said through gritted teeth, afraid that even the movement of her mouth could shatter the fragile balance she was keeping.

"If you keep your gait proper and straight, then they will not fall. Please relax your muscles," Lady Lily urged. Morrigan exhaled, a drop of sweat rolling down the side of her face, and slowly relaxed her muscles.

She started with her hands, trying to make their movements more natural and fluid. Then she relaxed her shoulders, allowing them to lower ever so slightly. And finally, she relaxed her legs, attempting longer, less shaky steps. The stack of books on her head wobbled, bumping against her horns. Morrigan panicked, stopping, and the stack tipped over completely and fell to the floor. Lady Lily sighed, and Morrigan slumped.

"This is impossible! Why would I ever need to walk straight enough to hold up a stack of books on my head?" she complained, picking up the books.

"It's not the books that are important, it's the ability to walk without losing your balance," Lady Lily explained as she helped Morrigan pick up the books. "Although such etiquette lessons are still too early for a small child like yourself. What was His Majesty thinking, promising those fallen scum to bring you along?"

"I'm sure there's a good reason." Morrigan chuckled awkwardly.

Father no doubt just wanted to brag about his prodigal daughter, which I suppose is fine, but why do it in front of a foreign delegation?

"The reasons don't matter when a child as small as yourself is involved," Lady Lily grumbled, then sighed in resignation. "But it's not like he will change his mind now. Don't worry, child. I'll do everything in my power to prepare you for the occasion."

"Thank you, Lady Lily. I really appreciate it," Morrigan replied, putting the last fallen book on top of the stack.

"Morri! Mom! How are you doing?" Deziara skipped into the room, smiling from ear to ear. However, seeing the books stacked on the floor, her smile faded. "Not too well, I guess."

"I don't how you do it so easily, Deziara. The only way I keep the books from falling is if I move as rigid as a..." Morrigan was about to say "robot," but stopped herself at the last moment.

"That is a problem. I wonder why it is more difficult for Morri than it was for me. I learned pretty quickly," Deziara said, and Morrigan felt her pride shatter to pieces. She knew her sister didn't mean anything bad by it, but it hurt nonetheless.

"It might have something to do with her body," Lady Lily said, looking at Morrigan thoughtfully.

"My body? Is there something wrong with it?"

"No. There's nothing wrong with it. It's just too small. You need to grow taller—keeping balance should be easier then," Lady Lily said soothingly, then took the stack of books and set it aside.

"How do I grow taller in one month?" Morrigan chuckled nervously.

"Maybe you could transform into a taller version of yourself?" Deziara offered, excitement radiating from her.

"Oh! I could do that!" Morrigan said, and was about to transform when Lady Lily put a hand on her shoulder.

"No. You won't be able to meet the delegation in your shifted form. Let's move on to a different lesson. We'll practice walking again if we have time," the demoness said. Morrigan slumped, her mind reeling from all the possibilities that could go wrong when meeting the people from the Fallen Kingdom. Without a doubt they would be critical of her every move.

That means that one mistake could instantly make me into a laughingstock, which in turn would enrage Alphegor and plunge the Demon Kingdom into a never-ending war with its neighbors. No pressure.

"Are you thinking of some ridiculous scenario again?" Deziara poked Morrigan's forehead, forcing her out of her thoughts.

"No..."

"You totally were. Whatever you were thinking, I am sure you were vastly exaggerating. It'll be just fine—Father will be together with you, after all," Deziara said with a smile.

"Deziara is right. You are just ten years old. Nobody is expecting you to have perfect manners," Lady Lily said, then paused, appearing thoughtful. "But let's learn as much as we can."

"Yes!" Morrigan nodded, internally praying that she'd be able to learn just enough manners and etiquette that the fallen wouldn't have a reason to belittle her.

* * *

Morrigan sat hidden under Haku's wing in the recesses of the giant dragon stable. The building had been reconstructed at least three times since the dragon's birth to accommodate his ever-growing size. However, at the rate Haku was growing, the stable would need another renovation in less than a year.

"You're getting really big, Haku," Morrigan said as she brushed his glistening red scales, making sure to get rid of any dirt and debris. The dragon hummed with delight, occasionally shifting this way and that to better scratch an itchy spot on his body.

"Sometimes I wish I could grow bigger more quickly." She sighed, thinking back on everything she had gone through in the past few weeks to prepare for the festival. Countless lessons in table manners where she memorized which one of the dozen table utensils she had to use for each dish, how to properly eat each dish—most of the time, it involved taking ridiculously small bites—and how to signal the waiter for whatever needs might arise at the table.

Why do I need to use some vague signals to call the waiter? Would it really kill somebody if I just called them over?

Haku lifted his head and looked at her, concern apparent on his draconic features. Or at least they were apparent to her. Morrigan could always tell what he was feeling, although Deziara claimed that she saw absolutely no change in the dragon's demeanor.

"I'm alright, Haku. I just wish there would be less of the delegation and etiquette nonsense and more of the festival fun," Morrigan huffed. Her politics lessons also hadn't really stopped due to the approaching celebration. In fact, Lord Weisedun had doubled the speed at which he spoke the names, making it sound like a weird rap of sorts. But her mind was so full with etiquette and manners and proper ways of speaking that there just wasn't enough space in her head to learn anything more.

The dragon crooned and gently nudged her arm, encouraging her to continue brushing. She giggled and obliged. The time she spent with Haku seemed like the only peaceful time she could get during the day. That, and whatever little time she had together with her father during the evenings.

"It's a shame you can't come to the festival. I bet it would be fun for you to look at something new. Otherwise all you see is this stable and castle yard," she said, wondering whether the dragon felt trapped, like she often did.

Haku shook his head and blew his breath at her, messing up her hair and forcing her to giggle. She grabbed his maw and gently shook his head, earning a puff of smoke in her face. Morrigan waved away the smoke and then put her forehead against Haku's, enjoying the closeness of her friend.

As they enjoyed the moment, the stable door opened, and Deziara peeked in, her black hair flowing down the side of her face. The girl smiled when she saw Morrigan and ran up to her cheerfully. "There you are, Morri! Mom has been looking for you—said it was time for the lessons again."

Morrigan groaned, and slumped over Haku's neck. The dragon stiffened, gingerly lowering his head so as to not drop her to the floor. Deziara's smile also waned as she walked up to the pair.

"My mom isn't that strict," Deziara said, poking Morrigan to get her attention, but the younger girl kept her face pressed into Haku's scales.

"It's not about your mom. It's about this etiquette thing as a whole. I've been learning every waking moment, but it feels like I haven't learned anything at all," she complained, scratching under Haku's chin.

"That's not true and you know it. You've learned more things in these few weeks than some of our older sisters have in years." Deziara pulled Morrigan off the dragon, setting her straight on her feet.

"But it's not enough. One mistake could cause a war," she said, waving her hands helplessly. Haku must have thought it was a game, as he began to gently nip at her fingers. Morrigan giggled and began to boop the dragon's noise while trying to avoid his mouth. Deziara laughed at the sight and, before long, joined the silly game.

"You know Father wouldn't allow that," Deziara said, grabbing Haku's maw and forcing it shut. The dragon shook his head and freed himself without any issues.

I'm not so sure about that. Sometimes it feels like Father wouldn't mind going to war and just wiping the Fallen Kingdom from existence.

"But I still don't want to make a fool of myself. I have to set a good example as the Crown Princess," she said, and her hands slumped to her sides.

"It doesn't matter how perfect you are—if they want to find something to fault you for, they will." Deziara pointed her finger at Morrigan.

"Great, so it doesn't matter what I do," the girl said. She sat on the rough stone floor, wrapping her hands around her knees. Haku whined, then put his head next to her in an attempt to cheer her up.

"No, wait..." Deziara waved her hands, as if it could erase the words she had just said. "No, it does matter, but you shouldn't stress over it just because you're not perfect."

Morrigan didn't answer, instead staring at the pile of straw on the floor.

"This isn't like you, Morri. The last time you acted this way, you ran away and disappeared for two years. You better not be planning to do that again," Deziara warned, then poked her forehead.

"No, I won't run away again!" She shook her head fervently.

"If you do, I'll chase you down myself and then tie you to Haku's back," the girl threatened, and the dragon whipped his tail back and forth in approval.

"I promise I won't. I just wish I had more time. There's barely two weeks left until the festival."

"I know, I know..." Deziara said, sitting down next to Morrigan. "I am worried too, you know. While most eyes will be on you and Viana, of course, people will be looking at all the princesses. All of us have to be a good example."

Morrigan nodded, realizing that Deziara must have been worried about the delegation as well. The whole kingdom was probably worried about the fallen coming at the time of their biggest celebration. Some might be angry, some might be worried, and some might even be scared.

"I just wish there was something we could do to help everything pass by peacefully. Us talking politely and curtsying at every guest isn't really going to ease the ongoing tension," Morrigan said.

"Well, it is a festival, so there shouldn't be any reason for there to be tension," Deziara said, then winced. "But then again, it *is* the Fallen Kingdom we are talking about. Nobody really likes them."

"Exactly. And I doubt they like us either. I have to do something truly extraordinary if I want them to consider signing a peace treaty afterward," Morrigan said.

"Your whole being is extraordinary. Whatever you show them, Morri, they will surely love it. Even if they are fallen," Deziara said with a smile, then patted her on the back.

"Whatever I show them..." Morrigan could feel an idea forming in her mind.

"Yeah. Just show them what you are good at, and surely they will forget and forgive any mistakes you could make."

"That's it, Deziara!" Morrigan jumped to her feet, startling both Deziara and Haku.

"What is it?"

"I'll just show them what I'm good at. Thank you, sister! I need to go and prepare now," Morrigan said before rushing towards the exit.

"Wait! Prepare? Prepare what, exactly?" Deziara called after her.

"You'll see!" she yelled back, her heart swelling with excitement. Deziara shouted something at her, but Morrigan was already in her shadow form, rushing inside the Demon Castle.

CHAPTER 13

ARRIVAL OF THE FALLEN DELEGATION

Morrigan rose from her bed a bit after seven, which was more than an hour earlier than usual. Her heart was beating fast and she felt nervous jitters all over her body. Like little pinpricks, they didn't allow her to remain still, forcing her out of the comforts of the bed. It was the day when the foreign delegations would arrive.

The preparation time for the festival had flown by in what felt like an instant. Between her lessons with Lady Lily, Azrael, and Lord Weisedun, as well as her own individual learning time, which she dedicated purely to honing her artistic abilities, she basically had no free time left.

Morrigan ran out of her room, through the living room, and knocked on Alphegor's bedroom door.

"Come in, little one," he replied, and Morrigan swung the heavy door open. The king was already up from his bed, browsing through his wardrobe.

"Good morning, Father!"

"Good morning, Morrigan. Couldn't sleep anymore?" He turned towards her and smiled.

"No. I feel so nervous. My mind is just going through a thousand scenarios where things go horribly wrong," she said, then peered into his wardrobe, wondering which outfit her father was going to wear. He pointed to a grand red one, and Morrigan shook her head. It was a wonderful suit, but a bit too fancy for welcoming a delegation. Alphegor nodded in agreement.

"And what's the worst-case scenario?" He pointed at a more demure black-and-gold suit. It certainly would look great on Alphegor, but this would be better suited for a smaller party or a dinner in a more relaxed environment. She shook her head.

"Worst-case scenario is that I accidentally lose control of my powers and set the Prime Minister on fire," she said. By "Prime Minister," she thought of the one coming from the Fallen Kingdom, not Lucius. She had no idea what kind of person they were, but they must be really important to have been sent to represent the whole country in their king's stead. Although Morrigan believed that the king was just too cautious to come himself.

"Worst case? That is the best-case scenario." Alphegor laughed, and she couldn't help but laugh along.

"Father! We need to establish a peaceful relationship." She elbowed him lightly, and Alphegor wrapped his arms around her and pulled her close.

"They could peacefully surrender to us," he whispered, and she laughed. For the most part, Alphegor was trying to find peaceful solutions; however, if things were not going his way, then he wouldn't be against using force.

I need to make sure that the relationship between demons and the fallen remains friendly, or at the very least civil.

Alphegor pointed at a royal purple suit with golden embellishments. It was neither too grand nor too simple. It would display Alphegor as the king that he was, but at the same time wouldn't make him look overly pompous.

"That's the one," she approved. "Shall I call for the servants?"

"Yes, I think it's time to get ready. Go call for Gunna, and wear that dress you showed me the other day. That alone should knock them off their feet." Alphegor smirked, and Morrigan blushed, remembering how he had praised her as the most beautiful demon in all of Doppelta, gushing over her and nearly calling over an artist to have her painted.

"It's just a dress, Father," she muttered, inching towards the door.

"It's not the dress that matters but rather the wearer. In my opinion, you look good in anything, but that particular dress is quite well matched." Alphegor hummed with satisfaction, and Morrigan made her escape before he went into another flurry of praises. Last time, he had kept talking about how nice she looked throughout the whole dinner.

Morrigan called out for Alphegor's butler, then returned to her room to ring the bell that would summon Gunna. Less than ten minutes later, the dwarf nanny was in her room with three maids alongside her.

"It's time to get ready! Today is an important day," she addressed the demon maids and Gunna, and all of them nodded, their faces stern, as if preparing for war.

"Do not worry, Lady Morrigan. We shall make sure that nobody will be able to turn their eyes away from you," Gunna said, and the maids nodded along with her. Usually, the demonesses didn't treat the nanny very nicely, but at times like these they all had a scary sense of unity.

* * *

After two hours of intensive preparation—washing, skin care, dressing, hairstyling, and makeup—Morrigan was finally ready. Her long red hair glistened like rubies, her skin shone with health, and the elegant black dress, with red embellishments that matched her eyes, fit her body like a glove.

Say what you will about demon personality, but their tailors are amazing. The level of detail on this dress would make every designer on Earth green with jealousy. Not to mention that it is actually comfortable.

Morrigan exited the bathroom, Gunna and the maids looking proudly over the fruits of their labor. It didn't matter who was a demon and who was a dwarf—the sense of camaraderie was undeniable.

"Ready to go, Princess?" Azrael perked up from the living room sofa, where he had been waiting for her. He was assigned as Morrigan's official escort, a position he was more than eager to accept. Morrigan had no doubt that he was cooking up some schemes involving the fallen delegation.

"Ready!" she said resolutely, then looked at him. Azrael was wearing a fancy white-and-purple suit, which matched his hair and eyes. Much to her dismay, she was forced to admit that he looked rather handsome. If only that mischievous glint in his eyes didn't give away his true intentions.

"Excellent! Let's show those fallen scum who's boss." He got up from the sofa and extended an elbow towards her.

"You cannot call them scum from this point on. Got it? I don't want the whole thing to fall apart just because you couldn't contain your tongue," she reprimanded, taking a firm hold of his hand. Despite her strong tone, her hands were trembling from nervousness.

Azrael probably felt it, but was kind enough not to comment on it. Perhaps he was planning to poke fun at her later when the big event was over. But at that moment, he led Morrigan through the castle, where maids and servants bowed their heads as they passed. After a while, they reached the entrance hall, where all the princesses, concubines, and other high-standing demons were gathered in groups.

The delegation from the Fallen Kingdom wasn't the only one who'd be arriving: so would the delegations from the other kingdoms. And since it was impossible and also unnecessary for the king to greet them all, each group would be greeted by at least one member of the Royal Family.

As Morrigan went downstairs, she saw Deziara and Lady Lily standing with the Commerce Minister. She gave them a small wave and Deziara waved back, while Lady Lily smiled in greeting. Some of Morrigan's other sisters also waved at her, although the majority acted like Viana, who was pointedly ignoring her existence.

And I'll have to spend the whole festival in her company. Great!

Much to Morrigan's chagrin, Azrael was leading her straight to Viana, who was dressed in an elegant dark red dress. She, Viana, Azrael, Lucius, and Alphegor would greet the main delegation from the Fallen Kingdom.

"Good morning, Princess Morrigan, Azrael," Lucius greeted.

"Good morning, Azrael," Viana said, curtsying ever so slightly.

"Is His Majesty not here yet?" Azrael asked, appearing rather bored.

"I have not yet seen Father today," she replied, twirling a lock of purple hair in her fingers.

"Do you know, Princess?" Azrael turned to Morrigan, who was taking in a deep breath in an attempt to calm her nerves a little.

"He should be here soon. I imagine he's still getting ready," she replied somewhat absentmindedly, and looked up the staircase in hopes of seeing Alphegor.

"Are you perhaps scared, little sister? You look somewhat nervous." Viana smirked, and Morrigan had opened her mouth to retort when the head butler, who was standing dutifully by the entrance, spoke up.

"The delegation from the Duergar Country has arrived!"

Deziara, Lady Lily, and the Commerce Minister all perked up and walked towards the entrance. Morrigan followed her sister with her gaze, wishing her good luck in her mind and praying for her success. Deziara managed to give her one last smile before the entrance door was shut again.

"So it begins..." Azrael noted. About every five to ten minutes after that, the head butler called out the arriving delegations, and the assigned groups went out to greet them. When only three groups remained, Morrigan's nerves felt as tight as bowstrings. Alphegor hadn't arrived yet.

Just as the second-to-last group was about to leave, Alphegor came downstairs, looking as regal as Morrigan had ever seen him. His hair was neatly slicked back and his dark purple suit with its gold ornaments complimented the magnificent crown on his head. It weaved around his horns and had sharp points, almost looking like a weapon.

"Good day to you, Father." Viana curtsied gracefully with a smile.

"Is everyone ready?" he asked, his stern, kingly persona turned on.

"Of course, Father," Viana replied.

"Sure," Azrael said nonchalantly.

"Morrigan?" Alphegor arched an eyebrow when she didn't reply. It might've looked demanding, but she saw the hint of concern in his eyes. She exhaled and nodded.

"I'm ready, Father!"

He allowed a small smile to pass his lips and then stood in front of them—strong, tall, and unyielding, like a mountain. A few more tense minutes passed until finally they were the last group that remained in the room. The head butler returned, and Morrigan felt herself go stiff as he opened his mouth and announced, "The delegation from the Fallen Kingdom has arrived!"

Alphegor strode forward, his gait confident and smooth. Viana flowed after him gracefully, like a river, Lucius extending his hand to her. Morrigan took a deep breath, then felt Azrael poke her in the side. She was about to glare at him, but then saw that he was offering his elbow to her in support. She smiled sheepishly at him and took it.

Azrael's hand and the sight of her father's strong back brought her courage, and she walked forward, allowing Azrael to lead her. As she exited the castle, she saw a carriage riding towards the castle entrance.

The carriages in the Underworld were a little bit different than the ones Morrigan had seen in history movies and books. They had no windows, their tires resembled tank tracks, and they were pulled by what looked like giant badgers. As if the miniature version weren't nasty enough.

Four more simplistic-looking carriages followed the main one, and around two dozen armored guards rode along their sides. Morrigan tried to catch a glimpse of their features, curious to see exactly what the fallen looked like, but their armor hid everything from sight. Finally, the main carriage stopped by the staircase, and Morrigan, along with the others, observed the guests.

"Announcing the arrival of the Prime Minister of the Fallen Kingdom—Allocen Heinspiel; his wife, Valeria Heinspiel; and daughter, Annabell Heinspiel," the head butler announced. The coachman hurried to open the carriage door, and for the first time in her life, Morrigan saw a fallen.

First came out a thin and tall man with pale skin, white hair, and sky-blue eyes. After him followed a short and thin woman with bright green eyes and platinum blonde hair tied in a neat bun. After them, a timid little girl scurried out, hiding within the confines of her mother's skirt.

Their appearance wouldn't have been anything special; however, all three of them had magnificent black, feathery wings coming out of their backs.

They have wings?!

CHAPTER 14

AWKWARD DINNER

As Alphegor descended downstairs to greet the fallen delegation, Morrigan couldn't help but stare at their wings.

What wouldn't I give up for the ability to fly? Why couldn't demons have wings? All we have are these scrawny, useless tails.

"Don't stare at them so much," Azrael whispered in her ear, and Morrigan blinked.

"But they have wings! Nobody told me that," she protested quietly, but tried her best to look somewhere else. She decided to inspect their servants instead. None of them had any wings, and they appeared to be from various races. There were dwarves, as well as duergar, their blue-skinned counterparts. There were also some demons, elves, and drow, as well as a few races Morrigan didn't recognize.

But one servant stood out among the rest. A young elven boy, approximately Morrigan's age, judging from his build. His hair shone like a golden sun while his eyes were like bright red rubies. It reminded her of her father's eye color when his bloodlust took over. But despite his eerie eye color, she couldn't help but be mesmerized.

Elves must have some superior attractiveness gene. I mean, pureblooded demons are usually attractive, but this boy is on a whole different level. It's a shame that he's probably a slave. This whole slavery thing needs to be forbidden.

"Welcome to the Demon Castle!" Alphegor announced in his booming voice, but his expression showed no sort of welcome whatsoever. In fact, he was nearly glaring at the Prime Minister.

"It is good to be here, Your Majesty King Alphegor," Prime Minister Heinspiel replied, his expression just as stiff as Alphegor's. The tension in the air was so thick that Morrigan could basically feel it on her skin. "This is my wife Valeria and daughter Annabell."

"Pleasure to meet you," Alphegor replied dryly, then turned towards Viana, his expression relaxing. "This is Viana, my eldest daughter."

"It is a pleasure to greet you, Prime Minister." Viana curtsied in a perfectly elegant manner, smiling politely.

"And this is Morrigan, my youngest daughter." A proud smile bloomed on Alphegor's face, and Morrigan curtsied to the best of her ability. It wasn't as graceful as her sister's, but she believed she'd done a good-enough job.

"It is a pleasure to meet you," Morrigan said, trying to smile at the fallen man.

"So this is the famed Crown Princess of the Demon Kingdom. To think that you would assign your youngest child as heir. It is unheard of," Prime Minister Heinspiel replied, his face becoming an unreadable mask. Morrigan couldn't tell whether he was making fun of her—which she thought was the most likely scenario—or whether he was just curious.

"Morrigan is the daughter of the late Queen Eirwen, so it is her birthright," Lucius intervened, noticing that Alphegor's glare had intensified.

"Is that so? Pardon me. I didn't know," Heinspiel apologized.

"Now you do. Let us proceed inside. We can talk more at the dinner table," Alphegor commanded. Without waiting for the guests' reply, he turned and walked back up the stairs. Morrigan thought it was rather rude, but perhaps a king was allowed to act this way. At least she hoped so.

Azrael led Morrigan back up the stairs and they headed towards the main dining hall, with the fallen delegation following silently behind them. Not a single word was uttered along the way, and Morrigan felt like she would suffocate from the excruciating silence.

Shouldn't somebody be talking about something? Anything? The weather, at least? Perhaps their journey on the way here? Should I speak up first?

Morrigan looked towards Azrael for answers, but he shook his head.

Even Azrael won't talk? What has the world come to?

Thankfully, the excruciatingly silent walk was soon over, as they reached the main dining hall. A table inside was long enough to accommodate about a hundred people, but only the very end of it had dishes set out for dinner. The rest of it had little Underworld flowers arranged in dark vases. The Underworld didn't have a wide variety of flowers, and their colors weren't nearly as vibrant as the ones Morrigan had seen on Earth. However, the maids had done their best to accentuate the larger flowers, using more demure buds of contrasting colors to bring out their vibrancy. The dark gray-and-silver tablecloth also helped to bring out their beauty.

The rest of the dining hall was also decorated with matching flowers, as well as with some sculptures and banners with the Demon Kingdom's symbol on it. Namely, it was a wingless dragon with large horns and a crown just like Alphegor's on its head. Apparently, it was the shape that the first Nachtstern King liked to take in battle.

Morrigan and the other demons went to sit on the right side of the table while the maids guided the guests to the left. Alphegor, of course, sat at the end of the table with the Prime Minister on his left and Morrigan on his right. She felt rather uncomfortable being seated right across from such an important person.

No, Morrigan. You're an important person too. You're the Crown Princess, so don't act like a meek little sheep.

So she straightened her back and put on the polite business smile she had been practicing with Lady Lily for the past month. The Prime Minister's expression didn't change, remaining an unreadable mask as the maids brought a wet washcloth for him and everyone else to wipe their hands. However, he rejected it.

"I would like to be served by my own servants, if I may," he announced, and the already tense air grew even thicker.

"As you wish," Alphegor replied, but Morrigan heard the dissatisfied note in his voice. The little elf boy went up to the maid and retrieved the washcloth from her. He inspected it carefully, then handed it to the Prime Minister.

Such a grim fate for a child. I've seen plenty of slaves around the Demon Castle, but at least none of them are children. Then again, it could be different outside the castle walls.

"So tell us, Prime Minister Heinspiel, how was your journey to the Demon Kingdom?" Viana said, putting on her most charismatic facade.

"It was a long and difficult journey. We all are quite tired and would love nothing more than to retreat to our chambers and rest," he replied.

"But surely you must be hungry as well. A good meal after a long journey will help you rest better afterward," Morrigan said, trying to ease the tension.

"The food in the Demon Castle is sublime," Viana added, giving Morrigan a knowing look.

I guess we're having a temporary truce now, sis? That is fine by me.

"Yes, I do hope your cooks can live up to the expectations," Heinspiel's wife said, her voice a little friendlier than her husband's. But only a little.

"They make wonderful meals for us daily. The desserts are especially tasty," Morrigan chimed in, hoping to catch the attention of the little fallen girl. Just as she expected, the child perked up, suddenly looking far more interested in the conversation.

"There will be dessert?" she said in a shaky voice. Heinspiel's face relaxed a little bit, and he looked fondly at the girl.

"Yes. No meal would be complete without one." Morrigan smiled, and the girl nodded shyly, her cheeks flushing a bit.

"I have to note, Your Majesty, that both of your daughters are eloquent speakers. I am surprised to see such an outspoken little child," Mrs. Heinspiel said, putting a gentle hand on her daughter's shoulder. "Usually children are really withdrawn at such a young age."

Really? I remember Deziara being pretty loud when she was about ten years old. Perhaps fallen children are quieter.

"Of course! Morrigan has been an extraordinary child ever since birth," Alphegor bragged. Viana's expression turned a bit sour when he failed to mention her.

"I've learned a lot from my big sister." Morrigan smiled and looked at Viana. She appeared a bit surprised at first, but quickly collected herself and smiled back at Morrigan.

"I'd do anything for my little sister."

"How sweet! I wish our little darling could have a sibling. You would love one more child, wouldn't you?" Mrs. Heinspiel gave her husband a knowing look. He tried to ignore it, sweat forming on his forehead.

"Annabell already has so much to do. Looking over a little sister would surely be too much," Heinspiel said, chuckling awkwardly.

"Children are a treasure, Prime Minister. I have twenty-four daughters, each one more beautiful than the next." Alphegor appeared more proud than a golden peacock flaunting its feathers, a wide grin spreading across his features.

"How do you manage so many daughters, if I may ask?" The Prime Minister leaned in closer to Alphegor and whispered so quietly that even Morrigan, who was sitting closest to them, could barely hear. "Sometimes I'm having trouble dealing with just one."

"Let me tell you." Alphegor lowered his voice and also leaned in closer. The two men became engrossed in their conversation, completely unbothered by everybody else. The atmosphere in the room relaxed and a pleasant chatter could be heard across the table.

Seeing this, Morrigan relaxed as well, and focused on her table manners instead. Alphegor would occasionally brag about one of her or her sister's achievements, so she had to keep up her good appearance. Soon the main dish arrived—a small leg of some sort of a bird on a bed of vegetables glazed with a dark sauce. Morrigan tried to remember which tools were proper to use in this exact case.

Was it the small fork with a knife, or the medium fork? Normally I'd go for the medium one, but the bird is so small that the medium fork feels like overkill.

Morrigan felt a gentle tap against her foot and looked at Viana, who was sitting next to her. She slowly took the small fork and a knife, then delicately cut the meat from the bone. She then set the utensils on the napkin above the plate, took the medium fork, and proceeded to eat.

She's showing me what I'm supposed to do?

Morrigan smiled at her and proceeded to repeat her sister's actions. As she finished cutting up the bird and was about to begin eating, she noticed Alphegor and the Heinspiel couple looking at her, giving her the same look one would give when seeing a cute kitten.

"Your daughters truly do get along. How sweet!" Mrs. Heinspiel noted. "Honey, we definitely need another daughter."

The Prime Minister nearly choked on the wine he was drinking, and everyone chuckled merrily at the sight.

"Enough about that, dear. Your Majesty, why don't you tell us more about the upcoming festivities?" Heinspiel suggested, then gestured to the elven boy behind him. The boy ran over to one of the diplomats sitting at the table and took an ornate box from him. "We have brought a gift as a gesture of goodwill."

Some of the previous tension appeared in the room again. The elven boy approached Alphegor with the box. What surprised Morrigan was how firmly he looked the king in the eye. Most demons usually lowered their gaze before him, and yet this young child looked at him head-on without fear.

"What is in the box?" the king asked, not reaching to open it.

"It contains a rare magical gem—a shadow ruby," Prime Minister Heinspiel announced proudly. The demon side of the table appeared shocked, while the fallen side looked awfully smug. Morrigan wished she could ask Azrael what it meant, but he was sitting two seats away from her. She looked at Viana, hoping that her sister was still in a helpful mood.

Viana leaned in closer to Morrigan and whispered, "A shadow ruby is said to possess the ability to adapt to the user's abilities. The only place where they have been found is in the Fallen Kingdom. That's the reason why they managed to gain such power."

Adapt to the user's abilities? What does that even mean?

But there was no time to ask Viana, as Prime Minister Heinspiel spoke up again. "If I understand correctly, there will be a competition during the festival."

"Of course. It is a custom, after all," Alphegor replied, taking the box from the elven boy. He opened it, and his lips pressed into a thin line. Then he turned the box towards Morrigan and the other demons, showing a bright red gemstone that sat cradled in protective fabric.

"We would love to offer this gemstone as a prize for the competition winner," Heinspiel said with a smile.

Oh, I understand. It is not really a gift. No doubt the fallen intend to win the competition and take the gemstone back. So much for a gesture of goodwill.

CHAPTER 15

LATE-EVENING TALKS

In the evening, when Morrigan was finally freed from the dinner table, she turned into a shadow and snuck through the busy castle hallways. They were brimming with demons, drow, and duergar, as well as other races. Not wanting to be escorted by Azrael and her two guards through the whole castle, she excused herself and went for the easy approach—sliding through the shadows.

Morrigan wasted no time and headed straight to Lady Lily's room, materializing from the shadow as soon as she reached the door. The two guards by the door appeared startled at first, but they recognized Morrigan and greeted her with a bow.

"Good day, Your Highness. Have you come to meet Lady Lily or Princess Deziara?" one of the guards asked.

"I've come to see Lady Lily. Is she back yet?"

"Yes, she and Princess Deziara came back a while ago. I shall announce that you wish to meet them," the guard said, then knocked on the door.

"What is it? I do not wish to meet anyone today," resounded the elegant, yet tired voice of Lady Lily.

"It is Princess Morrigan, my lady," the guard said. Before Lady Lily had the chance to respond, the door swung open and Deziara pulled Morrigan in, shutting the door behind herself.

"Morri! How did it go?" Deziara chirped, hopping around her in excitement.

"Deziara, give your sister some room to breathe," Lady Lily called out, an ice pack pressed against her head.

"I see it was rough on your end," Morrigan noted, and the demoness sighed in response.

"It wouldn't be so bad if this little one wasn't so excited about every new thing she saw."

"But, Mom! There were so many new people. The duergar were a little bit similar to Gunna, but much gruffer, and they looked annoyed at every little thing."

"That's because you kept pestering them about every little thing. I swear, all the training you went through was completely useless." Lady Lily sighed again, then looked at Morrigan hopefully. "Tell me it went better on your end, child."

"Yes, tell us everything! I saw the fallen from afar but I couldn't believe my eyes. Do they really have wings?" Deziara pulled Morrigan to the sofa across from her mother and sat right next to her.

"Yes, they do! They are so large and big and fluffy," Morrigan gushed, completely infected by Deziara's enthusiasm.

"Did they let you touch them?"

"What? I never asked. That would be inappropriate."

Deziara puffed out her cheeks, while Lady Lily nodded in approval.

"At least one of you girls has a good head on her shoulders. Tell me how the dinner went."

"It was really tense at first, but Viana and I managed to get some light conversation going."

"What? Viana? Really? Are you sure you're talking about the same Viana?" Deziara scowled in disbelief.

"Viana has her priorities set straight. She knows we cannot show any discord in front of our enemies," Lady Lily noted.

Enemies. I never thought of them as such. The fallen seemed like normal people, just like demons. It was rather heartwarming to see the Prime Minister and his wife gush over their daughter.

"Yeah, I was also surprised. She even showed me how to properly cut up the bird they served at dinner. Anyway, once the tension was broken, the conversation got really light and even cheerful, I would say. But..."

"But?" Deziara leaned closer, and Lady Lily narrowed her eyes.

"They brought this shadow ruby gem as a gift and asked for it to become the prize of the competition that will happen during the festival."

"So it is no gift at all." Deziara scowled, and both Morrigan and Lady Lily nodded at her conclusion.

"It's a rather rude thing that they did, but I understand why they did it. No doubt they wish for one of their own to win the competition and improve their reputation in the Underworld," the demoness said, then put a finger to her lips in contemplation. "But a shadow ruby of all things. That is a really valuable prize."

"How does it work exactly?" Morrigan asked. "Viana said it adapts to its user."

"She means that the gem gives the user the ability that is most suited for them. For example, if a lesser demon who works in the mines were to absorb a shadow ruby, it might grant the ability to locate ores more easily."

"That doesn't sound very impressive," Deziara scoffed.

"Indeed. But if for example one of you girls were to absorb it, it might give you the ability to control the shadows themselves."

"Control the shadows?" Both girls leaned forward, their eyes shining with interest. Moving as a shadow like Morrigan did was already considered a superior and rare ability. But controlling shadows in the Underworld, where there was no sun, meant that you were nearly invincible. Only Alphegor possessed this ability.

"Yes. Of course, that is not a given. Nobody knows what ability a shadow ruby will grant to the user, only that it will be beneficial to them."

"We must get that ruby, Morri!" Deziara jumped up to her feet, brimming with excitement.

"Wouldn't it be a bit difficult? The competition includes many tasks, and you have to be good at them all to be victorious," Morrigan said. The Nachtstern Festival Competition happened over the course of five days, and was the main attraction that garnered the attention of the whole Underworld. Apparently, it was a great way for demons and other races to search for employment, as those who managed to excel during even one of the tasks would be sought out afterward.

"It is worth a shot. And everyone is allowed to enter—even us princesses." Deziara hummed, and Morrigan saw how the cogs in her head were turning.

There's no stopping her now, but isn't the competition too dangerous? I'm pretty sure the tasks include monster subjugation or something similar.

"It wouldn't hurt to try. Why don't both of you girls enter?" Lady Lily smiled, the tiniest hint of mischief in her eyes.

"Wait? Me too? Am I not too small?" Morrigan protested. The thought that she could enter the competition never even crossed her mind. "Shouldn't someone like Azrael be competing and representing the Demon Kingdom?"

"He can't compete. He's the host of the competition. Everyone thought it would be unfair if he competed," Lady Lily objected. "And everyone is allowed to compete, even children."

"Isn't there a chance that I'll get hurt?" Morrigan asked.

"No, everything is carefully monitored. You'll be just fine. And in case something does go wrong, Azrael and your father will be right there, watching the whole thing."

"Morri, you should totally compete," Deziara urged. "I know for sure that you'd win the magic task and talent showcase in a heartbeat. Nothing can compete with your beautiful paintings."

The thought of showing off my art is exciting, but, still, I'm not too fond of the idea of wrangling monsters. What if they bring out something like that hydra that lives in the dungeon? Just thinking about that thing makes me shiver.

"But I can't wrangle any monsters, and I don't know that much magic yet," she objected.

"What do you mean? You got Haku soundly under your control and you mastered fire magic in just a few weeks. Not to mention all the other magic you've mastered over the years," Deziara praised.

Morrigan had learned levitation and how to create force fields by absorbing labradorite and quartz gems respectively, but those were just two abilities. Compared to adults who had hundreds of spells in their repertoire, her measly array of magic was nothing.

"Controlling Haku is one thing, but controlling some random Underworld monster is completely different," she objected, but Deziara was not about to budge.

"Morri, please! You have a better chance of winning this than I do. You got to try." Deziara took hold of Morrigan's hands and employed her best impression of puppy eyes. Morrigan tried her best to not look her sister in the eyes, but she couldn't resist for long.

"Alright, fine! But if anything happens, it is your fault," she grumbled as Deziara pulled her into a tight hug.

"I love you, Morri! You're the best sister a demon could ask for."

"Alright, Deziara, that's enough. I think it's best if we all rest for today. We need to gather our strength before the big day," Lady Lily said, although the smile on her lips didn't match her words.

"Aw, but I want to talk more about what we could do to win the competition," Deziara whined.

"Tomorrow, girls. Today we rest." She shook her head and stood up, gently placing one hand on Deziara's head and the other on Morrigan's. "Besides, I'm sure both of you will do just fine."

Both girls nodded and smiled in response. Then Morrigan unlatched herself from her sister and waved both women goodnight. As she exited the room, she let out a sigh, worried about the daunting task ahead of her.

Participating in the competition will be tough. But I have to admit that the shadow ruby is a very tempting prize. I wonder what sort of ability it would grant to me. Would it be shadow manipulation?

Morrigan was about to turn into a shadow and speed off to her room when she saw a flicker of gold pass through the end of the hallway.

"Princess Morrigan, shall I escort you back to your room?" one of the guards asked, appearing ready to follow her.

"No, that won't be necessary. I'll get there myself," she assured, glancing at the hallway ahead.

"With all due respect, Princess Morrigan, there are a lot of strangers in the castle. We cannot allow you to go by yourself," the guard insisted.

"I'll just turn into a shadow and go straight to my room. That wouldn't be an issue then, right?" She smiled at the guard, who thought for a moment, then nodded.

"Alright. If you go straight to your room as a shadow, then you should be safe."

"Thank you for thinking of me. Have a nice evening," Morrigan said before melding into the shadows. But instead of heading straight to her room, she zoomed into the hallway where she had seen the golden flicker before. It was empty, so she rushed to the next cross section, and to the left saw the same golden flicker heading upstairs.

Morrigan followed it and saw that it was the golden-haired elf boy sneaking his way upstairs. Well, he was trying to sneak, but it was rather obvious to anyone watching. He pretended to be nonchalant when somebody was walking towards him, but he appeared rather stiff. Luckily for him, the guests weren't interested in a scrawny elven boy, and the servants were too busy to pay any attention to him.

Where is he going? This way leads upstairs to where the Royal Family lives. Is he lost? Doesn't seem so.

Curious, Morrigan continued tailing him as he went higher and higher up the castle. He was actually sneakier than she initially thought, using servants as a sort of shield to hide himself from the tired guards or sneaking past them when they were distracted by something else. The fact that guards usually weren't wary of slaves also contributed to his success.

He's actually getting pretty close to my room. What the hell is he plotting? I can't just let him do as he pleases.

Morrigan materialized from the shadow, appearing right before the elven boy. He jumped back in surprise and glared at her.

"Where do you think you are going?" she asked, putting her hands on her hips and glaring at him. She had a suspicion that the fallen had sent him to do something nefarious, but at the same time Morrigan didn't feel threatened by a poor slave kid.

"None of your business," he snapped back, and was about to brush past her, but Morrigan stood her ground.

"I'm afraid it *is* my business. This is a private place. You're not supposed to be here."

"What are you going to do? Call your daddy?" the boy mocked, sticking out his tongue at her.

What a little brat! Perhaps I need to put him in his place. To show how much stronger I am. Surely that will scare him away.

"I could, but I don't need to call him to stop you from going farther." She smirked, then produced a fireball in her palm in an attempt to scare him off. Much to her dismay, the boy just scoffed.

"What? Are you going to light a candle with that? Good luck." He laughed, then tried to walk past her again. This time she produced a force field across the hallway, its shimmering presence stopping the elf in his tracks.

"If you know what's good for you, you will leave. This is my last warning."

The elven boy examined the force field, then extended his hands towards it. He touched the shimmering wall and pushed against it.

"Not a bad force field—for a girl," he scoffed, then plunged his hand into it, shattering the force field into pieces. Morrigan watched in horror as it disappeared completely, and the boy zoomed past her with a self-satisfied grin on his face.

CHAPTER 16

THE ELVEN BOY

The boy got rid of Morrigan's force field so swiftly that she didn't even register what he did to destroy it. She whirled around and then seized him with her levitation ability. It was rather tough levitating a moving, resisting person, but it was enough to stop the boy from reaching any farther.

"Will you stop that? I am not just going let you waltz into my room!" she grumbled, sweat forming on her forehead as she tried to keep hold of the levitation spell. But the boy redoubled his efforts, and Morrigan was forced to drop him.

"Your room? Why would I want to sneak into your room?" he retorted.

So he doesn't know these are the king's living quarters? But what else could he be searching for? The Royal Treasury? Could the fallen have sent him to steal some magic gemstones?

"If gems are what you're looking for, you won't find any in this room."

The elven boy paused, narrowing his eyes at her as if to assess whether she was telling the truth. After a while, it appeared he came to an entirely wrong conclusion, as he sprinted towards the door.

That suicidal little maniac. He's going to get himself killed.

Morrigan turned into a shadow and bolted towards him. However, before she could reach him, the elf lifted his hand and created a glowing orb of light. The glow coming from it was so strong that Morrigan couldn't remain in her shadow form and materialized. The feeling was so abrupt that she felt nauseous for a moment.

"Wha... What did you do?" She gasped, trying to catch her breath.

"Just created a bit of sunlight." The boy smirked, then ran straight into the hallway that led to Morrigan's room. She hurried after him, shielding her eyes from the bright light he still held in his hand. There were currently no guards at the door, which was odd. Usually, they were always there.

How did he time his arrival so perfectly with the time the guards change shifts? The fallen must have ordered him to do so and given him the necessary information to succeed. But how did they find out? In either case, I have to stop him before he does something foolish and gets himself killed. He's just a child, after all.

"Stealing whatever you were ordered to steal will not buy your freedom," Morrigan called out, her voice filling with bitterness as she remembered Faenor. The elf had traded knowledge of Morrigan's true identity for his freedom, but Asdeus had sent him straight into the Dead Bog. Most likely, he never made it out alive.

The boy stopped and looked at Morrigan with intense hatred. "So what? Am I supposed to just accept being a slave? Just enjoy being puppeteered by the likes of you for the rest of my life? No way!" He spat.

"So instead you choose to throw away your life on a foolish errand nobody will ever appreciate you for. You know, if somebody besides me catches you here, you're as good as dead."

"I'd rather die trying than not have tried at all."

Morrigan opened her mouth to speak when she heard familiar footsteps echoing through the hallway. The elf didn't seem to have noticed, and kept glaring viciously at her.

Oh no! If Father catches him here then he really is as good as dead.

She lunged towards him and took a firm hold of his hand. He

stared at her in shock and was about to shake her off when Alphegor appeared from around the corner. The king stopped dead in his tracks and stared at the scene before him. The elf visibly paled, sweat trickling down his forehead.

"Morrigan? What's going on?" Alphegor asked, glaring icy daggers at the boy.

"I'm just showing him around the castle, Father," she replied with a smile. Morrigan knew that Alphegor could probably see through her lie, but she also knew that he wouldn't press the matter if she insisted that everything was fine. Probably.

"Showing a slave from the Fallen Kingdom around the castle?" Alphegor arched an eyebrow. Morrigan crossed her arms over her chest.

"Slaves are people too. And this boy is just around my age. When's the last time I actually had a chance to talk to my peers?" she retorted, and the king actually looked a bit guilty for a moment.

"Well... You have many sisters to talk to."

"That's different. I want friends, not just sisters."

"Does it have to be a boy?" Alphegor narrowed his eyes, glaring at the poor elf again.

Oh, please don't tell me he's going to be like one of those dads who never lets his daughters date anybody. I'm not even old enough for that yet.

"It doesn't matter if it's a boy or a girl. Now, I will escort him back to his room, as it has gotten rather late. Well, shall we talk more tomorrow... err..." Morrigan realized she didn't even know the boy's name, and turned to him for help.

"G-Galandir..." he stammered, his eyes glued to the menacing king before him.

"Yes, I was just about to say Galandir. I shall return to my room in just a moment, Father," Morrigan said, then began pulling Galandir through the corridors. She felt a sort of menacing aura coming from behind but decided to ignore it and march on. As she led the boy ahead by his hand, she felt him shiver slightly.

"I warned you." She sighed.

As if coming out of trance, he yanked his hand free and glared at her. "Don't expect me to thank you," he snarled, then bounded downstairs without looking back.

"I wasn't..." she muttered before turning into a shadow, speeding back to her room.

I swear, a little bit of gratitude wouldn't kill him. But it's fine. At least I won't have to witness child murder this evening.

As Morrigan materialized inside her shared living room, Alphegor was pacing around it and mumbling something to himself.

"Are you alright, Father?" she said, cocking her head to the side.

Perhaps there was trouble with the fallen after dinner. Or maybe he is thinking about the competition. Was there a complication?

"Oh, Morrigan. You're back. That was fast." His bad mood evaporated, and he pulled her into a hug. She giggled as his long hair tickled her face.

"Yes, I just showed Galandir the way back to his room," she said. She felt a bit bad about lying, but there was no real need to escort him back. If he had managed to successfully locate her room without ever visiting the castle before, then his own guest room should pose no issues. Or the slave quarters that were probably assigned to him for the time being.

"Morrigan, you are still very young. You don't have to hurry with your choice. In fact, it is alright for you not to choose anybody for a hundred years. No, two hundred years." Alphegor held her tiny shoulders and looked at her with unyielding seriousness.

Oh, no! He really is the overprotective sort. This will be tough once I am older.

"Don't worry, Father. You're the only one I need!" she said, and Alphegor hugged her again.

"That's right! I'm so glad you understand, Morrigan!" He patted her hair, and she couldn't help but smile.

After a while, Morrigan broke free of his embrace. "Father, can I ask you something?"

"Of course. Anything," Alphegor said, then sat down on the couch, his kingly persona disappearing into the cushions as his expression and stature relaxed.

"I was wondering about the competition that happens during the festival. Deziara and Lady Lily suggested that I participate," she said somewhat timidly.

"I don't see why not. Do you not want to?"

"I'm just a bit worried. Isn't it dangerous?"

"No. It was made to be a fun experience for watchers and participants alike. While some tasks might seem more dangerous than others, there are demons on-site that will be monitoring everything. Azrael is one of them."

Morrigan relaxed, then sat down on the sofa across from her father.

If Azrael is there as a security measure, then I should be fine. His oath will compel him to protect me in the worst-case scenario.

"That's reassuring. Can you tell me more about it?" she asked.

"What do you want to know? I can tell you about the way the competition went last time, but the tasks themselves change every time."

"Aren't you the one determining the tasks?"

"No, it's the Culture Minister's job to do that. He's done a marvelous job every single time, so I entrusted him with it. Although he is rather old. I might need to find a replacement for him by the time the next festival comes."

"So you don't know what is going to happen this year?" Morrigan leaned forward.

"I do like to experience some surprises once in a while. But I can still recount what happened during previous festivals," Alphegor said with a smile.

She thought about it for a moment, then shook her head. "No. I think I would rather leave it as a surprise. If you say it's not dangerous, Father, then I'll trust you and do my best when the competition arrives."

Alphegor nodded approvingly. "I believe you should be able to win if you're careful and apply your knowledge correctly. You have all the tools you need. You just have to use them properly."

"I shall, Father!" Morrigan said resolutely, getting both nervous and excited.

* * *

Morrigan woke up with a fuzzy feeling running through her stomach. Despite it being early morning, she could already hear busy rustling and chattering both within the castle and outside its windows. The festival was here. She rang the bell by her bedside to summon Gunna and the other maids.

I have to look my absolute best today. Father is going to give the opening speech, and while I won't have to speak, I will have to stand alongside him.

The thought of standing in front of a giant crowd made her nervous, so she took a deep breath and exhaled to calm her nerves. She repeated the breathing exercise until she heard a soft knock on the door.

"Lady Morrigan, it is Gunna. May I come in?"

"Come in," she replied. The nanny had a big smile on her face as she carried the traditional festival dress worn by nobles and royalty. It resembled a Japanese kimono a little bit, except the fabric wasn't as thick and restrictive. And of course, it was mostly black, with a muted red dragon motif weaving through it. An homage to the first Demon King.

"Are you ready for the festival?" the dwarf woman asked, her eyes shining with excitement.

"As ready as I'll ever be," Morrigan replied with as much conviction as she could muster.

"Good. You have nothing to worry about. Your main task is to enjoy yourself." The nanny hummed as she began to untangle Morrigan's bed head.

"And not make a fool of myself in front of foreign diplomats. Also not to fail the competition to an extent that would make demons look down on me. Also, try not to cause a war."

"Please, do not worry. A Crown Princess you may be, but remember that you are, first and foremost, a child. Nobody expects a child to solve international problems. That is the king's job. Your job is to support him and enjoy yourself." Gunna gently stroked her head, and the warmth from her hand helped Morrigan relax.

"Yes. I'll try to do my best," she said firmly. Gunna hummed as she began combing Morrigan's hair.

A moment later, another knock sounded on the door, louder and stronger than before. "Morrigan, I am coming in!"

Alphegor strode inside, wearing the light underrobe meant for the festival. There would be another layer on top—an extravagant red robe with a black dragon motif. Morrigan was sure that nobody would be able to match the king in terms of looks.

"How are you feeling today, Morrigan?" he asked, taking the hairbrush from Gunna, who silently moved aside with a bowed head.

"Nervous, excited, worried, anxious, and curious." She grinned, and the king laughed.

"I understand. It is your first festival, so it's only natural that you are nervous. But remember that no matter what happens, I'll be right there beside you," Alphegor said as he combed Morrigan's hair.

"It is Deziara's first festival too. She must also be feeling nervous. Perhaps you could go reassure her as well," Morrigan suggested, and Alphegor nodded.

"Yes, I was considering that. I shall go do that while you get ready," Alphegor said, the hairbrush gently flowing through Morrigan's hair. "And remember, you are the Crown Princess! The highest-standing person in this kingdom besides myself. Keep your head high and your spirits even higher."

CHAPTER 17

COMPETITION SIGN-UPS

The crowd, filled with demons, drow, duergar, and other Underworld races, cheered as Alphegor raised his hand towards them in greeting. Morrigan stood a little bit behind him, on his right, while Viana stood on his left. All of her sisters stood on the large stage, each one dressed in similar kimono-styled attire with a dragon motif. However, each one wore a different color.

Viana's robe was dark blue with gold, while Deziara's, who stood right next to Morrigan, wore a purple robe with a black dragon. Morrigan was surprised that the tailors had managed to find a different, yet suiting color for each princess without any repetition among them.

"The princesses look so amazing!"

"Nobody could ever match our beautiful princesses."

"Is the Crown Princess really the smallest one?"

"She looks a lot like Queen Eirwen."

The crowd was chattering excitedly, their eyes darting from one princess to the next, often lingering on Morrigan. She did her best to hold her head high and retain the polite, serene smile that she had been practicing with Lady Lily. Her hands felt clammy as she held them together in front of her, thankfully hidden under the long sleeves of her black attire.

Just remain calm, Morrigan. All you have to do now is remain pretty and smile.

"People of the Demon Kingdom and dear guests. It is with great honor that I announce the start of our dearly beloved Nachtstern Festival. As the descendant of the first Nachtstern King, I promise that the glory of the Underworld shall never fall!" Alphegor called out in his booming voice, and the crowd went absolutely wild, cheering and hollering.

Morrigan glanced at the surroundings, her breath hitching as she saw people everywhere. They were in the center of Linberor Market Square, the same place Azrael had snuck her and Deziara to when they were small. All of the stalls had been cleared away to make place for the grand stage, illuminated by floating orbs and decorated to resemble the giant body of a dragon with crystalline scales that reflected the light, bringing as much attention to the stage as possible.

The surrounding square also had strings of bright lanterns going over the houses, held up by some sort of invisible magic. Meanwhile, the nearby streets were adorned with wingless dragon decorations, as well as anything that would pay homage to demons and the Royal Family.

"This time, just like during every festival before now, each and every one of you will be able to enter the glorious and noble Nachtstern Festival Competition. This year, in addition to the usual monetary prize and a favor from your King, you'll be competing for this." Alphegor pulled out a box from within his robes and opened it, showing the shadow ruby to the crowd. "As a show of goodwill, our guests from the Fallen Kingdom have given this shadow ruby as a prize to the winner of the competition."

The crowd gasped, and people began muttering among themselves.

"A shadow ruby? Isn't that the rare gem that grants you any power you wish?"

"I heard it can grant any wish!"

"Why would the fallen give us such a gift?"

"Who cares? I want that ruby!"

Cautiousness quickly grew into excitement, and one after the next, people began shouting that they wanted to participate.

Is it alright if all of these people participate? How would the logistics of that work? But then again, this is not the first time the festival has happened. Surely there must be measures to contain the amount of participants.

"Since the prize pool is larger this year, the entrance fee has also been increased. But fret not, for every noble who holds the title of marquess or higher in the Demon Kingdom, and every delegation from our foreign visitors, is allowed one free entry," Alphegor explained, and the crowd replied with an approving sort of muttering. Some appeared annoyed, as they most likely couldn't afford the price.

"Now then, to start off the sign-ups and encourage new participants to join, I shall announce that three of my daughters will also be joining the competition this time," Alphegor said, a confident smile appearing on his lips, and the demons in the crowd went wild again.

"Princesses will participate?"

"Does that mean we might get a chance to meet and talk to them if we join?"

"That is a prize in its own right!"

Morrigan tried to remain calm, but she felt a heavy knot form in her stomach.

I wonder if they'd still be excited if they knew that I'm the one participating. Watching a child compete probably won't be very fun.

"The first one to participate is my eldest daughter—Viana!" Alphegor said, and the crowd gave an excited cheer as she stepped forward and smiled at them.

"Next is my second-youngest—Deziara," the king continued, and the ovation continued as she confidently walked forward, appearing ready to take on the world.

"And finally, the Crown Princess—Morrigan!" Alphegor's smile grew just a little bit larger, and Morrigan stepped forward. She put as much grace as she could into each step, then nodded her head slightly at the crowd, just as Lady Lily had instructed her to do.

There was dead silence for a moment, and Morrigan's heart clenched. But then a roar of applause and cheers followed.

"The Crown Princess is participating despite being so young."

"Our princess is so smart!"

"Now I want to participate even more!"

The crowd, mostly demons, praised the princesses for a while longer until finally all three of them bowed their heads and stepped back to stand behind Alphegor.

"Now, I shall ask our foreign visitors to present their champions to us so we can all take a look at them. Let's begin with the Drow Kingdom!" Alphegor continued, and a smaller portion of the crowd cheered. One part of it was a bit rowdier than the rest, and Morrigan looked at them to see the drow delegation cheering.

She took the chance to carefully observe the drow. Largely they looked much like elves, with beautiful slender features and long, pointed ears. But their skin clearly had not seen daylight, ranging from light gray to grayish blue and even to deep, dark purple. They also had a certain air of arrogance around them, although it wasn't as pronounced as with some pure-blooded demons Morrigan had met.

A tall, muscular drow man with dark blue skin and black hair came out from their ranks and went up to the stage, bowing before Alphegor. He looked physically strong, and his gaze was sharp and focused.

I do not want to meet that guy face-to-face. I feel like he would have no qualms about putting a sword through my chest.

After the drow, Alphegor summoned the duergar champion, who looked just like a dwarf, except he had no hair and his skin was dark gray. He was even shorter than Gunna, making his walk somewhat wobbly, like one of those short-legged cats or dachshunds. Morrigan couldn't even spot the duergar delegation, as they were no doubt hidden by the taller people in the crowd.

She also couldn't see the delegation of deep gnomes, who were even shorter than the duergar and much more fragile-looking to boot. Some snickering could be heard from the crowd as the trembling deep gnome champion knelt before Alphegor.

These guys don't really belong here. Others will eat them alive. Even I look more menacing than them.

"Next, would the vampire delegation please present their champion?" Alphegor announced, and Morrigan barely managed to keep her cool.

How did I miss the fact that vampires have a whole country of their own? I had heard of them being mentioned before, but to think they had their own territory. I knew that studying geography would be more important than politics.

A seductive woman with long white hair and bright red eyes stepped confidently onto the stage and curtsied before Alphegor while giving him her most charismatic smile. A shiver ran through Morrigan's spine, and she noticed a similar reaction from Viana and Deziara, who scrunched up their noses at the vampire woman.

"I'll be sure to prove my strength to you, Your Majesty," she purred before seductively walking off the stage, every man in the crowd following her retreating form. Everyone besides Alphegor, at least, who thankfully didn't appear to be smitten by her charms.

If Father were to gain an interest in vampires... The horror. I have to make sure that woman doesn't get near him.

She gave a knowing look to Deziara, who appeared to have

thought about the same thing. Viana was mercilessly glaring at the vampire woman. It was clear that she was also not thrilled.

Morrigan realized how eerie the group of vampires actually were. All of them had skin as white as paper and bright red eyes. Demons could also manifest such features; however, when there was a whole group of people with those bloodthirsty eyes, Morrigan couldn't help but feel unnerved.

"And now, infernals, please present your champion," Alphegor said, and Morrigan perked up. She had never seen an infernal before. They were supposed to be people made out of fire and magma, and despite seeing the many renditions of them in books, she could never fully imagine a living person like that.

Morrigan also didn't notice anyone matching that description in the crowd, but that didn't surprise her, as the huge number of people could easily hide individuals. Not to mention that the assortment of demons in the crowd was so varied that it was hard to tell who was a lesser demon and who was a member of a different race entirely.

At one point the crowd shifted, and Morrigan saw a flame peak above some heads. It moved closer and closer, and she discerned a humanoid shape with flame burning instead of hair and eyes glowing like the inside of a burning furnace. She watched in awe as the infernal came onto the stage, looking just like the books had described him.

It's like fire has become alive. Amazing! I wonder if there are other races like this guy, only for other elements. Would a water elemental be made entirely of water? But then again, humans are already 70% water, so perhaps they look somewhat like jellyfish. Those are 95% water. I bet it would be fun to paint a jellyfish person, with all the reflections and transparency.

While Morrigan's thoughts wandered to her next painting possibilities, the infernal bowed before Alphegor and muttered something in a barely audible voice. It sounded very gruff and was hard to understand, reminding her of an angry fire crackling. Alphegor nodded in response to the infernal and then asked for the fallen to present their champion.

Their Prime Minister appeared rather smug, sitting along with the other fallen, while his wife looked somewhat uncertain.

I wonder who the fallen champion will be. The ability to fly will surely give them a great advantage in physical tasks.

Everyone watched and waited for their champion, but for the longest time, it seemed like nobody was coming. Then suddenly, Galandir clambered onto the stage and bowed before Alphegor.

"I am here to represent the Fallen Kingdom, Your Majesty," the boy said, and there was an echo of gasps in the crowd, followed by confused mutterings.

"That boy is not a fallen. He is not even from the Underworld."

"Why, he looks no older than the Crown Princess!"

"How shameless! They're sending a child to fight their battles. Only the fallen would resort to something so disgraceful."

But Heinspiel didn't appear even a little bothered by these mutterings. In fact, his smile widened as he listened to the accusations.

"Explain yourself, child. How can you represent the fallen when you are not a fallen yourself?" the king asked, his stern voice silencing the crowd in an instant.

"While I am not a fallen myself, I serve the fallen. And as Your Majesty is well aware of, the Fallen Kingdom is home to many races. My masters just wish to show our kingdom's open-mindedness to other people," the boy replied, his voice steady and composed.

Just let it slide, Father. It's not such a big deal. Certainly, it's scummy that they send a slave to a competition that is supposed to be a prestigious event. But it's not the boy's fault.

Alphegor squinted at the boy, then for a moment his eyes locked with Morrigan's. The king must have sensed her thoughts somehow, or perhaps he saw it in her face, as his expression relaxed.

"I shall allow it. It would be a shame if the Crown Princess were the only child participating, wouldn't it?" Alphegor announced, and the crowd cheered. Their attention returned to Morrigan, who smiled, trying to keep her composure under their watchful gazes.

"Thank you, Your Majesty." Galandir bowed, then quickly disappeared into the crowd.

I wonder what the fallen are really plotting by signing up Galandir for the competition. Surely it wasn't just because they wanted to annoy Alphegor and the demons a little bit. Isn't their goal to keep their ruby to themselves? Do they believe that Galandir can win?

CHAPTER 18

FESTIVAL FUN

"Father, please! I want to go. You promised me that I would be able to go." Morrigan held on to Alphegor's sleeve while he did his best to avoid her gaze.

"Morrigan, you know that we cannot take a stroll through the festival. Our presence alone carries a lot of weight," he objected, gently trying to free his sleeve from her grasp. But Morrigan wrapped her hands around his waist and looked up at him with large, teary eyes.

"Please, please, please! I have never been to a festival so large," she continued. While there certainly were festivals on Earth she had experienced, they were never on such a scale and never together with her family. "And we should take Deziara, and perhaps some of my other sisters with us!"

"No, that is completely out of the question. While I wish for all of my daughters to experience the festival, it will be from a safe distance, guarded from all potential dangers. Or have you forgotten what happened when you left the castle under Azrael's watch?" Alphegor scowled, but Morrigan was not deterred.

"That is different! This time I'd be together with you, Father. And there is no safer place than next to you," she said, then added in a hurry, "We could always just transform."

The king paused, considering the idea. Morrigan took it as a good sign and continued her onslaught.

"Please, Father! I really want to see it."

"Hmm... If we were to go transformed, then our transformation has to be good enough not to arouse suspicion of even the most skilled mage. One slipup and they could sense who we really are," Alphegor said.

"Azrael said that my transformation skills are excellent. And if somebody does notice us, then you could quickly silence them, couldn't you, Father? You're the strongest demon in the world, after all!"

"Do not think that flattery will work on me," Alphegor growled, and Morrigan released her hold on him. He cleared his throat and continued. "But if you are confident about your transformation abilities, then I suppose we could go out for a little bit."

"I love you!" she cheered, but the king narrowed his eyes at her, making her pause.

"But it will come at a price."

"Price?"

What price could I possibly pay him? Perhaps he wants me to do something? Or promise that I won't do something—like never leave the castle? I wouldn't want to promise that, but if that's what it takes to go to the festival...

Alphegor bent down and tapped his cheek with a smile. Morrigan giggled and pecked his cheek. He hummed with satisfaction, and his form began to change. A minute later he had changed into a shorter demon with darker skin and short black hair. His horns had also become much shorter, making him look more like a lesser demon.

Morrigan began her transformation as well, adopting the same dark skin tone and black hair as him. She changed her hair into short curls and made her horns barely visible.

"Will this do?" she asked, and Alphegor nodded.

"Very good. And remember—you are not allowed to leave my side." He held up his finger in warning.

"I wouldn't dream of it!"

* * *

Morrigan looked in awe at the various stalls lining the streets. Food, clothes, toys, trinkets of every size and shape. Her eyes eagerly darted from one stall to the next, unable to decide what she wanted to try out first. The disguised Alphegor, meanwhile, was cautiously scanning the surroundings, seemingly more concerned about the density of the crowd rather than the festival's colorful offerings.

"Father, look at all these things! It's amazing," Morrigan cheered, then walked up to the stall that had an array of colored potion bottles set out on the table. Alphegor quickly pulled her away, glaring at the stall owner, who instinctually flinched back.

"Some of these things have no business being at a festival," the king grumbled. "Perhaps I should impose stricter policies on vendors."

"None of that work stuff now! We are here to enjoy ourselves," Morrigan reprimanded, dragging her father deeper into the festive crowd. As she scanned the stalls, she noticed some demons lining up in front of what looked like a game. There were little metallic rods set out in a triangular pattern while the player tossed an orange ring. But the demons playing didn't hold on to the ring for long, instead throwing it before even properly lining up the shot.

"Father, what is that?" Morrigan asked, pointing at the game stall.

"Looks like a game of magma ring toss. If you manage to land a ring on the rod, you get a prize," he explained, looking rather bored by it.

"Can I try?"

"Absolutely not!"

"What? Why?" she whined, tugging on his sleeve.

"Those are magma rings. You will burn your fingers."

"Wait... you mean like, real magma?" Morrigan shuddered, remembering the heat she had experienced near the lava river.

However, I am resistant to fire now. Perhaps the magma rings wouldn't even burn me if their temperatures aren't too extreme.

"Yes. It starts off cool but quickly heats up, so the player doesn't have a lot of time to take aim. It's borderline illegal," Alphegor huffed.

"But I am resistant to fire. Could I at least try? Look, they have all sorts of prizes," Morrigan said, pointing at the shelf lined with various prizes clearly meant for children.

"I can buy thousands of such prizes and then a hundred thousand more on top of that," Alphegor said, trying to drag Morrigan away.

"But it's the experience of how you got it that matters! Please, Father," Morrigan whined, and some of the demons passing by chuckled at their display.

Alphegor rubbed his temples and sighed. "Alright, but I'll be playing. I don't want you burning your fingers," he said, then strode up to the booth. Morrigan wanted to protest at first but then paused to think about it.

Wouldn't it be fun to see Father play a game? How often does one see a king fumble at a silly carnival game? I cannot let this chance pass by.

Morrigan ran to stand by his side as they waited for their turn at the game. Alphegor tapped his foot impatiently as one after another, the demons failed to land the magma ring on the rods. Most just dropped it after a few seconds, while a few more resilient individuals were fast enough to toss it, but not lucky enough to actually land it on the targets.

"Would you like to give your daughter a try, sir?" the cheeky red-skinned demon man behind the counter said. He clearly felt some sort of satisfaction from watching all the people fail, children walking away from the stall sullen or even crying.

That nasty guy needs to be taught a lesson.

"I'll give it a try," Alphegor said, throwing a silver coin at the demon. He caught it swiftly in the air without missing a beat, then slid three magma rings towards him.

"You win a prize for each ring that you manage to land on the rods. Doesn't matter which one. And if you somehow manage to land all three then you get to choose from the special prize pool."

"Special prize pool?" Morrigan asked, leaning on the counter.

"Yes. Some of the rarest treasures the Demon Kingdom has ever seen can be found among them. Just feast your eyes," the vendor said, pulling out a large, transparent case. Inside it sat three objects—a potion that sparkled like a nebula, a pinkish gem, and a tube of paint, from the looks of it.

"What are those?" Morrigan asked, not seeing any value in them. Except the paint, perhaps.

"This is a potion of farsight. Drink it and you'll be able to see any far-away place you wish. Next is a pink tourmaline, said to give its user the ability to charm their enemies. And finally, a tube of golden magic paint."

"Magic paint? How is it magic?" Morrigan's eyes lit up, and she reached out her hand towards the case. The vendor pulled it back and hid it below the counter.

"If you want to see what it does, then you'll have to try it out for yourself!" the demonic vendor teased. Morrigan looked at her father with pleading eyes, but his gaze was already focused on the metallic rods.

He took the first magma ring, which instantly began glowing like a hot, raging flame. However, the king wasn't bothered in the slightest, instead aiming it and tossing it straight onto the closest rod. The vendor blinked in disbelief and raised his finger to say something, but Alphegor had already grabbed the second ring and, without hesitation, threw it onto the second rod.

"How?" the man uttered, his mouth agape in shock. Then Alphegor took the last ring and just as seamlessly threw it onto the last rod.

"Magic paint, please!" Alphegor slapped his hand on the counter, a victorious smile on his face.

"You cheated!" the demon protested, but the king glared so hard that even in his rather soft-looking disguise, the vendor took a step back.

"Are you implying that the game is impossible to win?" Alphegor glowered. Morrigan could almost see the dark, menacing aura coming out of him.

"N-No! Of course not. Go ahead and take your prize." The vendor shakily retrieved the case and unlocked it with a wave of his hand. Morrigan instantly grabbed the paint and clutched it close to her chest.

"Thank you, Father! You're the best!" she cheered.

"Of course I am! Let's go see what other things this festival has to offer." Alphegor outstretched his hand towards Morrigan, and she grabbed it, clutching the magic paint in her other hand.

Hand in hand they strode through the crowd, enjoying the festive atmosphere and admiring all the hard work people had put into the stalls, be it merchandise, food, or games. They bought two crepes—one with a savory, meaty filling and the other with a sweet, creamy filling—which they both shared.

The day went on, and Morrigan was beginning to feel tired when she noticed a demon child run by with a face that was painted to resemble a dragon. She watched him in awe, then saw a few more children with painted faces weaving through the crowd.

"Excuse me, where did you get that face paint?" Morrigan asked one of the children passing by.

"A lady in the stall over there is coloring the faces of anybody who asks." The child pointed towards one of the stalls, then continued on his way.

"Father, can I?" She looked pleadingly at Alphegor, who chuckled in response.

"Sure. We still have a bit of time."

Morrigan ran towards the stall, where a rather lanky woman with unusual pink hair swept on one side was painting a red dragon on a little demon girl's face. She went up to them and admired how she smoothly and precisely drew lines on the child's face, turning her skin into a canvas.

The woman was so engrossed in her work that she didn't even notice Morrigan at first. After a moment, she caught her watching, but chuckled at her enthusiasm. "Want to have your face painted next?"

Morrigan continued staring at her brushstrokes, not even daring to reply, lest she miss something. The artist took it as an agreement and continued working on her current client. Less than ten minutes later, the demon girl's face had been turned into what looked like a marvelous dragon. The woman gave the girl a mirror, and she cheered at her reflection.

"Thank you so much," she called out before sprinting towards her parents, who smiled at the girl.

"So, you're next? What color would you like?" the artist asked, pointing at the trays of paint she had laid out on a table next to her.

"Could I do the painting?" Morrigan asked as she admired the bright colors. The woman looked a bit shocked for a moment, but quickly regained her composure and smiled.

"We'd have to find someone who'd be willing to have you paint on them."

Oh, you're hoping that nobody would be crazy enough to allow a child to draw on them. You're out of luck!

Morrigan turned towards her father, who took a cautious step back.

"Father! Please!" She put her hands together and looked at him with the saddest eyes she could muster. Alphegor sighed and, with a resigned look on his face, sat down on the small stool where the girl had sat before.

"Looks like I have no choice."

The vendor laughed, then pulled out a clean apron and put it on Morrigan. "Always nice to see children be interested in art. There are too few artists in the Demon Kingdom."

"Do I need to set a base layer of paint first?" Morrigan asked, eagerly looking over the paints and brushes.

"Oh, not a beginner? Now I am curious as to what your little hands will create. Please, apply this clear base coat first. It'll protect the skin from harm and also allow the paint to remain vibrant and unsmudged."

Morrigan nodded and took the large, soft brush. Alphegor closed his eyes, and she began to gently cover his face with the base layer, making sure not to miss a single spot.

"Very good! Now you can choose a base color and start painting on your father's face."

Morrigan took the black color, setting it as a base, then used gray to set up highlights, not even listening to the artist's instructions anymore. Once the basics were laid down to her satisfaction, she took the gold color and began drawing in scales.

Alphegor sat unflinchingly the whole time, while the artist watched Morrigan work. After about twenty minutes, she announced, "I'm done!"

Alphegor opened his eyes, and the artist whistled. She handed the mirror to Alphegor, who looked at his face in amazement. The black and gold contrasted with each other, bringing out Alphegor's shifted facial features and making him look like a draconic being, rather than a demon.

"You've got real talent on your hands. I suggest you invest in educating your daughter in art. She'd go far."

Morrigan's shoulders slumped at this proclamation.

But I can never be an artist... My duty is to become the next queen. I can't abandon that just to frolic around and draw pretty pictures.

CHAPTER 19

TEST OF SPEED

"Welcome, contestants and our wonderful audience, to the Nachtstern Festival Competition!" Azrael announced in a magically amplified voice that echoed throughout the whole Underworld. "Each time we have an astounding number of competitors, but this year you all have beaten the record—1387 people have decided to participate. No doubt spurred on by the chance to see our lovely princesses closer!"

He pointed towards Morrigan, Deziara, and Viana, who stood close together, lined up along with other contestants in front of a pathway near the lava river. Cheers and applause resounded from the audience members, who were standing behind a special zone across from the lava river, just like people would in an auto rally.

Morrigan felt a bit overwhelmed being in the middle of such a huge crowd, but thankfully she and her sisters were placed among the honorary participants from other races and demon nobles. Of course, the three of them still stood out, even among the cream of demon society, but at least the nobles had enough decorum not to openly bother them.

She carefully looked over the competitors standing closest to her. All of them exuded confidence, even the deep gnome. Morrigan was surprised to see the fire burning inside the elven boy's eyes. The infernal next to him scoffed, clearly not thinking much of the boy, but he just looked head-on with an unyielding gaze. She wondered where he got all that confidence from.

"Our competition this year will begin with the Test of Speed. Some of you probably knew this was coming. After all, our contestants have to prove their physical prowess first. Now here are the rules, children. Listen closely, because if you break them—it's game over!" Azrael said enthusiastically, narrating from the raised podium where all the VIPs sat. Including the Demon King himself, whose gaze lingered on his three competing daughters.

Look at the bright side, Morrigan. Since you are here in the competition, you do not need to deal with the fallen delegation directly. Also, isn't Azrael enjoying this a bit too much?

"Rule number one—do not attack other contestants. You may use magic to hinder their path or slow them down, but physical harm is strictly forbidden. There are rule enforcers watching everyone along the path, and if somebody disobeys this rule they will be fed to Princess Morrigan's dragon," Azrael warned, then snapped his fingers.

Haku appeared from behind the podium, forcing a few people standing closest to it to scamper away. He looked around curiously at first and then wagged his tail enthusiastically when he noticed Morrigan among the participants.

"Be good, Haku!" she called to him, waving. The dragon nodded and lay down next to the podium. Participants from other races seemed particularly unnerved by Haku, as did the lesser demons.

Hopefully that will be enough to deter people from hurting others. However, I imagine some will still try it if they believe that there is nobody who could catch them during the act.

"Rule number two—no shortcuts! You can fly, glide, slide, or even dig to move forward, but you have to follow the designated path. The moment you try to take a shortcut, you are disqualified. Although you won't be fed to the dragon for that." Azrael laughed at his own joke, though the audience seemed rather unamused by it.

"Rule number three—no piggybacking on others! You have to cross that finish line with your own feet. If I see that you are using others to move forward in any way, then you'll be buried in the hot sand and left to cook there for three days. Let me tell you, it's not an enjoyable experience, folks. Tried it firsthand myself," Azrael warned. "The first four hundred participants to cross the finish line will be able to continue competing tomorrow. Now, are there any questions?"

A few hands shot up among the participants, but the white-haired demon completely ignored them, clapping his hands together loudly.

"Good, now prepare to run! On my signal."

Morrigan exhaled, staring at the craggy track ahead of her. If the competition were purely about running, then she would no doubt lose. She was younger and physically weaker than the others. But there was no rule against using magic.

"Three, two, one—GO!" Azrael yelled, and all the participants shot forward, trying to get ahead of each other.

Morrigan instantly turned into a shadow and sped forward, moving along the shadowy cracks in the ground. She saw how Deziara ran, swiftly avoiding collisions with other participants by either jumping over them or weaving out of their way. Her sister possessed special speed-enhancing magic, a gift from Alphegor. Deziara had been so ecstatic that she had trained hard with it and had mastered it within a few months.

Viana didn't have any speed-enhancing abilities; however, she had earth manipulation magic on her side. She moved the earth from underneath her feet, propelling herself forward and throwing the nearby contestants out of her way.

Morrigan slid over the crags Viana created with ease, speeding along with the group of fastest runners. She wasn't first, but rather was sticking close to the lead runners' shadows and using them as leverage points to move forward. Thanks to the proximity of the lava river, the area was rather well lit, so Morrigan couldn't just thoughtlessly rush forward. But there were still enough shadows for her to work with.

As she and the other contestants approached the first turn along the track, she noticed the elven boy, Galandir, pulling ahead of the competition by flying on some sort of transparent golden wings. The audience was not thrilled by this development in the slightest, booing at him angrily.

"Overworlder!"

"Cheater!"

"Disqualify him!"

These people are so judgmental. There are other people flying and you're not judging them. Although he does feel a bit overpowered for someone of his age. I'd like to have some golden wings too. I wonder if it's some sort of magic or an innate ability.

Resigned to her fate, Morrigan continued, occasionally checking on both of her sisters. Suddenly the track ahead of them erupted, hot lava spewing up in columns from random spots on the ground. The lava went so high up in the air that flying over it would almost certainly make you lose too much time.

"Oh, did I forget to mention—this is an obstacle course. So watch your step," Azrael cackled.

You son of a... You should have mentioned that before. I'll give him such an earful for this later.

The runners paused, looking at the lava pouring out like hot geysers, unsure of which path to take. The first one to take initiative was the duergar champion, who had kept up with the leading group by riding on a stone golem of sorts. He erected a tough rock shield around himself and headed straight for the field.

A hot burst of lava hit his shield, but the duergar didn't appear bothered, his golem marching on with his shield intact. Seeing this, several other participants moved into the lava field, using their own shields for protection. Viana was one of them, using earth and soil to block incoming bursts of lava.

"If you're worried about your safety—let me tell you something. Those worries are absolutely warranted. If you don't know how to avoid or block lava, then you'd better stop before you turn into a piece of charcoal." Azrael sounded absolutely delighted, narrating from the safety of the podium.

Isn't this supposed to be a safe, fun competition? Where did that bit go? I'm pretty sure getting hit by a burst of lava is deadly, even for a demon.

Deziara was about to run ahead through the lava field when a hot stream erupted in front of her, forcing her to step back.

"Deziara, are you alright?" Morrigan asked, emerging from the shadow. Deziara was breathing heavily but looked unhurt.

"Yeah. I am fine. Who came up with this? I thought this was supposed to be completely safe," Deziara huffed angrily, watching how more and more participants risked taking their chances. "How are we supposed to get through?"

Running through as a shadow is probably too risky. Lava would illuminate the area and force me out of my shadow form. While I am resistant to fire, I'll probably still get burned if I come in direct contact with lava. I could try using a force field, but I am not sure if it can withstand the force. The fact that Galandir managed to break it fairly easily makes it unlikely.

An idea struck Morrigan's mind. She outstretched her hand towards the lava field, feeling for the hot fire sleeping underneath. Within a few seconds, it was clear to her where exactly the lava moved and where it would erupt next.

"Follow me! I know where to go," Morrigan announced, attempting to run into the lava field.

"Morri, wait! We could get seriously hurt." Deziara pulled her back by her hand.

"Trust me. I know what I'm doing." She grinned, and Deziara relaxed. She looked at the flaming pillars rising up from the ground, then at Morrigan, who was a picture of confidence. Finally, Deziara relaxed and allowed herself to be led into the flaming field.

Morrigan walked slowly, her right hand extended forward. She grasped the hot tendrils of lava with her magic, trying to feel for their location underground. It was moving and shifting, converging together to escape outward with incredible force. Morrigan led her sister away from the hot spots, instead moving over the places where lava felt most stagnant.

"Princess Morrigan knows where to go. Follow her!" one of the participating demons yelled, rushing to follow them. Some other demons joined in the slowly moving column, and Morrigan noticed that the elven boy and the deep gnome champion had also followed her lead.

I didn't think they would follow me. I better make sure to lead them to the least dangerous areas that can accommodate a larger number of people.

As Morrigan slowly moved forward, feeling the lava flow with her fire magic, the infernal champion reached the lava field, having fallen behind the frontrunners. He didn't even pause at the threatening lava eruptions, instead marching straight through them. Morrigan and Deziara watched as he got hit by a flurry of lava, only to keep walking as if it were a gentle summer shower.

"Morrigan, he will catch up to us in no time. Is there any way we could move forward faster?" Deziara urged.

"Not if you don't want to be cooked. I don't think I could stop one of those lava streams with my magic, since it's not just pure fire," Morrigan explained.

"Don't rush. You'll be endangering not just your lives but also the lives of all these people too," Galandir called out, flying a little bit above them. Morrigan nodded, and continued her way slowly and carefully.

He's just trying to save his own skin. Not that I blame him. I don't really want anyone to get charred to a crisp.

"Well, would you look at that! Thanks to our lovely Princess Morrigan's efforts a whole bunch of participants managed to get over the lava field unscathed. Seems awfully close to piggybacking, but I'll let it slide since the Princess doesn't mind. But this strategy has lost them a lot of time. Will they be able to catch up to the frontrunners?" Azrael continued his magic-enhanced commentary while the audience cheered, chanting Morrigan's name.

Yes, we will!

As soon as they were out of the lava field, Morrigan turned into a shadow and zipped forward. Deziara and Galandir did the same, resuming their previous speeds. Viana, along with the duergar and infernal champions, was far ahead of them, but since this particular part of the tracks was farther away from the lava river, Morrigan had more shadowy places to work with, rapidly catching up to them.

"Uh-oh! It seems our frontrunners have reached our second obstacle—the Underworld mountain. I hope you're good at climbing, because going around means you're going off the track. And that's a no-no." Azrael laughed sadistically, to which the audience responded with disapproving mutters.

As Morrigan moved forward, she saw what really looked like a mountain ahead of the track. It was incredibly steep, and often participants would slide off it, forcing them to start anew. Viana was creating little handholds on the mountain, just large enough for her to grab. The duergar was having a bit of trouble as his golem kept sliding off, being too large to effectively climb.

Now's my chance! I'll regain the ground I've lost.

Once Morrigan reached the mountain, she moved straight up, neither the height nor the steepness being a real problem for her. The elven boy was moving at the same speed as her, flying over the hurdle without any issues. A few other contestants who could fly or levitate followed closely behind them.

"Alright, folks, our frontrunners have changed. I know most of you can't see it, but let me tell you that Princess Morrigan is currently in the lead. Her shadow form is terrifyingly fast. Trust me—I had to chase her once or twice," Azrael said.

"And you've never managed to catch her," Alphegor added.

"It's hard to catch something you can't touch, Your Majesty."

"Morrigan is far too clever to be caught by you," the king responded, and the audience laughed.

"Perhaps, but will she and the other contestants be clever enough to pass our third and final obstacle? Stay tuned, folks!"

Chapter 20

Fastest in the Underworld

Speeding over the craggy track, Morrigan could see the last obstacle in front of her. She was among the fastest runners, while both of her sisters had only just gotten over the giant mountain obstacle.

I wonder what the last obstacle is—hopefully, something where I can remain in my shadow form.

"And here our dear contestants are finally approaching the last hurdle! Can you guess what it is? Well, let me tell you—it is the Lake of Balance," Azrael announced, his enthusiasm having grown twofold since the start of the race.

Lake of Balance? Oh, please don't tell me there's more lava involved.

As Morrigan got closer, she could see a large basin that appeared to be filled with some shimmering liquid. Above the lake, there was a similar shimmering mist, which sparkled like stars in the night sky.

"Pretty, isn't it? But think twice about touching the shimmering water and mist, because the moment you do, it'll teleport you straight back to the shore. So wings won't work, digging won't work, and unfortunately for our leading princess, shadows also won't work, since there's too much light." Azrael cackled.

Really? I swear, he must have been the one to have come up with these sadistic obstacles.

As Morrigan reached the shore of the lake, she saw many wooden beams lying over the top of the water. They weren't very wide, and provided no shadows in which Morrigan could hide, as the water illuminated the bottom of the beams as well.

No worries, I did a lot of balancing exercises with Lady Lily and I am smaller than most participants. It shouldn't be too hard for me to cross.

Morrigan and the other frontrunners each chose their own beam and began a slow balancing act over the lake. She steadily put one foot in front of the other and kept her hands to the sides to help her balance. Her tail also acted as a counterbalance, which helped her confidently keep marching forward.

A few demon nobles saw her pulling ahead and sped up their pace to match hers, but they couldn't keep up with her for long, and soon fell into the shimmering water. A few seconds later, they were back on the lakeshore, drenched from head to toe. Morrigan looked back and saw that Deziara and Viana had also reached the lake and had begun to cross it.

Deziara made it over the mountain. Great. Now I can keep moving forward without worries.

The elven boy was close behind her, his small stature also making it easier for him to cross. She kept walking forward, making sure to utilize all of Lady Lily's lessons—straight head, straight back, uniform steps, calm breaths.

"Princess Morrigan is going to win!" The crowd began to chant her name, and before she even knew it, she was across the lake. Morrigan swiftly turned into a shadow again and headed straight for the finish line. There were less than five hundred meters left—she could already see the golden ribbon stretched across the finish line.

I can do it! I can win!

Morrigan's heart swelled with excitement, and she rushed forward as quickly as she could without looking back.

"Dear audience, please watch closely, because our dearest little princess is approaching the finish line! If you blink, you'll miss it!" Azrael cheered, and the crowd erupted alongside him.

Morrigan pushed herself to move faster and faster. The finish line was just a few meters away. Suddenly, bright light exploded right in front of her, and she felt herself being ripped from her shadow form and materializing onto the craggy track.

"Sorry, but I'll be taking this victory," Galandir announced, then crossed over the finish line, breaking the golden ribbon in the process. Morrigan quickly scrambled to her feet and ran across the last remaining meters to the finish, ending up in second place.

The crowd booed angrily at Galandir, calling him a cheater and demanding his disqualification.

"Settle down, folks! The slave won fair and square. I said that harming others is prohibited, but he never caused Princess Morrigan any harm. He merely forced her out of her shadow form." Azrael was arguing against the crowd, which only became more agitated.

Suddenly Alphegor stood up from his seat on the podium, and the crowd instantly settled down.

"Princess Morrigan, do you believe the actions of this boy to be fair?" he asked in his booming voice.

I can't say that I liked being forced out of my shadow form, but I'm not petty enough to hold a grudge over it. Better settle this peacefully.

"While I regret not taking first place in this race, I believe that Galandir's actions were fair. He knew my weakness and took advantage of it; however, at the same time it has not done me any harm," she said, trying to sound gracious.

There was a quiet muttering among the spectators at first, but then they slowly began to clap and cheer. Deziara approached the finish line, ending up in third place, and right after her came the infernal and vampire champions.

The crowd cheered as more and more people crossed the finish line, and soon it seemed like the matter regarding Galandir was forgotten.

* * *

"Demons, duergar, drow, vampires, and other guests, the Test of Speed is officially complete!" Azrael exclaimed for the whole Underworld to hear, and the audience responded with thunderous applause.

"Our four hundredth participant just crossed the finish line, which means that unfortunately, for everyone else still left on the track, your time of glory is over. But do not despair, you can always try again at the next festival. For now, however, let's move on to our winners!"

The crowd cheered so loudly that Morrigan wanted to cover her ears from the noise. Deziara, who was standing next to her, among the other winning contestants, was basking in the spotlight, waving at the crowd. She waved with extra enthusiasm at the podium where Alphegor sat, who responded with a satisfied nod.

"Now, I won't name each winner, since we'd be stuck here until tomorrow, but I will note that all of our princesses and the champions of each foreign delegation have successfully passed the Test of Speed," Azrael said. After a brief pause, he added, "The winner of today's task was the champion of the fallen delegation, Galandir."

The cheers disappeared, and silence settled over the scene like a heavy blanket. Galandir, who was standing in the very center of the winners, shifted uncomfortably as everyone stared at him. Morrigan could already imagine all the hateful things that were itching to escape from their mouths.

He's supposed to be the winner, yet everyone looks at him as if he were a murderer. I can't say that I like him too much, since he tried to steal something from us. But I cannot let this silence go on and fester into something unsavory. Perhaps I can ease the tension, at least a little bit.

Morrigan began to applaud for Galandir, each clap of her hands echoing loudly through the area like a bell. The scrutinizing gazes shifted to her; however, she kept applauding in hopes that somebody would join in. Alphegor stood up from his seat on the podium and began applauding as well. The moment everyone saw the king's action, they quickly followed suit, easing the tension in the air.

Thank you, Father!

Morrigan smiled at him, and Alphegor nodded at her, ending the applause and sitting down.

"Most excellent! Now, with today's task over, I suggest you all head back to Linberor Market Square, as many delectable treats have been cooked up by chefs from all over the Underworld. Trust me when I say that if you were waiting for a good day to treat yourself, this is that day!" Azrael announced, and the crowd slowly began moving back towards the city.

"I wonder what kinds of dishes they are cooking up in the square," Morrigan said, excited by the prospect of trying new foods.

"It doesn't matter to us. We have to attend dinner with foreign delegations and their champions," Viana said sharply. Some curious contestants, mostly demons, were beginning to approach the princesses. However, their private guards quickly surrounded them, creating a protective wall.

"What? I never heard of such a thing," Deziara protested, glaring at Viana. Some people were looking curiously at the ongoing ruckus, so Morrigan pulled on her sister's sleeve. Deziara looked around and quickly shrank back, noticing all the eyes that were glued to them.

"You should have listened carefully. Father talked about that this morning," Viana retorted, then strode off with her two guards in tow.

I think I remember something like that. But I was so nervous about the competition in the morning that most of what he said just went over my head.

Morrigan sighed, then gently poked Deziara's shoulder. "We better get going. Maybe we can enjoy the food next time."

"But next time it will be something completely different," Deziara whined.

"I know. But we don't have much of a choice," Morrigan whispered, and her sister finally relented. Both girls headed towards the Demon Castle, their moods dejected despite being winners.

* * *

If this goes on for much longer I am going to die of boredom!

The diplomats from various delegations were currently discussing the matters of establishing a friendly relationship. In theory, it seemed like a good topic—Morrigan firmly believed that the Underworld nations should live together peacefully. However, over time, it became a bragging contest of sorts.

Demons were great at doing this, drow were excellent at doing that, duergar were unmatched in this field, the fallen had the best whatever material in whatever-you-call-it place. While she was certainly no expert politician, she was sure that trying to outbrag each other wasn't a solid way of establishing a friendly relationship.

"You're beginning to slouch again," Viana reprimanded, and Morrigan quickly straightened in her seat. This was the other thing that irked her—whenever she or Deziara did something wrong, Viana took it upon herself to correct them. Each time she did it, Morrigan had the urge to singe a few hairs off her head.

Miss Bossypants could get off our backs for once. It's not my fault that this place is so boring.

Morrigan restrained a sigh and looked at her empty dinner plate. While the meal offered was certainly delicious, it wasn't nearly enough to satisfy her appetite after spending so much energy during the race. The guests weren't shy about asking for seconds; however, when she had tried to do that, Viana had reprimanded her once again, and Morrigan was forced to concede.

Looking around the table, she noticed how essentially everyone who wasn't involved in the "diplomatic" discussion appeared rather bored. Azrael being the most extreme example—completely slumped in his chair and openly yawning.

Geez, you could at least try to appear civil.

Their eyes met, and Azrael stuck out his tongue and rolled his eyes back, mimicking being dead. Morrigan glared at him and motioned for him to straighten. He just shook his head in response and slouched down even more. She motioned for him to straighten again, and suddenly Azrael perked up. A mischievous glint appeared in his eyes as he opened his mouth to speak.

Oh, no! He's plotting something again.

"Your Majesty, if I may be so rude as to interrupt..." Alphegor glared at Azrael, who continued speaking. "I couldn't help but notice that our precious princesses looked tired after the whole race. Wouldn't it be better if they retreated early?"

I'm sorry I doubted you, Azrael. Thank you!

Alphegor shot a suspicious glance at Morrigan just as the vampire champion spoke up, her voice as sweet as honey.

"I believe Lord Azrael is right. All participants performed most admirably. I think it would be fair for those who are tired to retreat and rest."

A wave of quiet agreements resounded in the dining hall. Alphegor carefully examined everyone, then finally nodded. "Very well. All participants of the competition may retreat to rest."

"I shall remain, Father. I do not feel tired at all." Viana smiled sweetly at Alphegor. Morrigan had the urge to remain just to prove that she wasn't tired in the slightest, but before she could say anything, Deziara had grabbed her hand and was dragging her away from the table.

"Thank you, Father! We shall take this opportunity to go rest," she said, giving Alphegor a quick curtsy before she resumed dragging Morrigan away. With the urgency she was pulling her, it felt like there was something Deziara wanted from her.

"What is it, Deziara?" Morrigan asked as soon as they left the dining hall.

"This is our chance to go see all the food being sold at the market square!" Deziara said excitedly.

"Wait... You mean we should go to the market square by ourselves?" Morrigan asked in shock.

"Not by ourselves. We have our guards with us," Deziara said, pointing at their guards, who looked at them nervously.

"This doesn't sound like you. Remember what happened the last time we went to the market by ourselves?" Morrigan said, recalling the horrible kidnapping incident.

"Admittedly, it was Azrael who gave me the idea. But this is different. We are older, we are stronger, and it's the festival. Who'd try to kidnap us at a festival? Besides, we can easily disguise ourselves," Deziara said excitedly.

"Princesses, please reconsider. His Majesty has not permitted you to leave," one of the guards said.

"Are you saying that you wouldn't be able to protect us?" Deziara retorted.

"No! Of course we would. We'd protect you with our lives," the guards replied in unison.

"See, there's no issue. Let's go, Morri!" Deziara grabbed Morrigan's hand and began dragging her towards the castle exit.

There's no changing her mind now. I'll have to be extra vigilant. If there's something even a little bit suspicious, I am instantly calling Azrael.

CHAPTER 21

OLD WOES

"Look at all these foods." Deziara, disguised in simpler clothes and a blonde wig, strode through Linberor Market Square. Delicious smells, both savory and sweet, were mixing in the air, attracting hungry mouths from far beyond the square's borders.

"I'm still not fond of this idea," Morrigan noted, transforming into a blonde, white-skinned version of Azrael. The four demon guards followed behind them through the crowd, wearing commoners' clothes and staying some distance away to not arouse any undue attention.

"This time everything will be fine. I know lots of magic now, so I can protect you, Morri," Deziara said, pulling Morrigan along.

"No, you are supposed to call me "Father." I hope that you will be on your best behavior, young lady," Morrigan reprimanded, lowering her voice for it to sound more masculine.

Her sister just laughed. "Of course, Father. When have I ever let you down?"

"Let's just be quick. I don't want to stay out here too long."

"It's not like I'm not worried, but we have taken precautions. Who would recognize us like this? And we have our guards with us this time," Deziara said consolingly, but Morrigan still felt anxious.

Odd that Deziara is so eager to get outside. Perhaps as she is getting older, she too is feeling more entrapped by the castle. Well, nothing bad happened yesterday when I was out with Father. It should be fine today as well.

"Look! What's that? It looks so pretty." Deziara pulled Morrigan over to a stall that was filled with an assortment of fruit on sticks. But they weren't the regular Underworld fruit that Morrigan had grown used to the last ten years. There were strawberries, grapes, oranges, and kiwis.

"Interested to try some Overworld fruit, young lady? I promise you—they are delicious." The stall owner, an elderly duergar man, picked up one of the colorful fruit sticks and waved it at them. Looking around carefully, it was clear to Morrigan that nobody else came to the stall, and it appeared that most of the fruit remained unsold.

"Overworld fruit? Who'd want to try those?! Let Overworlders eat them." Deziara was about to turn on her heel and leave when Morrigan grabbed her hand and pulled her back.

"Don't be so quick to judge," Morrigan said in her best impression of a man's voice. It wasn't very successful, but it would pass for somebody who had a bad cold.

I need to get some magic that helps me change my voice too. Otherwise, my transformations aren't completely convincing.

"Trust me, young miss, you will not regret it. These fruits were picked from the Gardens of Eldarar." The duergar picked up another stick of fruit and offered one to Morrigan and one to Deziara. Morrigan didn't hesitate to take hers, and her sister reluctantly followed.

"Just try it," Morrigan urged, then took a bite of the large strawberry. It was just as she remembered, sweet and a little tangy and most definitely delicious. Deziara eyed hers suspiciously until she finally relented and took a careful nibble of her strawberry.

"Wh-What? This is tasty," she called out, then began enthusiastically munching on the berry, all previous suspicion completely forgotten.

"Told you, miss." The vendor smiled and then yelled out, "Come try some Overworld fruit. Look how much this young demon lady and her father are enjoying them."

People who had been previously walking past the stall suddenly turned and looked curiously at them. Seeing the gusto with which Deziara was eating, some demons approached the vendor and asked for the fruity sticks. They were just as reluctant as Deziara, but after trying it, they began eating earnestly. Within ten minutes people were pushing each other out of the way to get to the front of the line faster.

"How much for the fruit? We never paid," Morrigan shouted over the crowd.

"On the house. You two helped me out." The duergar laughed, passing three sticks to eager demon customers.

"Thank you very much!" Deziara smiled, licking the last bits of fruit juice off the stick. "Now, come! We still have so many foods to try out!"

Both girls continued exploring the market, looking for the most appetizing and unusual foods. They came across something that reminded Morrigan of takoyaki, except this one was apparently filled with kraken flesh instead of the octopus. She was reluctant to try it at first, but since Deziara swore that krakens were supposedly delicious, Morrigan gave it a shot. The flavor was pretty much the same as takoyaki.

I guess a kraken is a giant octopus in the end. I wonder how many people one kraken can feed. It could probably keep a restaurant stocked for weeks.

Happy with the savory snack, the sisters decided to seek out something more filling next.

"I'm still hungry. That race really worked up my appetite," Deziara said cheerfully, looking from stall to stall like a hunter searching for its next prey.

"I know what you mean. Despite already having dinner and two snacks, I feel like I could still eat a whole horse."

"A horse? Where would you get a horse in the Underworld?" Deziara asked suspiciously.

"I… Nevermind, it's just something I read in a book," Morrigan said, correcting herself.

Have to be careful with what I say. Things that were normal to say on Earth do not make a lot of sense in the Underworld. I don't want Deziara to start thinking of me as some weirdo.

"In either case, you can't call that small dish we had in the castle a dinner. It feels like the portions are getting smaller by the day," Deziara huffed.

"It does! Maybe we should have a word with the chef," Morrigan said.

"Oh, I'd love to give them a piece of my mind. I want a proper meal. Princesses aren't even allowed to ask for seconds. The moment I tried, Viana glared at me."

"You too?" Morrigan replied, and both sisters laughed. Suddenly, a pleasantly familiar smell tickled Morrigan's nose. "Do you smell that?"

"You're going to have to be more specific. There's lots of things I can smell," Deziara said with a chuckle. Morrigan grabbed her by the hand and began pulling her along, following the pleasant smell. Before long, both girls were standing in front of a stall that looked to be lined with rather plain-looking pies.

"What's this?" Deziara asked the vendor, a chubby demon woman with a motherly smile on her face.

"These are cheese-and-meat pies. Fresh out of the oven," she said, pointing towards a large, round bread oven behind her.

How did she get that thing over here? It's huge!

"They look rather simple. Why don't we try something else?" Deziara said, trying to pull Morrigan away. But she stood and stared at the pie. It didn't look like anything special, but the smell reminded her strongly of something. She just couldn't recall what.

"Why don't we give it a try?" Morrigan said.

Deziara looked suspiciously at her for a moment, then relented.

"Alright. Last time you insisted, we tasted something really good. I trust your sense of taste."

"Two pies coming right up." The vendor smiled as she put paper wrappings around the two pastries, making them easier to carry. Morrigan paid, then each girl took one of the pies. She could still feel the warmth of the pie from behind the wrapping, spreading through her fingers.

Morrigan thanked the demon woman and bit into the pie. The flavor that exploded in her mouth could only be called one thing—bliss. Meat and cheese mixed with tomato sauce. It tasted just like a pizza.

"Wow, this is good! You have a knack for finding the tasty stuff." Deziara ate her pie with gusto, savoring each bite.

"Told you!" she replied, then continued enjoying her pizza pie.

* * *

"That was great. I finally feel full," Deziara said, wiping the last bits of the creamy dessert they'd just eaten off her mouth.

Morrigan nodded vigorously, her stomach filled to the point of bursting. "I wish we could eat like this every day."

The guards who were following them also looked satisfied, having bought their treats and eaten them in shifts so at least two guards were watching the transformed girls at all times.

"Me too. Unfortunately, tomorrow we'll have to return to the tiny portions. I really don't want to return to the castle when I think about that." Deziara groaned.

"We should be going back now. Somebody might notice our absence if we stay out any longer."

"I know, I know. But I still want to look around a bit. Maybe there's something fun around here," Deziara said, beginning to scan the market. "Oh, look over there. That looks interesting!"

Deziara ran towards a dark booth, in front of which sat an elderly demon woman with white hair. This was the first time Morrigan had seen a demon who looked elderly. Demons looked young throughout most of their lives, only truly showing signs of aging once they had lived for over ten thousand years.

"What is this?" Morrigan asked, looking at the odd stack of cards in front of the elderly demoness.

"Fortune-telling, young ones. Give me your coin and I shall tell you your future," the woman croaked in a hoarse voice.

"Fortune-telling? That sounds fun! Let's try it," Deziara said cheerfully, setting a coin on the table.

"Alright, alright, but quickly," Morrigan said impatiently, uneasiness gnawing at the pit of her stomach.

There's no way fortune-telling is real. Not even in this world. Who could ever predict the future? Not to mention that this demon woman is giving me the creeps.

"Give me your hand, young lady," the elderly woman said, wheezing.

"Is that really necessary?" Deziara scrunched up her nose in displeasure, looking up and down at the woman with barely hidden disgust.

"It is if you want your fortune told," the woman replied, reaching her spindly, wrinkly arms towards Deziara. The girl sighed, then placed her right hand on the old woman's. She closed her eyes solemnly and began humming to herself. She hummed for a minute or two, then finally snapped her eyes open.

"You will suffer great hardship because of a close family member. However, if you abandon them, you'll gain great prosperity." The old demoness cackled. Deziara instantly snatched her hand away.

"What kind of fortune is that? You just made that up," she accused.

"No, child. I only say the truth of what the future holds. But the truth is not always pleasant. Father, wouldn't you like to have your future told as well?" The woman reached out her hand towards the disguised Morrigan.

"N-No, thank you," Morrigan replied in a low voice, taking a step back.

"It's alright. This one is for free, since your daughter didn't appear satisfied with her fortune."

"It couldn't hurt, right? I'm curious to see what she'll say about you," Deziara said, but there wasn't a lot of conviction in her voice.

"No, I really am not interested. Let's just go home," Morrigan said. She took Deziara's arm, trying to pull her away.

"Do not think that I will let you escape!" The woman suddenly lunged forward, grabbing Morrigan's hand. She tried to free herself, but before she could, she felt herself and Deziara being teleported away.

The next moment, Morrigan and Deziara found themselves in a large, empty room filled with dust and cobwebs. There were only two candles for light, which gave the place an eerie and foreboding feel.

"What just happened?!" Deziara exclaimed, looking around in shock.

"Father, Azrael!" Morrigan instantly called upon their protectors. However, she could feel that the call hadn't reached them. The old woman began cackling and laughing while her shape morphed and twisted. The wrinkly skin smoothed out, and messy white hair turned into black locks.

"I'm afraid they can't hear you. I had this whole place warded just for this occasion." Asdeus laughed, removing the dirty rags and revealing an elegant black dress.

"Asdeus! Father will put your head on a pike!" Deziara roared, anger and fear contorting her features.

"The king will have no idea this ever happened," Asdeus said sweetly. She laughed again, her voice echoing against the walls.

"Oh, yes he will! Do not think you can keep us here for long. The moment he finds out we're gone he will turn this whole kingdom upside down to find us. Right, Morri?" Deziara turned towards Morrigan, only to find her reverted back to her demon self, her hands trembling.

"I don't think *Morri* has enough courage to say anything. Afraid of your retribution, lamb?" Asdeus stepped closer, her heels clattering against the wooden floor.

"Morri, snap out of it. She's just one demoness. Even without Father, we can take her on," Deziara said resolutely, then threw a fireball at the demoness. A watery shield appeared in front of Asdeus, and with a hiss, the fireball turned into hot vapor and dissipated.

"How naughty, Deziara. Throwing fireballs at your teacher. I'm afraid that won't do at all." Asdeus moved her hand up, and Deziara's body went completely stiff.

"Wh-What is happening?" the girl managed to say.

"The reason why you remained safe for so long was because I needed the time to master a forbidden bit of magic. With this mastered, not even your dearest daddy can oppose me." The demoness moved her hand down with a sharp motion, and Deziara fell to her knees, lowering her head to the floor in a bow. "Now that's better. How pleasant it will be once the king bows at my feet."

Morrigan took a shaky step back, but felt her body tense up and move forward against her will.

"And where do you think you're going? You're the whole reason we're in this mess, human! It's time to pay your dues," Asdeus snapped, and did the same motion as before with her left hand, forcing Morrigan on the floor just like Deziara.

"Human? Morri, what is she talking about?"

CHAPTER 22

PUPPETEER

Asdeus cackled. "You didn't know? Well, of course you wouldn't. Surely the little cockroach would guard her nasty secret as well as she could."

"Shut up!" Morrigan snarled, trying to break free from the invisible bonds.

"No, I don't think I will. Deziara is your sister, isn't she? She should have the right to know who you truly are." Asdeus walked up to Deziara and then, with a flick of her wrist, forced the girl upright. "You see that little maggot on the floor over there? That is a human."

"What are you talking about? She's clearly a demon," Deziara objected.

"Oh, but that's just a shell. Underneath hides a nasty little human. What shame you must feel, being related to such a disgusting creature." The demoness laughed maniacally.

Deziara's face was filled with shock and disbelief. "Morri, she's lying, isn't she?" the girl pleaded, and Morrigan's heart clenched.

Would Deziara even accept me as a sister anymore if she knew of my past? But I can't lie to her either. That would only make matters worse.

"I was a human before I was reborn as a demon. My mother Eirwen pulled my soul into the body of her child. While I couldn't accept it at first, I have come to understand that I am a demon now, not a human," Morrigan said, then felt her head slam against the floor below.

"Dirty little liar! You will always be a human and nothing more than a human. Your kind should be happy to lick the dirt off demons' shoes, yet you have the gall to argue against me!"

"Morri!"

Morrigan winced as pain radiated from her cheek.

I need to break free from these bonds and at least get Deziara out of here. I doubt Asdeus would be interested in chasing her.

"Let us go!" Deziara shouted, but then was promptly forced to the ground, her legs and arms painfully scraping against the floorboards.

"Leave Deziara out of this! It's me you bear your grudge against, isn't it?"

"Oh, still trying to act noble? Then again, maybe your disgusting human self has developed a twisted sisterly feeling towards Deziara. I wonder how you would react if something were to happen to her? Would you scream for her?" Asdeus twirled her finger, and Deziara's arm slowly began to twist. She screamed in pain, desperately trying to regain control over her body.

Something snapped inside Morrigan as she saw her sister scream. Unbearable heat and anger rose within her like a smoldering fire. It became hotter and hotter, until it felt like it would burn Morrigan from within. She directed this heat towards Asdeus, and a blue fireball appeared, flying towards the demoness as quickly as a bullet. She managed to erect a protective force field at the last second, but the impact was so strong that Asdeus was knocked off her feet.

The invisible strings holding Morrigan disappeared, and she took the opportunity to rush towards a stupefied Deziara. As soon as she had grabbed Deziara's hand, Morrigan imagined herself turning into a shadow and dragging Deziara along with her. She had never actually tried taking live people with her in her shadow form, as Azrael had warned that it could quickly eat away at her magic reserves. The sensation was odd—she still had the wide vision and freedom of movement, but she felt much heavier and more restricted.

"You're not going anywhere," Asdeus snarled, getting up from the floor. But Morrigan didn't wait for her to recover, instead slipping underneath the door and out of what appeared to be an abandoned warehouse from the outside. The surrounding area was dark, with similar warehouses populating the area.

Morrigan rushed some distance away, then materialized from her shadow form. Much to her relief, Deziara was right next to her, panting heavily.

"Father!" Morrigan yelled, just as a fuming Asdeus ran out of the warehouse. The moment the demoness heard her shout, she stopped dead in her tracks, anger contorting her features.

"We'll meet again, cockroach!" Asdeus spat, creating a portal in front of her with a wave of her hand. Just as two dark shadows appeared in front of both girls, the demoness and her portal disappeared.

"Morrigan, Deziara, what is going on?" the king called out, looking around the area, his eyebrows twisted in an angry scowl. "How did you two get so far away from the Demon Castle?"

Deziara's eyes filled with tears, and she launched herself at Alphegor, wrapping her hands around him. Alphegor looked at Morrigan for answers, his expression both angry and worried.

"It was Asdeus..." Morrigan said, then slumped to the ground, her legs giving out underneath her.

* * *

"I cannot believe you two would sneak out of the castle without even telling anybody!" Alphegor roared at the two girls, who were sitting on the sofa in the living room, looking like two guilty puppies.

"And you four—just allowing princesses to leave as they please? Have I not made it clear that they are not to go out without my explicit permission?" The king turned towards the guards, who were kneeling on the ground with their heads pressed against the floor.

"We are so sorry, Your Majesty!" they said in unison.

"Fired! All of you! Get out of my sight before I decide to turn your heads into castle gate decorations," Alphegor yelled, and the demons crawled away.

"We thank you for your merciful decision," they muttered as they retreated. Then Alphegor turned towards a dark figure standing in the corner of the room. Morrigan had seen him around occasionally and recognized him as the spymaster.

"Melanos, I want this castle and anything in its near vicinity absolutely teleportation-proof. I don't want anyone to be able to teleport around the castle anymore," the king commanded.

"I'll see that it is done at once, Your Majesty," Melanos replied quietly, then disappeared.

"Father, isn't that a bit excessive?" Morrigan objected, but seeing the icy glare on Alphegor's face, she quickly sank back into the cushions.

"Their job is to protect you! A job they have FAILED. As for teleportation, it was something that needed to be done a long time ago," Alphegor raged. "And I thought you two would have known better by now after that whole excursion with Azrael."

"Father, don't be mad at Morrigan. It was I who pushed the idea," Deziara said in a shaky voice.

"Then it'll be you who will suffer the punishment. What was going through your head? Do you not understand the dangers that lurk outside the castle? Do you not know how many would seek to harm you for just being my daughters?" Alphegor rubbed the bridge of his nose, then slumped down on the sofa across from them. "Tell me exactly what happened."

Morrigan looked at Deziara, hoping she would explain, but the girl was staring into her tightened fist, doing her best not to cry. With a shaky voice, Morrigan said, "Everything was fine at first. We disguised ourselves and strolled through the market, enjoying the foods that were offered."

"Deziara was disguised too?"

"Y-Yes, Father. I wore a wig and simple clothing."

"Go on, then."

"Once we had eaten, we saw this fortune teller. She offered to read our fortunes and Deziara went to have hers read first," Morrigan said, trying to leave out the part where Deziara was the one who wanted to check out the fortune teller. No doubt it would make the king even angrier.

"And this fortune teller turned out to be Asdeus, correct?"

"Yes. She pulled us into a portal. It took us to some sort of warehouse where we couldn't summon you," Morrigan continued.

"Anti-magic wards?" Alphegor pondered.

"No. We could still use magic. Asdeus did this weird thing where she could control our bodies and force them to move as she wished."

"Wait... She could control your bodies?" Alphegor's face went pale.

"Yes. We were unable to move."

"Then how did you break free?"

"Asdeus hurt Deziara, so I felt this surge of anger inside me. I was able to launch a blue fireball at her. While she was disoriented, I dragged Deziara into the shadows with me and escaped."

"Well done, Morrigan," Alphegor said, a small smile flickering on his face for a second. Then it was replaced with an angry scowl again. "So which one of you girls was the one who wanted to see the fortune teller?"

Alphegor's gaze was cold, sending a shiver through Morrigan's spine. She had never seen her father this angry.

"I-It was me!" Morrigan said, trying to take the blame. But the king narrowed his eyes at her, and she quickly lowered her head.

"It was me," Deziara admitted, large tears streaming down her face.

"You realize that it was a near miracle that you two escaped." Alphegor stood up again, his figure menacing. "Body control is something only the strongest of demons are able to break out of, and even then it is not a guarantee. If Asdeus really has this ability, then the problem is far larger than I initially thought."

"She said that she remained hidden to train this ability," Morrigan added, and Alphegor's face turned grim.

"So she probably hasn't mastered it fully. To think that you two got this close to being captured by her." Alphegor slumped down onto the sofa again, holding his head in his hands.

"But it all turned out okay?" Morrigan said, trying to lighten the mood. Heavy silence fell over them, and she looked at her shoes.

After what felt like an eternity, Alphegor spoke again. "Deziara, as you're the older sister, you will be the one to be punished. You're forbidden from participating in the competition."

Deziara opened her mouth to object, but seeing the king's unyielding expression, she nodded.

"Father, that's not fair. We are both at fault!" Morrigan jumped to her feet in objection.

"So you are. Do not think that you'll go unpunished. You will remain in the competition, but I am taking away that magic paint of yours," he announced, and Morrigan felt herself being shattered to pieces.

No! If I was withdrawn from the competition, I wouldn't have objected. But I really want to see what that paint does.

"But Father..."

"No buts! I am already being lenient with you two. If it was anybody else, they'd be confined to their room for months. Your only saving grace is that you actually managed to get yourself out of this mess," Alphegor said with finality, and Morrigan begrudgingly nodded.

There's no way I'm just going to give up on my magic paint. Maybe there's a way I could track where Father hides it.

Alphegor must have sensed her intentions, because suddenly the magic paint appeared in front of Morrigan.

"This will remain in my pocket dimension, so don't even think of sneaking around to get it," Alphegor growled, and the paint disappeared. Morrigan's eyes filled with hot tears and her heart clenched with desperation.

"Father, you dummy!" Morrigan yelled, emotions taking over her sense of reason. She jumped to her feet and ran to her room, slamming the door shut.

She heard a heavy sigh come from behind the door. She sat on the floor next to it, tears rolling down her cheeks. She knew she had no right to act this way—his punishment was just. But the thought that she wouldn't be able to use the magic paint was so painful. She was really looking forward to trying it out.

"F-Father, there is something I wanted to talk about..." Deziara said in a barely audible voice. "It's about something Asdeus said."

Morrigan's heartbeat quickened as she realized which topic her sister was about to bring up.

"What did she say?"

"She... She said that Morrigan is a human," Deziara stammered, and Morrigan's heart began thundering so loudly that she could hear it resounding in her ears.

"What did Morrigan say?" Alphegor's voice became cold and unreadable.

"She said that she used to be a human, but that she isn't one anymore. I don't understand. Morrigan is my sister, isn't she?"

"Do not worry, child. Morrigan is without a doubt my daughter and your sister. However, her birth is a bit different from that of a normal demon. I could tell you her story if you wish. But regardless of whether you hear it out or not, you must swear to never tell anyone about it, for it could put your sister in even bigger danger," Alphegor said in a barely audible voice. "That includes your mother as well."

"I... I want to hear it. If that's alright..." Deziara muttered after a long pause. Alphegor nodded, then retold the story of Morrigan's birth. How he had been unable to find a soul for his and Eirwen's child. How Eirwen had taken over the grueling ritual despite her exhaustion. How she had pulled Rosa's dying soul into Morrigan's body. And how Morrigan remembered her past life.

"So, Morrigan's soul comes from a human from a different world, while normally a demon child is imbued with a demon soul from the Underdark."

After the story was complete, an eerie silence stretched on. Morrigan's thoughts wandered to what she knew of the Underdark—the deepest sanctuary hidden somewhere in the Underworld, where every demon's soul went after death. It was like an afterlife for demons. Her heart hammered as she wondered whether Deziara would be able to accept Morrigan—a demon who had come from this sacred place.

"I... I need to think about this. I still love Morri to bits, but I need some time," Deziara finally said, and a brief silence was broken by the sound of a door closing. Morrigan wrapped her hands around herself and sat like that for a long time, slowly unraveling all the things that had happened.

Chapter 23

Monster Run

It was the second day of the competition and the third day of the Nachtstern Festival, but the cheerful atmosphere didn't reach Morrigan. She was still meekly sitting in her room with her eyes downcast as Gunna did her best to get her ready for the second task.

"What is weighing you down so heavily so early in the morning?" the nanny asked as she tied Morrigan's hair into a ponytail. Apparently, that day's task would involve a lot of moving, so it was important to style her hair in a way that wouldn't hinder her.

"I... I just had a bit of an argument with Father. And I think Deziara might be mad at me as well." Morrigan sighed.

"Then you just have to talk to them and set things straight, don't you?" Gunna chirped, finishing up with Morrigan's ponytail.

"But it was Father's fault. And I don't think I can make up with Deziara by just talking to her."

"There, there, no need to be so pessimistic. Just go talk to them and everything will be alright. You're a family, after all."

A knock resounded on Morrigan's door, and it slowly opened, Alphegor peeking from behind the door. It was a bit silly seeing the king peeking timidly with a guilty look on his face. Morrigan deliberately ignored him, looking the other way.

"Good morning, Morrigan. May we talk?" he asked, slowly shuffling into the room.

"Lady Morrigan was just speaking of you, Master Alphegor," the dwarf nanny said, earning a look of betrayal from Morrigan. Alphegor, on the other hand, visibly perked up.

"Wonderful! If you would give us a moment then, Gunna."

"Of course, Master Alphegor," she said with a gracious bow, then waddled out of the room with a self-satisfied smile on her face. An awkward silence stretched on as Morrigan pointedly ignored her father.

"Morrigan, I wanted to apologize for yesterday. I overreacted," the king admitted, sitting down on the bed next to her.

"I really want to try out that magic paint." She pouted, puffing out her cheeks. Her heart clenched as she remembered how the magic paint was stashed in the king's personal pocket dimension.

"I know," Alphegor replied, his expression becoming sterner. "And how do you think I felt when I suddenly heard you screaming for me from the city outskirts? When you were supposed to be within the safety of the Demon Castle?"

Morrigan stared awkwardly at her thumbs, knowing full well that her father must have been beside himself. "I'm sorry. I hoped that nothing would happen if me and Deziara went out disguised, like we did on the first day of the festival."

"That is different and you know it," he retorted. Morrigan hung her head shamefully, and Alphegor sighed.

"You must promise me that you will not leave the castle again without my explicit permission," the king said sternly. "No matter who tries to coerce you to sneak out, be it Azrael or Deziara or anybody else."

But that means that I would have to spend another twenty years cooped up in the castle. Even Deziara is getting sick of it, and she's never even seen anything besides the Demon Castle.

"Morrigan." Alphegor's tone turned cold as the silence stretched on.

She looked at him and finally sighed. "I promise. But then you have to promise to take me out sometimes," she countered.

Alphegor appeared a bit surprised at first but then smiled. "Alright, it's a deal. Everything's good, then." He outstretched his arms, inviting her for a hug, but Morrigan crossed her arms over her chest.

"There's one more thing."

"One more thing? What exactly?" Alphegor narrowed his eyes.

"You must allow Deziara to compete. She was really looking forward to it," Morrigan pleaded.

Even if Deziara doesn't see me as a sister anymore, I still want to do something nice for her.

"It was Deziara's—"

"I know, I know. But please overlook it. She was merely craving a bit of freedom," Morrigan interrupted. The two stared at each other for a while until the king finally relented.

"Alright, alright. She can compete. But she'll be confined to her room for a week once the festival is finished."

Morrigan wanted to object to that as well, but the stern look in Alphegor's eyes indicated that he would not budge any further. She nodded with her eyes downcast.

"Good, now come. We must tell your sister that she can compete today." The king stood up and outstretched his hand towards her. Morrigan felt nervous about going to see Deziara, but after taking a deep breath she stood up and took Alphegor's hand.

As Alphegor and Morrigan got closer to Lady Lily and Deziara's room, Morrigan got more and more nervous.

What will Deziara say once she sees me? Did she tell Lady Lily about me? Will she treat me just like Viana and our other older sisters do? Will things be awkward between us now?

"It'll be alright, little one," Alphegor said, squeezing her hand. She looked at him for a bit in surprise, then nodded, praying that her father was right.

Once they had reached Lady Lily's room, the guards outside their door instantly straightened, looking nervous.

"Your Majesty, shall I inform Lady Lily of your arrival?" the guard asked.

"I've come to see my daughter, not Lady Lily," the king explained.

"I shall inform her at once," the guard replied stiffly, then called out through the door. "Princess Deziara, His Majesty is here to see you."

There was a moment of silence before the door slowly opened, Deziara emerging from it looking depressed and tired. When she noticed that Morrigan was there too, she flinched, but then opened the door fully, allowing them to enter. Her reaction made Morrigan's stomach churn, and she couldn't force herself to look at Deziara anymore.

As they entered, they saw Lady Lily standing by the sofa and greeting Alphegor with a bow.

"Good morning, Your Majesty, Princess Morrigan. What has brought you here so early?" she asked politely.

"Deziara, you may take part in the competition if you wish," the king announced, and the girl instantly perked up.

"Really?"

"Yes. Morrigan spoke on your behalf, so I've decided to be lenient with my punishment. You will still have to spend one week confined in your room once the festival is over."

Deziara's face dropped for a moment, but then she nodded in understanding.

"That is fair. If it wasn't for Morri, then we never would have made it back…"

"I swear this girl is nothing but trouble," Lady Lily huffed, dropping the polite facade. She walked up to Morrigan, who was still clutching Alphegor's hand, and placed her hand on her shoulder. "Thank you for getting her out of there safely."

"Of course, she's my sister," Morrigan replied with a strained smile. *If she still thinks of me as her sister, that is.*

"Morrigan," Deziara said, looking at her with unusual seriousness. "I have thought a lot about yesterday. It really confused me at first and quite frankly I couldn't even believe it—it seemed so far-fetched. However, I realized that in the end, it doesn't matter. You are my sister no matter what."

Morrigan's eyes filled with tears at the heavy weight being lifted off her shoulders. Deziara began crying too, and before long, both girls were hugging and crying.

"Not sure what those two are on about, but I'm glad all is well that ends well." Lady Lily sighed, looking at the scene before her with a smile.

"Indeed. Now then, girls. Time to dry your tears. You two have a competition to win," Alphegor announced.

"Yes, Father," they replied in unison.

* * *

"Welcome, one and all, to the second day of the Nachtstern Festival Competition! Today we're all gathered in Linberor Market Square to observe our dearest contestants face the second daunting task," Azrael announced, standing on the very stage where Alphegor had given his opening speech. A massive crowd of demons and other Underworld races was gathered in front of the square, filling it to the absolute brim, with many onlookers watching from balconies or even rooftops.

Alphegor and the other VIPs were comfortably seated on a podium that had a clear view of the stage, which had a giant white piece of cloth hanging from the back.

"You all must be wondering—where are all the contestants? They are nowhere in sight," Azrael teased, then stepped to the side of the stage and pointed towards the white cloth. "Do not worry, my friends. They are right here!"

A bright blue crystal positioned in front of the stage lit up and directed its light onto the cloth. A misty image began to form—unclear at first, but slowly it gained more focus and sharpness. After a while, the crowd cheered as they saw all four hundred contestants standing in the old Linberor Market Square.

"I bet some have fond memories of this place. While the Old City has lost some of its charm over the millennia, it has certainly not lost its value. For today it will serve as grounds for our second task—the infamous monster run!"

Wait... Did he just say monster run?

Morrigan, along with the other contestants, heard Azrael's voice come from the blue crystal, which was hovering above the Old City of Linberor, illuminating it with its light. Morrigan's face paled as she stood among the rest of the contestants. She was huddled close to Viana and Deziara, who had similarly horrified looks on their faces. However, Viana hid hers a bit better.

"He doesn't mean actual monsters, does he?" Deziara whispered to Morrigan, and she could hear similar questions popping up from other contestants.

"I know what you're wondering—will you really let the contestants, especially our wonderful princesses, be chased by an actual monster? The answer to that is—of course not. The king would have my head for it." Azrael laughed, and the king responded with an affirmative nod. Morrigan and all the participants around her relaxed.

"But do not think that just because it's not a real monster, it'll be an easy task to win. Listen carefully, dear contestants, for here are the rules," Azrael called out, and everyone perked up.

"Rule number one—do not take off the armband provided to you.

It serves as an indicator to the monster that you are one of the targets. I know it sounds tempting, but we can see your every move. The moment your armband comes off is the moment you lose," he said sternly.

Morrigan looked at the metallic band wrapped around her left arm. There was a tiny stone embedded in it, no doubt the indicator Azrael had mentioned. She did get a tiny urge to remove it, but then shook her head, steeling her resolve.

It's not a real monster anyway. There is nothing to fear. All I have to do is outrun it. Surely it won't be much of a problem in my shadow form. The light from the crystal does leave me less space for movement, but there are still plenty of shadows I can hide in.

"Second rule—no stealth abilities. Anything that makes you invisible, hides you in the environment, or fools the senses is forbidden. That includes your shadow ability too, Princess Morrigan. I'm afraid it just wouldn't be fun if you just hid in some corner as a shadow while others got chased around." Azrael snickered, and Morrigan grumbled.

I'll sneak into his room later and cover his bed in ice while he is sleeping.

"And the final rule is simple. Do not leave the confines of the Old City. Everything is clearly marked, so no amount of whining that you 'didn't know' will save you," Azrael said sternly. "Are the rules clear?"

"Yes!" the participants called out back at him.

"Great! The last fifty left uncaught by the monster can advance to the next task tomorrow. You may now unleash the beast," Azrael bellowed, and a loud bell rang from the Old City's cathedral.

Morrigan looked on as the large wooden doors were slowly pulled open by two bulky demon watchmen. As they opened, she and all the others saw something black moving within. Two red eyes opened as the giant black monster awoke from the sounds of the bell.

Is this supposed to be a magical construct? It looks very much real to me.

Mesmerized and terrified, she watched as it took one step after another out of the cathedral, its footsteps making the surrounding area tremble. As it emerged outside, she noticed its form wasn't fully defined. There was a crystalline quality to it, shimmering and warping out of place as the monster moved.

"What are you doing, Morri? Run!" Deziara pulled her out of her contemplation, and she realized that the monster was staring right at her, while the other contestants were already scattering in every possible direction.

Oh, shit!

CHAPTER 24

OUTRUNNING A LANDWYRM

Morrigan looked in horror at the two crystalline eyes from the magical construct. They were locked on her, ready to capture her the moment she made any movement. Sweat began pooling on her forehead as she tried to think of how to escape from the beast.

The urge to just hide in the safety of shadows was unbearable. As a shadow, the monster would not be able to touch her—or even see her, for that matter. But if she did become a shadow, then it would be over. She would forfeit the competition and also the right to win that enticing shadow ruby.

"Not today," she whispered as the beast lunged for her. Morrigan erected a force field, protecting herself from the monster. It was stupefied by the force field for only a moment, destroying it with its giant paw as if it were made out of paper.

But that was enough time for Morrigan to put some distance between herself and the monster. Other participants fell into its line of sight, and it began chasing whoever was unlucky enough to be the closest. Among the chaos, Morrigan slipped into one of the narrow side streets, keeping as close to the walls as possible.

"Now, dear participants who haven't been caught yet, the magical construct chasing you is based on a landwyrm. It is one of the dragon subspecies that possesses no wings and prefers to live in the Underworld. For the record, the first Demon King liked to take a landwyrm's shape in battle," Azrael explained, as if he were telling a story in front of a class instead of announcing it to poor people being chased by the monstrosity.

"While you might think that because it is a construct, it is less ferocious, I'm sad to say that's not true. I worked very hard to make sure that it is as close to a landwyrm in both build and behavior as possible." He cackled as he watched the beast catch one participant after the next.

At one moment when Morrigan dared to glance back, she saw the construct's giant maw close around one of the contestants. It appeared like he would be eaten; however, when the beast's jaw opened again, the caught demon appeared completely unscathed, aside from the armband, which lay shattered on the ground. As the monster lunged for its next victim, the demon fell to his knees, no doubt scarred for life by such an experience.

Construct or not, I do not want to get caught by that thing. I need to move into places where it cannot follow.

So Morrigan moved deeper and deeper into the Old City, moving from one narrow side street to the next. Occasionally she would hear the landwyrm raging somewhere behind her or bump into another contestant trying to find a hiding spot. However, despite the large number of buildings in the city, their doors and windows were marked with a shimmering red light, indicating that entry was forbidden.

What's the point of all these buildings if I can't even hide in them?

Morrigan continued running through the streets, trying to keep ahead of the monster, whose snarls and growls always seemed to follow closely behind her. She ducked among the tiniest of buildings, hoping the lack of space would restrict the landwyrm. Unfortunately, it proved to be incredibly agile, often jumping over rooftops and landing in areas that seemed far too small to accommodate its size. But it always managed to squeeze in—like some oversized cat in a tiny box.

Just as Morrigan thought she had put some good distance between herself and the construct, she heard its sharp claws clatter on the rooftops nearby.

It is hunting us from above, now? I need to hide somewhere, and fast.

She darted into the closest side street and ran through it, avoiding the many scattered crates and barrels. The clattering followed her, so she ran faster, desperately searching for hiding places. The narrow street led to a larger street, and Morrigan saw a large building with dark pillars by its entrance from across the street. Much to her surprise, its entry wasn't marked, so she made a beeline to it.

Just as she closed the large entrance door behind herself, she heard some screams from outside.

Seems like a few more people got caught. I wonder if that thing will follow me inside. I guess that since the entrance wasn't blocked off, it probably will. Maybe there's some corner where I could lay low for a while.

Morrigan turned to head deeper inside, but was surprised, as she realized that she had stumbled into what appeared to be a museum—or *had* been a museum? A thick layer of dust had settled over every surface, and most of the furniture was either broken or half-rotten.

Intrigued by her findings, Morrigan hurried inside one of the open rooms. It was mostly empty, with large cobwebs sitting in the corners. However, there were also a few broken sculptures inside. She walked up to them and admired the handiwork on the smooth black stone. One sculpture depicted a demon woman carrying a torch, but sadly half of her body had been broken off. Another one portrayed a demon man with ram-like horns and a large build of a warrior. Unfortunately, one of his legs was missing, and his left arm lay shattered on the floor.

"What a shame! I bet these looked beautiful when they were whole," Morrigan muttered, gently pressing her fingers against the cold stone of the sculpture. Suddenly she heard a clatter from the main hall as the landwyrm made its way into the museum.

Oh no! It's found its way inside.

Morrigan hurried to the adjacent room, using the connecting doors instead of running back to the main hall. However, just as she made her way into the next room, the construct crashed into the sculpture room, destroying the last remnants of the exhibit.

"Did you have to break that, you uncultured worm!" she called out angrily to the construct as she ducked out of the empty room, back into the main hall. Morrigan tried to run for the exit, but the landwyrm cut her off, snarling and hissing at her. She ducked under the staircase and then ran to the exhibit rooms across the hall, hoping to find a window that she could use as an exit.

This room was filled with old paintings, some weathered and muddled from neglect, while others had been torn, perhaps by some bored hooligans.

I swear, some people have no appreciation for the finer things in life.

She was looking longingly at the paintings when the landwyrm's maw appeared at the entrance. Morrigan grabbed a large, broken table with her levitation magic, straining a little bit under its weight, and tossed it straight at the construct. Its head was forced back, and she took the opportunity to climb through the broken window.

The window turned out to be rather high up, so in her hurry to get away from the beast, she fell painfully to the ground. Morrigan feared she might have broken or sprained something during her fall, but after carefully inspecting her legs, she concluded that aside from a few minor scrapes, she hadn't suffered any serious injuries.

Now to get as far away from here as possible.

Morrigan dove into the nearest alleyway, and it wasn't a second too soon, as the snarling form of the landwyrm appeared right where she had fallen. A few demons who had been hiding in the alleyway scampered to their feet as they heard the beast rage, running as fast as their legs could carry them. But before they and Morrigan could make it out, a stone wall was erected before them.

"Sorry, lads. Better you than I," resounded the gruff voice of the duergar champion.

That dirty little cheater! When did he even get there?

The construct ran straight into the alleyway, heading towards Morrigan and the demons with jaws wide-open. She grabbed a few rogue boxes that littered the alleyway and flung them at the beast using her levitation magic in an attempt to stop it. Unfortunately, it just swatted the heavy boxes away like they were mere twigs.

"We're done for!" one of the demons screeched, pressing close against the wall. But Morrigan refused to give up. She levitated the remaining boxes and formed a way for herself to climb up to the rooftop. Then she erected a force field in front of the beast to buy herself a little bit of time. The landwyrm collided with the force field, dazed by the shimmering wall for a moment, before destroying it just like it had the first time.

I really need to train more with my force field ability. It is far too weak in its current state.

But it had bought Morrigan enough time to get up to the roof. One of the demons who had been stuck in the alleyway with her was trying to follow her up to the roof, but the construct closed its jaws around him before he could reach it. Then it went for the remaining two demons in the alleyway before making its way up to the roof.

Morrigan ran as fast as she could across the shingles, the clatter of her feet resounding across the area. She paused for a moment as she reached the edge of the roof, unsure of where to go next.

I wonder if I could use my force field as a bridge of sorts.

She created a shimmering force field bridge from one rooftop to the next, testing it with her foot before fully committing to her steps.

It held her weight just fine, so she sprinted across to the next roof. The landwyrm ran after her, occasionally jumping into a nearby side street to eliminate a poor participant who happened to be hiding nearby.

"My, oh my. Do you see that, dear audience? Our little princess is leading the monster according to her whims. Truly the daughter of our powerful King!" Azrael announced, and the crowd responded with a loud cheer.

I am just trying not to get caught!

Morrigan screamed inwardly as the beast got closer and closer to her with each rooftop she crossed. Her feet were beginning to tire, and she knew that if she didn't end the chase soon, she'd get eliminated.

I need to lead it to an area where there are other people it can focus on. But where would most people go?

As she surveyed the area over the rooftops, she realized that the most obvious choice was the starting point. The beast was very unlikely to wander back to the place it had emerged from, instead chasing participants into the depths of the Old City. No doubt many had realized that and gone back as soon as they felt it was safe to do so.

Morrigan changed her running trajectory, focusing on getting back to the cathedral in the center. It seemed like her plan worked well, as the landwyrm got distracted more often before resuming its chase after her.

I wonder if it's just inclined to chase after the easiest prey. Unsuspecting, hiding people are easier to catch than I am, but once they are caught, it switches back to me. I should try getting off the rooftops, but how can I do that without breaking my neck?

The landwyrm jumped down into an alleyway again, and a scream resounded as yet another person got caught.

"And with this catch, dear participants, everybody else remaining uncaught officially moves on to the next task. But don't think the competition ends here. The one who remains as the last uncaught person will gain a boon in the next task. And trust me when I tell you that it could be what decides your victory or defeat," Azrael announced smugly.

You really could have told us that at the start while explaining the rules. Does there have to be a surprise each time?

Morrigan had no intention of running herself ragged to obtain first place. But if the boon could help her win in the next task, she should try to earn it. She began to search for a place where she could descend back to the ground—a stack of boxes, a staircase, or anything else that could serve as the middle ground. She even considered levitating herself to it, but self-levitation was very difficult. If she wasn't careful, she could easily lose control and injure herself.

The landwyrm's heavy form became too much for the old roof, which started to crumble under its weight. The shingles under Morrigan's feet began to cave in, and she fell, desperately trying to keep hold of something. The monster fell into the half-decayed building, flailing and thrashing about all the while. Its heavy tail tore through the supporting beams like matchsticks, forcing the roof to come tumbling down.

Morrigan couldn't grab hold of anything. She fell straight down, along with the heavy debris.

CHAPTER 25

UNCATCHABLE PRINCESS

The audience watched with horror as the buildings collapsed on the raging construct and Morrigan. Lady Lily had gone deadly pale as she watched the projection at the screen from the podium. She turned to the king for help, but he was nowhere to be seen.

"Now, dear audience, before you panic, let me assure you that our dearest Crown Princess is alright," Azrael said, pointing at the screen. Everyone focused their gaze on it, watching the debris for any movement. The landwyrm wriggled its way from beneath it and continued chasing the participants, some of whom had also stopped to observe the situation.

"Where's the Princess?" somebody from the crowd asked.

"She is right here." Alphegor's amplified voice resounded through the area, and everyone looked towards the podium. Morrigan was standing right next to the king, uninjured aside from the bruise she had gotten when she fell from the museum window.

"As you can all see, Princess Morrigan is unharmed. But since it is clear that the landwyrm would have caught her had His Majesty not pulled her to safety, I declare that her participation ends here, earning the fiftieth place," Azrael announced. The crowd cheered and applauded for Morrigan, which she accepted with a courteous nod. Then everyone returned their attention to the projection in front of them.

"I'm sorry, Father," she said, lowering her head in front of Alphegor.

"Keep your head up. You have successfully completed the task," Alphegor said sternly, and she straightened. He nodded before pointing towards the empty chair next to him. It was supposed to be the place where the queen sat, so Morrigan wondered whether it was alright for her to take it. But from the intense stare her father gave her, she realized that she didn't have much of a choice and sat down.

"I shall have all the old buildings reconstructed. This is far too dangerous," the king muttered in annoyance, loud enough for only Morrigan to hear. She chuckled, and decided not to dwell on the matter. She had completed the task. Even though she hadn't obtained the boon, that didn't mean she still couldn't win. So Morrigan decided to relax and watch the other contestants.

The landwyrm construct didn't appear to have been fazed by the incident in the slightest. It kept chasing whichever poor participants happened to be closest to it, mercilessly closing its jaws around them. One after another, their armbands shattered into pieces, leaving them trembling and horrified until the beast was well out of their sight.

Much to Morrigan's delight, Deziara was still in the competition, weaving and running out of the landwyrm's reach whenever it got even remotely close to her. Her speed magic, which was trained to nearly its maximum potential, gave Deziara an unbeatable edge over the other contestants, who were forced to fight the landwyrm back with less reliable methods.

The duergar who had previously trapped Morrigan in the alleyway was flinging a barrage of rocks at the construct in an attempt to stop it. However, the beast deflected the rocks with its paw, quickly closing the distance between them. Seeing this, the duergar erected a thick shell around himself, encasing himself in stone. But this didn't hold the monster back for long, either. It scratched at the shell with its razor-sharp claws, and before long, the duergar was dug out like a rabbit from its den.

The monster's jaws closed around it, and the arm brace shattered to pieces, leaving a cursing, angry duergar behind.

"Duergar champion, would you please hold your tongue? This is supposed to be a family-friendly event," Azrael called out, but the smile on his lips indicated that he in fact found the duergar's outrage amusing.

I'm not even sure what some of those words mean. Nobody ever bothered to teach me something like that. Perhaps I could ask Azrael.

However, the stern gaze from her father clearly said that finding out the meaning of such words was the last thing she needed to do. Morrigan returned her gaze to the projection and decided to ask Azrael the next time they'd have a magic lesson.

The landwyrm construct continued rampaging through the area, chasing the remaining contestants with even more ferocity. Those who were previously able to hide from it due to their size were picked off one by one. Morrigan watched the deep gnome champion desperately bury himself in a flower bed to mask himself and the bracelet. But the beast was done playing games. It found the deep gnome cowering inside the flower bed and dug him out as if he were an earthworm.

Thrown out of his hiding spot, the deep gnome tried to scamper away as quickly as his stumpy legs would allow him. Alas, the beast had caught him in his jaws before he managed to even take three steps. When the monster retreated, the gnome was curled up on the ground with a thumb in his mouth.

Maybe it's a good thing I never ended up in the construct's mouth. Seems like many participants will require some therapy after that experience. Do they even have therapists in the Underworld? I don't even know the demon word for therapist.

The next one to fall was the infernal champion, who, despite his best attempts to scare off the beast with powerful fireballs, was unable to truly damage its formidable hide. At least he took the loss far more gracefully, merely shrugging and walking to the cathedral, where the rest of the caught participants were gathered.

Finally, only three contestants remained scattered in the Old City—Deziara, Galandir, and the vampire champion, who was fluttering about in her small and speedy bat form. Morrigan wasn't surprised to see her sister remain among the last three, nor was she surprised about the vampire. But Galandir was unexpected.

I didn't even notice him at any point. Did he fly? No, I surely would have noticed that. So how did he avoid the landwyrm for so long? Did he hide? Or perhaps outrun it? Or a mix of both? I wish I would have focused on his movements a bit earlier.

The landwyrm attempted to chase down Deziara first, heading to the side street where she was hiding between some houses. But as soon as she sensed its approach, Deziara swiftly ran from her hiding spot, forcing the beast to give chase. Morrigan feared that it might catch up to her, but her sister always kept a little bit ahead of the monster, no matter how long it chased her.

She's trying to lead it somewhere? Perhaps to lure it towards the other participants.

Deziara suddenly turned into one of the side streets, and the spooked vampire champion, in her bat form, tried to flutter over the rooftops. Deziara jumped onto the same roof and swiftly overtook her, leaving her in the monster's path. The landwyrm closed its mouth around the tiny bat, making it disappear for a moment. Before anyone even realized what had happened, the tiny bat fluttered out of its mouth and landed on the ground.

The vampire woman transformed back to her humanoid shape, breathing heavily. She glared at Deziara, who kept leaping from rooftop to rooftop, leading the beast while no doubt trying to find the elven boy. For a while Deziara was chased by the beast much like Morrigan had been before, but after it became clear that she would not be able to find the sneaky boy, she sped up, leaving the landwyrm far in the dust.

It chased her for a while, then gave up, seeing that it wasn't going to catch up anyway. The landwyrm took a sharp turn in the direction of the cathedral, and after a few minutes, Galandir surfaced from one of the side streets on his shimmering wings. He tried to fly up out of the construct's reach; however, as it turned out, landwyrms were rather good jumpers. With a strong push from its legs, it was high up in the air, and Galandir was between its teeth.

The beast landed with a loud thud, then opened its mouth to release Galandir. The boy slid to the ground covered in drool. He tried to get the nasty sludge off himself, but it stuck to him like glue. Morrigan laughed as she watched him try to desperately get it off by wiping his legs against the cobblestones.

"Demons and guests, we have our winner for the monster run—Princess Deziara!" Azrael announced, and the crowd erupted into cheers. Morrigan applauded enthusiastically and cheered for her sister, while Alphegor and Lady Lily were trying to show some restraint—though she had no doubt that they wanted to applaud just as loudly as others.

"I knew that monster wouldn't be able to catch me!" Deziara called out, and Lady Lily sighed heavily at her daughter's lack of proper decorum. Thankfully, the crowd was too caught up in her victory to really care, instead chanting her name over and over again.

"With this victory, Princess Deziara has secured herself a special boon to use in tomorrow's task. As for what it is—I'm afraid that will remain a secret until tomorrow," Azrael said cheekily, and everyone groaned. "Now, now. Good things come to those who wait. Let's give a loud applause to all contestants continuing on to the next task. Coincidentally, all three princesses and almost all of our foreign champions continue on."

The delegations cheered, as did the demons, who roared with enthusiasm, many of them directing their cheers towards Morrigan. She felt a bit unnerved by their attention but managed to keep her composure and wave at them.

* * *

"Really, you two. I was supposed to be getting drunk on magma ale out in the town, but instead I am stuck babysitting. Why'd you have to sneak out like that yesterday?" Azrael grumbled, kicking a piece of chewed-up wood away from himself. Meanwhile, Deziara and Morrigan were hard at work, foaming up Haku's body to get hardened lava pieces off him.

Apparently, after the Test of Speed, the little dragon had taken it upon himself to go for a little walk along the lava river, occasionally submerging in the hot lava. Morrigan was happy to hear that her friend got his own bit of freedom and fun during the festival. But he had really scared the festivalgoers, as they had gone to complain about the dragon to the Demon Castle's guards. Haku had refused to go with them, so in the end Azrael had to be the one to bring him back to the stable.

"We just wanted to try some food and have some fun, like Haku over here," Morrigan said, scrubbing away a piece of hardened magma with a rough brush. It crumbled away after she applied some force but left Haku's scales intact. It was quite possible that at this point his scales had become nearly impenetrable.

"And almost get caught by Asdeus again. Yes, that sounds like fun," Azrael scoffed.

"But we didn't—that's all that matters. Besides, nobody could have predicted that she would appear in the festival, and be equipped with that weird body control magic to boot," Morrigan grumbled.

"Can we not talk about such glum topics? In the end, everything was fine. Let's focus on something else," Deziara interjected, her expression dark.

"Like your absolute victory today?" Morrigan cheered, and Haku wagged his tail, sending foam flying all over the stable. Azrael jumped out of the way of a rogue cluster of bubbles and waved another away with a gust of wind magic.

"Yeah! Wasn't I amazing?" Deziara exclaimed, lifting her foamy brush high in the air, but Morrigan sensed that the gesture was a bit forced. It appeared that the incident was still eating away at her.

"While the other princess nearly got crushed by deadly debris. Do you have to endanger your life every single day? Can it not be every other day? Or like twice a week?" the white-haired demon grumbled. "You know that every time you are in danger, this oath stabs at me like a knife, urging me to go to your rescue. It's not a very pleasant feeling."

Deziara sneered. "Aww, Azrael is too shy to admit that he cares for you, Morri."

"It's alright to be honest with your feelings," Morrigan added, playing along with the joke.

Azrael walked up to her, swiftly covered her in foam from head to toe, then poked her forehead. "I am serious, you little menace! Even if the oath urges me to protect you, it cannot magically save you on its own."

"It's not like I wanted those things to happen…"

"Yeah! Don't blame Morri for them!"

"I wouldn't, if she didn't have a knack for finding trouble. At least try not to have an incident tomorrow," Azrael said, groaning.

As if I can control what is going to happen. But I do hope nothing bad happens tomorrow.

CHAPTER 26

MAGIC MAZE

"Welcome, dear audience, to the most awaited day of the Nachtstern Festival Competition. As most of you probably know, the theme of the third day is magic. But what you don't know are the exact details of today's task. Most of you are probably curious to know why we are gathered in the Demon Castle's gardens today," Azrael announced from his place in the podiums, which were erected across the Demon Castle's wall.

The majority of the audience were gathered in front of the podium, curiously stretching their necks and trying to see past the giant hedge that stood before them. Morrigan and the other contestants stood on the other side of the hedged-off area, which spanned through the majority of the Demon Castle's gardens.

How did they even get this ready overnight? There wasn't even a single sign of activity in the backyard yesterday when I was coming back from the stable. Is there a convenient magic that lets you grow giant hedges overnight? I know there is magic that allows you to teleport things to another place, but could it teleport something as large as this?

"Well, let me tell you, dear audience. This year we decided to put a spin on our regular magic test. We have a magic maze—that giant wall of bush in front of you all is part of it." Azrael snapped his fingers, and a giant projection appeared on the Demon Castle's wall. Morrigan couldn't see it from where she stood, but judging from the audience's applause, it must have been impressive.

"In this maze, our participants will have to display their magic skills to try to get past the many, many obstacles within. Their goal is to find a special gem that will teleport them to the winners' circle right here in front of us. The first ten people to find the gem and teleport here win!"

The crowd cheered in response, clearly eager to get the show started. Azrael smiled mischievously and then pointed dramatically in the direction of the contestants.

"Now the rules! There's only one rule today—do not kill anyone. Other than that, go wild!" Azrael snickered, and Morrigan could feel bloodlust rising from some of the other contestants.

Is this alright? The only rule is not to kill. But that still allows you to hurt other participants...

She looked at Deziara, hoping her sister would share her worries, but she had a giant smile on her face.

Not you too, Deziara.

"Before anyone objects that I forgot, I shall explain Princess Deziara's boon. At any time during the maze, she has the right to call for me, and I shall go and clear an obstacle in her stead. But this boon can only be used once, so keep that in mind, Princess," Azrael explained quickly. "Now, with the boring stuff out of the way, would the contestants please go and pull a number out of the bag."

A demon woman came up to them, carrying a bag of what sounded like stones. She offered it to them, and everyone took their turns pulling out their stone. When it was Morrigan's turn, she stuck her hand in the bag and pulled a smooth stone with a "7" clearly written on it.

"Those, my dear contestants, are your entry points. Each number corresponds to a different entry point. Do not worry, the maze was designed so you all have equal chances of finding the gems from any entrance."

Morrigan looked at the giant hedge in front of her and saw numbers flickering above the many entrances. She watched as Deziara headed for entrance 1, then proceeded to go to her own starting point. Much to her dismay, that was exactly where Viana was going, too.

"Best of luck to you, youngest sister," she said with a smile, but Morrigan felt the sting of hatred coming from her words.

I hope she doesn't decide to attack me. She probably won't, since there are so many people watching. Or perhaps she just won't do it directly. I'll have to be careful.

As Morrigan stood in front of the giant entrance, she saw the vampire champion approach her. Besides them, two more demons—nobles, judging by how they were dressed—joined them, looking awfully smug and satisfied with themselves.

"It is a pleasure to be in your presence, Your Highnesses." They bowed towards her and Viana, although Morrigan got the feeling that the greeting was meant more for Viana than for her. Her sister returned their greeting with a smile, and they took it as a sign to start buttering her up, singing praises to her power and intelligence.

"So quick to jump at the first opportunity thrown at them." The vampire lady tutted, giving Morrigan a knowing look. She decided to ignore the vampire for now and instead peered into the maze ahead. Tall, bushy walls stretched high up, no doubt with the intention that nobody would be able to look over the edge.

I wonder if it will be possible to just burn through the hedge and move forward that way. Or perhaps somebody who can fly could just fly and scour the maze from the top. Heck, somebody could just climb up. But I doubt it will be that easy—no doubt there's some magic set on it to prevent all those things from happening.

"All of our contestants are in place. Excellent! I wish all of you good luck. Start!" Azrael bellowed, and the contestants rushed into the maze. Viana ran straight inside, the two demon nobles following right after her. Morrigan expected them to separate at the first intersection but was surprised to see that they all went together.

"It appears your elder sister decided to use underlings to help herself get farther into the maze. Why don't we work together as well?" the vampire woman offered, smiling sweetly at her all the while.

"Why? We are supposed to be competing against each other," Morrigan replied, then hurried inside the maze.

The vampire kept pace with her, not put off by her rejection in the slightest. "Because nobody said that we each have to find an individual stone. We can both find the same stone and teleport to the winners' circle. And by working together we'll have a larger array of spells, which could help us overcome different obstacles."

As much as I hate to admit it—she is right. I don't have a wide variety of spells in my arsenal yet, and I can't be sure that I can solve every problem I encounter here. Perhaps it is beneficial to stick together with this woman, at least for the time being.

"Alright, we can work together," Morrigan conceded.

"Excellent! I knew Your Highness would make the wisest choice," the vampire woman said. "By the way, my name is Larissa."

"Pleasure to meet you, Larissa. I am Morrigan Nachtstern," she replied formally, trying to make it clear that she had no intentions of being chummy with this woman.

The two of them continued in the opposite direction of where Viana went, following the path deeper into the maze. But they didn't get far before the ground in front of them shifted, and nasty-looking thorny vines grew out of it, blocking their path. They grew so densely that there would be no way of climbing through it, and crawling over them would likely result in many scratches from the sharp thorns.

"I'll just burn it," Morrigan announced, then threw a fireball at the growth. It easily caught aflame and burned to ash in a matter of seconds, leaving purple smoke behind itself. What surprised Morrigan was the fact that the hedge, which at one point had been connected to the nasty plant, was completely untouched by the flames.

So it is protected by magic. I knew it!

Morrigan was about to walk up to the hedge to inspect it more closely when Larissa blocked her path.

"Your Highness, the fumes from the plant are a strong paralytic. You should not inhale them," she warned.

"Paralytic?"

"Yes. It was without a doubt demongas bramble. The real danger of the plant is the toxin within its thorns. If you were to poke your finger on it or inhale the fumes from the plant, you'd be left paralyzed for several weeks."

Morrigan took a step back from the smoke and covered her mouth. A few more steps and she would have surely inhaled it.

"Don't worry, Your Highness. I'll take care of this," Larissa said, waving her hands around in a fluid motion. The wind rose up and began to flow around the paralytic cloud, moving it higher and higher up.

That's amazing! She is able to control the flow of air so perfectly that all of the gas is being contained. Then again, I probably could have just passed through as a shadow and it wouldn't have done me any harm.

Morrigan nodded gratefully at Larissa, and both women proceeded forward. Once they had passed the area, the vampire woman moved the cloud back to its original place.

"We wouldn't want to give our foes an open route, now, would we?" she explained with a smile.

I wouldn't mind keeping the poisonous cloud up above so nobody can get paralyzed.

Morrigan and Larissa continued through the maze, memorizing

which paths they had already taken. They used one of the Demon Castle's spires as a landmark, moving towards it when possible in order to avoid circling back to the entrance. The vampire woman was doing most of the navigating, however, since Morrigan's sense of direction had not improved much over the years.

At one point, a pitfall trap appeared before them, but it wasn't a real obstacle for either of them, one slipping past it as a shadow and the other just flying over it in her bat form. However, despite the lack of danger, Morrigan felt like they weren't getting anywhere. The castle spire still appeared at the same distance as before, despite them desperately trying to move closer to it.

"Something isn't right," Morrigan said, coming out of her shadow form. "It's like we are stuck in the same place."

Larissa also came out of her bat form, and nodded at her. "Yes, I was also thinking that. We've likely been caught in an illusion."

"Illusion?" Morrigan asked, poking at the hedge wall. It felt real to her.

"Yes, and a very powerful one at that. More likely than not, we've been circling around the same area for a while," Larissa explained, examining the hedge carefully.

"How do we break out of the illusion?"

"There are several ways. One would be to find the caster and either incapacitate them or force them to end the illusion."

This is no doubt Azrael's doing, so we probably won't be able to end the illusion that way.

"And what are the other ways?"

"We could try to block our senses and find our way out of the illusion blind. This, however, could take a long time," Larissa said. "Or we could find an anchor."

Morrigan furrowed her brows. "An anchor?"

"Yes. Something that exists outside of the illusion. If we can hear something or see something outside the illusion, our senses could latch on to the real thing and dispel the rest."

"Shouldn't the castle spire be outside of the illusion?" Morrigan asked.

"Most likely the spire that we see is the one created by the illusion, not the real one," Larissa explained. They paused to think.

What could be something outside the illusion we could latch on to? Perhaps I could call out to Deziara and then I could latch on to her voice as the real thing. But her entry point was rather far away, so it's unlikely that she will be nearby.

"Should we just try calling out to somebody and hope that they respond?" Morrigan suggested.

"We could certainly try."

"Hello! Could somebody answer us?" Morrigan called out.

"Is somebody nearby?" Larissa followed.

For a while there was nothing but silence, and both women called out again. Nobody seemed to answer them, or if they did, Morrigan certainly couldn't hear them. Then, just as Morrigan opened her mouth to try again, a low growl resounded through the area.

CHAPTER 27

GUARDIAN OF THE MAZE

"Well, that's not... ideal," Larissa muttered, having clearly heard the threatening growl.

"No. This is perfect!" Morrigan cheered before calling out again. "We are here! Where are you?"

"Your Highness, I understand that you are confident in your magical abilities, but calling out to a monster like that is dangerous," the vampire woman objected. A louder growl reverberated through the area.

"Haku is not a monster!" Morrigan retorted, then closed her eyes.

I cannot trust anything except for Haku's call. I need to follow it if I want to leave the illusion.

"Haku, I am here! Help me out of the illusion," Morrigan yelled, and the dragon roared back. Larissa seemed apprehensive to follow at first but eventually went after Morrigan. Haku continued calling out to her, and she followed his calls, slowly and carefully moving forward.

Eventually, Larissa spoke up again. "I believe we have left the illusion now."

Morrigan opened her eyes. Before her was a rather unusual scene. Haku was sitting in the middle of a large clearing with a giant red egg in front of him. There were a bunch of other participants in the clearing, most of them huddled in a corner as far away from Haku as possible.

"Dear audience, as you can see, our Crown Princess and several other participants have reached one of the major checkpoints in the maze. Pass a checkpoint and you can be sure that you are getting closer to the gem. Unfortunately, if you cannot pass it, then you either have to look for a different checkpoint or give up altogether," Azrael announced in his amplified voice.

I should have expected something like this. But Haku is one of the checkpoints? I wonder who decided to do that?

"How are you doing, Haku?" Morrigan called out to her friend, who instantly dropped his stern dragon facade and wagged his tail happily. "Azrael set you up as a guard dog in here? How rude!"

"Princess, do not think that just because this is your pet, you'll be able to get a free pass. You still have to complete the task," Azrael warned, but she just strode up to Haku and reached her hand out. The dragon lowered his head, allowing her to scratch the scales under his chin. It was evident that the dragon had no intention of blocking her way.

"What is the task?" she asked curiously.

If I can complete it, I should do so to appeal to the public. If I just walked past Haku, then it probably wouldn't leave a good impression.

"You must open the dragon egg by either hatching it or breaking it," Azrael instructed, and the participants in the clearing began muttering among themselves.

Oh, it's like that time Azrael hatched Haku. I doubt this is a real dragon egg, probably just a magical contraption that was made to react to certain conditions.

"No problem." Morrigan smiled as she extended her arms towards the egg. Hot flames came out of her hands and surrounded it, heating the egg up from all sides. She knew that the temperature required to hatch a dragon egg was extreme, but she doubted it would be required for the competition as well. As Morrigan recalled, there were only a few people who could produce temperatures high enough to hatch one. She wasn't even sure if she could do it yet, despite her high affinity with fire magic.

But before Morrigan had to push her fire magic to its limits, a crack appeared in the egg and it came apart. Inside lay a piece of fire salamander meat, one of Haku's favorite treats. The dragon eagerly took it and swallowed it with great satisfaction.

"Enjoy, Haku! I'm going to continue now." She gave him one last pat on his neck, then ran towards the exit behind him. Larissa followed her, making sure to sidestep Haku. The other contestants, however, were too slow, and by the time they realized that the dragon was distracted, Haku had once again blocked their way.

"You have a truly ferocious pet, Your Highness," the vampire woman commented.

"Haku isn't ferocious. He is actually a big softie," Morrigan retorted.

"He certainly didn't appear that way..."

"He's just shy with strangers, that's all. How do we best continue through the maze? We have reached the spire that we followed before," Morrigan said, pointing towards the tower they had used as a guidance point.

"According to what Azrael said, we shouldn't be able to circle back to the beginning. Perhaps I could try looking from above, although I have a feeling that there'll be magic to block that sort of thing," Larissa said, then turned into her bat form. She flew up carefully, watching the surroundings for any traps. However, at one point it seemed like she was unable to fly any higher.

"Seems like there's a magic seal that prevents anyone from getting above the hedge," she explained once she had turned back into her vampire form.

"How about we follow either the right or the left wall? I heard that this strategy is guaranteed to lead one out of the maze. Besides, we don't have to worry about circling back to one of the entry points now."

"But we are not really looking for an exit, are we? We need to find the gem."

"This way we'll at least know we're not wandering the same path over and over."

"It would certainly be a safer approach. But we'll have to move fast, because this method will take more time."

Morrigan nodded, then took her shadow form while Larissa returned to her bat form. She flew surprisingly fast for such a small creature, but Morrigan had no trouble keeping up with her. At one point, they passed through a trap that shot a flurry of arrows in both directions, but in their alternate forms, it didn't pose a challenge. Larissa just flew as high as the magical barrier allowed her to, and naturally, Morrigan was not bothered by regular arrows in her shadow form.

As they continued on their way through the maze, the girls heard some sort of bickering ahead. Moving closer, it was clear that there was some sort of scuffle going on among the participants.

"Ignore it. We'll have fewer competitors to worry about," Larissa called out, zooming ahead.

I hope that nobody is trying to hurt anybody else. This is supposed to be a fun event, after all.

"Why is scum like you participating in this honorable competition, anyway?" Morrigan heard a male voice sneer from somewhere very close.

"Yeah! Slaves like you should be polishing our boots!"

"No, he's an Overworlder! Scum like him are only good for cleaning the stable and toilets!"

This doesn't sound good at all. They are most likely bullying the elven boy from the Fallen Kingdom.

"Princess, let's go ahead!" Larissa urged, sensing her hesitation.

"You dare to glare at me, you scum! Take this!" There was an audible thump and a pained groan. Morrigan couldn't endure it any longer. She materialized from her shadow form, heading straight for the source of the racket.

"What is going on here?" she called out, seeing one young demon noble restraining Galandir while the other one beat him like a punching bag.

They are doing this in the middle of an event? Really? How petty must you be to do such a thing? To a child, no less.

"Princess Morrigan!" Both nobles instantly straightened, dropping the beaten-up elf to the ground. "It is a most pleasant surprise to encounter you here in the maze!"

Pleasant, my ass. There's nothing pleasant about this. I wish I could just send these bullies to Haku and have them be chased around by him for a bit. That would certainly teach them a lesson. But the whole Underworld is watching, so I need to handle this in a way a princess should. Damned politics!

"What is going on here?" Morrigan repeated, crossing her arms over her chest and glaring at the two nobles. They didn't appear bothered by her hard stance and instead smiled pleasantly at her.

"We were just taking care of the scum. There's no need for you to worry about that, Princess," the taller and lankier noble said, his eyes glinting as if some golden opportunity had just fallen into his lap.

"Indeed. The slave will not bother you any further. In fact, why don't you allow us to accompany you? We will help you overcome any trials and safely deliver you to the gem and the winners' circle. We only ask that you remember our favor in the future." The noble smiled, slowly inching closer to Morrigan.

"He never bothered me in the first place. What bothers me is that two fully grown demons decided to gang up on and beat up a child in what is supposed to be a fun event." Morrigan channeled the ferocity she had seen in her father when he was scolding his subjects.

The nobles flinched back for a moment, but they quickly recovered their smiles. "This child, Your Highness, is an Overworlder. It is a mistake for him to participate in this prestigious event." One of them sneered at Galandir, who was trying to sit up, clutching his injured chest.

Have they broken his ribs? That means they weren't even holding back. If I had any say in this, I'd just send them to prison for a couple of months. Or perhaps years, since demons have such a long lifespan.

Morrigan wanted to go check on Galandir's condition, but she knew that the nobles had to be dealt with first.

"This elven boy is the representative of the Fallen Kingdom, and should be treated as such," Larissa intervened.

"Shut your mouth, vampire! Your lowly kind has no right to talk to us," one of the nobles spat.

"Are you telling me that my father, the king of the Demon Kingdom, made a mistake by accepting these two as champions?" Morrigan said in a low, threatening voice.

The nobles' faces dropped at the mention of the king. "N-No! We would never question His Majesty's judgment!"

"But you just clearly said that it was a mistake to let Galandir participate," Morrigan pressed, taking a step towards them.

"No, we didn't say that!"

"So now you're claiming that I, the Crown Princess, just made that up?"

"We apologize, Your Highness." The two nobles bowed their heads, their teeth clenched together in anger.

Doesn't feel nice to be pushed around by a little kid, does it?

"Leave! And do not make the mistake of thinking that you can decide who deserves and who doesn't deserve to participate in the competition," Morrigan ordered, and the two nobles begrudgingly skulked away.

"You might have just turned them and their families against you," Larissa said, watching the two nobles leave. But Morrigan didn't care for them and instead ran up to Galandir.

"Hey, are you alright?"

"I... I don't need your help!" he snarled, trying to get to his feet.

But the pain proved too much and he fell back to the ground, groaning and clutching his ribs.

"You clearly do." Morrigan crouched next to him, trying to remember what the correct procedure was in case somebody had broken ribs. But before she could come up with anything useful, Galandir pressed his hand against his chest. The spot began to glow with warm light but then dimmed again as the elven boy nearly screamed from the pain.

"What happened?" Morrigan asked, wondering if the movement had shifted the rib and punctured some of his organs.

"Healing magic. He's trying to fix his rib, but the process is incredibly painful. It's best if you give up, boy. No sane person would be able to endure that sort of pain. Just wait here until the healers arrive," Larissa said. But Galandir glared at her and instead focused back on his rib.

Sweat formed on his forehead and he bit into his lip, making it bleed. The light glowed for a while before it proved too much for him, and he removed his hand from the wound.

"Dammit! If only I hadn't exhausted my magic getting past that dragon, I could have shown those assholes and healed myself without any issues," he muttered in a barely audible voice.

So he doesn't have enough magic to heal himself. I could channel some of my magic into him, but it would no doubt cause a horrible stir among demonkind. After all, you're only supposed to give your magic to those you deem to be your equal. Stupid rules.

"Larissa, do you perhaps have a spell that could mask us from view for a short while?" Morrigan asked hopefully, as she didn't want to leave the elf boy to just writhe in pain.

"I do have a spell that allows me to create mist. But why exactly, Your Highness?" the vampire woman asked, her eyebrow raised.

"Because I'm going to give Galandir some of my magic."

CHAPTER 28

RIDDLES OF THE SPHINX

"Are you insane? I don't want your demon father to come and murder me!" Galandir protested.

"I am going to agree with the boy. It is not the best move a princess could make. Not to mention that it could leave you exhausted for the trials still hidden in the maze," Larissa objected.

"Oh, hush. It's a little bit of magic to help him recover. Just create that mist for us real quick," Morrigan said, dismissing their complaints.

Father might not like the idea of me giving my magic to others, but I am certain he's not going to flip out over something like that. It's the other demons that worry me. I do not want to fuel any unsavory rumors, since my position as Crown Princess isn't all that stable.

"As you wish, Your Highness," the vampire agreed with a sigh. After a moment, dense fog settled over the nearby area.

"I already said that I don't want your help!" Galandir hissed like an angry kitten.

"Just settle down and let me help you already," she said, taking his left hand. He tried to pull it away at first, but she held it firmly and began to channel her magic into him. Azrael had taught her how to do that a few years ago so she could power any appliances that required magic for activation, like that water-magic ball Gunna used to fill up the bath.

"Slowly! You're channeling too much too fast," the boy protested, and Morrigan reduced the magic flow to a small trickle. Galandir scowled at her for a moment, then put his right hand back onto his injured rib. The healing light glowed, and his grip on her hands tightened. He squeezed so hard that Morrigan winced from the pain, but she refused to let go, continuing to gently trickle her magic into him. After a few minutes, Galandir's grip loosened.

"I am done now," he announced, pushing Morrigan's hands away.

"You're all healed?" she asked, looking at him in amazement. He got up from the ground and moved his torso left and right, then bent down and straightened back up to demonstrate the results.

That's amazing! To think that there's magic that can heal a broken rib. I mean, I knew healing magic existed, but seeing it firsthand is a different thing entirely.

"We should get going. We've already lost a lot of time on this," Larissa said, reducing the density of the fog but not dismissing it entirely.

"I will guide you to the next checkpoint," Galandir suddenly said, looking straight at Morrigan with a hardened expression.

"You know the way to the next checkpoint?"

"I used wind magic to scour the layout of the maze," he explained briskly, then began walking, not waiting for Morrigan's reply.

"Wait, how does that work?" she asked, catching up to him.

"I'm not telling you. Follow me if you wish to win," the boy said.

He could use a lesson in manners, but I guess this is his way of saying thank you. Well, I'm not passing up the opportunity of finding the checkpoint easily, instead of wandering around like a fool.

"Hey, vampire! Keep up the fog. It'll make things harder for others," Galandir commanded.

"I would have done so even if you didn't ask," Larissa replied, sounding annoyed at the boy.

* * *

They continued through the dungeon at a brisk pace but without altering their forms, as it would apparently be too difficult for Galandir to pinpoint their location if they moved too quickly. This prompted Morrigan to begin asking questions about how exactly he managed to navigate using wind magic, but the boy just ignored her and kept walking.

He probably doesn't want to reveal it so we can't duplicate the method. I wonder how he even does it? Is he just "feeling" the maze out with his wind magic, just like I did with the lava? But that's different. The lava was already there to begin with, but there are no concentrated pockets of wind magic here. Perhaps he can feel the general layout? Or maybe he can find the larger areas. I need to ask Azrael to teach me wind magic later.

As they kept walking through the maze, it was clear that they were effectively avoiding any traps or obstacles, since they hadn't encountered a single one yet. Morrigan was beginning to wonder if they would even be able to find the gem at this rate when Galandir stopped.

"There is a large clearing up ahead, which I think is the second checkpoint. Some large creature is in there, so be ready," he warned. Morrigan and Larissa hardened their expressions, tightening their focus. They peeked around the side of the hedge to see the monster lurking in the clearing.

The moment Morrigan saw the creature, she felt like she had been transported to Egypt. A large monster with a lion's body was lying in the middle of the clearing. It had large, eagle-like wings on its back, but the most unusual feature was without a doubt its head. It was the head of a beautiful woman with distinct Egyptian features and raven-black hair. The sphinx was looking in their direction, its expression unreadable.

"What the hell is that thing?" Larissa whispered, taking a step back.

"I don't know... a chimera of sorts?" Galandir guessed.

"Isn't that a sphinx?" Morrigan asked, but her companions just cocked their heads in confusion.

"A sphinx? I have never heard of such a creature before, and trust me when I tell you that I have encountered all sorts of beasts in my time," Larissa said, narrowing her eyes suspiciously.

Just as she said that, a scream resounded from the clearing as another group of contestants reached it. Morrigan peeked out from behind the hedge and saw that it was Viana's group; one of her demon noble companions had fallen to the ground in shock.

Azrael's amplified voice resounded through the area, startling everyone. "Dear audience, it seems that two of our groups have reached the second checkpoint. I bet many of you are wondering what this unusual creature is."

"That guy is starting to get on my nerves," Galandir noted, looking annoyed.

"How do you think I feel after having to deal with him for ten years?" Morrigan retorted.

"My condolences," the elf boy said solemnly, and Morrigan accepted it with a nod.

"Well, this is none other than the mighty sphinx, master of riddles. If you wish to get past it, you must answer its riddle, or perish," Azrael announced dramatically, then chuckled. "Don't worry, it is merely a magical construct, much like the landwyrm from yesterday."

"If it is a construct, then there's no harm in just killing it, is there?" The infernal hero strode into the clearing, holding a large fireball in each hand. "There's no need to hold back since this isn't anyone's pet."

A shiver ran through Morrigan as she imagined what could have happened to Haku if he had clashed with the infernal. While the dragon was certainly strong, he was still a juvenile, and probably wouldn't be able to overpower a seasoned warrior with a vast magical arsenal.

"You're welcome to try," Azrael cackled in response. The infernal champion didn't wait any longer before unleashing a barrage of fireballs at the sphinx. The construct covered its face with its wings, fireballs hitting the feathers and then sizzling out without doing any damage whatsoever.

"What?" the infernal called out in shock.

"Oh, did I forget to mention? The sphinx is completely unaffected by magical attacks." The demon laughed, and Morrigan could imagine the delighted, smug expression on his face.

"Is that so? If magic doesn't work, then I'll have to beat it physically." The duergar champion came out of the maze and charged straight at the sphinx, brandishing a giant stone axe. However, the construct swatted the axe away with its paw, sending it flying across the clearing. The axe lodged itself in the hedge while its owner looked at it, flabbergasted.

Azrael laughed. "I'm afraid it is also pretty tough physically."

"So how are we supposed to get past him?" Viana complained, having watched the whole scene unfold from the sidelines.

"You answer the sphinx's riddle," Morrigan said, walking out into the clearing and approaching the sphinx. It looked at her, its wise gaze seemingly boring straight into her soul.

This creature... It doesn't have the same mindless stare that the landwyrm construct did. And it looks solid without that crystalline obstruction that the landwyrm had. Could it actually be alive? But why would Azrael lie about it being a construct, then?

"Ping-pong! Somebody has been listening well. To proceed, you must answer the sphinx's riddle. A group is allowed to pass through together, but then you must receive the riddle together as well," Azrael explained, and Morrigan stopped in her tracks, looking back at Larissa and Galandir. They came out of the maze as well and joined her side.

Meanwhile, Viana wasted no time and approached the sphinx first.

"Tell me your riddle!" she commanded, and the sphinx turned its gaze towards her. It stared at Viana for a while, then finally spoke in a beastly sort of voice. It felt like it was a woman's voice and yet at the same time not, like two creatures talking in unison.

"To be me you must not know me, but with me comes true bliss, to unlearn me is to learn another, and without me, you will better know your place."

Everyone stared at the creature, flabbergasted by its words. They didn't seem to make any sense, and even the usually collected Viana let her elegant mask slip for a second.

"That makes no sense," the demon noble by Viana's side called out. The sphinx turned its gaze towards him and he took a step back, intimidated by its unyielding gaze.

"We will take some time to think on the riddle," Viana replied, retreating from the sphinx. It nodded ever so slightly at her and sat down, waiting for another to approach.

"Alright, tell me your riddle, beast!" the duergar called out, and the infernal walked up to stand by his side.

"I shall join you. Two heads are better than one," he announced in a gruff voice. The duergar nodded and looked at the sphinx.

"To keep this, you must first give it to another," it said.

"That makes no sense either!" the duergar complained, stomping angrily against the ground.

"Sphinx, would you kindly tell us your riddle?" Morrigan finally approached it with Galandir and Larissa. The creature once again stared her in the eyes, as if it were able to analyze her mind.

"Tree without roots, bread without taste, live together but not freely, home but needs no place."

It seems nonsensical at first, but if I know anything about these sorts of riddles, it's that they usually have a rather simple solution. It should be a common thing, or a concept that is well known to everyone. Like how "where it walks on four legs in the morning, two during the day, and three in the evening" signifies a human and their lifetime. I just need to piece together what the riddle is trying to represent.

"It must be some sort of large creature," Larissa whispered to Morrigan and Galandir. "A tree without roots could signify its treelike appearance. The bread without taste could mean that its flesh has no flavor, and the part about living together could mean that it has multiple heads. The last part could signify that it could live anywhere, no matter the environment."

"That does make sense, but I do not know of any multiheaded, plantlike creature that could live anywhere," the elven boy protested.

"No, it is not a creature," Morrigan said, shaking her head. "Or at least I don't think it is. The answer should be simple, something everyone would know."

"How do you know that?" Galandir narrowed his eyes, looking at her suspiciously. "Did your demon friend tip you off?"

"What? No! I've just read about riddles before," Morrigan replied. "They are meant to confuse, but the answers are usually simple."

"Do tell us what the answer is if it's so simple."

"I... don't know it..."

"Let's think about it carefully. If the thing that creature is referring to is something everybody knows about, we should be able to figure it out," Larissa said.

As they were thinking, Deziara ran into the clearing, but abruptly stopped when she saw the sphinx.

"What the..." she exclaimed, but stopped herself mid-sentence before saying anything rude. "What is that thing?"

"It's a sphinx. You answer its riddle to get further," Morrigan explained.

"A riddle? Alright. How hard could it be?" Deziara stood in front of the sphinx. "Tell me your riddle."

"I speak without mouth and hear without ears, I have no body but I come alive with the wind," the sphinx said after assessing Deziara for a moment.

"There is no bloody wind in the Underworld," Deziara shot back at the creature, but it did not react to her complaints. She stared at it for a while, then her shoulders slumped. "I had hoped to save this for later, but I guess I have no choice. Azrael, I'd like to use my boon now."

Azrael appeared in the middle of the clearing, looking smug and satisfied.

"Our princess has decided to use her boon. A wise choice. Dearest sphinx, the answer to Princess Deziara's riddle is 'echo.'"

Dumbfounded, everyone looked at Azrael as the sphinx nodded solemnly at the answer and then moved aside, revealing an exit behind itself.

"You may proceed now," Azrael said to Deziara, who nodded, then ran farther into the maze.

"Good luck with your riddles, dear participants. I suggest you think hard," the white-haired demon said before disappearing just as quickly as he had appeared.

Why does this guy always have to make things difficult?

CHAPTER 29

WORKING TOGETHER

The riddles of the sphinx left many participants stumped, muttering among themselves as they tried to figure out the answer.

"What could be a tree with no roots?" Larissa mused.

"Most likely it isn't a tree at all," Morrigan said.

"Something plantlike, perhaps? Or maybe something made from a tree," Galandir added.

"Alright, so let's assume that it is something made out of wood. But how could it also be bread with no taste?"

"It's probably edible then, but doesn't have a flavor."

"A wooden thing that is edible? Perhaps the thing itself is not edible. Perhaps it can merely hold edible things. Or drinkable things. Like a water jug, perhaps," Larissa suggested.

"Those would usually be made from glass or metal, wouldn't they? Although it wouldn't be impossible for it to be made from wood. Alright, if we assume it's a dish of some sort, how does that tie in with the second part?"

"Live together but not freely. Perhaps it may be a chest that holds some treasure. Treasure is usually plundered from various places, so that could be interpreted as not living together freely."

As Larissa and Galandir continued their discussion, Morrigan's thoughts wandered in a completely different direction.

I still think they are taking the things from the riddle too literally. The answer to Deziara's riddle was an echo, so perhaps our riddle could also allude to something seemingly obvious. But what could it be?

Morrigan began thinking of her sister and wondered how far Deziara had already gotten while everyone here was busy trying to decipher these riddles. Part of her felt happy, because even if she didn't win, Deziara would most definitely find that gem.

"Wait... I got it!" Morrigan exclaimed, startling Larissa and Galandir out of their discussion.

"You got it?" The elven boy narrowed his eyes suspiciously. Morrigan grabbed their hands and dragged them in front of the sphinx.

"We know the answer to your riddle."

"State your answer," the beast said solemnly, her eyes focusing on Morrigan.

"Tree without roots, bread without taste, live together but not freely, home but need no place. It is family!"

"You're correct." The sphinx nodded, then moved aside to let Morrigan pass.

"That answer makes no sense," Galandir pouted as they continued running forward.

"No, it does. A tree without roots would symbolize a family tree—"

"Yeah, yeah. Whatever," the boy interrupted. "As long as we got past, that's all that matters."

How rude! This guy could at least not interrupt others while they are speaking.

However, Morrigan said nothing. Their relationship was one of mutual gain, so she would put up with him for the time being. After all, Galandir's skill allowed them to navigate through the maze with ease.

"We won't be able to avoid obstacles going forward. Seems like they have been laid out in a way that you have to pass by at least three of them," Galandir said after slowing down his pace.

"Can you find the gem?" Larissa asked, but the boy shook his head.

"I can only get a general sense of the maze. I can't find something that small."

"Well, if there are obstacles in the way, then the gem has to be hidden somewhere behind them," Morrigan concluded, and the other two nodded.

"Alright, let's take the path with the fewest obstacles," Galandir said, and they continued forward at a fast pace.

Soon enough, they ran into a part of the maze where the hedge wall was replaced with menacing-looking dragon statues. They stood along the whole path, their red eyes glowing with eerie light—as if they were watching.

"Something tells me that just running past them wouldn't be a smart idea," Morrigan noted, looking at the creepy statues. Larissa took a small lock of her white hair and cut it off with her nail as if it were a knife. Then she took the lock and threw it in front of the statues. A red beam of light came out of it, covering the whole area in front of it. Once the light disappeared, so did Larissa's hair.

"I thought this contest was supposed to be a fun event!" Morrigan complained, wondering what exactly had happened to the hair.

Azrael cackled with delight. "And it *is* a fun event! The statues in front of you are completely harmless. They merely teleport you to a random location in the maze."

Being sent to a random location isn't the worst thing that could happen. It might actually get us closer to the gem. But knowing my luck, it'd just teleport us back to the beginning.

"We need to disable these or find a way to block the teleporting light," Larissa noted. She snipped off a few more strands of her hair and threw them at various locations—above the statue, close to the ground, and in the gaps between statues. However, no matter where she threw them, the statue activated and teleported them away somewhere.

"Let me try something," Morrigan said, pulling out a strand of her own hair. She then sent it into the maze while creating a force field around it. However, as soon as the strand touched the red light, it was teleported away.

"So the force field is a bust. Perhaps we need to block it physically?" Galandir said. He created a wall of ice in front of the statue. However, the red beam appeared and a moment later, the wall was gone.

I wonder where that ice wall got teleported to? Would be funny if it blocked Viana's way to the gem. But how does Galandir know so much magic? I doubt that the fallen would hand their magical gem to somebody who they consider to be a slave. Who is he really?

"Seems like it'll teleport away anything that comes into its range. But there definitely must be a way to circumvent it," Larissa pondered, looking over the statues. Morrigan dared to take a step closer to it, and she noticed how its eyes sparkled a little as she did. She stepped back and the sparkle disappeared.

"Could it be that it will teleport away anything it sees?" she guessed.

"Sees?" Galandir wondered.

"I'm going to take a risk," Morrigan said, slipping into the shadows. Before either of her companions could object, she positioned herself in front of the statue. Nothing happened. The statue's eyes remained dull.

"It worked?" Galandir exclaimed.

"So it did. Unfortunately, it means that the Princess will continue on without us," Larissa said with a twinge of regret in her voice.

Morrigan went out of the statue's range and materialized again. "I could take one of you along with me in the shadow form, but two is too much," she said, looking from Larissa to Galandir. The elf boy glared at Larissa, but she just chuckled lightheartedly.

"No need to get prickly, boy. You two go ahead. It'd be shameful for an adult to take advantage of children," she said, then transformed into her bat form. Before anyone could object, Larissa was already out of sight.

"At least that vampire has honor," Galandir noted, then turned towards Morrigan. "Let's not waste any more time."

"I feel bad for just leaving her behind. I could have made two trips," she said.

"By the time you did, other contestants could have already reached the end," the boy said, and Morrigan nodded. She took his hand and turned into her shadow form, pulling Galandir along with her.

The feeling was rather unusual and heavy. Deziara had also given Morrigan a sense of heaviness, but she was a familiar presence, so melting into a single shadow hadn't bothered her. Galandir felt foreign, and he had a bright presence that made it difficult for Morrigan to maintain her shadow form.

As she passed by each statue, the heaviness seemed to grow, and her hold on her shadow form began to slip. Morrigan pushed herself to move faster, hurrying to get past the last statue. As soon as they were out of its range, she instantly materialized out of it, breathing heavily from exertion.

"That was... so weird..." Galandir noted, looking as if he had seen something he hadn't wanted to.

"I am not doing that again," she replied.

"Agreed."

After a brief pause, they continued through the maze in silence. It turned out that Larissa had been the one to keep the conversation going before. With her gone, Morrigan wasn't sure what to talk about. On the other hand, it didn't appear like the elven boy was interested in making conversation, instead focusing on finding the path ahead.

"We're close to the second obstacle, although I think this one won't be much of an issue," the boy said. As they turned the corner,

Morrigan saw that the maze floor had been replaced by a long, deep pit. At the bottom of it, odd dark plants floated in a pool of water, upon which sat some disturbing-looking toads. They were oversized, and their gazes seemed to follow them.

"What are those?" Morrigan asked, pointing at the toads.

"I don't know, and quite frankly, I don't want to find out. Let's just fly over them," he said, a pair of translucent golden wings sprouting from his back. Morrigan turned into her shadow form and was about to go over the pit by crawling along the side of its wall. However, as soon as she approached the edge of the pit, the toads jumped towards her, sticking their large tongues out at her.

"Here, dear audience, we have a rare treat from our Underworld fauna: the famous—or, rather, infamous—shadow-catcher toads. Afraid somebody will break into your house while hidden in their shadow form? Do not worry, for these toads will catch them without any issues and paralyze the intruder with the use of their special venom," Azrael announced, mimicking the voice of salesmen in ads.

I never should have given him access to my laptop. To think that he would be so influenced by things he got to see for only a few days.

"Oh, and these toads will attack anything that moves. So do not make the mistake of thinking that you are safe." The demon cackled, and Morrigan materialized from her shadow form.

"Great. Thank you, Azrael!" she called out in annoyance.

"You're welcome, Princess!"

"I'm surprised the king hasn't disposed of him yet," Galandir whispered.

"Oh, trust me. He has tried. I just made the foolish mistake of stopping him." She sighed and rubbed her temples, trying to think of a way to get across the pit.

I could try levitating myself across it, but it is very likely that I'll drop myself. Levitation isn't very effective on moving objects and living beings.

Perhaps if I were to make a makeshift platform from the ground or those plants in the pit...

Before Morrigan could ponder any further, Galandir hoisted her up into his arms, holding her like a princess. Well, she *was* a princess, but it was still awkward.

"Not sure what you're thinking about, but this will be much faster. You got me over the last obstacle, so I'll get you over this one," he said, then took off. Morrigan was surprised to see that such a scrawny boy had enough strength to lift her and fly as if he were completely unhindered.

"Do you even eat? You weigh nothing," he said when they were about halfway across the pit. The toads were chasing them from below, shooting their slimy tongues at them. However, they were too high for them—even with their long tongues.

"Can't say the same thing about you. You were really heavy to carry in shadow form," Morrigan grumbled.

"Should I drop you?"

"Sorry."

It didn't take long for them to get across the pit and continue on their way through the maze. After a while, Galandir slowed down again and then stopped completely.

"Is something wrong?" Morrigan asked, looking at the concerned boy.

"There's something weird about the next obstacle... it's just a large, empty space," he said, his eyebrows furrowed.

"It's probably a trap of some sort, isn't it?"

"It could be. Wait... I think there is something small in the middle of it?"

Curious, Morrigan peered around the corner to see exactly what Galandir was talking about. In the middle of the maze stood a long, thin pedestal, upon which sat a small gem encased in glass.

Chapter 30

Breaking the Glass

"Is that it?" Morrigan said, looking at the gem sitting on the pedestal. But she didn't dare to rush towards it, as the empty space around it looked like a prime place to put traps.

"Without a doubt. But we should approach it cautiously," Galandir said. He conjured a small ball of ice in his palm, rolling it across the ground towards the pedestal. Much to their relief, nothing happened, but they took slow and measured steps regardless, looking around carefully each time to make sure that no hidden traps or monsters would suddenly jump at them.

At this pace, they slowly reached the pedestal, then took a careful look at it. The gem inside it was a beautiful translucent blue—without a doubt, this was the one they were supposed to find. Morrigan's heart swelled with excitement at the thought that they'd be the first to reach the winners' circle.

"We actually found it," she uttered, and Galandir nodded in response, his hands inching closer towards the glass casing. He grasped the casing firmly and pulled... and then pulled again, and again, and again, without any result.

"It's not coming off," he huffed, desperately trying to remove the glass.

"Let me help," Morrigan said, also taking hold of it. They both pulled at it with as much strength as their little hands could muster, but it wouldn't budge.

"Of course, they couldn't have made it easy…" the elf boy said in annoyance, glowering at the pedestal.

"This is supposed to be a magic maze, so perhaps we have to open it with magic."

"But that's what you had to do with the dragon egg. Would they really make you do the same thing twice?"

"I don't know, but it's worth a shot." Morrigan motioned for Galandir to step back, and the boy obliged. She took several steps back as well and then launched a steady stream of fire towards the glass casing.

If it's not triggered by magic, then perhaps I can just melt the casing.

"Doesn't look like it's doing anything," Galandir commented. "I don't think it's going to pop open magically."

"Then I'll just melt it into a puddle!" Morrigan said, then increased the heat of her flames, channeling more magic into it. The flames turned from bright orange, to purple, to finally blue, signifying the power within them. The surrounding temperature was steadily rising; however, the casing didn't show any signs of giving up.

"Cut it off. You're more likely to set us both on fire at this point," Galandir grumbled, and Morrigan stopped her flames. She walked up to the casing, hoping that it would be at least a little bit deformed, but much to her dismay it remained completely unscathed.

"What is this thing made out of?" she muttered in annoyance.

"Magic-resistant glass, no doubt. There must be a trick to opening it," he said, then pointed at the pedestal. "Look at that."

Letters had appeared right underneath the glass, stretching around the whole length of it.

"If you wish to open me, you must show me true magic first," Morrigan read, then frowned. "How are my flames not true magic?"

"Maybe it just needs a different kind of magic? Let me try," the boy said, motioning for her to step back. She did so and watched how he encased the whole pedestal in a thick layer of ice.

"How does that help? Now it'll be only harder to get to it," she grumbled.

"Oh, shush! Melt the ice, maybe it will have triggered something," he retorted. Morrigan used her flames again, this time to a much more modest degree, and melted away the ice. As she did so, a little sparkle emanated from the glass casing, but it disappeared as soon as the ice had melted.

"Did you see that?" she asked, looking at Galandir. The boy nodded, peering at the glass as if trying to understand its structure.

"It seemed to react when your fire melted my ice."

"Let's do that again!"

Galandir encased the glass in ice again, and Morrigan melted it, making the glass shimmer ever so slightly at the interaction. However, as they repeated the sequence, increasing the strength of their magic each time, it was clear that their efforts were not enough to trigger the glass to open.

"I think it needs more," Morrigan said.

"Should I make the ice layer even thicker?" the blond boy asked, his eyebrows furrowed in contemplation.

"I don't think it'll change much. It has a limited surface area. We should try to make the stream of magic continuous."

"Surface area?" The boy cocked his head quizzically.

"It means that no matter how much ice you pile on top, only a small amount of it will ever touch the casing."

"Okay, but it won't be easy to have fire and ice touch the case at the same time. If you hit my ice too soon, then it'll melt before even touching the glass."

"Can you create something more akin to snow? Make it snow down on the glass steadily and then I'll make it melt?" Morrigan suggested.

"I can. Just make sure you don't make your fire too hot," Galandir warned. He held up his arms, creating a gentle stream of snow that fell upon the case. The initial layer was too thick and quickly covered the glass, but he adjusted it to a more moderate pace.

Morrigan lifted one hand and imagined a gentle candlelight. A tiny warm flame swirling around the glass. Enough to melt the snowflakes that had fallen on top of it, but not enough to affect the still-falling flakes. But the ring of fire she created around the pedestal was too strong and melted the snow long before it reached the glass.

"You need to lower the heat. Imagine something calm and serene," Galandir said.

"I'm trying..." she said, remembering how she had learned to control flames from Haku. The peace she imagined from flying on his back. However, the fact that the dragon was forced to fly in the dark Underworld scenery marred the image, giving fuel to her flames.

"That's better, but the flame is still too strong."

"I'm having trouble imagining something peaceful..." she admitted, pressing her eyes shut and trying to think of her time together with Father and Deziara. They were happy memories, but the constant gloom weighed heavily on these images, like a suffocating prison.

"Think of your fire as a gentle morning sunlight. Wait... you've never seen the sun before, have you?" Galandir said, trying to come up with a different image.

Gentle morning sunlight? I've almost forgotten how it feels. How it wakes up the world, dries the dew from the grass, and warms up the day after the cold night, slowly but surely.

Morrigan's breath steadied, and the ring of flame became a mere gentle flicker. It only melted the snow closest to it, making the glass shimmer with increasing intensity.

"Oh, you're doing it! Keep it up!" Galandir said encouragingly. Morrigan kept her focus by thinking about the warm Overworld sun, and after a few minutes of careful control, the glowing glass case finally disappeared.

"We did it!" Morrigan cheered, pulling Galandir into a quick hug. The boy appeared stupefied by the gesture; however, she was too happy to care and instead ran to retrieve the prize. "Come, let's go to the winners' circle."

"Sure," he said lamely, then put his hand on the gem. It shimmered, and a moment later, both of them were standing in front of the podium with an audience exploding in cheers.

"And the winners of today's task are Princess Morrigan and the champion from the Fallen Kingdom—Galandir! Give them a big round of applause," Azrael announced, and another wave of cheers erupted from the crowd.

Morrigan saw Alphegor applauding with a proud smile on his face. She felt her own heart swell with pride as she waved at the king and then at the audience, who began chanting her name—and her name only. She looked at where Galandir had been standing, but the boy had already disappeared somewhere, leaving Morrigan to claim all the glory for herself.

* * *

You have got to be kidding me. I spent the whole morning and the better part of the day trying to get through that maze and now I have to attend a ball. Who thought this would be a relaxing way to spend the evening?

Morrigan fumed internally as the demon maids worked their hardest to get her ready for the evening ball. Apparently, it was a celebration meant for the ten victorious participants of the competition. She understood that it was probably a grand opportunity for many people, as the king himself was attending, along with the representatives of the foreign delegations.

But she had already had enough of dealing with diplomats and nobles. The only thing Morrigan wanted to do was sink into a bubble bath and rest her tired body. Instead, she had to accept the quick rubdown the maids did and wear the special gown prepared for the winners. These outfits were apparently magical in nature and would adjust their size according to the wearer's body.

It was beautiful in Morrigan's opinion—a white dress with gold and black accents. However, the skirt of the dress was far too puffy for Morrigan's liking, and the many frills felt like they would crawl up her nose. She had managed to remove such clothing from her own wardrobe—after many arguments—but her particular taste was not accounted for in these dresses.

Once Morrigan was dressed, her guards escorted her to a large ballroom on the first floor of the castle, where winners, diplomats, and nobles alike were already chatting and mingling happily. Among them, she spotted Viana, along with the two nobles who had decided to team up with her, Deziara, Larissa, the infernal champion, and the deep gnome champion.

How did the deep gnome make it so far? I was sure that the drow and duergar would have a better chance of getting to the end. I guess you can't judge a book by its cover.

As Morrigan entered the ballroom, trying to keep her head high and her gait straight, she saw her father and Lucius enter from the other side. Their eyes met briefly, and a flicker of a smile passed Alphegor's lips.

"Dear contestants who have made it to the last part of the competition, I am most delighted to see you here in the ancient halls of the Demon Castle! I hope you will enjoy this special evening of the Nachtstern Festival. We are honored to host you in the Demon Castle and we wish you the best of luck in tomorrow's task. Please relax, eat, drink, and dance to your heart's content, for this evening is meant for you!" Lucius announced, and everyone erupted in thunderous applause.

Wait, did Lucius just say dance? That's not mandatory, is it? I haven't had much time for any dance lessons. The only dance I know is the waltz, and I'm pretty sure they don't have it here in the Underworld.

As if somebody had heard her thoughts, musicians began playing a rather energetic tune using violins, saxophones, and something akin to drums. While it was not the first time Morrigan had heard demon music, it always felt odd and mismatched to her ears. Some of the braver guests went to the large open space at the end of the hall. Demon men and women came together and began dancing under the fast rhythm of the music, weaving and moving their bodies like agile cats.

I definitely cannot dance like that. Better lay low and head towards the food table.

Morrigan was sneaking her way through the ballroom, using her small size to avoid unwanted attention, when black feathers suddenly blocked her path. She barely prevented a collision with the fallen girl, Annabell, who appeared shocked by her sudden appearance.

"I'm sorry for almost bumping into you. I didn't notice you." Morrigan curtsied, hoping that this mistake wouldn't cause an international incident.

"Oh, n-no! Don't apologize! I... I was trying to find you," she said in a meek voice. Her parents were nowhere near Annabell, but Morrigan saw their black wings somewhere on the other side of the hall, where diplomats were gathered together in a dense cluster.

"Oh, really? Was there something you wanted?" she asked, and the girl flinched. Morrigan wondered whether she was too direct, and was thinking of how to soften her words when Annabell spoke up.

"Yes, I just wanted to tell you how amazing you were during the competition today!" she blurted out, her cheeks tinged red from embarrassment.

Morrigan blinked, stupefied by her sudden enthusiasm. "I... Well... Thank you," she stammered awkwardly.

"Would you please t-tell me how you got the courage to do all those things?" Annabell asked, her eyes sparkling with barely contained excitement. "You are not much older than I am and yet you can do such brave things."

It was Morrigan's turn to blush, and she wondered how best to answer. Her mind was drawing a blank.

"I just tried to do my best. Most of it was done out of instinct," she replied somewhat awkwardly.

"Really? That makes it even more amazing! The way you faced that landwyrm the other day was nothing short of a miracle. I could never do something like that. It looked so scary!"

"It *was* scary. The only thing I thought of was that I didn't want to get caught by it. So I just ran from it as fast as I could."

"That's so amazing! And today when you opened the glass case with magic—that looked so beautiful!"

"It wasn't just me. Galandir also helped." Morrigan chuckled, and Annabell cocked her head in confusion.

"Who is Galandir?"

"The champion from your kingdom," she replied, somewhat stupefied by her question.

"Oh, you mean Slave Thirteen. It was only natural that he would do as you ask—he is a slave, after all."

Slave Thirteen? This girl doesn't even know Galandir's name? But if they care so little for him, then why would they name him their champion? This is getting weirder and weirder.

CHAPTER 31

DANCE WITH THE KING

It turned out that Annabell was not the shy girl Morrigan initially thought her to be. Once she became entranced in conversation, she kept going. And going. And going. Initially, the fallen girl was raining praise at Morrigan; then the topic switched to the competition in general, and later Annabell was explaining the difference between her pet arachnoids—a sort of spider monster.

"They have the cutest little black eyes and they look at you so intelligently. Truly, arachnoids are the most amazing creatures on Doppelta," she gushed, completely unaware that the corners of Morrigan's lips were beginning to twitch.

Somebody, please save me! I don't think I can endure any more "lessons" on arachnoid physiology.

Deziara's familiar form passed through Morrigan's peripheral vision, and she turned towards her, hoping to find salvation in her sister. However, before she could truly catch her, Deziara disappeared somewhere into the crowd.

So much for that escape route. Just how much longer do I have to listen about spiders? They'll be showing up in my nightmares at this point.

"And did you know that their pincers secrete a special type of venom that can..." Annabell carried on unperturbed even as the whole hall went silent, their gazes turning towards the far side of the ballroom, where Alphegor was standing. Morrigan gently poked the girl, who looked around dumbfounded at first, then blushed and quickly shrank back, muttering a quick apology.

"Dear contestants! I want to congratulate you all for getting this far in the competition. I wish you all luck in tomorrow's performance and invite you all to dance to your heart's content. As a reward for your hard work, you may request a dance from anyone within this hall," the king announced with a smile.

Morrigan felt cold sweat form on her hands as the attendants' eyes went from Viana, to Deziara, then to her. As the Demon King's daughters, they were the most desired prizes in the ballroom. One of the quicker demon noblemen was already bowing before Viana and asking her for a dance, while a few more were approaching Deziara and Morrigan.

No, no, no, I can't let all these important people see me fumble on the dance floor. I need to find a way to not dance. Would it be all alright if I just pretended to be tired and left? It's not exactly a lie. That probably isn't the best solution, but it's better than becoming a complete fool in front of everyone.

Another demon nobleman was bowing in front of Deziara, to which she responded with an elegant nod and extended her hand for him to take. While she could be brusque and even tomboyish at times, Deziara was still a princess, and had proper etiquette drilled into her. She already had plenty of dancing lessons, so something like this wouldn't be a problem for her.

As one of the demon noblemen approached Morrigan, she realized that her time was short. She needed to act or become a laughingstock. From the other side of the room, she saw her father looking—no, glaring—at the approaching nobleman, who was completely unaware of the death stare directed at him, and an idea crossed her mind.

Morrigan decisively strode through the ballroom, ignoring those who wished to approach her for a dance. She headed straight towards Alphegor and then curtsied in front of him.

"Your Majesty, would you please dance with me?" she said with a smile. The king stared at her for a moment and then smiled, extending his hand towards her. As she took his hand, she saw him doing his best to keep a calm expression, although the corners of his lips were twitching upward from happiness.

"Of course," he announced loudly as he put his arm on her waist and held her right hand firmly. Those who had previously tried to approach Morrigan instantly shrank back. She doubted that any of them would have enough nerve to ask her for a dance after she had danced with the Demon King himself.

"Father... I can't dance..." She whispered so only Alphegor could hear.

"Do not worry. I'll take care of it." He smiled at her. "You could have just told me you were tired, but I am glad you've decided to dance with me."

"I was thinking of doing that, but I figured it would be more impressive if I asked for you to dance," she whispered.

"Right you are, little one." Alphegor chuckled, and the song began to play. The king instantly took a firm lead in the dance, guiding Morrigan by not only using his hands but also some sort of magic. It felt like she had become an extension of her father as he twisted and turned in perfect rhythm with the music. The whole ballroom looked at them with awe, nobody daring to dance with them taking the center stage.

Despite Morrigan not knowing the dance, she actually enjoyed it. Alphegor guided her without any issues, not allowing her to make any mistakes, instead taking absolute control of the situation. Once the song came to an end she found herself breathing heavily, but it was a pleasant sort of tiredness.

"Thank you so much for the dance, Father!" She gave him a deep curtsy.

"It was my pleasure," he replied. As soon as Morrigan moved away from the king, Viana strode towards him with resolute determination, her previous partner completely forgotten.

"Father, may I request a dance as well?" she said boldly, then gave Morrigan a sharp look.

"Of course you may," Alphegor replied, taking Viana's hand. She appeared a bit surprised at first, but then smiled shyly. This smile seemed different from the ones Morrigan was used to seeing. Those were just polite smiles that she wore to please people. But *this* smile, this one was genuine. And Morrigan thought it made her look beautiful.

However, she wasn't about to remain in the ballroom and wait for somebody to muster the courage to ask her for a dance. Instead, she headed straight to the open door that led out into the gardens. Some people were already gathered outside, taking a breath of fresh air between the night's festivities. Morrigan didn't want to remain among them, and instead headed deeper inside the gardens.

Nobody will mind if I disappear now, right? I went there, I socialized, and I danced with Father. Surely that's enough.

Haku's familiar growl resounded from somewhere nearby, and Morrigan headed towards it. She was worried that perhaps some of the guests might have gone too close to the dragon and agitated him. But as she got closer, she realized those were not angry growls; rather, they were the growls Haku made when he was curious about something.

I wonder what has caught his interest.

"Good dragon! Look at your beautiful scales," Morrigan heard Galandir say as she peeked from behind one of the bushes to observe the scene. The elven boy had climbed—or perhaps flown—inside Haku's enclosure and had his hand extended towards the dragon. Haku looked a bit apprehensive, but made no move to stop the boy from approaching.

"That's impressive. Haku usually doesn't like strangers approaching him," Morrigan said before momentarily turning into a shadow to get through the surrounding fence.

Galandir flinched back and glared at her. "Shouldn't you be twirling around on the dance floor like a good princess?"

"Shouldn't you be doing the same?" she retorted, then went up to scratch the scales under Haku's chin. The dragon purred happily, leaning into her touch.

"I can't believe it. He actually is your pet dragon."

"Why wouldn't he be? You thought Azrael was lying?"

"Yeah."

"I... I honestly can't blame you for that. But Haku is my dragon through and through. I watched him hatch," Morrigan said proudly, patting Haku's neck.

"So he's never actually seen the blue skies," Galandir said, looking at Haku with eyes filled with sadness.

"No," Morrigan admitted. Her gaze fell to the dark ground beneath her feet.

"Poor guy. You said his name was Haku?" Galandir moved closer to Haku, taking slow, careful steps. He held his arm out in front of him, reaching towards the dragon. Haku appeared a bit unnerved at first, but Morrigan patted his neck, soothing him. "I bet you'd love to fly freely, wouldn't you? To soar in a sky with no limits."

Galandir's expression was gentle as he looked at the dragon, who lowered his head and cautiously sniffed at the boy. He inched closer and closer until Haku's snout touched the elven boy's hand. Morrigan could see the excitement glittering in Galandir's eyes, a wide, boyish grin spreading on his face.

"Haku gets to fly often here," Morrigan argued weakly, but there was no strength behind her voice.

"It's not the same and you know it, Otherworlder," Galandir retorted, rubbing the scales on Haku's snout. The dragon snorted but didn't seem to mind the gesture, continuing his thorough inspection of the elven boy. Morrigan, on the other hand, was frozen in place, barely able to keep a calm expression.

"Otherworlder? Is that how you refer to people in the Underworld?" she retorted, trying to keep her composure, despite her racing heart.

"Don't play dumb. You know how the sun feels. You've seen it before, and not for a mere brief moment. The flame you created perfectly mimicked the morning sunlight. A true Underworld princess wouldn't be able to do that," he said nonchalantly, looking for the spot underneath Haku's chin that Morrigan had scratched before. As soon as he found it, Haku purred with delight, accepting Galandir as a new friend.

"You..." she uttered, unsure of what to say. It felt like the whole incident with Asdeus and Faenor was repeating itself again. For a moment, she wondered whether she should just call for Azrael and nip the problem in the bud. But seeing Haku lowering his head to the ground—an invitation to play—and Galandir smiling back at him with a wide, childish grin dispelled such thoughts.

"It must be hard. You've been trapped in the Underworld for longer than I," he said. He looked her straight in the eyes, his eyes portraying pain and suffering a child of such age shouldn't have lived through.

"I'm not trapped," she objected, feeling a bit offended by his pity.

"I suppose deluding yourself into thinking that must make it easier. But don't you want to feel the warm rays of the sun again?"

"The Underworld has given me something more than just the sun. It gave me a family."

"The Underworld took away my family," Galandir said, and Morrigan flinched back. His eyes were filled with hatred and sadness, and she realized that the boy would no doubt seek revenge for those he had lost.

"I'm sorry…" she stammered, unable to hold his gaze for any longer.

"If you are truly sorry, then make a change."

"What?"

"You're the Crown Princess now, aren't you? The next ruler of the Demon Kingdom. If there's anybody who can make a change and anybody who understands that changes need to be made, then it is you, Otherworlder," the elven boy said, then turned towards Haku. "And I suggest you start by freeing your dragon."

"I'm not just going to release Haku!" She clung to her draconic friend, who, sensing her distress, covered her protectively with his wing.

"This dragon is ready to give his life for you, yet you are denying him his birthright—his freedom. You know he'll never thrive in the Underworld. He will slowly wither away and become a husk of what he could be," Galandir said, then turned to leave.

"Wait, you can't—"

"I have no intention of exposing you, Princess. I'm not foolish enough to believe it would ever do me any favors," he said dismissively. He flew out of Haku's enclosure, heading towards the castle.

Haku jumped up and down excitedly, wanting to follow the boy, while Morrigan just stared at his retreating form, dumbfounded. She looked at Haku, who was spreading his wings, ready to take off and fly.

"Would you really be happier if you were free? Away from me?" she asked the dragon, who jumped up in the air and began circling around the Demon Castle. It took him no time at all to do a full lap around the castle, and she realized that the Underworld indeed might be too small for this magnificent creature.

CHAPTER 32

TALENT OF THE UNDERWORLD

The fifth day of the festival came with a new wave of excitement, as it was the last and most important day. Morrigan donned a new beautiful kimono-style dress. Its black color made a stark contrast to Morrigan's light skin, while the lava flower motif complemented her red hair.

She sat on a special podium made specifically for the last remaining contestants, Deziara sitting on her right while Viana sat on Deziara's right. The podium was positioned on the right front side of the stage that had been used the previous days, while a crowd of enthusiastic watchers were excitedly chattering among themselves and occasionally stealing glances in their direction.

"Dear audience, we have reached the final day of our wonderful festival, and also the last day of the competition. And how better to end it than with a wonderful performance where everyone has a chance to show off their talents!" Azrael strode across the stage, talking in his amplified voice and looking exactly like the big show hosts Morrigan had seen on TV.

I wonder if he has seen some of those popular talent shows. I don't really remember what he was watching while we were on Earth.

"Of course, we need to determine a winner, and to do that I have gathered a council of judges," Azrael said. He pointed towards a different podium that was set up on the other side of the stage, right across from the participants. "Among our judges, we have representatives of our foreign delegations, our King's four beautiful consorts, and none other than His Majesty himself."

That has got to be the most biased group of judges I have ever seen. Viviana and Lady Lily are there too. It's quite obvious they are voting for their daughters, while Father will probably vote for me. The representatives will no doubt vote for their champions. Although the winner is likely to be a demon, since the remaining two consorts will vote for one of us princesses.

The audience, however, didn't seem to have any issues with the judges, and greeted them with applause. Or more likely was that nobody dared to show their disdain since the king was one of the judges. Would anyone even dare to oppose his vote and vote for somebody else? Consorts could probably get away with it, but what about the diplomats? Morrigan prayed that her father wouldn't try to intimidate them.

"Now, let's get this started!" Azrael cheered as he shot sparks of lightning from his fingertips, making the crowd go wild. "We'll begin with the participant who finished last in the maze and then move our way up to the winners. So would our lovely vampire Larissa kindly take the stage?"

Azrael retreated from the stage with a flourish, and Larissa gracefully strode over to take his place. The men in the crowd couldn't take their eyes off her, staring unabashedly at her beautiful form, which was accentuated by the long black dress she wore.

"If I may request some music," she said, addressing the group of demon musicians who sat on the side of the stage. They nodded, no doubt already well aware of what she wanted them to play, and began. A melodious tune began playing, the violin taking the lead among the instruments, and Larissa began to dance.

As soon as she began moving, Morrigan became entranced. She

moved so fluidly, so perfectly along with the music that it felt like Larissa had become the music itself. She embodied it perfectly as her body twisted and turned in a delicate and beautiful balance. But all too soon the song came to an end, and she stopped, her piercing red eyes looking at the audience.

There was a moment before everyone realized that it was over and then the crowd erupted into cheers. The men were especially enthusiastic, and Morrigan noticed that even her father was applauding, his gaze glued to Larissa.

"Father is liking this a bit too much," Deziara grumbled.

"Her dance was very good," Viana said, but it was clear that she didn't want to admit that.

"We need to keep her away from Father. She's too good," Morrigan said, and both of her sisters agreed with a firm nod. A vampire concubine was the last thing they needed in the Demon Castle.

Larissa left the stage, escorted by thunderous applause. The next participant was the infernal champion, whose fiery form attracted everyone's attention in a different sort of way. Morrigan looked at him with deep curiosity and wondered what sort of talent he would display.

The infernal snapped his fingers, and a little infernal child ran onto the stage, holding a large box in his hand. The boy put it in front of the champion, then with a bow, and with what Morrigan assumed to be a smile, left the stage. The infernal broke the lid open and turned the box, showing its contents to the audience. It was sand.

"Why is he showing us sand?"

"Is he going to do something with it?"

"This is disappointing."

The audience muttered in dissatisfaction, but the infernal didn't appear put off by their reaction. Instead, he jammed his hand deep inside the box. When he finally pulled it out, the sand within had formed into what looked like molten glass.

He began molding the molten glass as if it were modeling clay. First, he formed an elongated body with what looked like a tail, then he grabbed more sand from the box and melted it, putting the resulting blob on the figurine's head. Then he formed the wings, the legs, and finally used his fingernails to perfect the little details on the dragon.

As he revealed the fragile little dragon statue to the judges and the audience, everyone began clapping. It wasn't the same sort of applause that Larissa got, but it still was a good reaction. Morrigan was applauding the most enthusiastically of them all.

"What are you so happy about? He's your competitor," Viana grumbled.

"But that is amazing! He just made a dragon sculpture out of glass in such a short amount of time. That must have taken a lot of practice before he managed to perfect it," Morrigan gushed, her eyes glued to the little glass statuette.

"Oh, please. He's an infernal—melting sand into glass is no big deal for them. Their whole country survives from the glasswork," Viana retorted, not looking impressed in the slightest.

You really can't appreciate the finer things in life. I still think it was really impressive. Not sure if he beat Larissa's dance, but it certainly is a close call. Unfortunately, I don't think the majority of the crowd understands such complexities.

The next one to perform was the little deep gnome champion. He was holding an instrument that resembled bagpipes and looked really eager to play. However, as soon as he began blowing the instrument, the whole crowd, Morrigan included, covered their ears at the loud screeching sound. It sounded like somebody had grabbed a metallic pot and was grating the bottom of it with a fork and then added a trumpet into the mix.

"That is quite enough," Alphegor's voice boomed over the grating noise, making the deep gnome jump up in surprise and stare at the king with fear.

"Let's move on to the next performance," Azrael said awkwardly, shooing the deep gnome away from the stage, who ran off, his cheeks red from embarrassment. Morrigan had expected the deep gnome diplomat to be mad at this, but instead, he looked relieved.

Even the diplomat didn't like it, so this is not something that deep gnomes would enjoy. But why send him to represent your race if you knew he couldn't perform well? Did they expect him to do something else?

But the question remained unanswered as the next participants took their turns on the stage. The demon nobles Viana had gone with into the maze both performed some sort of sword dance, displaying various sword techniques Morrigan knew nothing about. But the audience appeared impressed by their display, so she had to accept that they did well enough.

Then it was Viana's turn to show her talent. The audience seemed to be leaning forward as they watched her walk onto the stage, her violet hair flowing behind her like a veil. One of the demon servants brought her a violin, which she hoisted onto her shoulder, then began playing without hesitation.

The song Viana performed was a well-known and loved tune that Morrigan had heard before. It was often played during official parties and was associated with royalty and their strong rule. But although Viana's play was great, Morrigan couldn't force herself to be moved by it. It was as if the song were mechanically played by a robot rather than a live person.

Once Viana's song was done, the demons in the crowd went wild, cheering and praising their princess. Lady Viviana appeared especially satisfied, applauding for her daughter without reserve.

"Was I the only one who thought that something was missing?" Deziara whispered, leaning close to Morrigan.

Morrigan nodded in agreement. "I don't think her heart was in it."

"So odd. It was perfect, and yet I couldn't bring myself to like it."

"Maybe it's just because we know how Viana really is," Morrigan said with a shrug.

"Maybe. Well, it's my turn next, so wish me luck," Deziara said, then stood up from her seat.

"Good luck," Morrigan called out. She watched Deziara walk towards the stage, meeting Viana halfway through. Viana appeared very smug and satisfied with her performance, giving Morrigan a condescending look as she sat down in her place.

"That is how one is supposed to perform," she said. Morrigan decided not to reply, and instead concentrated on Deziara. She had a good feeling about what she'd do. It was a well-known fact that Deziara was an incredible dancer, but would her dance outperform Larissa's? The vampire woman had the mature allure that Deziara still lacked.

However, as soon as the music began playing and Deziara's body sprang into motion, Morrigan's doubts disappeared. Her fluid and agile movements exuded such confidence and strength that it felt as if her body were the one that created the music rather than just moving along with its rhythm. Not to mention that some of Deziara's moves were nearly acrobatic in nature, as she moved her body at angles that a normal demon definitely could not achieve.

Once her dance was over, the ovation from the crowd was no less than it had been for Larissa. But the strongest praise of all was the proud smile on Alphegor's face as he applauded for Deziara, whose cheeks flushed a bit as she curtsied for the audience, soaking in their cheers. Even Viana, who had not applauded for anyone before now, clapped for Deziara—if only a few times.

"You did great!" Morrigan said as Deziara returned to her seat.

She snickered. "Hehe, now we won't need to worry about that vampire woman."

"Indeed, you did well," Viana admitted, and both younger sisters stared at her in disbelief. "Close your mouths, you two. It is unsightly for a princess!"

The girls laughed happily before turning their attention back to the stage, where it was Galandir's time to perform.

I wonder what he can even do to impress the audience. As a young boy, he wouldn't have had the time to hone any talents like others did. Even I have an advantage over him, since I've had time to hone my art skills in the human world. I just hope he doesn't fail like the gnome.

It was clear that nobody was expecting much from him, a large portion of the audience chattering among themselves instead of paying attention.

"Could you amplify my voice?" he asked Azrael.

"Sure thing, buddy," Azrael said, then waved his hand. Judging by his snicker, the demon also wasn't expecting much from the boy. But then Galandir began singing, and the whole crowd went completely silent.

CHAPTER 33

KING'S PORTRAIT

The moment Galandir began singing, the crowd went completely quiet, surprised by what they were hearing. A voice so pure, melodious, and beautiful that it contrasted with everything that the Underworld was, like warm sunshine after a long winter. Morrigan couldn't understand the words he was singing, as they were in the elven language; however, the emotion and meaning behind them were clear.

It was a song about freedom and his yearning for it. His voice was filled with the deepest sadness, overtaking Morrigan's senses completely as she felt her very soul being touched by his performance. However, the sadness was not the only thing she could feel—there was also unyielding strength and determination.

The words Galandir had told her the other night only strengthened his song, and she felt a strong resolve form within herself. A strong desire to change things—to make them better. As this desire formed within her, Galandir's song came to a close, leaving complete silence behind.

He didn't bow or smile at the audience like the other contestants had. Instead he just left the stage without a word and went back to his seat. Nobody applauded. Nobody said anything. Only when Azrael spoke did the crowd awaken from its trance.

"Al-Alright, let's move on to our last contestant, then—Princess Morrigan!"

It took a moment for Morrigan to realize that it was her turn to perform. She wanted to applaud Galandir for his song, but the boy had already disappeared from the stage. The audience turned their attention to her and cheered, encouraging her. Morrigan put on her polite mask and got up, walking towards the stage with measured steps. Her heart began to beat fast as she once again found herself at the center of everyone's attention.

It's alright, just take a deep breath and relax. You'll do just fine.

As Morrigan stepped onto the stage, the gazes from the audience seemed to pierce into her like arrows. It felt like she could barely breathe under the pressure.

I can do this, just be calm.

"I-I'd like to request my supplies," she announced, trying to keep the shaky smile on her lips. Gunna emerged from behind the stage, first bringing out an easel with a canvas already set upon it and then bringing Morrigan all the paints, brushes, water, and a palette.

"You can do it, Lady Morrigan," the dwarf nanny whispered as she handed her the supplies. There was an intrigued sort of muttering in the crowd.

"Is she going to paint?"

"She's a child. It's normal for children to enjoy painting."

"But shouldn't a princess show something a bit more impressive?"

Morrigan did her best to ignore the comments, but she felt herself being constrained by them. She began doubting whether it was a good idea to show her artistic talent for the whole Underworld to see. Demons weren't big enthusiasts for art, so perhaps it was a mistake.

She turned to look at the audience and saw her father sitting in front of everyone. His eyes were sparkling with excitement as he watched her every move. He wanted to see her paint, and this knowledge settled Morrigan's nervous heart. She looked towards the contestants' podium and saw that Deziara had the same sort of excitement in her eyes.

It doesn't matter what all of these people think—as long as Father and Deziara and other people who are close to me support me, I can do this.

"And now I'd like to request for His Majesty to come and pose for me," she said with a smile, looking her father straight in the eyes. Without a moment's hesitation, the king stood up and strode onto the stage.

"I shall oblige your request," he announced, then snapped his fingers. A dark throne with red upholstery, the same one that usually sat in the throne room, appeared on the stage and Alphegor sat down on it, looking as kingly as one ever could. The crowd had gone quiet, but Morrigan couldn't tell whether it was the good kind of silence or the judgmental kind.

There's no need to worry about them. Just do what you do best, Morrigan.

The easel was positioned in a way that the audience could see everything that she was doing. Morrigan, however, had her eyes only on her father. She took a deep breath and then began.

First, I'll begin with the background. The black dragon ornament makes for a really nice black background, so I can just paint the whole canvas black.

She took a large brush, applied a generous amount of black paint on the palette, then painted the whole canvas black with large, generous strokes. Then she mixed the black color on the palette with white, creating a dark gray color, which she used as a base for the throne.

Alright, now to set up the basic form for father. He's wearing the deep purple robes that are customary for the Nachtstern Festival, so that will make it easier to give the whole painting a "royal" feel.

She took the purple paint and mixed it with a bit of black, making it richer, and then painted the basic contours of her father's body and outfit. Afterward, she used light gray for his skin and a rich red for his hair.

That is a good base. Now it's time to start defining shadows.

"That is cute," somebody whispered in the crowd.

"My children also like drawing. It seems that royal children are not so different from normal children."

"Shouldn't a princess be a bit better than normal children?"

But their words couldn't bother her anymore, as Morrigan was already in her own world. She began by defining the background—adding more shadows to the dragon ornament, accentuating the scales and defining the shape of the throne, making it appear three-dimensional rather than just a plain shape.

Okay, this is shaping up nicely. Now to the main part. I need to make sure that Father is painted in the best way possible.

She looked past the canvas, taking in every detail of her father's appearance. She measured how the colors of his robes appeared in the strong stage lights. She took in how the features of his face interacted with each other, making a single whole. She admired the strength that he exuded by merely sitting on a throne.

Her hands seemed to move of their own accord as she mixed one color after the next, matching the tones, creating deeper shadows and slowly bringing the painting to life. The fabric of her father's attire became more detailed, the face on the canvas reflected the same one that sat in front of her, and the strands of hair gave volume and lifelike beauty to the portrait.

The audience had gone completely quiet. Morrigan could feel them watching her every movement.

Now it's time for the best part—lights!

Morrigan put a generous dollop of white paint on the palette and began applying light to the various elements in the painting. First the scales for the ornament in the background, but not enough to bring much attention to it. Then the almost metallic reflection of the throne, the shine of Alphegor's hair, and finally the reflection in his eyes, which looked at Morrigan as she painted.

Finally, Morrigan took the smallest brush and began applying the final touches to the painting—the darkest of shadows, the motif of Alphegor's kimono. She defined his facial features even further and added the ridges on his horns. Once that was done, she gave the painting one last look, then nodded with satisfaction.

"It is complete!" she announced, stepping aside to show her masterpiece to the audience. They stared at it in amazement, taking in the details she worked so hard on.

"I-It looks just like the king..."

"I can't believe that the little princess could create something like this."

"But will His Majesty accept it? He's rejected every single portrait that has been made for him before."

Wait... what?!

The last comment threw Morrigan off, and she looked to her father for explanation. But before the king could get up to look at the painting, Azrael appeared on the stage.

"Demons, demonesses, and guests, you've seen it firsthand—the artistic talent that Princess Morrigan possesses. The question is, will it finally be the one portrait that our King accepts? We all know that no artist has ever been up to His Majesty's standards," Azrael said, and Morrigan felt herself break into cold sweat.

I've never heard of this! Father even asked me to paint him once, so I couldn't even imagine that he would have rejected artists before. But he has always praised my paintings, so it'll be alright. Right?

Alphegor got up from the throne and strode towards the painting, his gaze stern. She almost began feeling nauseous but then noticed a small smile appear on his lips. As he finally looked upon the painting, the smile only grew wider and wider, turning into the same fatherly smile she was so familiar with.

"Those previous artists clearly had no idea what they were doing. This is what a portrait should look like," the king announced, and the crowd went completely wild, cheering, applauding, and hollering at the top of their lungs.

"You heard it from the demon's mouth himself, folks! The king has accepted the Princess's painting!" Azrael cheered as well, and everyone began chanting Morrigan's name. The sudden positive change made her flush from embarrassment.

"Thank you..." she muttered, and after a quick curtsy, she returned back to the contestants' podium. Deziara was already expecting her, her eyes brimming with excitement.

"Morri, when did you get this good? I knew you could paint well, but this is something else entirely!"

"I practiced drawing Father a lot. In the evenings when he'd work, I'd sketch him and then try to paint that the next day," Morrigan explained. Creating a painting so quickly was only possible once you already knew exactly what you were painting. If she had painted somebody besides her father, the result would have been vastly different.

"That practice clearly paid off. That's the best painting I've seen in a long while," Deziara said, then gave Morrigan a quick side hug.

"Alright, settle down, everyone. All of our participants have shown us their talents, so now it is time for us, or rather the judges, to determine the winner!" Azrael announced, moving to the stage's center.

Everyone turned their gazes towards the judges, Alphegor having rejoined them—although the king's gaze was still glued to the portrait that stood in the center of the stage. Morrigan wondered whether she should have taken it with her when she left the stage, but it was too late to do that now.

"To determine the winner, we're going to do something simple—a vote. Each judge will vote for their favorite performance. The person who gets the most votes wins the competition, earning themselves a boon from the king, the shadow ruby, and a nice stack of gold," Azrael explained, then turned towards the judges. "Now, let's begin with our delegation representatives."

"I vote for Larissa," the vampire diplomat announced.

"Princess Deziara," the duergar diplomat said, although it clearly pained him that their champion hadn't made it to the last task.

"Princess Morrigan," the drow representative said, and Morrigan's heart fluttered with excitement at the mention of her name.

"Princess Morrigan," the deep gnome diplomat agreed. Apparently, they were too embarrassed to support the performance of their champion.

"Lionell," the infernal representative said curtly, and it took a while for Morrigan to realize that he was talking about the infernal champion, as she had never pinned down his name.

"Wonderful answers from our wonderful judges. But before we go any further, I'm afraid we're going to have to take a little intermission. We've been enjoying the show for a while now, and I'm sure my dearest audience could use a break. We'll resume our vote in twenty minutes."

Everyone groaned in disappointment, but it was undeniable that the competition had gone on for quite a while. Begrudgingly, Morrigan, Deziara, and the other participants got up from their seats and went to get some refreshments.

CHAPTER 34

WINNER

After the intermission, everyone eagerly returned to watch the conclusion of the competition. Some people had never bothered to leave, worrying that they would miss it. Morrigan was on pins and needles the whole time, doing math in her head and wondering if there was any chance for her or Deziara to win. Part of her just wanted to win, another part wanted Deziara to succeed, and there was a little bit of her that hoped Galandir would win, as his performance had truly touched her heart.

"Is everyone ready to continue the vote?" Azrael took command of the competition again, and the crowd responded with a loud cheer.

Azrael would really make a great showman. It's a shame there's no TV in the Underworld. Although... there are these projection crystals, so perhaps something akin to TV could be created through magic. I'd need to understand it more to make any actual conclusions.

"Alright, Prime Minister Heinspiel, I believe it is your turn to vote," the white-haired demon said.

"I vote for the fallen champion, of course," he answered curtly. Morrigan wished that he would have voted for Galandir because he believed in his talent, but obviously, it was only because he was representing the Fallen Kingdom. After all, he didn't even bother to say his name.

"Wonderful. Now it's time for our lovely consorts to cast their vote!"

"I'm voting for my daughter, although I do wish I could cast a vote for Princess Morrigan as well," Lady Lily said forlornly.

"I'm afraid it's one vote per judge, Lady Lily. But I do understand your sentiment." Azrael chuckled, then turned his gaze to the third consort, Henrietta. She was a demoness with short blonde hair and blue eyes, a real beauty. However, Morrigan rarely ever encountered her, as she was very withdrawn and rarely left her room.

"I vote for Princess Morrigan," she said briskly, not even sparing Azrael a glance. This surprised Morrigan a bit, but then again, Lady Henrietta's daughter hadn't entered, so it was clear she would choose one of the princesses.

"I vote for Princess Deziara," Lady Julia said, still sporting her usual cute pink attire, standing out from among the crowd of demons like a sore thumb. Morrigan would have found her refreshing if her reactions weren't so over the top all the time.

"Obviously Princess Viana's performance was the best one," Lady Viviana announced with a twinge of sorrow in her voice. No doubt she had expected her daughter to receive more votes, and looking at Viana, it was clear that she was less than pleased by this development.

"That leaves one final vote. Your Majesty, would you please do us the honor of announcing the winner?" Azrael said, and Alphegor got up from his seat and went back up to the stage. Morrigan's heart beat like crazy, as it was clear who her father would vote for.

"I believe you all are already aware who the winner of this Nachtstern Competition is. The youngest participant of all, who has shown her physical prowess, magical aptitude, and her wit. It is my daughter—Princess Morrigan," Alphegor said with a warm smile, reaching his hand towards Morrigan. Her cheeks flushed red as the crowd cheered and chanted her name.

She took a moment to take a deep breath and then walked towards the stage. The feeling was exhilarating—people cheered for her and not just because she was the Demon King's daughter, but because she'd actually shown them something worthwhile. Something that they liked.

As Morrigan stood before Alphegor, he put a hand on her shoulder and said, "Congratulations, my daughter. You have accomplished something most demons could only dream of. With this victory, I grant you any boon you wish, and the shadow ruby."

Alphegor produced the box that contained the ruby and presented it to Morrigan. She opened the box and looked at the red gem in awe. It glistened with a radiant light, unblemished and utterly perfect. But as she admired it, she noticed something in the corner of her eye.

While the crowd was focusing on her and the king, a few fallen had grabbed a struggling Galandir and were dragging him away through the crowd, who paid no mind to them.

They're going to punish him because he didn't win. But they wouldn't be too harsh towards a child, would they?

Morrigan tried to calm herself down with that thought, but deep inside she knew that he'd no doubt be beaten half to death. They didn't care about some slave boy unless he could prove himself useful to them. And since he hadn't...

I can't let them drag him away!

"Thank you, Father! But I am afraid I'd never have gotten this far if I didn't have the help of Galandir, the champion of the Fallen Kingdom," Morrigan said loudly, and the crowd grew quiet, their gazes slowly turning towards the struggling boy. The two fallen that were dragging him away paused, dumbfounded by the sudden attention.

"Let go of me!" Galandir snarled, then wriggled out of their grasp. Hushed murmurs went through the audience as they observed the scene before them.

I feel like I'm digging my own grave here, but I won't let a child just be dragged away and beaten if I can help it.

"I believe that Galandir's valiant efforts should be rewarded, as he not only reached the final task of the competition but also performed a beautiful song that I believe deserved far more votes than it got. But since he is a child and a slave, nobody here has recognized his effort," she said, noticing how her father's eyes had narrowed a bit.

Father doesn't look pleased with this. I am probably overstepping my boundaries here, but what is the point of being the Crown Princess if I can't do even this much?

"I also believe that it is unfair to grant a boon to me since I may ask my father, the king, for help at any time, while others will never have such a chance. So I'd like to give this boon to Galandir instead," she finished, trying to keep a serene expression. However, it proved to be increasingly difficult as more and more demons looked at her with distaste.

"Are you sure about this, Princess Morrigan?" Alphegor asked, and the tone of his voice indicated that the answer should be no.

Oh, dear. Father is mad at me. Maybe I...

She looked at Galandir and all of her doubts disappeared, as she saw the boy looking at her with what looked like hope. Previously, his eyes had always looked dark, as if there was no joy left in his life. But now there was a spark.

I'll just have to accept whatever punishment he gives me later. It might be harsh, but if it saves somebody's life then it will be worth it.

"Yes, I am absolutely sure!" she said resolutely. The muttering increased in intensity, but Galandir didn't intend to wait for anyone to step forth and object. He strode onto the stage and bowed in front of Morrigan.

"Thank you for your graciousness, Your Highness. I will accept the kindness you have bestowed upon me." There was no mockery in the boy's voice; his words were sincere.

Alphegor's fist clenched and a flash of red went through his eyes. However, once his eyes went back to Morrigan, his expression relaxed, resigned to her whims. "Very well, elf. Tell me what you wish to ask of me," the king said, and the crowd went quiet, listening intently.

"I wish to be free," he said resolutely, and Prime Minister Heinspiel jumped up from his seat.

"That is not something you can grant him! He is our slave!" the fallen man called out in anger, and the rest of the fallen called out in agreement.

"I said that I shall grant any boon, and I will fulfill my word." Alphegor looked at Heinspiel with a gaze so cold that nobody dared to even squeak. The minister tried to hold the king's gaze at first, but was unable to do so for long. "How much do you want to have for the boy?" Alphegor continued.

"Three million gold," the minister stated, and everyone gasped. With that much gold, one could feed the whole of the Demon Kingdom for a year. Morrigan's heart sank as she realized that her father would never pay that amount for a slave. Nobody would.

"Very well," Alphegor replied coldly, and Heinspiel fell back into his seat. Clearly, he had called out the outrageous sum just to dissuade the king. But Alphegor was not somebody to be taken lightly. He turned towards Azrael and said, "Inform Lucius of this and take the boy to the castle."

"At once, Your Majesty," Azrael said, grabbing Galandir by the scruff of his neck. "Let's go, boy!"

A moment later, they both disappeared into the shadows, leaving Morrigan and Alphegor alone on the stage. The crowd resumed their cheers, celebrating and congratulating her on her victory. However, she felt a distinct coldness coming from her father, giving her an unpleasant sense of dread. And it only grew stronger once she saw the hatred with which Prime Minister Heinspiel was looking at her.

* * *

"Everything is ready for the grand finale, Your Majesty," one of the servants whispered to Alphegor, who nodded approvingly. Morrigan sat to his right, while Viana sat on his left on a grand podium that was erected in front of the stage after the competition had concluded.

Morrigan couldn't help but feel amazed at the speed at which demons always managed to set things up. Within twenty minutes, a dozen demons could transform the whole market square into what reminded Morrigan of an opera. The stage also had a completely different background now—with dark castle walls and bushes for decorations instead of the black dragon.

Apparently, it was a tradition for each Nachtstern Festival to end with a play that portrayed the historical events of the past—the reason why it existed in the first place. Morrigan was eager to learn exactly what happened between the Overworld and Underworld to make their inhabitants hate each other so much.

All the magic lights that were in the area turned off, leaving only the lights that were illuminating the stage. Two figures strode onto the stage, one dressed in all black and the other in all white.

"Dear Underworlders, you all know our wonderful world of Doppelta, but do all of you know how it came to be?" The narrator spoke in a deep, masculine voice, something Morrigan would compare to that of an audiobook narrator. His tone was friendly and indicated that the story was meant for the younger inhabitants of the Underworld.

"For not always have the Underworld and Overworld been separate. Once it existed as one," the narrator said, and the two figures on the stage came together in a hug. "The passages between the two were open. Races of the Underworld could be found in the Overworld, and the Overworld races could be found in the Underworld. It was a wonderful time of peace and mutual understanding."

A flurry of actors of different races appeared on the stage, dancing and weaving together while a wonderful melody played in the background. The black and white figures stood at the center of it all, holding each other in a tight embrace.

"But one day everything changed..." All the actors ran off the stage while the hugging figures retreated to the very back. "A young human man, seeking to become a *hero*, came to the Underworld in an attempt to become stronger."

A man in armor strode onto the stage, and Morrigan's pulse quickened, believing that he was an actual human. However, looking at his features more carefully, she realized that he was actually an elf, his ears hidden underneath the metal helmet. To this day, she had not yet met even a single human in Doppelta.

"Of course, he was not the first to seek his fortune and fame. There were many before him. However, this man went beyond where any person should venture—he descended into the deepest recesses of the Underworld." The stage went dark, only one lone torchlight being held by the elf.

"There he met the king of all dragons—the ancient, almighty landwyrm. It warned the human to turn back, but he didn't listen, and the two clashed in a battle. However, the landwyrm was already old and weak, so the human warrior defeated him," the narrator said while a smaller version of a landwyrm construct grappled with the elf on the stage. After a while, the red light shone on the scene and the landwyrm fell to the ground before disappearing into smoke. Once the smoke cleared, a pile of gems stood in the landwyrm's place.

"As the ancient landwyrm died, the magical gems he had collected over his long life emerged from his body. The human took them all and rushed back home, telling everyone of the treasure he had discovered." The scene rapidly changed, the dark background switching to bright green trees and the lights turning nearly blinding.

"Once the other humans learned of the Underworld treasures, they began to venture into it more and more often, each one seeking to slay a beast with magic within them and obtain their power for themselves."

Chapter 35

Tale Older Than Time

"More and more humans came to the Underworld, killing one Underworld creature after another in hopes that one of them would bring them the same riches the first human warrior got from the landwyrm. But their greed wasn't sated by the gem or two each monster dropped, so they began slaughtering any beast they found," the narrator said as the actors on the stage re-created the scene, magical monster constructs littering the stage.

Morrigan noticed that the black and white figures in the back were slowly separating from one another, going from a deep hug to holding hands.

"The inhabitants of the Underworld began to notice that it had become harder and harder to find monsters to hunt and that magical gems, which were previously in abundant supply, had begun to dwindle. They searched for the cause and soon discovered it to be humans," the narrator continued, his voice turning slightly grim.

"The demons went to the humans and asked them to stop, hoping to solve the matter peacefully at first. But the humans had discovered a power they'd never held in their hands before, and became arrogant and greedy. They rejected the demons and continued to kill the monsters of the Underworld.

"But the demons weren't willing to accept it, so they took up arms and fought against the humans. They were stronger, and soon it became near impossible for humans to venture underground. For a short while it felt like peace had been restored in the Underworld," the narrator said. The scene changed to happy-looking demons and other Underworld races. The black and white figures were barely touching fingers, their heads turned away from each other.

"While the demons were celebrating, humans were hard at work, trying to come up with a solution to overcome the magically more powerful demons. And one day they discovered the secret of demonkind," the narrator said, and the music became melancholic, with heavy drum beats playing in the background.

He must be talking about the fact that demon children are born without souls. I guess they wouldn't announce that with so many guests of other races around.

"They created magic that could summon demons and bind them to their will, giving up their own souls as payment." The tone of the narrator's voice indicated how worthless the payment actually was. On the stage, the same human warrior from before had a demon woman locked in chains.

"With this newfound power, humans continued to pillage the Underworld until there was nothing left. But their greed knew no bounds, and they began to look to their neighbors in the Overworld for more. They conquered the elves, the dwarves, and all other Overworld races, taking everything for themselves."

"Meanwhile, the people of the Underworld suffered. Stronger demons were forced to fight their wars while weaker ones were used for hard labor. Demon, drow, and duergar alike died from starvation and exhaustion." The narrator's voice was low and full of sorrow, while actors on the stage portrayed the misery demons had felt. The black and white figures in the back were clashing against each other in battle.

"But one day, a young demon, who was enslaved by the same human warrior who first invaded the Deep, learned how to break free of his chains. He killed the warrior and began teaching the demons how to free themselves of human contact. A bloody war began between humans and demons."

The scene on the stage showed demons and humans clashing with swords while magic swirled around in the air, making it both beautiful and gruesome at the same.

"A war dragged on for many centuries. Demons grew weary and exhausted, while humans could continue without remorse, one generation replaced by the next. The young demon, now the king, understood that the war could not drag on for much longer. And so he gathered all of the strongest demon mages and closed all entrances to the Underworld," the narrator said, and the black and white figures took center stage ahead. Only this time, they were separated by a giant wall.

"Since that day, the Overworld and Underworld have been kept separate, and this world has been known as Doppelta—the Dual World. The Underworld has continued to live in peace under the first Demon King's rule, and to this day, we honor the king that freed our world. We honor the First King, Nachtstern!"

All actors came onto the stage and bowed, and the crowd followed suit, turning their gazes to Alphegor and then bowing before him. Even the concubines and all of Morrigan's sisters rose to their feet and bowed, so Morrigan hurried to follow their lead. It felt a bit odd, bowing to their Father like that, but she understood that it was her duty.

"Praise King Nachtstern!" the crowd began to chant.

"Praise King Nachtstern!" the concubines and Morrigan's sister repeated.

"Praise King Nachtstern!" she repeated too, but there was a sort of unpleasant nagging at the back of her mind.

I understand why the demons hate humans so much, but is this really all that there is to this tale? It felt rather... one-sided, painting humans as the absolute bad guys.

* * *

After the play, the people were shooed away from Linberor Market Square to prepare the grand evening feast. Apparently, all of the best food and drinks were brought out for the celebration, and everyone could have their fill—even the poor, who were already eagerly lining up on the side streets, waiting for the preparations to finish.

But the Royal Family would not partake in this feast. Instead, there was a different one prepared in the Demon Castle, where all of the notable demons and representatives from Underworld countries would come together to mingle. It was considered the grandest event, and anyone who was somebody even remotely important was set to attend.

Morrigan, however, wished that she didn't have to attend, and groaned as the maids once again set upon the task of dolling her up for the occasion. The fact that she had won the competition had made her into the main attraction of the show, so she expected to have a very long and exhausting evening ahead of her.

"Gunna, perhaps I could just slip away to my room and pretend to be sick?" she asked her dwarf nanny, who was busy preparing her a fresh new hairstyle for the night.

"I wish I could allow you to do so. It is too much for a small child." Gunna sighed, gently patting Morrigan's head, comforting warmth radiating from her palm. She enjoyed the soothing sensation, letting her worries fade, if only for a moment. "But do not worry. You will not be alone. Master Alphegor will always be there to support you."

"He looked a bit angry at me before," Morrigan noted, remembering the cold gaze he'd cast upon her after she begged him to free Galandir. She did not regret her decision, although three million gold was definitely an infuriating amount.

Slavery as such just shouldn't exist, especially when it comes to children. They should be growing and learning instead of doing hard labor.

"Even so, he wouldn't just leave you alone during such an important event," Gunna said, and the demon maids nodded in agreement as they fixed her dress. "Not to mention that your sister will be there too."

Deziara being there is definitely a relief, but Viana... I feel like she'll be eager to make even more trouble for me than the others will. Perhaps I should make a point of avoiding her if possible. Just to be safe.

"There, all done," Gunna announced, patting down Morrigan's shoulders. "Now everyone will be too stunned by your beauty to say anything."

The maids once again nodded vigorously in agreement, their eyes shining with pride at their hard work. Morrigan looked in the mirror and saw that her long hair had been styled into a high ponytail with elegant locks weaving down her shoulders. Meanwhile, her dark red dress with gold accents truly made her look like the Crown Princess of the Underworld.

"Wish me luck," she said with a sigh, then left the dressing room, going into the adjacent waiting room. Azrael was sprawled on one of the couches there, looking bored.

"Oh, finally! I thought you'd never come," he grumbled, getting up from his seat.

"It takes time for a lady to get ready," she replied, mimicking what she had once heard Viana say.

"Where's the lady you're talking about? I only see a kid that I need to babysit."

"How interesting, because I also only see a kid," she retorted, and they both stared at each other for a while. Morrigan felt her lips slowly curl upward, as did Azrael's, and they both broke out into laughter.

"If somebody tries to ask me to dance, please stop them," Morrigan said as she walked up to Azrael and took hold of his extended elbow.

"Don't worry, this isn't technically a ball. It's supposed to be a feast. There will be music playing, and there's a small space for dancing, but you can reject anyone without any repercussions tonight," he explained, then began leading her out of the waiting room.

"Wait, before we go out there, I wanted to ask. Where'd you put Galandir?" She pulled on him and stopped him from walking any farther.

"In the prison, of course. Where else?" He shrugged, completely unperturbed by his words.

Morrigan gaped at him in shock. "Prison?! Isn't he supposed to be free?" she snapped, anger bubbling inside her.

Azrael laughed in a mocking sort of fashion. "The king paid three million gold for that pipsqueak, and you expect he'd just be allowed to march free? Although by the look on your face, it seems like you fully expected us to open a portal to the Overworld and send him on his way with a gift basket in tow."

The last bit seemed a bit over the top, but Morrigan had indeed hoped that Galandir would be able to return home, wherever it may be.

"But why imprison him? He didn't commit any crimes," she objected.

"Oh, but he did, even if you tried to hide it. But we'll deal with that tomorrow. Today we still have work to do," Azrael said, then resumed walking. Morrigan followed him numbly as the sense of dread she'd had before grew stronger.

Father probably knew what Galandir tried to do that night when I stopped him, but decided to ignore it at the time because of me. Could it be that he'll have to suffer punishment for that now? Oh, dear... That could be even worse than whatever punishment the fallen wanted to inflict upon him.

She remembered how the fallen had dragged the elven boy away in the middle of a big celebration without any care for keeping appearances. It was clear that he would have gotten more than just a stern lecture. Morrigan took solace in that thought, and began thinking of ways to convince her father to overlook Galandir's transgression, or at least soften whatever punishment he deemed to be right.

Before long, Azrael and Morrigan reached the grand ballroom, which was already buzzing with excited chatter. The whole place was lined with tables that had all manner of foods set upon them. Many were already happily enjoying the decadent dishes.

Waiters hurried left and right, bringing food and drinks to the guests while they sat at a table and enjoyed chatting with others. The atmosphere was more relaxed than yesterday, although as soon as Morrigan entered the room, the chatter stopped and all eyes fell upon her.

"Dear guests, I am proud to present the winner of the Nachtstern Festival Competition—Princess Morrigan," Azrael announced in his amplified voice, and everyone applauded. Morrigan gave a small curtsy and plastered on her most polite smile.

"Princess Morrigan, would you please join our table?" a burly demon with twisted horns asked, and she recognized him as Duke Ramhorn from a painting she had studied before.

Seems like looking through those demon noble portraits was not a waste of time after all.

"My son was most impressed by your display and wants to discuss more about the topic," the demon continued, pointing towards his son, a scrawny-looking demon who most certainly did not look interested in the topic.

"No, Princess Morrigan, you should join our table. My son was absolutely blown away by your magic and would love to learn more about it," a corpulent demoness called out, despite sitting three tables away.

"No, Princess Morrigan, you should sit at our table. Our house has specialized in magic for generations. I am sure there is much we could discuss," another demon called out, and soon a whole swarm followed after them.

Oh, dear God. If you exist in this world, please grant me the strength to endure this night.

Chapter 36

Debt of a Lifetime

As a human, Morrigan had believed that she could never come to hate any gathering where lots of food was involved. Especially if the food was good. And the one made by the Demon Castle's chefs was most certainly top quality in terms of both presentation and taste. Even something with an unappetizing name, like salamander liver pâté on volcano-baked bread, turned out to be a delicious treat. However, the Nachtstern Festival feast was most certainly now on the list of gatherings Morrigan resented.

The whole evening she was being ping-ponged from one table to the next, forced to listen to demons and demonesses brag about their sons and suggesting that she get to know them better. Some of these sons showed no interest in Morrigan, since they were still children themselves and had no idea that their parents were buttering them up for marriage.

But many of these suitors were much older demons, and were eager to charm Morrigan in their favor. The only thing she could feel for them was disgust. While technically she had the mentality of an adult human, nobody here knew that. To them, she was just a child. And yet they had the gall to try to groom her into their good graces.

Azrael watched the whole charade with much amusement, although she didn't know whether he was amused at Morrigan's misery or the knowledge that the demons were flirting with somebody who was a human before. Morrigan guessed that it was probably both. A few times she tried to coax him into helping her, but he had no intention of doing that, instead leading her from one table to the next with a wide smile.

By the time she finally reached the royal table, where Alphegor sat with his four consorts and their daughters, Morrigan was too tired to pay any proper attention anymore. All congratulations and cheers melted into a jumbled mess as she mechanically recited her thank-yous and tried to keep her ever-heavier eyelids open. Before she realized what had happened, she found herself in her own bed.

"Huh? How did I end up here?" she said groggily, then looked at the clock on the wall. Its shorter dial was pointed at nine, meaning that she had already slept in.

Oh, God! Galandir! I need to get dressed quickly and try to get him out of prison before Father decides to punish him.

Morrigan didn't bother to call for the maids, and instead put on the first dress she found in her wardrobe. She quickly combed her hair and was about to rush out when she noticed the shadow ruby standing on the nightstand next to her bed. It felt wrong to leave behind the treasure she'd worked so hard to win, so she quickly snatched it and put it in the hidden pocket of her dress.

Now I need to go to Father and have a serious talk with him.

She left the room in a hurry, only stopping to ask the guards about the king's whereabouts. Apparently, there were some documents to take care of, so he had gone to his office. That made things easier for her, as it meant that nobody would interrupt them.

She turned into a shadow and without a second thought headed straight to Alphegor's office, not paying any mind to the guards as she slipped inside from underneath the door. The king was busy scribbling something, his brows furrowed in a scowl.

"Morrigan, I'd appreciate it if you could at least knock before barging into my office," he said, his voice filled with irritation. However, it appeared that this irritation was directed more at the paper in front of him, rather than her.

"Good morning. There's something I wish to discuss with you, Father," she said after materializing from her shadow form. As she did, she was startled by another figure in the room, a sleek demon with dark skin and vivid blue eyes. Most of his body was covered, and his attire vaguely resembled that of a ninja.

"Leave us, Melanos," the king commanded, and before she could even properly blink, the demon was gone.

"Who was that?" she asked.

"Our spymaster. What is it that you wanted, Morrigan? I am very busy at the moment. There was an incident yesterday that needs to be dealt with," the king grumbled, looking rather tired.

"An incident?"

"Nothing you need to concern yourself with," he replied briskly as he continued writing. Morrigan felt a bit annoyed that he wouldn't share exactly what troubled him, but decided to brush it aside for the time being. There were more important matters to deal with.

"Father, I wish to know why you imprisoned that elven boy," she said, and Alphegor's hand stopped for a moment. His scowl deepened, then he resumed writing at double the speed.

"That was merely a temporary measure to ensure that he doesn't get any ideas in his head and escape," he said.

"And why couldn't he just leave? Didn't he ask you to grant him freedom?" she retorted.

"And so I have. He has been freed of the fallen and is no longer a slave." His voice was so cold that Morrigan could barely recognize her father. It felt like she was talking to a ruthless king.

"Then why is he imprisoned?"

"Because he owes us a debt that needs to be repaid," the king explained, still not bothering to look up from his document.

"Three million gold is an insane amount. It'll take him centuries to repay that if he works a simple servant's job," she objected, stepping closer to her father's desk.

"Then it's a good thing that elves live so long. He'll spend a few centuries repaying his debt and then will be free to go," Alphegor said matter-of-factly.

Morrigan raised her voice, frustrated by his cold and heartless response. "How can you even say that?! He is just a child."

"He came to steal from us." Alphegor finally looked up, his eyes, as cold as daggers, piercing into Morrigan. She was taken aback by his statement. Not because he had known—she had long since learned that the king knew everything that was going on in his kingdom, and especially his own home. No, she was shocked by his demeanor, as he had never talked to her with such cold anger.

"He was most likely ordered to do that by the fallen," she protested.

"Yes, Melanos got as much from him. But the boy was stubborn. We had to use a truth potion for him to admit it," Alphegor retorted. "Turns out his whole goal was to get your blood."

"My blood?" Morrigan paled. Why would Galandir need her blood?

"Yes. He was supposed to give it to his fallen masters, although he had no knowledge of what they would use it for," Alphegor said through gritted teeth. "I cannot let someone like him just walk freely. He might still decide to turn on you in an attempt to please his masters."

"He wouldn't do that. He just wishes to be free. Let me talk to him. I'm sure he'd be willing to explain himself then."

"No. It is too dangerous. The boy is skilled in magic, and clever to boot. He might attempt to use you to gain leverage over me," Alphegor said.

"So what is going to happen to him? Is he just going to rot in prison for the rest of his life?" Morrigan felt anger growing inside her from this injustice.

"No, he'll be working in the dungeons to repay his debt. Once he's done with that, he's free to go, just as I promised. As long as it is outside the Demon Kingdom's borders."

"The dungeons?!" Morrigan exclaimed. That horrifying place never failed to foul her mood, since its only purpose was to make unwanted guests suffer. Those few times she'd been down there, she felt like a bit of her happiness was permanently drained out of her. Not to mention that anybody unlucky enough to work in the dungeons always looked like they had lost all hope in life.

"Father, you can't be serious! That is no place for a child. She had raised her voice out of her frustration, and Alphegor rose up from his seat, looking down at her.

"Morrigan, enough! I understand that it is your human past that is compelling you to say this, but it is time for you to learn the ways of the Underworld. If you remain soft towards those who wish to harm you, you'll get stabbed in the back and killed," he said sternly, and Morrigan took a step back. She felt as if he had slapped her across the face. A twinge of regret passed through Alphegor's face as hot tears filled Morrigan's eyes.

"So my human past is a mistake after all," she said bitterly. She slipped into the shadows, unable to face her father anymore.

"Morrigan, wait... I didn't mean that..." he called out after her, but she didn't stop and instead headed straight back to her room. As soon as she was back, she fell onto her bed, letting hot tears stream down her face.

I only wanted Galandir to be free again. That child was no doubt taken away from his home by the fallen and forced to do their bidding. But now I've condemned him to an even worse fate. And Father seems to be unwilling to feel compassion for anyone who isn't a demon.

She understood that her father had mentioned her human nature largely out of anger. However, the fact he wished for her to change that hurt. Morrigan had always believed that Alphegor would accept her the way she was, no matter what happened. That was the reason she'd given up her life on Earth and returned to Doppelta. But it appeared that even here there were expectations that she had to meet.

"Alright, Morrigan! Enough moping. I need to do something about the elven boy. I can't just let him rot in the dungeons for hundreds of years." She slapped her cheeks to get rid of the unpleasant feelings within her. Those would be addressed at another time.

Father certainly isn't going to change his mind, at least not anytime soon. And talking to him right now wouldn't lead to anything productive. I could try asking Azrael to bring me to the prison so I could at least talk to Galandir. But Azrael is largely a wild card—I never know whether he'll be in a mood to cooperate.

As Morrigan was thinking of the best course of action, a knock sounded on the door.

"Lady Morrigan, are you awake yet?" Gunna's friendly voice came from behind the door.

"Yes, come in," she called back, wiping away any residual tears from her cheeks.

"My, you're already dressed! Couldn't wait to get up this morning?" the nanny said cheerfully, waddling over to Morrigan's side.

"Something like that," she replied awkwardly.

"That's wonderful. Today is a sacred day in the Underworld—a time for rest and peace. It's a great day for contemplation and time with your family," the nanny explained. "It means you'll be able to rest a bit.

Sadly, it will be necessary to send the guests from foreign countries back tomorrow, so there will be an event to attend before their departure."

"Oh, joy..." Morrigan muttered, imagining yet another stuffy party. Hopefully this one would be on a smaller scale.

"That is a worry for tomorrow. Today you may rest alongside everyone else," Gunna said.

"Yes, rest would be nice..." she said absentmindedly, and an idea crossed her mind. "Is this a day when the whole kingdom is resting?"

"That's right. Most businesses are closed today, and it's a time when even the Demon Castle's servants get to relax a little," the nanny explained.

"Even the guards?"

"Yes, I believe a large number of guards have also gone to rest with their families. Only the bare minimum are kept."

Bare minimum. That means there won't be as many guards watching over the prison. Perhaps a certain little princess could sneak in.

CHAPTER 37

PRISON BREAK

As the silent day after the festival continued, Morrigan used the opportunity to sneak into the prison. She had never actually been there before, since obviously a princess had no business going to the prison. However, from her trips down into the dungeons, she knew that its entrance was located right across from the dungeons' entrance, guarded by Chad. The stoic guard had never tried to stop her from going into the dungeons, but it certainly would be different if she tried going into the prison.

Sneaking in as a shadow wasn't an option, since the place prevented anyone from using their shadow form. Nonetheless, Morrigan had already figured out a solution to this problem and knew how she'd get past Chad without any issues. She would turn into Alphegor. After all, the king could go wherever he pleased.

With this plan in mind, she turned into a shadow and quickly zoomed into the part of the castle where the main living space intersected with the servants' quarters. The castle felt deserted, with only one or two guards snoozing away at their posts. Morrigan probably could have snuck past them in her physical form—that was just how lax they were.

Once Morrigan reached the narrow corridor that led down into the prison and dungeons, she shape-shifted into her father. It was an easy task, since Alphegor was the person she could mimic perfectly, down to the last strand of hair. Nobody would be able to tell the difference between her transformation into Alphegor and the real King.

The main problem is my voice. I have yet to learn magic that would allow me to change it. That should be the next thing on my learning list.

As Morrigan descended down the corridor, her pulse quickened and she began doubting herself. While she believed that Galandir certainly should not be in prison, was sneaking inside really the best course of action? What would she do once she got him out? Did she even want to free him right away, or would it be better to just talk to him and have him admit that the fallen had forced him to sneak around the castle? Could she use his confession to free him afterward? Or would that anger her father even further?

The more she thought about it, the more she doubted herself. Before long, she had already reached the dead end, where she began stomping against the ground in a pattern now well known to her. After a minute, the wall began to shift and move out of the way, and she proceeded down to come face-to-face with Chad.

The stoic demon guard didn't show any emotion at her appearance, barely inclining his head in acknowledgment. Morrigan didn't say anything either, and instead just strode past him while her heart hammered in her chest like crazy.

"Wait," Chad said, and Morrigan stopped. It felt like her heart would leap out of her mouth.

Is he on to me? No way, the transformation is perfect. Could it be that Father always says something to him before going farther?

"Keys to the prison, Your Majesty," the demon said, and Morrigan exhaled in relief. She turned around and took the keys without a word, trying not to show how shaky her hands actually were. Then she hurried into the prison, praying that her behavior had not seemed weird to Chad.

As she went through the dimly lit corridor and realized that nobody had come running after her, her breathing relaxed and her heart calmed down. She reached a barred door, where two guards who were equally as stoic as Chad—if that was even possible—stood. As they saw her approach, they bowed their heads but said nothing.

With as much confidence as she could muster, she took the key Chad had given to her and inserted it into the keyhole. A wave of purplish energy glittered across the bars, and the door sprang open. It was difficult to retain a calm expression in front of the guards, and Morrigan felt her hands become clammy with sweat, but somehow she managed to retrieve the key without dropping it to the floor.

As soon as her foot crossed the threshold, it felt like the world had transformed. Moans and groans of pain and misery echoed around the long hall, which had large metallic doors spanning on both sides as far as she could see. There was barely any light in the prison; only occasional torchlight on the verge of going out provided a minuscule amount of lighting. The stench within was also horrid—a mixture of sweat, vomit, and other unpleasant body odors wafted through the air, forcing Morrigan to cover her mouth and nose with her hands.

What a horrid stench! And they sent a child down here? The thought that anybody would have to spend more than a day in this place is just horrifying. Better to find Galandir quickly and get out.

But as she looked at the identical metal doors, she realized that she had no way of knowing where the elven boy was locked away. There was only a tiny hole at the top of the door, and it was covered with a metallic lid.

I can't just go from cell to cell, checking each inhabitant one by one. But how else am I supposed to find him? Calling out his name in a clearly girlish voice would certainly alert the guards.

With a sigh, Morrigan went up to the first cell and slid the metallic lid aside. Inside sat a scrawny demon man, all skin and bone, his hair long and tangled and dirty. The man looked up when the hole opened, perhaps expecting his next meal to be brought to him. But when he saw Alphegor's face, the prisoner instantly dropped to the floor and began groveling and muttering "Sorry, spare me, don't kill me," over and over again.

Her heart clenched at the sight, but she reminded herself that the people here were criminals and had no doubt been thrown inside their cells for a good reason. Thieves, rapists, and even murderers no doubt spent their days here, reflecting on the crimes they had committed. Well, aside from Galandir. He was just an unlucky child.

Morrigan closed the lid and resumed checking the cells. The guards, who were positioned at every tenth cell door, never questioned her behavior, and merely bowed in greeting. It seemed like Alphegor was not a rare visitor here.

Morrigan had reached the thirtieth cell when the prisoner she saw inside caused her to pause. The demoness inside seemed somewhat familiar, and it took her a moment to realize that it was the same spindly demon that had kidnapped her all those years ago. One of her arms was completely cut off and there was a horrid scar running down the left side of her face. When the demoness gathered enough strength to look at Morrigan, she smashed her head against the floor and apologized with double the vigor of other prisoners.

I should feel some sort of satisfaction that she got punished, but somehow the only thing I feel is pity. At least I can rest easy knowing that she won't be sending more children to Phantom.

Morrigan's mood grew darker and darker with each cell she checked. Just as she started thinking that she would never be able to find Galandir, she finally saw him. He was in a much better state than the other prisoners, but he by no means looked happy. Once he saw Alphegor's face appear in the small opening, he just turned his back to her.

Well, it's good to see that he hasn't been hurt. But how do I even speak to him? I can't just turn into myself with guards around.

She gently tapped the metallic door in hopes of attracting the elf's attention, but all she heard was a *hmph* as he huddled deeper into the corner.

Oh, why does this boy always make it so hard to help him?

"Your Majesty, shall I open the door?" one of the guards asked, pulling Morrigan out of her thoughts. She was about to say yes, but caught herself before she opened her mouth. Instead, she nodded firmly, like she had seen her father do before. The guard unlocked the door without question.

"Will you be taking the boy with you, Your Majesty?" the guard asked. "He's tough, but I don't think he'll endure it here for long."

Obviously not. This place is just horrible. But thank you for asking, kind guard. I shall take advantage of this opportunity.

Morrigan nodded solemnly again, and the guard strode inside the cell and pulled Galandir out. He was rather rough with the boy, and Galandir was resisting with all his might.

"The boy is very stubborn, Your Majesty. Shall I help you escort him?" the guard asked, trying to contain the flailing elf.

"Let me go, you overgrown monkey!"

Morrigan shook her head and grabbed Galandir's arm, pulling him away from the guard. He was doing everything in his power to resist, and it was difficult for her to keep a steady hold on him. She bent down and whispered in his ear.

"I am trying to help you."

Galandir instantly stopped flailing and looked at her with a shocked expression, no doubt trying to process how the Demon King managed to sound like his daughter. The guard, however, took it as a sign that she had everything under control and returned to his post.

Morrigan didn't give Galandir the chance to change his mind and began pulling him along. The walk through the prison felt long with the guards watching them leave and the prisoners wailing miserably behind them. But once they finally reached the entrance, Morrigan felt relieved. The smell and the noise disappeared right away. She looked at the door and hurried out of the prison, only stopping to return the key to Chad.

"What exactly are you doing?" Galandir whispered once they were out of the hidden pathway. Morrigan's eyes darted nervously around the castle corridor, wondering what she was supposed to do next.

I should have actually thought of what to do with Galandir once I got him out of prison. But I couldn't ask him anything without arousing the guards' suspicion.

"I don't know," she admitted as she turned back to her normal self, still holding on to his hand.

"What do you mean you don't know? Did you drag me out of prison without even knowing the reason why? Are you stupid?" he snarled.

"Should we go back?" she countered, and the elven boy shook his head. "For now, let's go somewhere people won't bother us. I believe I can convince my father to spare you, or at least lessen your punishment, if you just give us more information."

"Oh, I see how it is. This was the king's plan to get me to speak. Forget it!" Galandir stubbornly tried to pull his hand free, but Morrigan held it firm.

"Listen! I never intended for you to be thrown into the dungeons. I've been there, I know how awful that place is. The fact that you tried to steal from us before is working against you. You need to explain exactly what it is that the fallen wanted. But this isn't the place."

Galandir scowled at Morrigan but didn't resist her anymore.

I don't like doing this, but I think I'll have to move around like a shadow with Galandir in tow.

Morrigan slipped into the shadows, dragging the boy along with her and feeling his bright presence like a heavy rock on her form. She couldn't move as fast as usual and soon began to tire; however, after some time, she managed to reach her destination—the dragon stable.

As soon as she was inside, she materialized with Galandir, who had a disgusted sort of expression on his face.

"That is too suffocating," he grumbled.

"It was the only way for me to get you through the castle unnoticed. Now, let's talk!"

CHAPTER 38

UNDER THE EYE OF A DRAGON

Haku was elated to have visitors and without a second thought began jumping around Morrigan and Galandir in joy, his tail whipping around and sending his chewed-up toys flying. Morrigan had to dodge a few random toys as she tried to calm the dragon down.

"Yes, I am happy to see you too, Haku," she cooed, gently rubbing his snout.

"Still keeping him locked up, I see," Galandir noted bitterly, looking around the stable. It was by no means a small structure, as it could easily fit four double-decker buses inside it; however, there was certainly not enough space for a dragon to feel free. And Morrigan knew that before long, it would be impossible to make the stable any larger. What would happen to Haku then?

"He's too young to leave," she argued weakly, pressing herself against Haku. He picked up on her sad mood and nudged her gently in an attempt to cheer her up. "I'm alright, Haku. You don't have to worry about me."

Galandir sighed, then picked up a large, half-chewed wicker ball that was lying in the corner and threw it. Haku bounced after it happily and caught it, chewing on it mercilessly and making the material crack between his teeth.

Morrigan changed the subject, not wanting to dwell on Haku's lack of freedom at the moment. "Anyway, Haku is not the reason we are here. I need you to talk."

"Talk about what?" The elven boy looked to the side, deliberately avoiding her gaze.

"You know what!"

"You're just going to tell your daddy and make everything worse again," he retorted, and Morrigan felt a heavy pang of guilt in her chest. She really had made everything worse in a way. Instead of being a fallen slave, he had essentially become a demon slave—confined to the dungeons, no less.

No, you don't know what would have happened if you had let them drag Galandir away. Perhaps they wouldn't have even allowed him to live.

"I'm sorry that you got sent to the prison, but tell me, would you really have wanted to accept whatever punishment the fallen deemed right for you?" she said seriously, and his expression turned grim. Haku sensed the heavy mood and gently padded over to the elven boy, throwing the wicker ball in front of him. Galandir smiled bitterly and threw it again, watching the dragon bound after it.

"They would have killed me," he stated.

"Y-You don't know that..." Morrigan objected, but mostly because she didn't want to accept the fact that there was somebody wicked enough to kill a child for not fulfilling the impossible task they had set out for him.

"No, I do. They wanted to kill me on that night when I failed to get your blood, but they allowed me to live *temporarily* to serve as their champion and retrieve the shadow ruby," he said, and Morrigan gasped in shock.

"Why'd you need my blood?" she asked, not daring to meet his eye. The fact that someone wanted her blood made her stomach churn.

"I already told your spymaster everything I know. Which admittedly is close to nothing," Galandir explained. "My guess is to open the Royal Treasury. As far as the fallen know, there are only two people in the whole world who can open it—the Demon King, and his direct heir. And guess who is the easier target."

"Me."

"Without a doubt."

"But what do they want from the Royal Treasury? The magical gems? The gold?" She asked him this despite knowing that there wouldn't be an answer that would make it all alright.

"My guess is that they wanted it all. Gems to strengthen the warriors, gold to strengthen their kingdom, and use whatever else they could for their gain." Galandir shrugged, then once again retrieved the wicker ball, which was barely holding together, and threw it for Haku to catch.

Morrigan paused, trying to process the information. The fallen had always bitterly opposed the Demon Kingdom, but to go as far as to steal something right from the Royal Treasury? It was a rather desperate move. Or perhaps they were just sure that they could get away with it. But what gave them the confidence?

"How'd you know the layout of the castle so well?" she asked, remembering how flawlessly Galandir had navigated through the castle corridors, which had taken Morrigan a long time to learn properly.

The elven boy went silent for a moment, contemplating something. He narrowed his eyes at her as if trying to determine whether he should trust her or not. But as Haku nudged him with the wicker ball, he took a deep breath and said, "A demon woman provided the information about the castle layout."

"A demon woman? Who?" Morrigan's mind reeled as she thought about which demon would sell out their own kingdom to their enemies. Demons didn't like other races, and thinking that demons would betray their own for the fallen, whom they actively hated, was unthinkable.

"I don't know who she is. I only caught a glimpse of her once. A black-haired demoness with red horns and glasses," he said, and Morrigan felt her blood run cold. There was a demoness who fit that description perfectly.

"Asdeus," she muttered, clenching her fists. "To think that she'd stoop so low."

"So you know her?" he asked curiously.

"She used to be my teacher when I was four years old, but she tried to use me for her own gain and made my life in the Underworld miserable. Because of her actions, I ran back to Earth, thinking that my father would hate me if he found out that I was a human. But that wasn't true," she explained through gritted teeth, remembering the unpleasant memories.

"Wait... So the Demon King knows that you used to be a human?" The boy's mouth gaped in shock.

"Of course he does. He's my father. Although I didn't realize it back then."

"That is... That is actually rather shocking. I didn't think the Demon King would accept a child with a human past, considering how much demons hate humans," the boy said.

"He is much kinder than many people think. And I am sure he will be sympathetic towards your situation if we explain everything you just told me to him," Morrigan said. She grabbed Galandir by the arm, preparing to meld into the shadows and head straight to the king's office.

"Wait, wait, wait. He was sympathetic towards you, but that doesn't mean he'll be that way towards me. You are still his flesh and blood, but I am not even a demon. Heck, I am not even from the Underworld. You might as well have dragged a human in front of him and asked him to spare it." Galandir pulled his hand back and hid behind Haku, who looked content to act as his shield.

"Explaining yourself will certainly not make matters any worse. Besides, I do not believe that the fallen will have given up just because you failed to meet their expectations. It would be foolish to base their whole plan on the success of a child." Morrigan gently pushed past Haku and took Galandir's hand again. The boy looked visibly uncomfortable.

"But what if he—"

"It'll be alright. Trust me on this," she said reassuringly, then began to gently pull him along. He didn't resist anymore, instead allowing her to lead him towards the door. But before they could reach it, Haku began snarling viciously, his pupils dilating to catlike sharpness.

"We'll come back later, Haku," she said, trying to console the dragon, but he only snarled more viciously.

"I don't think he's snarling at us. Listen," the elf said, then pointed towards the door. Morrigan tried to listen for whatever it was Galandir was talking about, but couldn't hear anything. At least not at first. After a few tense moments, she noticed something resembling a whisper from outside the stable. Haku's growls intensified, and Morrigan had a feeling of dread growing in her stomach, so she did the only logical thing.

"Father! Azrael!" she called out at the top of her lungs in an attempt to summon them. But the only thing that happened was laughter, which came from behind the stable's door.

"Clever princess," a man's voice said, and the door was flung open. Inside strode a tall, white-haired fallen with vivid green eyes. His facial features reminded Morrigan of Mrs. Heinspiel to such a degree that he definitely had be related to her in some way. However, she'd never noticed this man among the guests.

"Who are you?" Morrigan asked, sticking close to Haku, who looked like he was ready to attack the man at any moment.

"It doesn't matter who I am. What matters is that you're coming with me," he said, striding towards her. Haku launched a warning fireball at him, but the fallen man blocked it with his wing, the fire harmlessly dissolving against the tough feathers. He raised his hand and some sort of shimmering powder came from his palm, floating towards Haku, Morrigan, and Galandir.

Before the dust could reach them, Galandir waved his hand, summoning his wind magic and blowing the particles back at their producer. They blinked out of existence before reaching him, and the man looked at the elven boy in annoyance.

"You dare to oppose me, slave! You should bring the Princess to me," the fallen man commanded, but Galandir shook his head, despite the fact that his features were marred with fear.

Think, Morrigan. You need to somehow summon Father or Azrael, but it seems like they have somehow blocked the summoning ability, just like Asdeus did. But if it's the same type of hindering ability, it means it has a limit. If I slip into the shadows and reach outside that limit, I should be able to call for help.

But before Morrigan could turn into a shadow, the fallen man threw an ice spear straight at Galandir. She produced a wall of fire, melting the incoming ice attack. This, in turn, triggered Haku, who leapt at the fallen with the full intent of biting into his flesh. The man dodged the dragon's attack and directed his ice spears at him instead. Thankfully, Haku's scales had no problem deflecting them.

"Quite a powerful dragon you have here, Princess. We could find a good use for him. Men, secure the dragon. I'll deal with the Princess," the fallen ordered, and two dozen men dressed in black clothes from head to toe poured into the stable. Morrigan's breath hitched as she recognized their outfit as the same one as the assassin that was sent to kill her when she was a baby.

This is really bad. I need to get Father or Azrael as soon as possible.

However, as the dark figures and the fallen man got closer, Morrigan couldn't help but feel weak and defenseless. Her hands trembled, but she knew that there was no time to cower in fear. She looked around frantically, hoping to come upon a solution somewhere in the stable. However, all she saw were broken scraps of Haku's toys.

"Princess, we need to get out of here," Galandir called out frantically as he began flinging ice spears at the black figures. But it was obvious that he was fatigued from his stay in prison, as he had trouble conjuring his magic and began breathing heavily.

The masked figures deflected the icy attacks without any issues. The fallen man jumped towards Morrigan, using his wings for balance, but Haku blocked his way, furiously flapping his wings and swinging his tail to keep the attackers away.

"Focus on the dragon first," the fallen commanded, and two men charged at Haku, pulling out the shortswords that sat at their hips. In an attempt to protect him, Morrigan launched a fireball at them, forcing the two men to stop their assault and fall back.

Galandir threw more of his ice at the fallen man, who growled in anger. "Enough of you, slave. You've gotten in my way far too many times." The man pulled out a vial with some sort of a red liquid inside. He held it in his hand and then grinned triumphantly. "This is where you die."

Galandir suddenly clutched his chest and fell to his knees, gasping for breath.

"What are you doing to him?" Morrigan called out.

"What I should have done a long time ago," he cackled, and she watched helplessly as Galandir lay on the floor, convulsing in pain.

He's killing him. He is killing him! No, no, no!

"FATHER!" she screamed, the anger and fear she was feeling taking over her and growing in intensity. She channeled this energy into a fireball, but instead of shooting the flaming orb at her enemies, she shot it straight up. It burned through the ceiling, blazing like the sun and illuminating everything in the area.

"Oh, shit..." the fallen man said as he watched the fireball rise, reaching the Demon Castle's highest peaks.

CHAPTER 39

BLOOD SPILT AND BLOOD TAKEN

"Our time has been cut short, it seems," the fallen man snarled as he looked at Morrigan, who was clutching Galandir. All she had to do was hold out until the guards, or ideally her father, came to her rescue. "Forget the dragon and the boy—get the Princess's blood!"

Morrigan paled as the dark figures turned their attention to her. Before she could even realize what was going on, a barrage of various spells flew her way. Haku stepped in front of her, spreading his wings and protecting her from the majority of spells. Meanwhile, Morrigan erected her force field, trying to protect herself and Galandir from any spells that got through.

"Haku, are you alright?" she called out. The dragon growled in confirmation, his scales undamaged. The same couldn't be said about her force field, which had been destroyed in some places. Another barrage of spells was launched straight at her, but the dragon blocked them. This time it proved too much for Haku and he fell limp to the floor.

"Haku!" she called out, and her concentration on the force field slipped. The fallen man took the opportunity and broke through it, grabbing Morrigan by her neck. She grabbed his hands, struggling to free herself, but the pressure on her neck was increasing and she felt like it would snap at any moment. Instinct took over, and she allowed angry blue flames to come out of her palms and burn the man. He howled in pain and dropped her, but as he did so, his nails painfully scratched against her neck, drawing blood. She coughed and sputtered as she tried to regain her breath.

"I got what we needed. Retreat," he commanded, and the black-clad men tried to leave the stable. However, before any of them even had the chance to register what had happened, the Demon King had appeared inside the stable and cut down most of the intruders in a single swift attack.

His red eyes bore into the fallen intruder as dark tendrils wrapped around him, capturing him in an instant. Morrigan looked at the scene in horror—Haku and Galandir, lying limp on the floor, and her father, a bloody sword in hand, standing above a pile of corpses.

"Morrigan! Are you alright?" Alphegor ran up to her, checking for injuries. He must have seen the deep scratch mark on her neck, as his face contorted with rage and fury, and his red eyes almost began to glow in anger. "Whoever did this is going to pay!"

"Galandir and Haku need help!" Morrigan said frantically, not caring about the cut on her neck. But it was merely a scratch when compared with what had happened to her friend.

"The elf? Why is he here?" Alphegor growled.

"I got... him out, Father," Morrigan explained, clutching at her injury and feeling the blood seep through her fingers.

Seeing that, the king's expression turned to that of worry. "We're going to get that healed right away," Alphegor said.

"Never mind that scratch, I can barely feel it. That fallen did something to Galandir! And to Haku as well. You need to help them first," Morrigan pleaded, and the king relented.

"Azrael!" He tried to call for the mage, but nothing happened.

"That won't work. They did something to the stable to prevent summoning," she explained.

"Those annoying pests. Messing with magic in my own home," Alphegor growled.

"Your Majesty. Your orders?" Melanos appeared out of seemingly nowhere, making Morrigan flinch in surprise.

"Get Azrael here to take care of the dragon. Take the elf to the healers immediately and summon one to come here and take care of Morrigan," he commanded.

"At once." Melanos bowed and then disappeared as quickly as he'd come, with Galandir in tow. Merely half a minute after the spymaster had left, the whole castle seemed to come to life, and guards rushed into the stable.

The guards looked around the gruesome scene in horror. "Your Majesty, what—"

"You lot are too slow. Rally the guards and strengthen the defenses in the castle. Remove the ward placed upon the stable. Investigate for any stray magic," Alphegor commanded.

The guards nodded, each one taking on a different task, with most of them turning their attention to intruders. They began hauling away the bodies while Alphegor pulled the fallen man closer, glowering at him with an intense red gaze. Meanwhile, Morrigan focused on her dragon, who still lay limp on the ground.

"Haku, are you alright?!" she called out desperately, inspecting him for any injuries. There were a few gashes on his tender wing membranes; however, his scales looked largely unharmed. But the lack of reaction from the dragon made hot tears well from her eyes.

"He's been knocked out cold, but he'll be fine. He's still breathing," Alphegor explained, pointing at Haku's chest, which rose each time he took a breath. Morrigan relaxed a little, then looked at the man who had attacked her. Despite being captured, he didn't appear very fazed by it. He almost appeared satisfied.

"Speak. Why did you attack my daughter?" Alphegor demanded, but the fallen man just laughed.

"As if I'd tell you anything," he cackled.

"Fine, then. I'll guess we'll do it the hard way." Alphegor eyes glinted with malice as the dark tendrils pulled the fallen man into the darkness. Morrigan's stomach churned—she knew that her father would use any method necessary to get the information out of him, and she doubted that he'd be as nice to him as to Galandir.

But I suppose it has to be done. We cannot let this kind of attack just slide.

Azrael finally appeared in the stable as well, his eyes widening as he saw the limp dragon on the floor and the corpses of the intruders. "What in the name of darkness happened here?"

"Take care of the dragon, then check for any stray magic or magical interference. The enemy launched an attack right in the middle of my home," Alphegor raged, his eyes glowing red.

"The enemy? Who?" Azrael asked, perplexed.

"The fallen. They're the ones behind this attack," Morrigan said, and Alphegor and Azrael looked at her with grave expressions.

"You're going to explain everything that just happened. Including the reason why the elven boy is outside his prison cell," Alphegor growled, and Morrigan shrank back, hiding behind Haku.

I am in deep trouble now.

* * *

Morrigan sat on the couch in Alphegor's office while Alphegor and a very confused-looking Lucius sat on the couch across from her.

"Your Majesty, what exactly is going on? Why is Princess Morrigan covered in blood? And what was that blue fireball earlier? I also received a report that the elven slave was out of prison and is now being tended to by our healers," the older demon said, his gaze darting from one person to the next.

"Is Galandir alright?" Morrigan asked, her voice filled with worry. She feared that the fallen man might have killed him with whatever strange magic he'd used.

"He's alright, merely unconscious. May I have an explanation now?" Lucius asked, his eyebrows furrowed.

"Morrigan will explain everything. From the beginning," Alphegor commanded, tapping his finger impatiently against his knee.

She took a deep breath, mustering the courage to speak.

"I snuck into the prison to get Galandir out of there," she admitted, her head hanging low.

"Wh-What?!" Lucius sputtered in shock, then looked helplessly at Alphegor, who looked mildly annoyed. "You snuck into the prison to get a slave out of there, but..."

"Seems my daughter has developed a bit of a soft spot for the boy," the king noted bitterly.

"But even so... sneaking into prison... Princess Morrigan, I had always thought you were more mindful than that. If people were to find out..." Lucius's face paled in horror, and Morrigan feared that her action might have added a new wrinkle to his complexion.

"Yes, that would instantly ruin public opinion of you, and make them rally against you as the Crown Princess," Alphegor explained, and Morrigan realized just how bad that would be. More assassination attempts, a possible uprising, or maybe even worse.

"Even so, the way you treated Galandir was unfair. Putting a child in prison to later have him work in the dungeons is absurd!" she protested, looking her father straight in the eyes.

"So I should just let him go free?" he challenged.

"That is what he asked of you. And you promised to fulfill his request," Morrigan objected, not wavering under his intense stare.

"Three million gold is not a small amount."

"You promised him freedom."

The two stared at each other stubbornly, not willing to budge. After a long, tense minute, Lucius spoke up.

"Let the boy repay his debt through hard work once he wakes up," the older man suggested.

"What?" Morrigan looked at him incredulously. "Have a child work in the dungeons?"

"The boy already agreed to repay his debt when I interrogated him," Alphegor said. "And so he shall work to repay it."

"Father, sending a child..." Morrigan objected, but Alphegor held up his hand.

"I understand your concern. I shall not send him to the dungeons. He'll work as a servant in the Demon Castle instead. However, he will not be able to leave the castle, as I do not trust him to simply not run away at the first opportunity."

"That is a very wise resolution, Your Majesty," Lucius agreed.

"Alright, I'll consider this matter settled. Morrigan, tell us what happened once you left the prison," Alphegor said, not allowing her to raise any objections. She huffed a bit in annoyance, but since there was no time to spare, she continued her explanation.

"According to Galandir, the fallen were planning to get my blood right from the beginning to get into the Royal Treasury. Or at least he thinks so—they never explicitly told him. The one who scratched my neck was a fallen, and he looked a lot like Mrs. Heinspiel," Morrigan said. Alphegor's and Lucius's expressions turned grave at this.

"Now that I think about it, there certainly was a resemblance. But you say that he was the one who injured your neck? It must have been their son. But they claimed that he remained in the Fallen Kingdom," Alphegor growled.

"Your Majesty, did this intruder manage to get the Princess's blood?" Lucius asked, his face turning pale.

Morrigan thought back on the attack and remembered how he definitely had some of her blood on his hand. He'd even ordered them to retreat. She nodded. Alphegor's expression grew dark, and the room grew silent as the king got up from his seat and began pacing around the office.

"But he's captured, so it doesn't really matter, right?" Morrigan said hopefully. "Whatever he wanted to do with my blood, he can't do it while captured."

"I need to make sure of something," Alphegor muttered. Morrigan noticed how Lucius's eyebrows had twisted into a deep, concerned scowl.

"Your Majesty, what if he actually managed to..." The older demon trailed off, his voice sounding as if all hope was lost.

"We have no choice then. We're going to have to negotiate with them," Alphegor said, clenching his hands into tight fists.

"Negotiate? Why would we negotiate with intruders?" Morrigan looked at her father in confusion. She then looked at Lucius for an explanation, but the demon would not meet her gaze head-on.

Something else is going on here. They shouldn't be so worried about the attacker being captured. It feels like I am missing some crucial bit of information.

"Lucius, summon the fallen Prime Minister. Tell him that it's time to negotiate," Alphegor ordered.

"At once, Your Majesty," Lucius said. He left the room in a hurry.

"Father, what is going on?" Morrigan grabbed her father's sleeve, hoping to receive some answers.

"It is possible that the the fallen who attacked you managed to teleport your blood to his allies," Alphegor said grimly, and Morrigan could see that this fact scared him. It scared *him*, the almighty Demon King, whose power was unrivaled in the Underworld. And even if Morrigan didn't understand why, she knew that if he was scared, she should be too.

CHAPTER 40

RAT IN THE HOUSE

Alphegor strode through the hallway with heavy steps, his piercing gaze cursing seemingly everyone who dared to cross his path. Lucius followed him, holding Morrigan's hand, and they in turn had the dozen best demon warriors following them, fully equipped and ready for combat.

She didn't fully understand why their reaction was so grim. After all, the intruder had been captured and was probably being *interrogated* for any information by the spymaster. It was only a matter of time before they found out exactly what the fallen wanted to accomplish with that stunt. And yet simply because of a possibility that the fallen man might have somehow given her blood to his allies, Alphegor acted so... nervously.

Morrigan also couldn't understand why Alphegor had decided to talk with the fallen Prime Minister. It wasn't like she supported wanton murder, but this seemed like a case where the king would just slaughter the enemies. And yet, he was being overly cautious.

But Morrigan was relieved that Galandir was fine at the very least and wouldn't be forced to work in the dungeons. He'd live along with the other servants and slowly work off his debt. It was not an ideal scenario, and it would certainly take him a long time to be free again, but at least he'd be doing honest work and wouldn't be beaten for it.

Or so she told herself. Morrigan knew that members of other races weren't treated particularly well in the Demon Castle. But she'd never seen a demon actually harming slaves. Then again, such matters probably would be done out of her sight. Who'd deliberately beat up slaves in front of the Crown Princess?

They soon reached one of the main audience chambers, where another dozen demon warriors stood by, armed to the teeth. Across from them stood half a dozen warriors from the Fallen Kingdom, as indicated by the dark blue coat of arms on their armor, which portrayed two crossed wings.

The guards parted, two of them opening the door for Alphegor. Behind him, Morrigan saw the Heinspiel family sitting nervously on the guest sofa. Annabell was clutching her mother, whose eyes were darting from one demon guard to the next. Clearly they had no idea what was going on. The Prime Minister also looked nervous; however, it was clear from his gaze that he knew exactly why the situation was the way it was.

I feel sorry for Annabell. She has no idea what is going on. She is just suffering on account of what her father likely plotted. If worst comes to worst, I should beg Father to spare her and her mother. Although I am not sure if he'll listen this time.

"Your Majesty, for what purpose have you summoned us here?" the Prime Minister said nervously, trying to appear oblivious. However, in his haste he had completely forgotten good manners. This fact did not go unnoticed and the demon guards tensed, their hands inching towards the swords at their hips.

"Last time I checked, I am the king in this castle. You will show me due respect before asking me questions." The king's voice turned the air heavy, making it hard to breathe. It seemed to affect the fallen the most as they clutched at their chests and gasped for breath. Annabell hands spasmed.

"We apologize. We did not want to antagonize Your Majesty," the Prime Minister said with a deep bow, even managing to force out a smile. His wife also got up, pulling Annabell along with her and bowing before the Demon King. Alphegor lifted the pressure off the room by striding towards the sofa opposite the fallen, sitting down with a flourish. Morrigan quickly followed him, sticking close to his side.

"So, tell me a good reason why I should not raise an army and wipe the Fallen Kingdom off the map of the Underworld right this instant," Alphegor said in an ice-cold voice, wrapping his hand protectively around Morrigan.

Prime Minister Heinspiel emitted a sort of hiccuped squeak, sweat profusely pouring from his forehead, while his little daughter was barely holding back tears. "There is no need to resort to such actions. I am sure we can come to a peaceful agreement," Heinspiel said in a trembling voice.

Alphegor glared at him and then snapped his fingers. A dark shadow appeared in the middle of the room, and out of it rose the dark tendrils that were firmly holding Morrigan's attacker.

Mrs. Heinspiel gasped, while Annabell outstretched her arm towards the captured fallen. "Big Brother!"

"So he is your son?" Alphegor growled, his eyes turning red from anger. The Prime Minister flinched back. It was likely that he wanted to keep that detail hidden, but there was no hiding it now. Although, in Morrigan's opinion, their son resembled his parents so much that there was no doubt about who he was. Heinspiel's eyes darted from Alphegor to his son, and then he bowed deeply before the king.

"He is my son, Theobold Heinspiel, the next Prime Minister of the Fallen Kingdom," the fallen said, keeping his head low. "Please, spare his life."

"Spare his life." Mrs. Heinspiel bowed even lower, and so did

Annabell, although it was clear that the girl had no understanding as to why her big brother was bound like that. The sight must be horrifying for her, and Morrigan felt sorry for the girl.

"He had the impudence to attack my daughter and injure her in my own home," Alphegor snarled. The air in the room grew colder, and the magic lights grew dimmer. Demon warriors drew their swords and pointed them towards the fallen, ready to strike. The fallen warriors also drew their swords, prepared to defend their lieges, even though the odds were not in their favor.

"I did what I had to do to protect my country. It was rather obvious after the festival that no peace would come between our countries unless given the right push," Theobold snarled through his restraints.

"Silence, you impudent worm!" Alphegor growled. The dark tendrils wrapped around Theobold's mouth, preventing him from speaking.

"Please, be merciful." Mrs. Heinspiel was bowing so low that her forehead was touching the ground. Meanwhile, Annabell was crying and trembling, her little eyes darting from Alphegor to her captured brother.

"Call your king here if you wish this worm to survive," Alphegor said with a menacing glare.

"If we could arrange for a neutral meeting place, I am sure His Majesty would—" Heinspiel began, but Alphegor cut him off.

"We will negotiate here, or you will receive your son in pieces," he growled mercilessly, then stood up, pulling Morrigan along with him. She looked back and saw the dark tendrils, with Theobold in tow, sink back into the darkness, while Annabell cried at the top of her lungs.

As soon as they were out of the audience chamber, Morrigan tugged at her father's arm.

"I don't understand. Why do you want to negotiate with their king? Can't Melanos get the information from Theobold?" she asked, although she had a nasty suspicion in her mind already.

"It's a bit difficult to explain, but essentially the fallen can…" Lucius began, but the king glared at him, cutting the older demon off.

"I'll explain it to her. For now, secure the castle. Triple the amount of guards for each concubine and princess. Monitor the fallen's every movement. I want to know everything that they do," Alphegor commanded.

"Yes, Your Majesty," the warriors responded. Before Morrigan could ask anything further, she felt herself being dragged into darkness, then realized that her father had teleported them back to their room.

"Father, what exactly—" She looked up at him, but felt herself being pulled into a hug.

"It'll be alright, Morrigan. I'll protect you," he whispered, and she felt his hands tremble.

Protect me? But I am not in danger. Is it because Father believes that they have my blood that he's so worried? But what can the fallen do with my blood that would make him this afraid?

"Of course, Father," she said. She wrapped her tiny arms around the king, gently stroking his back in a calming motion.

"Look at me! Soothed by my own child. It seems that I have grown old," Alphegor said with a bitter smile, then let go of Morrigan.

"Father, what is it exactly that the fallen can do with my blood? That's what you're worried about, isn't it?" she asked.

The king sighed. "It has to do with the way the fallen were born. You see, the fallen are a counterpart to a race called angels."

There are angels in this world? Overworld races are still a mystery to me. Nobody really talks about them much, and the books that have any mention of humans have been removed from the library.

"The angels are a race that has the innate ability to cure those whose blood they possess. With just a single drop, they'd be able to determine what ails the person and would be able to heal them from even the deadliest of diseases. People would willingly give their blood to the angels, who in turn would cure them. Humans, who are especially prone to illnesses, began worshiping them like gods.

"However, not every angel was satisfied with that. Some became greedy and demanded more and more payment from people. When the demands became too high and people refused to pay them, they became resentful. They began experimenting with the blood they received, trying to find a way to use it for their own gain," the king said, then put a hand on Morrigan's shoulder. It felt heavy and tired, and she could feel the seriousness behind his words.

"These resentful angels succeeded in twisting their magical gift into something completely different. Instead of curing ailments, they learned how to inflict them. Their feathers changed to reflect that, and their angel brethren, enraged and embarrassed, banished them to the Underworld. These angels became known as the fallen. Over the millennia, the ability, which once required diligent refinement and study, became innate. Now, any pure-blooded fallen may bring death upon anyone whose blood they possess."

Morrigan felt a shiver go through her body as the heavy realization hit her mind.

"They can kill me with just that one drop of blood?" Morrigan asked, and the king nodded, clutching her shoulder.

"But if they have taken your blood, I shall retrieve it. We also have a bargaining chip on our side. Their king will not be able to just throw away the life of the Prime Minister's son."

Alphegor straightened, then looked outside the window with determination. He called for Azrael, who appeared within a minute, his expression serious.

"Your Majesty, the dragon is fine, merely weakened from magic attacks," he informed the king.

"Good. Prepare yourself for a possible battle. The fallen may have gotten their hands on Morrigan's blood," the king explained.

"So that's why the oath has been clawing at me so insistently this whole time. I couldn't understand it, since she's supposed to be safe," Azrael said, clutching at his chest, where the oath had been placed.

Alphegor nodded. "You have to try and find out whether they truly have acquired Morrigan's blood," the king commanded. "Although the fact that the oath is acting up is a bad sign."

"I will do my best," Azrael said without hesitation.

"Maybe I can help somehow?" Morrigan asked, feeling utterly helpless and useless in the situation.

"Absolutely out of the question!" Alphegor said.

"You'll only get in the way," Azrael exclaimed at the same time.

"But..." she muttered, feeling fear gnawing at her chest. If somebody could kill her with just a drop of her blood, then she had to get it back.

"Morrigan"—Alphegor knelt down in front of her and looked her straight in the eyes—"this is not something you are able to do. Please, trust us to resolve this. I promise that nothing bad will happen to you."

She nodded at her father, who gently caressed her hair. It was comforting to know that Alphegor would protect her no matter what.

The king got up to his feet and looked at Azrael. "Go now. I wish I could go with you, but I must remain by Morrigan's side. You're the only one I can trust with this task," Alphegor said, putting his hand on Azrael's shoulder. The white-haired demon looked almost touched by the trust the king placed in him. He nodded firmly and then disappeared into the shadows.

CHAPTER 41

ELUSIVE MAGIC

The next morning, Morrigan and Alphegor sat at their breakfast table, poking at their food. Neither had slept very well, Morrigan catching a few winks towards the morning while Alphegor diligently watched over her, not having slept a wink all night. Nor did they have the appetite to eat, their minds constantly going back to Azrael. The demon had left on his mission last night, taking along some of the most skilled spies to find out whether the fallen truly had Morrigan's blood. And if they did—attempt to retrieve it.

The only small consolation came in the form of Haku's recovery. According to the doctor, the dragon had been merely exhausted from enduring so many magical attacks, and would recover in due time. This knowledge brought some peace to Morrigan, although it didn't lessen the heavy feeling in the pit of her stomach.

"Lady Morrigan, Master Alphegor, you should eat something." Gunna was the only one brave enough to speak up, the other maids staring gloomily at the floor. Due to the large number of guards who had witnessed the whole exchange, it was impossible to keep the matter hidden from the castle's staff. So, in the morning, the whole Demon Castle knew exactly what had happened.

"I'm not hungry..." Morrigan mumbled, setting down the fork on the table.

"Even if you're not, you should eat. It'll make you feel better," the nanny insisted, and Morrigan gave in, cutting herself a small piece of bacon from a creature unknown to her and putting it in her mouth. The meat was delicious and tender, and as soon as she had swallowed it, Morrigan realized how hungry she actually was. Seeing his daughter eat, the king also forced himself to do so.

"Morrigan!" The door to the dining room burst open, and Deziara ran inside, Lady Lily following closely behind her. The girl instantly pulled Morrigan into a tight hug, tears streaming down her face. "I can't believe the fallen would stoop so low as to attack you in our home."

"And on a day when even attacking your enemy is sacrilege. The fallen should be banished from the Underworld," Lady Lily huffed angrily, placing a comforting hand on Morrigan's shoulder. She buried herself in her older sister's embrace, enjoying her comforting warmth.

"Trust me, I'll do it as soon as the opportunity arises," Alphegor growled, clenching his hands into fists.

"No matter what happens, we must not give them what they want," Lady Lily said.

"But we shouldn't go to war," Morrigan said, remembering the horrible scenes from the war documentaries she'd seen. It only ever brought misery and suffering, especially to common people and soldiers. The Underworld would become a living hell, and that was the last thing she wanted.

"We'll do whatever needs to be done," Alphegor said sternly. "If the fallen refuse to cooperate, then war might be the only option we have."

This is not good. It seems like one tiny thing will be enough for Father to just go into an all-out war with the fallen. I cannot let that happen.

Just as she thought this, a second wave of shocked gasps broke into the dining room, this time with less force. A few more of Morrigan's sisters had come to complain about the fallen. She was surprised to see how angry they seemed about the fact that the fallen had attacked her, as most of the time, they didn't really care much for Morrigan. Except, of course, for how to best take her position.

Viana walked into the dining room. "Enough with your clucking. You are princesses, not maids spreading rumors in the kitchens."

"Why are you here?" Deziara narrowed her eyes, still clutching Morrigan's hand.

"Why do you think I have come? You believe I'd just stay mute in the middle of this crisis, just sipping tea in my bedroom?" she retorted.

"Well... yes," Deziara admitted, and Morrigan had to admit that she was kind of expecting the same thing.

"Clearly you do not understand the gravity of the situation then. This is not some personal slight towards Morrigan alone. This is an attack against the Demon Kingdom as a whole," Viana explained, walking towards Morrigan. Their other sisters parted to let her through, and even Deziara released Morrigan's hand.

Alphegor nodded grimly. "Viana is right. We need to take this matter seriously."

"Father, if the Fallen King agrees to come and negotiate for the life of his subject, I'd like to participate in the negotiations," she said resolutely. Alphegor arched his eyebrow at that, and then the other princesses begged to be allowed to participate in the negotiations as well. Morrigan could see her father's irritation rise with each second, no doubt aggravated by his poor night's sleep.

"Quiet! This is not some party to show off your dresses and jewelry," he barked, and all of his daughters simmered down, looking guiltily at the floor. "Morrigan will attend, and I'll allow Viana to come too."

"Why Viana? Why not me?" Rosalie, the third-eldest daughter, asked, her cheeks puffing out in a pout.

"Because Viana knows how to behave herself properly," Alphegor retorted, and she skulked back. He was right, and she knew it. All of the princesses knew. Despite them being much older than Morrigan, all of them, with the exception of Viana, acted rather childish. Even when they were trying to spite Morrigan, in the end it was no better than school bullying. Not that they had many chances to bully Morrigan, since she was with Alphegor or Azrael most of the time.

As the princesses pouted and grumbled, one of the royal messengers ran into the dining room, huffing and puffing. "Your Majesty, I have a message from the fallen Prime Minister."

"Speak," Alphegor commanded.

"He says that the Fallen King will arrive in Linberor in three days," the messenger said, his face pale. If there was any semblance of cheer left in the room, now it was completely gone. The princesses suddenly didn't look very eager to participate in the meeting anymore.

"Good. That means we have time to prepare for the worst-case scenario," Alphegor said. He threw a short glance at Morrigan, then disappeared into the shadows.

Worst-case scenario. He means war, doesn't he?

* * *

Two days remained until the Fallen King would arrive at the Demon Castle. Everyone was busy preparing for his arrival, one meeting of nobles happening right after the next. Alphegor was so busy with them that Morrigan barely ever saw him during the day. She asked to attend at least a few of those meetings, but was completely shot down. Apparently it was no place for children.

You're going to allow me to meet the Fallen King, but not with the demon nobles. That just isn't fair. Viana is allowed to attend.

With the tension high and having nothing better to do, Morrigan had hoped to maybe distract herself with some magic lessons—only to remember that Azrael was away on a mission and unable to teach her anything. So in the end she had nothing better to do than pace around her room and stare at her many paintings, both finished and unfinished. She wasn't even allowed to leave her room until the whole matter with the fallen was settled.

She looked at the half-finished sketch of Haku she had done some time ago. Perhaps it was time to finish it. But at the same time she felt far too nervous to actually draw or paint anything properly. Morrigan never could manage to draw anything nice while she was stressing out, so it was best to leave it for some other time.

But what do I do then? There aren't many ways to entertain yourself in the confines of your room, aside from painting and reading. And I'm pretty sure I've already read everything that is in this room, excluding Father's documents.

Morrigan went to her bedroom, hoping to find something to do there, and noticed the ruby sitting on her nightstand. The treasure she had worked so hard to win was completely forgotten due to recent events.

Since I have nothing better to do, I might as well absorb it and see what ability it will give me. What if it gives something like forcing your enemy to obey your every command? Now that would be useful. I could force the fallen to return my maybe-stolen blood, go back to their kingdom, and never attack us again.

Yeah, as if anything that convenient could ever happen.

Morrigan sighed before picking up the shadow ruby. It shone with brilliant red light, and she could feel the power within it resonating with her touch—as if it wanted to know more about her, to understand her from deep within and adapt to her needs. It was almost creepy in a way, but incredibly fascinating at the same time. What could have happened for this stone to give the user whatever ability suited them most?

Magic. There's no other explanation, if it can even be considered one. I still know so very little about magic and how it works, it's embarrassing. Azrael never bothers to explain the theoretical stuff. As long as I can shoot fireballs or change to look like him, he's content.

Morrigan shook her head, trying not to think about Azrael at the moment. He was away on a mission, and thinking about him would only make her nervous about the Fallen King arriving in two days. No matter how hard she thought about it, the result could either be bad or worse. Best-case scenario, they did not have Morrigan's blood (unlikely), Father would return their prisoner, and they would only resume their attacks the next day. Worst-case scenario—a bloody battle would begin right in the center of the Demon Castle, plunging two kingdoms into instant war.

Morrigan had considered various solutions that could help avoid that. She'd even thought about arranged marriage, since that was apparently how her father had solved many political issues in the Demon Kingdom. But she quickly dismissed that thought. She didn't want to marry some fallen prince or demand that one of her sisters do it. Besides, there was no guarantee the Fallen King would even consider that beneficial.

Oh, enough thinking about all that. Better absorb that ruby and see what kind of ability it will give me. Maybe it really could be something useful for this situation.

Morrigan closed her hand over the ruby and imagined its power flowing into her like a steady stream of water. But as its power started going into her, she noticed that it felt different from the other times she'd absorbed gems. Instead of a cool stream of magic spreading throughout her body, this felt almost electrifying. Not in a painful way, but rather in a tingly sort of way. The energy also flowed much slower, so she had to concentrate on keeping the flow of magic steady within her body.

After several minutes, the gem had finally disappeared from her hand, its energy fully ingrained in her body. She smiled, happy that she had finally absorbed it, but then paused, looking down at her now empty hand.

"But what ability did I get?" she asked herself, blinking. Morrigan knew that there was some new power within her, but there was no mysterious message in her head telling her exactly what it was. It only told her that something was there.

Alright, let's try doing various things then. Maybe something will click.

She extended her hand forward, imagining dark tendrils appearing from the shadows and grabbing the clock on the wall. Nothing happened. She imagined creating a spark of lightning coming from her fingertips. Nothing. A giant icicle appearing from the ground. Nothing.

It's supposed to be an ability suited for me, so maybe it has something to do with painting and art.

Morrigan imagined a sculpture rising from the ground and becoming her protective golem. No. She imagined paint coming from her fingertips and swirling around her. No. She even imagined a giant paintbrush appearing in thin air. Still no. No matter how many times she tried, Morrigan could not figure out what ability she'd obtained from the ruby.

CHAPTER 42

VALUE OF LIFE

Two long days came and went far too slowly for Morrigan's liking. The whole time she was sitting in her room and trying to figure out what ability the ruby had given her. But no matter what she tried to do, it never resulted in anything. She would have loved to get some advice from her father or Azrael, but she never got the chance to meet either of them.

Alphegor didn't even return to his room to sleep, so she had to wonder where he slept. Azrael apparently had returned to the Demon Castle late last night, but unfortunately nobody had told her exactly what the results of his mission were. Although judging by the fact that there were more soldiers pouring into the Demon Castle, they couldn't have been good.

I suppose it is safe to assume that the Fallen King truly has my blood. But how did that fallen... What was his name again? Theobold. Yeah, I think that's what it was. How did he manage to send my blood to the king in that short span of time between when he injured me and Father arrived and captured him? Oh, who am I kidding? It was magic, of course. It's like anyone can do anything in this world as long as they wish for it hard enough.

Gunna came into the living room, appearing nervous, no, even shaken. "Lady Morrigan, your father has summoned you to the grand conference hall."

"Is everything alright, Gunna?" Morrigan asked.

"I... Well, the Fallen King has arrived," she said. Morrigan gasped and ran to her window. Looking down from the high tower, she saw around twenty unfamiliar white carriages parked within the castle yard and more than a hundred soldiers with an unfamiliar coat of arms standing opposite the Demon Castle's soldiers. She could sense the tension going on between the two sides even from up in her room. It was like all of them were ready to grab their weapons at a moment's notice and attack.

Oh, no. Whatever happens, it cannot turn into a fight. That would plunge the Demon Castle into a bloody battle that would no doubt spread throughout the country. No, this has to end peacefully.

Morrigan took a deep breath, exhaled, then hurried out of her room to the conference hall. Her heart was racing and her hands trembled, not out of fear for her own life, but out of fear for her family and her kingdom. It was ironic, in a way—once she wished for nothing more than to return to Earth and forget about the Demon Kingdom, but now she wished to protect it. She wanted to protect her family and its many inhabitants. To protect their beautiful traditions like the Nachtstern Festival and allow them to continue their daily lives in peace. And she would do everything in her power in order to achieve this.

* * *

When Morrigan arrived at the entrance of the conference hall, she saw her father, Viana, and a bunch of demon ministers, including Lucius, standing by the door, surrounded by what appeared to be a small army. When they noticed her arrival, all of their gazes fell, and only the king met her eyes. From his gaze alone, she could already tell that the situation was bad.

"The Fallen King is already inside. Let's go," he said simply, and Morrigan nodded. Her hands trembled, and she tried to squeeze them together to prevent that from showing. However, as the doors were opened and she saw the fallen sitting at the table, her hands only began to tremble harder.

"Keep your head up, Morrigan," Viana whispered in her ear, then gently touched her hand. Morrigan flinched at first, but Viana took her hand and held it firmly. Her skin was soft but her grip was strong, preventing Morrigan from shaking any further. "Do not show them any weakness. Remember that you are the Crown Princess of the Demon Kingdom."

Morrigan looked at her sister in shock. She never expected her to show such support. Straightening, Morrigan dutifully followed after their father, trying to show as much confidence and grace as Viana.

Before long, the representatives from the two kingdoms were seated around a long roundtable, guards from both countries standing nearby, armed to the teeth and ready to jump into action at any moment. Morrigan sat between her father and Lucius, while Viana was sitting on Alphegor's right. Right across from them sat the Fallen King and Prime Minister Heinspiel.

Morrigan took a moment to carefully assess the Fallen King. Just like all the demons, he looked really young, with long blond hair cascading down his back and his sky-blue eyes analyzing everything with measured coldness. In a way, he seemed almost angelic. Almost. The dark wings on his back gave no doubt about what he really was—a fallen.

"It is most wonderful that you have invited me here, King Alphegor. I am sure that today we'll finally be able to find peace between our two countries," the Fallen King said with the sweetest of smiles. However, it was not a friendly smile, and Morrigan could feel how powerful and dangerous the man really was.

"There will be no peace until my daughter's blood is returned, King Uriel," Alphegor growled in return, not bothering to keep up any pleasant appearances. It appeared that Azrael had confirmed that the Fallen King indeed had it.

Uriel shrugged nonchalantly. "Whatever are you talking about? How could I have your daughter's blood when I was on the other side of the Underworld?"

Alphegor glared at him, and suddenly a dark shadow arose at the end of the conference table. Within it was Theobold, looking limp, his gaze completely apathetic to his surroundings. Heinspiel noticeably flinched at the sight, his face growing pale.

Even Morrigan felt a bit uncomfortable. It was clear that he had been tortured for information. She had already known her father would do that, but seeing someone who had actually been tortured was not pleasant, even if he didn't have any visible injuries on him.

"No need to play this charade. This worm already admitted that he teleported the little bit of blood he got from Morrigan to you," Alphegor snarled.

Silence took over the room as all eyes fell on the Fallen King. Then he smiled and looked at Morrigan. A shudder ran down her spine, but she did her best to not look away. That would be a sign of weakness, something he could take advantage of.

"Well, since you've already confirmed it, I suppose there's no reason to hide this." The Fallen King put his hand inside his white robes and pulled out a little vial. At the very bottom of it sat a little red dot. It was so small, so meaningless. But everyone in the room knew exactly what it was. The tendrils on Theobold tightened and he groaned, making Uriel drop his smile.

"It appears we both have something that the other wants back. Let's make this easy. I shall return this scum back to you in exchange for Morrigan's blood," Alphegor said.

"But do you really believe that would be a fair exchange? Do you believe the heir of the Demon Kingdom is worth the same as a Prime Minister's son?" Uriel said, while Heinspiel turned a shade paler at his words.

"Nothing in this world is worth as much as my daughter's life," Alphegor growled, and Morrigan furrowed her eyebrows. While she really appreciated that her father cared for her this much, this was not the right time to show how much he cared about her. It would have been better if he had said something along the lines of "I have twenty-three more daughters that can take her place."

"Then I believe it would be fair for the Fallen Kingdom to receive some extra recompense along with the return of our Prime Minister's son," Uriel said, beginning the true negotiations. "As you are probably well aware, the Fallen Kingdom has been suffering from poverty for a long time now. Our citizens are dying of starvation every day while the demons frolic and cheer, organizing festivals and eating to their hearts' content. These are things my citizens can only dream of."

For a king of a supposedly starving nation, he sure doesn't look like he is starving. And the clothes he is wearing are so extravagant, far more so than what Father is wearing right now.

"The vast land that the Demon Kingdom possesses is filled with riches and resources our lands do not have. I merely wish to improve the lives of my citizens, many of whom have already suffered under the injustice of others," he continued. Despite the supposedly tragic story he was telling, Uriel's smile never wavered.

"So what is that you want?" Alphegor asked, no doubt trying to forgo any other sad stories the Fallen King was trying to tell.

"I do not ask for much. It would be a mere sliver of the wealth the Demon Kingdom possesses. 300 million gold, five thousand magic gems of various grades, and the Duchy of Lendmar," he said nonchalantly.

This time Morrigan lost control of her expression for a moment, as did many other demons in the room. The gall of this guy!

That is not a mere sliver! It's an outrageous sum. Not to mention the territory of Lendmar Duchy. It certainly isn't the richest duchy in the Demon Kingdom, but in terms of size, there is no place larger. Not to mention that it houses no small portion of demon citizens. What would happen to them if we just handed the duchy over to the fallen?

"Outrageous. Your greed surpasses even that of humans," Alphegor said.

Uriel just chuckled in response. "Greed? No, this is no greed. It is merely what the Fallen Kingdom deserves. Especially after the destruction you brought upon our country a few years ago."

"I was merely cleaning out a rat infestation from my kingdom," Alphegor retorted, and despite Uriel's smile, the tension in the room grew very heavy.

"Of course. And I am merely looking out for my citizens. Or are you saying that your daughter's life isn't quite worth the price I am asking?" the Fallen King said.

Alphegor slammed his fist against the table, making it crack and creak. "As I already said, there is nothing worth more to me than my daughter's life," he growled, his eyes turning a murderous shade of red.

"Then I am sure the price I am asking is not an issue."

There was a tense silence in the room. Morrigan knew that this was the time for her to speak up; however, her mouth felt dry and she couldn't bring herself to open it. But she had to. At the rate this conversation was going, the Demon Kingdom would remain as the losing side, as Alphegor wasn't willing to risk Morrigan's life, even if they were supposed to be on equal negotiation grounds.

"I believe what you are demanding is outrageous," Morrigan said, and the demon ministers nodded eagerly at her statement. "One life should not be worth more than another life. Or are you saying that the life of your subject does not matter to you?"

Heinspiel looked at his son, who was still trapped within Alphegor's dark tendrils, mostly unresponsive to the conversation that was going on. The other fallen looked at their king too, and Uriel grew a bit more tense.

"One life is not equal to another. The life of a king cannot compare to the life of a peasant. Same as the Prime Minister's son cannot be compared to the next queen of the Demon Kingdom," Uriel said with a smirk.

"Who says I'm going to be the next queen? I might be the Crown Princess now, but do not forget that I have twenty-three older sisters. Any one of them can easily take my place. Like my eldest sister Viana, here—she was the Crown Princess before me. Why can she not be one again?" Morrigan said.

"Even if you are not to be queen, you are still a princess of higher rank than a mere fallen noble," Uriel retorted.

Morrigan pressed the attack, hoping that the already tense fallen ministers would speak out against their King. "So you're saying that your subject's life is worthless to you?"

"That is enough!" King Uriel said, and Morrigan suddenly felt as if somebody had gripped their hand around her heart. She gasped, barely managing to remain upright. "You will know your place, pup!"

"Release your magic at once!" Alphegor jumped to his feet, his eyes glowing bright red.

"Not a step further or the princess will be stuffed out like a candle," Uriel snarled. "You will meet your demands or the princess will die."

Morrigan clawed at her chest, tears rolling down her eyes from the pain. She was completely powerless before this invisible force. Seeing that, Alphegor took a step back, raising his arms up to show surrender.

No... No. We cannot give in to their demands. We cannot just give up part of our kingdom to the fallen. Demonkind would surely be enslaved. If only there was some way to counter their magic.

Suddenly a bright light shone brilliantly in the conference room, illuminating everything just like the sun and forcing demons and fallen alike to shield their eyes. Morrigan recognized this magic—it was one of Galandir's spells. As soon as the light orb reached the Fallen King, the pain within Morrigan's chest disappeared. The suffocating hold on Morrigan was broken.

CHAPTER 43

PEACE TREATY

Galandir stood by the entrance, his hand outstretched as he concentrated on the light. He was breathing heavily and sweat ran down his forehead from the strain, while Azrael supported him with his hand.

"Y-You will not harm her," the elven boy exhaled. "I will not let you do to her what you have done to me."

King Uriel jumped up to his feet in outrage and pointed at Galandir. "Kill the slave!"

The fallen warriors unsheathed their weapons at once and were about to jump towards the boy; however, Azrael conjured a fireball, making them all falter for a moment.

He snickered. "You have to go through me to attack the boy."

"Father, the magic holding me is gone!" Morrigan called out, and Alphegor reacted without hesitation. He unsheathed his sword and with a swift movement lunged towards the Fallen King. Uriel jumped out of his way and erected a force field, blocking his attack.

"What are you doing, fools? Get rid of the boy! Get rid of that light!" Uriel bellowed, but now the demon soldiers had their weapons ready for an attack. Morrigan watched the scene in horror. A few more moments and the whole room would erupt into a bloody battle. She had to get her blood back as quickly as possible.

It appears that the fallen's blood magic does not work in light. Theobold must have failed to kill Galandir because I had conjured that bright fireball. And now Uriel can't harm me because Galandir created this light.

I have to get my blood back before somebody gets to Galandir or he runs out of magic. It doesn't look like he has fully recovered yet.

So Morrigan called upon her fire, the one power that never failed her. She couldn't just outright attack the Fallen King, since that would trigger a battle that she was so desperate to avoid. So instead of flinging flashy fireballs, she concentrated on the vial within his hand. She imagined it getting hotter and hotter, invisible embers burning at the glass.

"What the—" Uriel dropped the vial, his hand unable to withstand the heat coming from it. Morrigan didn't hesitate and engulfed the flask in bright blue flame, instantly destroying it and the contents within. A few seconds later, nothing remained, just a scorch mark on the pristine conference table. Everyone stared at the spot in shock, the chaos in the room coming to a halt.

"Good job," Galandir said weakly, then collapsed. But before the boy could hit the floor, Azrael caught him and flung him over his shoulder.

"Good job, kiddo. Now, with this matter settled, I'm going to take him back to the medical ward. He still needs some rest," Azrael said with a toothy smile before disappearing with a nonchalant wave of his hand.

King Uriel's face filled with rage as he stared at the scorch mark. Then his eyes locked on to Morrigan, his fist clenching with fury. Morrigan feared he might just attack her openly, but before he could go forward with the attack, she was pulled into the safety of Alphegor's embrace, his sword pointed towards Uriel.

"I believe you have lost your trump card, King Uriel. All because you didn't value the pawns you were given. Had you valued that elven slave more, perhaps he wouldn't have turned against you," Alphegor said triumphantly. Uriel's face turned red with anger; however, he sat back down in his seat, motioning the fallen soldiers to sheathe their weapons.

They hesitated for a moment, then slowly backed away. There was nothing the fallen could do anymore. Without Morrigan's blood as their leverage, the fallen were completely at the Demon King's mercy.

Suddenly Uriel began laughing hysterically. His ministers looked at him incredulously, wondering if their king had gone mad. "Alright, you've beaten me, Alphegor. Once again, I am at your mercy. So tell me, what horrors will you enact upon my kingdom? More gold? More magic gems? More slaves? Will you take everything from us, leaving the fallen to starve and suffer?"

"You will give us whatever we deem to be the right price. It was YOU who ordered the attack on my daughter in my own home. It is only fair that YOU pay for what you have done," Alphegor said, his gaze merciless and cold.

"What choice did I have? You demons keep rampaging and pillaging us without mercy. My people are dying while yours prosper and thrive," Uriel spat.

"Oh, don't start with this pity nonsense again. You don't appear to be starving to me," the Demon King retorted.

"What do you know about me? Or about the Fallen Kingdom? Have you seen the devastation across our lands? Of course not, because you were the one who brought it there in the first place, hundreds of years ago. Our land is already poor, being in the deepest recesses of the Underworld. But even what little we had, you took away from us." Uriel pointed his finger at Alphegor, who just narrowed his eyes at him.

"So to fix that you decide to raid my kingdom. Attacking my people and stealing from them."

"It was either that or we die," Uriel said bitterly.

"No, it is your people dying. Your soldiers are dying for your arrogance. I never saw you on the battlefield. You were too cowardly to even attend a festival. Instead you sent your Prime Minister. Not to mention that instead of sending a proper champion like everyone else did, you sent a slave," Alphegor said.

"Why should we honor some old demon tradition? All you ever did for us is spit on our face."

"It is not a demon tradition, it is a tradition of the whole Underworld. But you are too big of a fool to see that, being cocooned in your bubble of misery and pity."

The two kings continued bickering among themselves, both of them clearly using the occasion to vent some pent-up frustrations. Ministers from both sides initially vehemently supported their own king with enthusiastic nods and even the occasional clap, but as the argument dragged out and became more nonsensical in nature, they started looking annoyed.

"What do you know about raising children? You had five nannies for each of your daughters. I couldn't afford so many servants, so my two sons were raised purely by me and my wife!" Uriel shouted.

"As if you've ever even changed a nappy in your lifetime," Alphegor retorted. "Best-case scenario, you looked over your wife's shoulder as she did. I remained by Morrigan's side constantly for the first four years of her life. Until you decided to invade my lands, and I was forced to leave her alone!"

"That's enough!" Morrigan yelled, her irritation reaching its boiling point. The two of them looked at her in shock, while the ministers, as well as guards from both sides, sighed in relief. "If you two keep squabbling like this, we will never come to any conclusion."

"What conclusion could there be? You demons will just take whatever you want again," Uriel said, crossing his arms over his chest. Morrigan had to suppress a laugh—he looked just like a pouting kid.

"Let's just look at this objectively and lay down the facts," Morrigan said. "The Fallen Kingdom is suffering. There's not enough food, not enough resources. Is that correct?"

"That is correct. A large portion of our population struggles to earn enough money to buy food," the Fallen King confirmed.

"So your people are suffering, and in order to fix that, you attacked the Demon Kingdom in hopes of gaining some wealth from us," she continued, and Alphegor nodded in confirmation.

"That is correct. This kind of pillaging has been going on for centuries, but six years ago, the fallen army itself led the raids, instead of it being some small groups assembled by the citizens."

"You attack us and then expect us to not retaliate. That's not very logical, is it? Would a dragon spare a snake attacking it just because it felt sorry for it?" Morrigan asked.

"We are not snakes!" King Uriel said, looking offended.

"It was just an example. I'm not saying you are snakes. My point is that you cannot just expect us to not fight back. Even if we know you are suffering, we cannot just let you attack us," Morrigan said. King Uriel remained silent, but some of the fallen ministers begrudgingly nodded.

"So when you attack us, we fight back, which starts this whole cycle of hatred. However, this cannot go on. After all, we are all people of the Underworld. Instead of working against each other, we should be working together," she continued, and the Fallen King sneered.

"Pretty words coming from someone in a position of power. Where are you even going with this, little princess?"

"Alright, I'll just cut to the chase. Instead of our two countries arguing and fighting, we should sign a peace treaty," she said resolutely.

A wave of murmurs passed through the room as everyone considered the option.

"Peace treaty? What use would a peace treaty be?" King Uriel scoffed.

"It's to establish a friendly relationship between our countries.

Wasn't that the whole point of the Nachtstern Festival—to unite the races of the Underworld? It's not that we demons want to keep fighting. Isn't that right, Father?" She threw a glance at her father, who coughed, looking away awkwardly.

"Right."

Uriel narrowed his eyes on Morrigan. "Alright, let's say we sign your peace treaty. How would the fallen even benefit? It's not like it would solve our issues."

"First, it is not our job to fix the problems of YOUR kingdom. That is your own job. If you wish to improve the conditions of your citizens, then you should have come seeking aid instead of pillaging our villages," Morrigan retorted.

"Establishing trade routes and allowing fallen citizens to search for jobs in the Demon Kingdom could be a significant boost to your economy," Viana chimed in. Morrigan looked at her, and the two sisters smiled at each other.

"Why would you want to do that?" One of the demon ministers slammed his fist on the table in anger. But Alphegor glared at him, forcing the man to flinch back.

"Because then the fighting would stop. The people near the Fallen Kingdom's border wouldn't have to suffer anymore. Not to mention that the fallen have access to shadow rubies, which don't exist anywhere else in Doppelta. Trading for those could prove invaluable to us," Viana said.

Thank you, Viana! I'm not quite as knowledgeable in these things yet, so your support is much appreciated.

Uriel scratched his chin in contemplation. After a moment, he looked at Alphegor. "Would you really return Theobold to us and sign a peace treaty?" he asked suspiciously.

"You heard my daughters. I have no use for fallen prisoners. It's just another useless mouth to feed. But those rubies of yours, I'd be willing to trade for," the Demon King said.

For a while, a tense silence descended upon the room as the Fallen King contemplated this information. Morrigan feared that her words might have been useless after all and more battles would follow between their kingdoms. But finally, Uriel sighed and nodded.

"Very well. I shall sign this peace treaty. For the sake of my people!"

CHAPTER 44

UNCERTAIN FUTURE

Morrigan woke up in her bed in the Demon Castle. Gunna was snoozing on a chair next to the bed, and judging from how her shoulders sagged, it appeared that she'd been there for a long time.

How long did I sleep? My body feels so stiff.

She slowly slid out of bed while rubbing the sleep out of her eyes. Despite how much she'd slept, the mental exhaustion still lingered. When it was time to forge the magical contract for the two kings to sign, things had gotten... heated. There were long debates on what to add to the contract, how to properly phrase things, and also how to avoid any loopholes.

At that point every minister got involved and argued about every single part of the contract, saying how it could be misinterpreted in that way or there was this possible loophole in this clause. It was a nightmare and it took no less than six hours for the whole thing to be written. And then it took another hour to convince both kings to sign it.

As Morrigan clambered out of bed, Gunna began to stir, and her eyes soon opened. The nanny looked confused for a moment, but she saw Morrigan and instantly pulled her into a deep hug.

"Oh, poor child. I heard everything that happened to you. It is just awful what those fallen have done. You know I'm never quick to judge a race as a whole, but in this case, the demons were right. The fallen truly are scum—attacking such a young child and using her life for political gain," the dwarf woman huffed, her eyebrows scrunched up in anger. This was probably the angriest Morrigan had ever seen her nanny.

"It's alright, Gunna. It's over now. The peace treaty is signed with a binding magical contract that cannot be broken," she replied.

"Even so, it is absolutely barbaric. Good thing about that magical contract. With it we don't need to worry, since there isn't a single case of a magical contract being broken," Gunna said encouragingly.

Not even a single case? With the civilization in this world being so old, far older than the one on Earth, if nobody yet has discovered how to break a magical contract, then what are the chances of it ever happening? Plain impossible. That puts my mind at ease.

"This matter is now settled, Lady Morrigan. How about we forget all about that unpleasant event and instead get ready for the day ahead? The whole Royal Family is going to eat breakfast together," Gunna chimed in.

Morrigan barely managed to suppress a groan. Seeing all the concubines and her sisters was the last thing she wanted right now. But it wasn't like she had a choice, so she nodded and allowed Gunna to get her ready.

* * *

This is the worst.

The concubines and princesses were gathered at the large dining table in the main hall, chattering and happily enjoying their meal. However, their gazes would constantly travel to Morrigan, hidden sneers occasionally appearing on the corners of their lips. Nobody dared to say anything openly, but what they were thinking was clear—Morrigan had made a mess of things again.

After all, the fallen had taken her blood and used it as leverage against the Demon Kingdom. It didn't matter that it was taken forcibly or that she'd helped with solving the issue. She could have single-handedly saved the world, but if she made a mistake while doing it, these women would latch on to it. They would still sneer and point their fingers at her behind her back. Rosalie, Miriam, and a few other of the oldest princesses, as well as their mothers, looked awfully satisfied with this outcome. It was clear that this was a golden opportunity for them. A chance to claim the title of the Crown Princess for themselves.

Viana, however, didn't appear pleased in the slightest. Her expression was glum while her mother chattered happily with the other concubines, her spirits as high as they could be. Morrigan looked at her eldest sister, who looked back at her. She looked forlorn and even somewhat guilty, and soon lowered her gaze to the still-full plate in front of her.

"I'm glad that was resolved nicely, wasn't it?" Deziara said, looking hopefully at Alphegor and Morrigan, trying to cheer them up. But the king looked rather glum, no doubt already dreading all the paperwork he would have to go through to make the peace treaty with the fallen actually long-lasting and sustainable.

"Yes," he replied in an absent-minded sort of manner.

"I have to say, Your Majesty, this is truly a once in a lifetime opportunity. A peace treaty with the fallen. We should cherish and strengthen it further," Lady Viviana said, the wine clearly getting to her head already. "Imagine if we were to connect our kingdoms through the sacred vows of marriage? We could gain an effective spy on the inside and rule the Fallen Kingdom from within. We should send out our strongest princess to—"

"Silence," Alphegor growled, and the whole room went deadly silent as he glared at Viviana.

"It's alright, Father. There is no reason to get angry. It was merely a joke," Morrigan said. Not that she felt sorry for Lady Viviana, but she'd seen the look of horror Viana had when her mother spoke up. Morrigan would hate for her to get punished along with it. After all, it felt like they were finally starting to understand each other, if only a little bit. "It was most pleasant having breakfast with you, but I am afraid I have to excuse myself. I want to check on Haku's well-being."

She walked out of the dinning hall with her head held high; however, as soon as the doors closed behind her, she melded into the shadows and rushed to the dragon stable outside. Much to her relief she found Haku chomping on a large piece of meat, unscathed and uninjured.

"Haku, you're alright!" she said, then went to hug her dragon friend. He quickly swallowed the meat he was eating and cooed at her. He flicked his tongue in an attempt to lick her, but she dodged him.

"No licks. You stink like meat." She wagged her finger, and he whined. Morrigan scratched the scales underneath his chin, and Haku wagged his tail in satisfaction.

"I'm really glad you're okay," she whispered, pressing her forehead against her friend.

"Dragons are not so easy to injure or kill," Galandir said, and Morrigan jumped back in shock. The boy was carrying a bucket of water, which he poured into Haku's bowl.

"Can you just walk around like that? Are you okay?" she asked. It wasn't like she was unhappy to see the boy walking around freely. But it felt a bit odd, knowing that just a few days ago he was still imprisoned. Even if her sneaking him out of the prison felt like a lifetime ago.

"Of course I can. I am not a slave anymore!" he retorted, setting the bucket down.

"You're not?"

"Why are you so surprised? You're the one who demanded my freedom in the first place. I've been assigned to care for Haku by that annoying white-haired friend of yours," the elven boy explained. He went up to the dragon and patted his shoulder affectionately. Haku blew a puff of smoke at the boy, as if to confirm his words.

"Really? That's great! I mean... you're not really free to return to the Overworld, but…" she stammered, wondering whether the boy felt bitter about this outcome.

"Maybe I am not free to go there yet, but in retrospect, this actually might be better. It's not like I have a home to return to, and who would even want to deal with some orphan kid? It is not too far-fetched to say that the fallen might try to send somebody after me for revenge. After all, I foiled all their plans," Galandir said, then sighed. "I do miss the sun and the sky and the wind, but I'll be safer here. I have a job, warm food to eat every day, a safe place to sleep, and a giant debt to repay."

The boy chuckled, and there was a bit of hope in his eyes. Previously they seemed resigned to his grim fate, but they now shone with new determination. A warm feeling bloomed inside her chest. She had done something good. She had managed to save this child, and that thought gave her strength and hope. Hope that perhaps one day she could free more slaves. Or perhaps end slavery as a whole, even if the path to doing that would no doubt be a long and hard one.

"It truly is a huge debt. I hope Azrael pays well for being a dragon keeper." Morrigan chuckled, but the smile on Galandir's face vanished.

"It pays well enough, but that is not the kind of debt I was talking about," he said, looking her in the eyes. She cocked her head in confusion as the door swung open and Azrael came into the stable, whistling without a care in the world.

"Hello, squirts. Up to no good again?" he asked, snickering.

"We were just talking. Besides, you're the one who is always up to no good," Morrigan retorted.

"Oh, I certainly used to be the biggest troublemaker around these parts, but I'm afraid at this point you have taken that title from me." The mage grinned and pointed at Morrigan, who crossed her arms over her chest in annoyance. She didn't cause that much trouble, did she? Maybe a little, but she certainly wasn't as bad as Azrael.

"What do you want?" she grumbled.

"It's like you forget what my job is around these parts. It's to teach you magic. With this whole fallen debacle over, we need to return to your lessons. Bring that shadow ruby, and let's see what ability it gives you."

"About that—I already absorbed the ruby," Morrigan admitted sheepishly.

"Oh, good. Saves us some time. What ability did you get?" the demon asked, excitement flickering in his eyes. "No, actually, never mind. Just show me."

"Well, there's a bit of a problem..." she stammered.

"What problem?" Azrael raised his eyebrow, and Galandir also cocked his head curiously, having listened to the conversation.

"I have no idea what ability it gave me!"

EPILOGUE

"Perhaps you can make flowers bloom from your fingertips," Deziara guessed while sitting on Haku's front paw. The dragon was lying on the ground at the back of the Demon Castle, observing Morrigan. She did her best to imagine the flowers blooming from her fingers, furrowing her brows in concentration, but after several minutes it became clear that nothing would happen.

"No, it's not flowers," Morrigan groaned. It had been three weeks since she'd absorbed the shadow ruby into her body, and yet she still had no idea what ability she had. "Why isn't there a way to just find out what abilities you have? Like a list of sorts? Or like a system in a video game? That would make things way easier."

"System in a video game? What's that? Is that one of those human things?" Deziara asked curiously.

"I've never heard of the term *video game*," Galandir added. Since the elven boy was assigned to take care of Haku, the dragon stable were the place where he hung out most often. And since Morrigan and Deziara always came to visit Haku, they had slowly formed a friend group of sorts.

"I doubt humans have them in this world. It is a rather complicated thing to make. You'd need to have plastic and microchips and all sorts of other complicated stuff I don't think this world has," Morrigan said.

"Aww, bummer! The stuff from your old world sounds so interesting, Morri. I wish I could have seen it too. Just like Azrael and Father." Deziara pouted.

"Azrael could open a portal to Earth, but if you were to spend just one day there, more than a hundred days would pass on Doppelta," she said.

"Yeah, we can't leave for that long, especially not now, when all of our sisters are eager to take your place as Crown Princess," Deziara grumbled. "I swear, they're some monsters, not people. Their sister gets attacked and they turn the matter on its head and call her incompetent. The greedy leeches only want power. Even Viana has more tact than them."

"Let's not talk about that. I honestly don't even want to think about all the things I'll have to do to keep the title."

"Why do you even want to keep it?" Galandir asked, poking at the ground beneath him with a stick.

"Isn't it obvious? It's because..." Morrigan paused as she thought about the answer.

But why do I want to keep the title of Crown Princess? Wouldn't it all be much easier if I just gave it up to Viana and lived as a simple princess? I know Father really wants me to inherit the throne, but is it what I want?

"It's because Morri has the biggest magical potential of anyone since Father was born. No other demon can even compare to what she can do," Deziara announced proudly, getting to her feet. Haku growled in agreement, producing a tiny, flaming crown above Morrigan's head.

"Oh, he's exaggerating. You and Viana can do magic too," she retorted, waving the flaming crown away from her head.

"No, I'm really not. You could shadow step when you were just a baby and you learned how to shape-shift at age four. Age four! That is insane. Even Azrael, who is supposed to be a magical prodigy, could only do it when he was twenty, and at nowhere near the same level as you. Mom told me so," the girl objected.

"Maybe demons just aren't that great at magic. I mean, I could light step when I was a baby too," Galandir said, clearly unimpressed.

"Light step?" both girls asked curiously.

"Yeah, it works the same as shadow stepping, except in the light. Not very useful here in the Underworld," the elven boy scoffed.

"No, I refuse to believe that elves are better at magic than demons. It is well known that Underworld races have stronger magic because the Underworld is where the magic is born. We breathe it in with each breath. Everything you have in the Overworld is just magical residue," Deziara scoffed.

"I wonder if that's how it really is. I wish I could go to the Overworld and compare," Morrigan said, thinking about the green forests, blue sky, and the warm glow of the sun. How she would love to paint just a simple nature scenery with a meadow full of flowers!

"Yeah, like that's ever going to happen. I'm pretty sure Daddy won't let you out of his sight now." Galandir shook his head, and Morrigan's shoulders sagged.

"Don't worry, Morri. You'll be able to go wherever you want once you're an adult," Deziara said cheerfully, but Morrigan didn't share her enthusiasm. She'd have to wait until she was forty years old for that to happen, and even when she reached adulthood there was no guarantee that Alphegor would just let her go in and out of the Demon Castle whenever she wanted.

"For a princess you sure lack any sense of tact," Galandir pointed out.

"What?" Deziara grumbled. "What did I say wrong?"

"Never mind that. Let's just try to figure out what ability I got from that accursed ruby," Morrigan mumbled, the unpleasant heaviness once again settling over her heart.

"Oh, perhaps you can create light now," the elven boy suggested. "That would certainly be ironic for a demon princess."

"It's worth a shot," Morrigan said with a sigh. She imagined creating a ball of light above her palm. However, all she got was a gentle, flickering fireball. It shone rather brightly and illuminated a large portion of the surrounding area, but it was without a doubt her fire magic, not some new light magic ability.

Haku seemed mesmerized by the fireball and touched it with his claw. It disappeared just like a soap bubble. The dragon growled and lowered his head, begging to play.

Morrigan giggled. "It's no new magic, but it seems that Haku likes it," she said, then created enough magic fire lights to fill the yard. The dragon chased after them and popped them one after the other. Soon Galandir joined in on the game, popping the fire with his stick; it was so gentle that it merely charred the end of the wood a little bit. Deziara also joined in, and Morrigan followed after her.

Soon the yard was swirling with small, gentle fireballs, while the four of them ran around and played.

* * *

Morrigan returned to her room rather late, having spent the whole day with Deziara, Haku, and Galandir. Though she'd had a lot of fun with them, they still couldn't figure out exactly what ability she had acquired from the shadow ruby.

When Morrigan entered her room, she saw Alphegor sitting at his work desk and diligently writing something on a piece of paper. He stopped the moment he saw her enter.

He smiled and got up from his seat. "Welcome back, little one." He opened his arms, inviting her for a hug, and she obliged, burying herself in his embrace. "Have a nice day?"

"Yeah, it was fun. Unfortunately, we couldn't figure out what ability I got." She sighed into his chest, and he gently patted her head.

"I'm sure we'll figure it out soon," he said, releasing her.

"Is there really no way of finding it out? Some magical artifact or something?" She groaned as she sat down on the sofa, sinking into its soft and comfortable cushion. Some of her tiredness seemed to melt away.

"There are rituals that could tell us. However, they require you to spill your blood, so those would be the absolute last resort. Actually, I would rather not find out what ability you got if we'd have to perform one of those rituals," Alphegor said sternly, and Morrigan sank deeper into the cushion.

"But it is supposed to be an ability suited for me. Shouldn't I just know what it is?" she grumbled.

"I'm afraid magic is not that simple. Some abilities can be sensed. I imagine you can sense to an extent where you can slip into shadows and where you cannot," he said, sitting down next to her.

"Now that you mention it, yes. I don't really want to become a shadow in a place that is well lit, but in dark places, it feels as natural as breathing," she said thoughtfully. "Am I supposed to concentrate on something to feel this new ability?"

"It is possible that could help you discover it. However, the majority of abilities are undetectable until put to use," he said, then placed a comforting hand on her shoulder. "Don't worry. I'm sure you'll discover it in time. There's no need to rush."

"I suppose you're right," Morrigan said, her eyes landing on her father's portrait. It hung in their living room, having become the grand centerpiece. Alphegor was very proud of it and often looked at it with a big, satisfied smile on his face. "It's been a while since I've painted anything. I think I'll do that to distract myself."

"Sure. I still have some work I need to finish," he said, then returned to his desk.

Morrigan went to change her clothes first. She put on a simple black dress with short sleeves and then wore an apron over it. It was already covered in various colorful splotches, proof of her previous work. Gunna had wanted to replace it with a new one, since the color didn't exactly wash out from the cloth, but Morrigan insisted on keeping it. She felt like it had a nice character. A clean apron felt like it was inexperienced, not yet ready for the task ahead.

Once she was dressed, Morrigan prepared her private painting corner. She propped up a canvas and set out her colors, looking at them thoughtfully and pondering what to draw.

"Father, is there something you'd like me to paint?" she asked as she measured the small canvas in front of her, wondering what she could fit in there.

"You've already given me the best portrait I've seen in nearly ten thousand years," he said proudly, looking at the portrait.

She chuckled. "You haven't even lived for that long."

"But I am sure that I will not see a better one. Unless it is painted by you, of course."

She shook her head with a smile and then turned her attention to the colors before her. Her eyes fell upon the vibrant green color. She thought of green grass and lush trees.

It's been such a long time since I've actually experienced any real greenery. And who knows if I'll ever even touch grass again. No, don't think about it. Those gloomy thoughts won't do you any good. Just focus on the happy feelings.

So Morrigan picked up the green paint and the paintbrush, and began painting. She did her best to remember the scenery from Earth. A calm meadow far away from the city. A warm breeze blowing and rustling the long, soft grass. She imagined the small flowers growing through the grass, gentle white and pink buds reaching out towards the sun, along with a forest somewhere far away in the distance, a small line compared to the vast blue sky above.

With a satisfied hum, Morrigan began putting down colors on the canvas. Just like the image in her head, the scenery slowly came to life. With each stroke of her brush, it felt like the picture became more real, more complete. But there was something odd as well. She was feeling tired. And not just a little bit tired, but really, really tired.

It must be because of all the running I did before.

But she dismissed her tiredness and continued painting. She could almost feel the soft grass beneath her feet. She could smell its freshness.

Oh, the smell of grass. How I have missed it. There's nothing like it in the Underworld.

"Morrigan!" Alphegor suddenly called out to her. Her eyes snapped away from the painting.

"What is it, Father?" She turned her head to look at him, then gasped in shock, dropping her paintbrush to the floor. Or to be precise, she dropped it into the grass. The soft green grass that was growing on the living-room floor.

"Look at what you've done!" the king exclaimed, his voice filled with wonder and a giant grin growing on his face.

"I... I did this?" she asked, dumbfounded, then bent down to touch the grass. It felt exactly like she expected it to feel like. She plucked a strand of it and brought it to her nose. It smelled wonderfully fresh. It was without a doubt real grass.

"This is amazing, Morrigan! I've never seen such an ability before in my life. Your painting just turned into reality. Do you realize how powerful that is?" Alphegor gushed, his eyes sparkling with an excitement she had never seen before. Morrigan staggered, exhaustion taking over her body. Her father quickly ran up to her and caught her.

"It seems to take a lot of energy from me..." she muttered. She felt so exhausted, but at the same time so elated with this discovery.

"It's alright. I'm sure that in time, you'll learn how to manage the energy consumption better," Alphegor said, lifting her up in his arms. She leaned into his embrace, allowing her eyes to close. Before falling asleep she heard him say, "With this, you'll become a ruler far more powerful than I could ever hope to be."

Need another story to keep you satiated until book three of *Demon Queen Wants to Paint* is released?

Check out *Tiny Dungeon Core* by The Bearded Man!

A new Dungeon Core is born… and it's unlike anything the world has seen.

In a realm of epic quests and powerful gods, the tiniest Dungeon Core ever created is about to prove that size isn't everything. Armed with a mysterious System, and a handful of fiercely loyal creatures, the Core must grow, adapt, and defend itself against a world that sees it as prey.

But building up a dungeon is no easy task when you're practically pocket-sized. Every upgrade, skill, and creature summoned is a gamble for survival. One misstep could spell destruction.

Grab your copy today and discover a dungeon worth rooting for.

About the Series: *Tiny Dungeon Core* is a LitRPG adventure with a non-human protagonist, strategic base-building, and a unique take on dungeon fantasy. Expect a story that blends light progression, loyal monster allies, and slice-of-life with rising stakes. Ideal for readers who enjoy magical creatures, clever worldbuilding, and underdogs that grow into something far greater.

Available now on Kindle Unlimited and Audible!

Thank you for reading a MoonQuill original novel. More exciting stories can be found on at www.moonquill.com.

We would greatly appreciate it if you could take a moment to leave a review. Each one helps the author and supports their ability to continue writing fantastic books for everyone to enjoy!

Scan the QR code below to subscribe to our mailing list and be notified of new releases. You'll receive a few ebooks for free!